SET AT RANDOM

ABOUT THE AUTHOR

Declan Dunne has written *"Peter's Key – Peter DeLoughry and the fight for Irish Independence"* and a bestseller in Ireland, *"Mulligan's – Grand Old Pub of Poolbeg Street"*, both published by Mercier Press. He has also written *"Palais Royal – Musée du Louvre"* a screenplay in French and several plays in English including *"Whispers to the boy unseen"*. He lives in Dublin where he works as a journalist with Ireland's national broadcasting company, RTÉ.

DECLAN DUNNE

SET AT RANDOM

THE BOOK THAT WOULDN'T LIE DOWN

First published in 2018.

© Declan Dunne, 2018.

ISBN-13: 978-1724899620

ISBN-10: 1724899627

A CIP record for this title is available from the British Library.

www.setatrandom.com

Printed by CreateSpace.

EPISODES

To my mother, Nessa.

Time present and time past
Are both perhaps present in time future,
And time future contained in time past.

T. S. Eliot, 'Burnt Norton', *Four Quartets*

The past is not past. It is present here and now.

James Joyce, *Exiles*

1

THE SUITORS

Mr. and Mrs. Boldt stood arm-in-arm on their porch looking out at their neighbors who had gathered to watch them being buried alive. The couple were dressed in their dark Sunday best. It was Friday. Mrs. Boldt held a small box made of Canadian pine. Inside, was a milk jug made of Dresden china. Two men in suits waited for them, one big, one small. They were made of greed.

I didn't know what to do.

"I am so."

That's what Lukas Shaefer always said when his daddy told him he couldn't go somewhere he wanted. Mr. Shaefer generally won but, this time, he was busy helping Mr. and Mrs. Boldt. That's how Lukas managed to get his own way and come along with me to see what was going to happen to the Boldts. The way I saw it, Lukas was made of defiance while Mr. Shaefer was most made up of patience.

We were all there that day because of something that had happened about a month or so after the '29 season, the '29 cotton-picking season, that is. The work meant we didn't go back to school until late September so one of our neighbors, Mrs. Taylor, made sure I didn't fall behind. I remember writing a story for her about my daddy and what had happened to him when he was about my age. She wrote in all the punctuation after, corrected my spellings too.

And so, when I was fourteen, I was sent away from our home in southern Texas to the lighter days of the Central Plains, north, between the Piney Woods and the Hill Country, not knowing what the future held. My father, it was – your grand-father – who sent me away to this place; this place of the prairies and the lakes where my uncle lived. My uncle lived here, in this place.

Written by Set Wright,
The '29 season
Pendleton, Troy, Bell County, Texas

"You must remember to punctuate. And how do we know who's talking?"

I told Mrs. Taylor I wanted no truck with punctuation.

"Mrs. Taylor, my daddy says 'Tayke-siss' not Texas like what you's writing there."

"The way people speak is not the way it is written."

"You saying my daddy's wrong, Mrs. Taylor?"

"No. If you really want to write the way he speaks then underline it so the reader will know that you are meaning to write that way, that it's not a mistake."

"Why, Mrs. Taylor, I done laid out all them words real careful like."

She put her hands to her head like there was a mouse running around the floor. "Dear Lord, how many grammatical mistakes can a body make in one sentence?"

When I got home I started thinking about what Mrs. Taylor had said so I set about writing my story again. I thought about underlining some of the words but changed by mind because I didn't see no reason to. That's the way I saw it anyways.

An' so, when I woze fohteen, I woze sent away from ah home

in sutthen Tayke–siss to the light–ah days of the Sayntral Plains, nawth, buh–tween the Py–nay Woods 'n' the Heel Kawn–tray, not known what the few–chah hailed. Mah fawtha, it was – your granfawtha – who sent me away to this place; this place of the prairies 'n' the lakes where mah uncle lived. Mah uncle lived here, in this place.

Written by Set Wright again,
The '29 season
Pendleton, Troy, Bell County, Texas

When I read it over, I realized that Daddy had spoken to me with more of an accent than he normally did. This was like him getting a red pen out and doing his own underlining, underlining what he wanted me to hear by hanging a weight on his Texan voice, the real him. I wanted to have this power, to be able to speak one way all the time and then bring in my army of Texan sounds when I wanted people to sit bolt upright and listen. I figured the only way I was going to do this was to learn to read and speak English proper. Then, I thought, I'd be able to do what my daddy did; ring a bell to whoever's listening to me when I changed back to my own manner, my Texan voice, the real me, Texas proper. I was a bit concerned, though, him telling me that story about when he was fourteen and having to leave home and all. I was thirteen, see?

As I was writing, the door opened and Daddy came in.

"Mr. Taylor's down. Cotton-weigher's acting up. Neighborly of him."

Mr. Taylor was good with his hands. His wife was good with her head. That's what they all said. I looked out to see if I could spot Mr. Taylor working. I couldn't. All I could see was Ops facing the wind. That's what she did. She was Carrizo. They came from Peru where they were called Incas but that was a long time ago. Ops didn't like thunder and lightning and she didn't like the fact that she was born in 1900 because most folk remembered her age.

"Cotton's nearly all in," Daddy said. "You finished your schooling?"

"For today anyways."

Ops started walking toward the house. Good thing too. I was hungry.

"Mr. Shaefer's coming," she said when she came in.

I looked out and couldn't see nothing. No rise of dust from a truck. Nothing. Ops did that. The only way she could know Mr. Shaefer was coming was if he had told her the week before. I wasn't sure how she knew. Ops fixed us something to eat.

"Can I go up to Mrs. Taylor after, Daddy?"

"What for?"

"Schooling."

"Thought you was through with schooling for today. Wouldn't be to get biscuits now would it?"

"Well if she has some, it'd be impolite to refuse 'em."

Mrs. Taylor made biscuits in the evening.

Daddy smiled. "What an obliging child I've raised. See if the Boldts need chores doing first, son."

Mr. and Mrs. Boldt lived just over the hill. I spent many days there. Every time I finished hanging up their washed Irish linen, tending to their garden or painting the outhouse I banged the back of the large tub that was hung up on a rusty nail just beside their back door.

Mrs. Boldt used to give me a glass of milk as a reward. She poured the milk from a jug made of Dresden china. She sure liked that old jug. When she had poured all the milk out, she washed the jug, checked it and then showed it to me.

"It's made of Dresden china. My aunt sent it over to me in this box. That's made of Canadian pine. Someone must have sent her something the size of this jug in this box from Canada, don't you think? It was stuffed with newspaper to keep it from breaking. You know what was on that newspaper?"

"That Queen Victoria was dead," I said.

"That's right. She came over with the jug. Queen Victoria. The first time I met your mother, we had a glass of milk from this very same jug. Imagine that."

The conversation didn't change much. Mrs. Boldt then put the jug back in the box, closed the lid and patted it. She sure liked that old jug.

After chopping some fire-wood, I banged the tub. It was still bonging when I went inside. Mrs. Boldt didn't like me banging the tub but I couldn't resist. I loved the *boing, boing, boing* sound it made. Mr. Boldt said that I should be a drummer.

"I don't think I'm too musical, Mr. Boldt."

He didn't answer me. I sat down and ate the biscuits that Mrs. Boldt always had for me. I held my hand underneath my chin because those biscuits sure made a lot of crumbs.

Then Mr. Boldt put back his head, closed his eyes and began speaking German. He was Texas German:

> *Schlage die Trommel und fürchte dich nicht,*
> *Und küsse die Marketenderin!*
> *Das ist die ganze Wissenschaft,*
> *Das ist der Bücher tiefster Sinn.*

He asked me what it sounded like.

"German."

"Not like a drum?" he asked.

"Yeah, like a German drum."

"No, a universal drum," Mr. Boldt said.

"What's it about?" I asked.

"A universal drum."

"Oh."

"I was compelled to go to New York because of him," Mr. Boldt said.

"Who?"

"Heine, Heinrich Heine. He wrote the poem."

"Does he live in New York?"

"He does now," Mr. Boldt said. "He always will. They refused to put up a statue to him in Germany. At least, the people in power wouldn't allow it."

"Why not?"

"He annoyed them and he threatened their power. So Germans in New York had the statue transported over but the politicians in New York wouldn't allow them to put it up."

"Why not?"

"Because *we* annoyed *them, we* threatened *their* power. We eventually found a place for it in The Bronx.

"Could you write it down for me, Mr. Boldt, the poem? Like, write it down in English too? Would you do that, Mr. Boldt?"

"Why?"

"I'd like to learn it."

"All right then, so long as you understand you don't need to be musical to be this drummer boy."

Schlage die Trommel und fürchte dich nicht,
(Sound the drum and hold your nerve,)
Und küsse die Marketenderin!
(And kiss the girl, why don't you?)
Das ist die ganze Wissenschaft,
(Why, that's what it's all about, ain't it?)
Das ist der Bücher tiefster Sinn.
(Ain't it?)

When I left the Boldts, I ran up to the Taylors. Even though I couldn't find Mrs. Taylor in the house, I knew she was around because Hannah was there and the gramophone was playing. I hollered. Mrs. Taylor shouted back that she'd be there in a minute. I called out again.

"Can I take Hannah, Mrs. Taylor?"

"Yes, but be careful with her."

"I will, Mrs. Taylor."

I took Hannah from her cot and sat down with her on my lap. Her arms reached up trying to grab me and she was smiling. She was only a couple of months old, I guess. I got lost thinking, so I didn't realize that Mrs. Taylor had come back in.

"Set." She tried again. "Set! Are you gone deaf, son?"

"No," I replied. "I couldn't hear with all that blaring going on."

"Blaring?" Mrs. Taylor asked.

"Well, the gramophone, I meant."

"That's not blaring. That's Caruso."

She was real annoyed. She took Hannah from me and put her back in the cot. I followed her over and looked at Hannah who was wriggling and laughing. I let her clench my little finger.

"Do you miss your little sister?"

"Yeah. Some."

"And your mother too, of course?"

"Yes, Mrs. Taylor."

My mother died when I was young, after giving birth to my sister and then my sister died a few months later. I used to like to hold my sister.

"Well?" Mrs. Taylor asked.

I was still looking at Hannah.

"Well?" she asked again.

I had forgotten why I was there.

"I –"

"I haven't got all day."

My mind started racing because I didn't want her to think I had just come looking for biscuits.

"I finished that book, Mrs. Taylor. Forgot to say earlier. The one about Troy, the one in Europe."

"It's not in Europe. It's in Asia Minor."

"Wherever. The one with the blue and purple cover."

"I know the book. I gave it to you. Well, tell me what you think?"

"It was real good, Mrs. Taylor."

"Real good? What did you like about it?"

"What did I like about it?'

"Yes. What did you like about it?"

"Well, I liked the bit about where they couldn't find no way into the castle and then they built a big old horse out of wood. Do you remember that bit, Mrs. Taylor?"

"Yes. Go on."

"Well, they all snuck in and hid in it and then them fellers on the other side, like in the castle, they couldn't believe it so they opened the gates and wheeled the horse in. It was on wheels, see, and then all them other fellers came out and killed them and then they had a big meal like with steaks, you know, the ones Mr. McGlassop sells. Real tasty, they are. That's about it, Mrs. Taylor."

"Anything else?"

The gramophone stopped playing.

"What's his name again? The man singing."

"Caruso and he was singing 'Santa Lucia'."

"Is that like Carrizo, the tribe that Ops is from?"

"No, Set. It's nothing like that. Anything else I can help you with."

"Did you make any biscuits?"

✝

I arrived back empty-handed to find Mr. Shaefer's truck parked where it normally was. Lukas was swinging on the porch rail. He was only about eleven then, I guess.

"*Wie geht's?*"

"*Wie geht's?*"

That's how we greeted each other. The Shaefers was Texas German too.

"You two go on up to the Boldts and help 'em out," Daddy said.

"Aw, dang, I was up there already, Daddy."

"None of your lip now," Daddy said. "Go on."

"Do we have to?" Lukas asked.

"You heard Mr. Wright," Mr. Shaefer said. "There ain't a lick of common sense between the both of them."

Lukas kicked a stone as we walked off. I noticed the silence behind us and it wasn't until we were a good distance away that we heard, with the help of the wind, Daddy and Mr. Shaefer laughing.

We saw the Mexican children, Eduardo and Gabriela, playing a long way off. I could hear their voices; the wind helping again. I asked Lukas if he had ever heard of *Schlage die Trommel* and he started reciting it. We walked in step with the rhythm.

Mrs. Boldt hobbled into the house when she saw us coming over the hill. I challenged Lukas to a race. We got to the Boldts' house in no time.

Mr. Boldt was standing in the tub steadying himself by resting his hands on the backs of two chairs. "Evening," he said.

"I want him nice and clean for the rubbing-down doctor," his wife told us. "He's coming tomorrow."

"Yes, Mrs. Boldt."

"Sure, Mrs. Boldt." Lukas was always less formal.

We got to it, dipping the cloths in the sudsy waters and cleaning Mr. Boldt's hide as he stood looking into the distance. It reminded me of grooming the horse but Mr. Boldt shifted on his legs a little more. Lukas and Mr. Boldt began talking German. I felt left out but I caught a word here and there. They mentioned Pendleton, Deer Creek and Sterling, which I thought must be the Sterling delivery truck that Mr. Shaefer drove.

When we had finished, Mrs. Boldt put a towel on the ground and we helped her husband step out of the tub and onto it. Then she gave us towels and we dried him down. Mr. Boldt always finished by doing the last bits himself. His clothes were laid out on an easy chair. We dressed him and put him sitting down. Then, Lukas and me took the handles of the tub, brought it out back some distance and emptied the water out. We hung the tub up and went back into the house. *Boing, boing, boing.*

After we had washed our hands, we noticed there were two glasses of milk waiting for us. We started drinking and Mrs. Boldt began telling us the story about the jug. Well, it sounded like all the other times she told it but, at the end, she put her hand on Lukas's arm. She took a cloth and wiped the milk moustache from his lip.

"Do you know who's going to get this when I go?" she asked him. "You are. I'm going to give it to you."

"Well, thank you very much, Mrs. Boldt," Lukas said. "I'll look forward to that."

"Here, son," Mr. Boldt said, handing me some money.

"No thank you, Mr. Boldt," I said. "You's neighbors."

"Take it," he said. "Buy something nice."

"Thank you, Mr. Boldt," I said.

"Gee, thanks," Lukas said.

The sun was strong and we found it unpleasant to walk back up the hill that had been so easy to run down. I heard Gabriela cry; the wind again, sending me a message. She was sitting down. Her brother, Eduardo, was standing beside her.

I saw Skeeter Grasshop Nestor walking away from them. He was carrying a shotgun. When he beat children, he hopped around them in a sideways dance, like a crab. It was his victory dance.

We ran over to Gabriela. Her crying had turned to hiccups. A line of dark red blood crawled down Eduardo's upper lip. He didn't have to say nothing. I got the end of my shirt and pinched Eduardo's nose with it. I had to stand up on the tips of my toes. He knew the drill. Thirty seconds. I felt the wind on my stomach because my shirt was up and my legs began to shiver because of the way I was standing. It's what we always did. When I released my fingers, Eduardo stared at me for the sign.

"Yep," I said. That meant he had stopped bleeding. The only other way to know is to rub your nose but then you get blood smeared across your face and people start asking questions.

Lukas and me resumed our journey home. Skeeter shouted at us, "Who's your friend?"

I didn't answer.

"Hey," Skeeter said. "I asked you a question. Who's your friend?"

"Lukas," I answered.

"Ain't you going to introduce us?" he asked.

"No," I replied.

We walked on a bit, quickly.

"Who's he?" Lukas asked.

"Skeeter Grasshop Nestor," I told him. "He dances round people after he beats 'em up. You know what else he does?"

"What?"

"He kills deer up at Deer Creek," I said. "The young ones, and then he leaves 'em there. They's all just ah-decomposing."

"Well that's just plain wrong," Lukas said. "He ain't got no business doing a rotten thing like that. Does he dance around them too?"

"Don't know," I replied. "He was boasting to me about it in Troy last week."

"That's not right. Killing fawns. That ain't right at all."

We heard the sound of a shotgun barrel being clicked into place. The wind didn't need help with that. Lukas looked back and then began running up the hill.

"He's going to shoot," Lukas called to me. "Come on."

I didn't run. I just kept walking. He wasn't going to scare me. I heard a shot. I kept on walking. He fired another. I kept on walking.

"Who's been shooting?" Mr. Shaefer asked.

We didn't say nothing.

"Who were you fighting with?" Daddy asked me.

He had seen the blood-stain on the front end of my shirt.

"Well?" Daddy insisted.

"Answer your father," Mr. Shaefer said.

So now I had Mr. Shaefer and Daddy focusing in on me. Lukas broke the silence.

"Skeeter Grasshop Nestor."

"What's he been doing?" Daddy asked.

"Shooting, that's what he's been doing," Lukas said. "One of them bullets near took the hairs offah my ear."

"You don't have any hairs on your ear," I said, "and he shot above us anyways."

Lukas ignored me and kept on telling. "You know he shoots deer too, Mr. Wright. The young ones, and he just leaves 'em there. And he dances round them. That's why they call him Grasshop. And he beat up the two Mexican kids as well for no reason. Just over the hill there. They wasn't bothering nobody."

"He seems to have had quite a busy day, this Skeeter Grasshop Nestor," Daddy said.

Before the Shaefers left, I pulled Lukas aside and scolded him for telling on Skeeter.

"Why you want to protect him?" he protested.

"I don't. You just don't tell on people."

"Well I wasn't telling on people. It was the deer. They can't speak. They needs us to speak on their behalves. Don't you see?"

Lukas always had some kind of an answer that made sense. He got into the truck and stuck his tongue out at me, smiled and then waved. In a moment, the Shaefers were gone. I was mad with him for another reason. Mrs. Boldt had favored him over me with that jug even though I went up there most days not like Lukas.

Ops and Daddy were sitting on the porch when I went to go back into the house. I didn't say nothing.

"What's the matter with you?" Daddy asked me.

"Oh, he's sad that Lukas is gone," Ops said.

"No I'm not. He's not my friend."

I went to bed without having to be told. They must have known there was something wrong then. Ops came in.

"Well, come on now," Ops said. "Spit it out."

"Nothing."

She tried to kiss me on the forehead but I turned away. She got up to leave.

"Mrs. Boldt is going to give Lukas her Dresden jug," I told her.

"That's mighty kind of her," Ops said.

I sat up.

"Kind?" I asked. "After all I done for them?"

"Well, I never thought I'd see you so wound up over an old milk jug," Ops said.

I lay down and turned away. "I ain't going up there again."

Ops came back and sat on the bed.

"Maybe there's a reason," she said.

I sat up again and faced her.

"There ain't no reason."

"Promise not to tell?"

"Tell what?"

"The Boldts are leaving their house to your daddy so they probably felt they had to give Lukas something. Something small. I'm a witness to the will. They told me over a cup of coffee in their house last Fall. Important things are decided over a cup of coffee, I find. Even your daddy doesn't know about this so you don't say nothing. Promise?"

"Why are they doing that?" I asked.

"Well, they don't have no-one else," Ops answered. "Mrs. Boldt was very close to your mother and she loves you very much, your daddy too. Feel better now?"

"Why didn't she tell me?" I asked.

"They don't want everyone knowing especially your daddy. Likely be an argument. He'd refuse it. You know what he's like. Feel better now?"

"Yeah."

"You keep this to yourself, promise?"

"I promise."

Ops was at the door when I spoke again.

"Ops?"

"Yeah."

"How do you know when thunder and lightning's coming?"

She waited a while before answering.

"Strange light, different kind of breeze, the way the birds hop about. The signs are there. Everyone can see them. Just that I look out for them. Scares me because they come close together. Maybe I wouldn't curl up like a sleeping dog if I could deal with them one at a time, with a lot of space in between."

"Ops?"

"Yeah."

"I didn't want that old jug anyway."

About three days later, Mr. Shaefer arrived back. He carried Lukas from the car and put him sitting down beside me on the porch swing seat.

"Been drinking my brew," he told us and then he went back to the car to fetch a bundle of newspapers wrapped in twine with too big a knot.

Lukas turned, put his hands against my left shoulder and laid his head on them. I didn't much like being his pillow.

Ops snapped open the bundle with a knife and began reading. Mr. Shaefer always brought a newspaper from whatever place he went to. There was *The Houston Chronicle, The Rusk Cherokeean* and *The Shamrock Texan* but a lot more as well. He even brought *The New York Times*. Mr. Shaefer did a lot of traveling in that old truck of his. He stayed talking for a while and then drove off, leaving Lukas behind.

Daddy took his rocking chair and brought it down beside the steps to the porch. He sat down and put his feet up against the steps so that the rocking chair was kept still, rolled back to the point that it'd fall over if a puff of wind blew at it. Then he began reading.

"Don't like rocking when I'm reading," he once said. "The words must land in the right place in my mind. Can't have that if my head is moving with the chair."

After a while, Lukas woke up and looked at me as if he had never seen me before. He sat up but his eyes were still half-closed.

"What's going on?" he asked.

"C'mon," Ops said and brought him inside to put him to bed. When she came back out she was nervous.

"*Catequil*," she whispered.

That was her word for thunder. She started walking towards the outhouse where she slept. On her way, she took out a black and white bald eagle feather that she kept in her pocket and held it up. It was her way of warding off the thunder. Daddy went inside and continued reading. The thunder and lightning began. I ran over to the outhouse and found Ops lying down on her side, chanting and shivering. I lay down beside her and put my arm over her, holding her hands.

"Don't worry, Ops," I said. "That old lightning won't get you when I'm here."

I felt her body getting tense just before the lightning struck. She knew it was coming. She kept chanting. It was like she was crying, really afraid. After a long time, her body stopped getting tense. She knew it was over. She stopped chanting and fell asleep. I left and found Daddy out on the porch again, drinking Mr. Shaefer's brew.

"Best get to bed."

I sat down. He started talking or maybe it was Mr. Shaefer's brew talking.

"Last year, down in Houston, something like eight men, they went in and took a man out of a hotel, bellhop, a black man and lynched him, killed him. His body was found hanging from a bridge about eight miles outside the city on the West Heimer Road. That was last year.

"So they all started saying, 'We have to get these people. This can't go on'. And then I get the *Orange Leader*, Mr. Shaefer brought it, and I find out that four of the people made confessions but the District Attorney had lost the papers. That's what happened there. That's what you're dealing with."

I asked Daddy why bad things happen.

"There's no design, Set. It's random. Cotton's all in."

"Yeah, I know," I said and went to bed.

Lukas was knocked out beside me. I couldn't sleep. I knew that Daddy was only sounding off about life, how tough it is or was or will be. I thought he was mad that he couldn't do anything about it. That was the only connection. He was furious that all these people up there on the hill in the city didn't treat us right and he was disappointed and saddened that the laws to protect us were just ink.

We sat out on the porch after Thanksgiving dinner. Mrs. Taylor left down some grape jelly. She started telling me how to make biscuits, maybe because I was always getting biscuits from her or because she knew something else. She told me to use baking powder with sweet milk and if you use sour milk you mix it with soda and baking powder. I wasn't much interested in making biscuits, just eating them.

"They all talking about Wall Street," Daddy said. "The Crash. The world's come tumbling down."

He was drinking Mr. Shaefer's brew.

"Yeah," I said. "I heard them at it again today in Troy, in the General Store."

"Well, they talk about everything there," Daddy said. "Be surprised if the country going bankrupt didn't come up in conversation. I got a letter from your uncle."

"Yeah?"

"Says there's a job going – grocery boy. He knows someone. Could keep it for you if you like."

"I don't want to go to New York, Daddy."

"Up to you. Says he can put you up."

"I don't want to go."

Daddy didn't seem to mind. He started talking about something else or at least I thought it was about something else.

"Ops was standing in the wind earlier," he said. "Says there's been no-one shooting young deer lately."

"Did the wind tell her that?"

"I don't know," he said. "She said it's going to rain too. Said it's going to get worse. It's not only Wall Street. Poverty is going to spread like a prairie fire around the country. We'll be the worst hit. We always are."

"How do you know New York'll be any better?" I asked. "That's where it all started."

"I don't," he replied, "except that you'll have a guaranteed job and a place to stay. That's all."

"But I have that here."

"Sure you do."

"How does Ops know it's going to get worse anyway?" I asked. "Did the wind tell her that too?"

"No, she read it in the *Chronicle*."

We moved from 1929 to 1930 without much fanfare. I thought the sky might light up but nature didn't seem to think that changing from one decade to the next was worth getting all that worked up about. Neither did a lot of people.

I had just been told that Mr. and Mrs. Boldt were about to lose their farm when the Shaefers arrived. I was sitting on the porch steps with Eduardo and Gabriela. Lukas joined us. I wasn't in the mood for listening to him but then something caught my attention.

"What's that?" I asked. "Who's selling deer?"

"No-one is selling deer," Lukas said. "They're selling the John Deeres, the tractors."

"Why?" I asked.

Lukas was impatient with me. "Ain't you been listening? The whole country's seizing up. Everyone's selling everything. Some people reckon it's the end of the world."

"But why are they selling the tractors?" I asked.

"It's because they got no money and needs some," he explained. "That's why. Everywhere we drive, there's people on the move. They always stop and look at us. They look like they just came out of a grave."

"Why are they on the move?" I asked.

"That's because they've been kicked off their land. That's why. When we goes to New York next, I'm going find me that feller in Wall Street who done all this and I'm going to punch his nose in real good. That's what I'm going to do. Everywhere we go. They all have suitcases or bags. People don't smile anymore."

I told him about Mr. and Mrs. Boldt having to leave their house and live with us.

"Hope they don't forget about my jug," Lukas said. "It's mine. No grubby stock-broker's getting his filthy paws on that. No, sir. I'll break his nose too."

I was a little jealous of Lukas Shaefer because he could travel around all over the country. There I was, back in school and still having to go over to Mrs. Taylor because my daddy insisted on it. I wanted to have the life Lukas Shaefer had. He always knew what was going on. I thought maybe being a grocery boy in New York wouldn't be so bad. I'd be living in a big city. Lukas Shaefer wouldn't.

I went up to Mrs. Taylor's one time for more schooling.

"Mrs. Taylor?" I asked because I was having real problems with the French lesson we were doing.

She wasn't herself.

"Mrs. Taylor? I don't know. It's too difficult for me."

Still no answer. I looked at the phrase again.

Il s'est alors produit un silence absolu.

"Yeah," she said. "Too difficult. Too advanced for you."

I felt she was mocking me. She still hadn't answered my question. She went off on a different course.

"What if you took a slice of this American cake?" she asked. "A thin slice, here, in this place? Is it all like here?"

"I don't understand, Mrs. Taylor."

Even though she went on to explain, it seemed as if she hadn't heard my question.

"Mr. and Mrs. Boldt having to get out. All your father's stories; about the black man put in jail, the other black man lynched and marked, same thing really, the corruption and now all this poverty. Is it just all in our slice of cake?"

"I don't know, Mrs. Taylor?"

"No, of course you don't. Go home. I'm finished."

I didn't like the way she spoke to me. I gathered up my books, put my flat cap on and walked to the door but, as I did so, anger started pumping inside me. I opened the door and looked back. She was staring out the window and didn't even seem to be aware that I had gotten up and was at the door. The anger shot out of me.

"I'm doing my best, Mrs. Taylor."

I banged the door behind me. She called after me.

"Set. Set! Come back."

I kept walking.

"I'm sorry," she shouted.

I wanted to go back but I just kept walking, my anger driving me away.

"Daddy?" I asked. "Is that job still there, the one in New York? The one for me?"

"Job won't become free for another month or so," he replied. "That's what your uncle said."

"Well, I want to go to New York."

"Is that because you're fed up of schooling?"

"No. I just want to go."

"Better get you fitted up for a suit then. I ain't having no son of mine looking like a tramp in New York."

"A seersucker suit?"

"No. Tweed."

I decided for some reason, perhaps because of my row with Mrs. Taylor, that I would improve my punctuation and my writing. I wanted to show her that I could do well. So, I began to punctuate and write as well as I could.

I spent New Year's Day 1930 moving stuff from the Boldts' house to our house. We had to leave some chairs in the Boldts' house because there wasn't enough room to store them anywhere. Daddy had asked them to move in with us because they had nowhere else to go so they weren't exactly in a position to decline his offer. We also had to move my things out of my room. There wasn't much. Ops insisted on having my stuff put in the outhouse where she slept. It was school-books mostly and the book about Troy with the blue and purple cover.

I went up one time to the Boldts' house to see if they wanted anything else doing. Only Mr. Boldt was there. I felt uneasy saying anything to him. I didn't know what to do.

"Mr. Boldt."

He was sitting where he normally sat.

"Sit down, son."

I sat down where I normally sat.

"Folks have stopped saying to me, 'How are you?' or '*Wie geht's?*' Guess they know the answer."

"Where's Mrs. Boldt?" I asked.

"Mr. Shaefer's taken her to Troy. Selling a few odds and ends. Ends."

I looked at the dresser and there it still was, the box made of Canadian pine.

"Never thought we'd end up like this," Mr. Boldt said.

"Can I do anything, Mr. Boldt? You want anything else brought down?"

"Having to rely on the kindness of neighbors for shelter."

There were long silences.

"They have a phrase in German, you know, *zu lebendig begraben*, to be buried alive. In debt. Roof is gone, floor is gone, walls are gone, dignity is gone. Worse than being buried alive."

"We're honored, Mr. Boldt, to have you in our house," I said.

"You been working on that for a while, have you?" he asked. "Your father told you to say that? Well-rehearsed, it was."

Another silence made me shift on the chair.

"You want to swap places?" Mr. Boldt asked me.

I didn't answer.

"Don't blame you," he said. "Here I am. Mrs. Boldt ain't talking to me. All my fault, see. Buying stocks and shares. Putting the house and farm on it. If only I had sold them. No use now. I hear we're taking your room."

"It's your room now, Mr. Boldt."

"How did he put it to you, your father? Great adventure, New York? Didn't tell you that he can't afford to feed so many mouths no matter how hard you work? He didn't tell you that, did he? Did he?"

He was snarling at me and at my daddy.

"But I want to go to New York, Mr. Boldt."

"Oh, I'm sure you do and ain't you lucky while me and my wife rot here?"

"I'm sorry, Mr. Boldt."

"Yeah. I'm sure you are."

I shifted in my chair again.

"Your father often tells me about his friend Ira. I didn't know him but from what your father says he was a good friend to him. Said that Ira once told him never to leave a guest standing at the door. Seems to have been a civilized kind of feller."

"Yeah, they put him in jail for stealing oxen."

"Eight years, your father said. He likes to talk after drinking Mr. Shaefer's brew, does your father. Told you about the Klan, the people they lynched and killed, about the Fergusons, the governors, voting for them, making his mark?"

"Yes, sir."

"Told you all that? Told you what he thinks now? Wall Street?"

"Yeah. Lukas Shaefer says he wants to punch all them brokers in the nose. Well, one of them anyways. That's what I want to do too."

"They're coming tomorrow to take the house," Mr. Boldt said. "Men in suits. The suitors, I call them. They're all the same, these powerful people. They're the same ones who took away eight years of that man's life when he was in prison. Stole those eight years on him. Same with the Klan who marked that man's face. Stole his identity with three letters and a bucket of acid. Your father's right. You know who was among them, Hiram Wesley Evans, the Exalted Cyclops of the Ku Klux Klan. And here I am, my house being stolen off me. I suppose I'll have the honor of becoming one of your father's anecdotes when he's drunk next time."

"I wouldn't say that, Mr. Boldt."

"I would. You know what their great weapon is? Censorship. They even tried to censor Heine. You remember me telling you about him? About Heinrich Heine?"

"Yes, Mr. Boldt."

"Censoring eight years of a man's life, censoring a man's identity with KKK on his forehead, censoring my house. I had plans for this house you know. I wouldn't punch them in the nose like what your friend is planning on. No. Noses heal."

"What then?"

"Find someone in New York, maybe someone on a street corner, someone they're trying to shut up. They being those people up there with their fine offices on the top floor of them skyscrapers."

"What'll I do then?"

"Make sure they're heard – the people they're trying to silence."

"What if they're saying the wrong thing, Mr. Boldt?"

"They won't be. The fact that them suitors are trying to button their cakehole means that whatever they have to say will be worth listening to. I had plans for this house you know."

"It's all right, Mr. Boldt."

He answered me calmly.

"No, Set. No. It's not all right."

We sat in silence on the chairs we normally sat on.

"She'll be leaving you the jug. We wanted to leave you something much better."

We would never sit on those chairs again.

Other people would.

✝
✝

Mr. and Mrs. Boldt stood on their porch arm-in-arm looking out at their neighbors who had gathered to watch them being buried alive. The couple were dressed in their dark Sunday best. It was Friday. Mrs. Boldt held a small box made of Canadian pine. Inside was a milk jug made of Dresden china. Two men in suits waited for them, one big, one small. They were made of greed.

It might have been the sun in his eyes, the effect of the eviction on him or just old age but Mr. Boldt stumbled on the first porch step. We all stumbled with him. His wife did her best to steady him and succeeded but there was a price to be paid. The sound said it all, the sound of a Dresden china milk jug breaking. She had dropped the box of Canadian pine.

She bent down and, as she picked up the box, the broken pieces rattled. It made her stop for a moment. Blinded by the sun, Mr. Boldt waved his arm beside him, its tempo revealing his panic. She stood up, her body bringing her husband's waving to an awkward halt.

"I'm here," she said sternly.

"Is it broken?" he asked.

"Fool," she said under her breath.

We all heard.

They grappled to link their arms again. It wasn't the most elegant of exits.

Mr. Shaefer obeyed the order Mrs. Boldt had given him. They would walk unaided to his Sterling delivery truck. Mrs. Boldt's prized 1921 Singer sewing machine had already been loaded on to it. He was waiting for them with the door open. They got in. Mr. Shaefer took the wheel and drove them round the hill to our house.

Gabriela began to run around. Eduardo stopped her and put his index finger to his mouth. She looked at me, wondering why she had to be quiet. I shook my head, reinforcing Eduardo's order. She obeyed. We held her hands.

Even though the Boldts were gone, we remained. The two men in suits, one big, one small, made their way to the house. People were standing on the hill. Some had come all the way out from Troy. Lukas Shaefer broke the silence. He roared in his boy's piercing voice at the men in suits.

"Don't come looking to us for no sugar."

The bigger suit looked over and smiled. They continued walking.

"What's the matter? Cat got your tongue?" Lukas roared.

"Best go home, son. You're trespassing," the bigger suit said.

"No, *you's* ah-trespassing," Lukas said. "*You's* ah-trespassing."

The suits ignored Lukas and kept walking.

"So which one of you ladies does the knitting?" Lukas asked.

Laughter reached us from nowhere discernible. We all heard.

The smaller suit turned quickly to face Lukas but the bigger one restrained him.

"Go home, son. All of you, go home. We're not the ones going to be living here."

Lukas wouldn't stop.

"Well ain't you the fast learner, boy? Darn right you won't be. Now you two dumbasses clear out. This is our neighbors' home. Go on. Get back to the rat-hole you come out of. Go on. Git."

Lukas launched the last word as he raised his arm quickly and dismissively in front of him and then lowered it. He turned his head to the side, spat, wiped his mouth with his shirt sleeve and walked away. The men in suits glared at him. We all drifted off, silently following the decision of Lukas to go.

A few days later, we had a party in our house, not for the Boldts but for me, not so much celebrating my departure but marking it. The days in between had not been the easiest.

Several times, Ops left for the outhouse without saying anything because Mrs. Boldt insisted on taking over every housekeeping duty. She felt she must earn her keep.

Mrs. Boldt also made it clear in several casual remarks that she wasn't overjoyed at the prospect of living in a house where alcohol was consumed. We were told stories – many, many stories – of how liquor had brought misery and destitution to the greatest and noblest of men.

My daddy did not drink much and did not want to make Mrs. Boldt feel uncomfortable so he took himself off to Mr. Nestor's house when he wanted to relax. In fact, he took himself off to Mr. Nestor's house most evenings. I found it odd that Mrs. Boldt's attempts to make my daddy stop drinking made him drink more. His absence from the house in the evenings eased the tension a little before it was racked up again by Mrs. Boldt; she'd ask my daddy if he had been up to Mr. Nestor's which, we all knew, meant had he been drinking again.

On top of this, Mr. Boldt had decided to help out on the farm because he felt he should earn his keep as well. This was not a good idea. Why, he even shuffled and groaned when he was sitting down. Only the strong words of Mrs. Boldt managed to stop her husband from taking up a shovel or cleaning the John Deere. There was a sad and ugly silence after this particular argument. It seemed as if all of us were thrown into a barrel to chase and annoy each other.

I got to thinking about all this on the day of my party and realized that not only had the Boldts' house been taken over by the brokers, so too, had my daddy's.

Lukas Shaefer enjoyed the party more than anyone else. He crouched on a piece of wood, his legs shooting up to his knees. There he was, a toadstool in human form, full of mischief. He couldn't find enough enjoyable things to do like leaving down his bowl and chasing Gabriela, returning to his pie and nearly falling over backwards laughing when Eduardo tumbled while trying to do a handstand. I thought that this playful Lukas Shaefer, the one at my party, could not have been the one on the hill who had humiliated the suitors when they took possession of the Boldts' house but it was.

I should have been at the center of my going-away party but I was not. Another being was. All the punctuation, grammar and underlining in the world that I had learned up to that point, was not enough to describe this creature. In other words, while I knew it existed then, I could not have described it then. I can only describe it now. Only the future can explain this past.

This unwelcome guest at my going-away party was formed of many distressing parts. The bad luck which it visited on my neighbors and on my daddy pulsated in our midst. It had the power of a stirring and unnerving nightmare the day after a troubled sleep. It had the temerity to leave my celebration – for me – bereft of joy by possessing it with an undercurrent of desolation. This unwelcome spirit surfaced relentlessly above the water-line for air it really didn't need, raising its decomposing head for the sole purpose of attracting attention to itself. It reminded me of a fawn felled for no reason. It was made up of the tension caused by the Boldts being in the house, of the belly-churning when I thought about my unknown and future life in New York and of the untouchable but fleshy feeling that a vexatious spirit had engulfed our waking and sleeping lives. It was fueled, this feeling, by the stories of families wandering aimlessly and uselessly on dusty roads across the United States stranded between hopelessness and hunger, between humiliation and poverty and subjected to the effects of all. It was made up of anger that could not, at that time, be directed at any person or thing. It had a name, this being. It would become known as the Great Depression. It preyed on powerless lungs, clapped out livers and exhausted hearts. The things it did to us were beyond all bearing. I felt it was smiling, gleeful, reveling in our ordeal and in our tortured lives.

At my party I sat down beside Mr. Shaefer and he told me the Taylors had left the neighborhood.

"Didn't you see their car all hitched up? They're gone, son."

"Gone where?"

"Dunno."

"Why didn't they say goodbye?"

"Guess it's not easy when you have to leave," Mr. Shaefer said. "The men in suits were at their place – saw them off."

"But why didn't she say goodbye?" I asked.

"Maybe she doesn't like to cry in front of people," he answered.

"She wrote a phrase in French," I said. "I don't know what it is."

"I speak French," Mr. Shaefer said.

I fetched my French book. Mr. Shaefer scratched his head.

"*Il s'est alors produit un silence absolu.* That's mighty highfalutin' French."

"She said it was advanced," I told him.

"It describes an aftermath, you know," he said, "what it's like after something has happened so it means that complete silence followed. Maybe she was trying to tell you something. She's gone now so there's silence or maybe it was just part of the lesson and doesn't really mean anything."

"Mr. Shaefer, you know that poem by Heinrich Heine, *Schlage die trommel?*"

"You mean *Doktrin?*" he said.

"That's what it's called?" I asked. "I didn't know that. What does that mean?"

"Philosophy."

"Oh," I said. "I was wrong then. I thought, you know, when I listen to it, Lukas knows it, when I listen to it, it's like a drum and it's like you should bang a drum and keep banging it until you get what you want."

"That's exactly what it says."

"Why's it called *Philosophy* then?"

"Philosophy as in your philosophy," Mr. Shaefer explained. "What *you* believe, *your* way of dealing with life. Imagine that, a poet being able to tell someone what he thinks purely by the rhythm. It's all about freedom of speech, banging the drum so you'll be heard. Freedom of hearing, too."

"Thank you, Mr. Shaefer. Mr. Shaefer, what'll I do in New York?"

"Keep your money in your hand at all times and keep the other one clenched just in case."

✝
✝

I woke on the mattress in our living room with Lukas Shaefer beside me sleeping soundly. This is where I had slept since the Boldts' arrival. I could make out the shape of Mrs. Boldt's prized 1921 Singer sewing machine that had been placed on the small table near the door as soon as they moved in. It was a constant reminder of their presence but we didn't need a constant reminding. Lukas moved and laid his arm across my chest, still sleeping soundly. It was hard to believe this ball of energy could ever sleep. I never had a purer friend than Lukas Shaefer.

They gathered from near and far to see me off as the first week of the New Year was coming to an end. Mr. Shaefer would take me on his wandering journey from Bell County to New York because he had business all the way there and in that great city. Lukas would be my constant companion. After the hugs and hand-shakes, I felt uneasy. Then Eduardo came along. He had Gabriela in his arms. He said goodbye and wished me luck. I said goodbye to Gabriela and kissed her on the forehead. She was shocked. She knew something was wrong, saw the car, Mr. Shaefer with my suitcase, waiting. Eduardo carried her off. She began to scream.

"No. Set? Set?"

She tried to defeat the distance she was being brought away from me by screaming louder. Her little legs were paddling rapidly on either side of Eduardo. He held her close so the only way she could fight back was to punch his shoulders. I didn't know she loved me so much. I didn't know I loved her so much. She went into a fit, her voice loaded with all the force that her small frame would allow. It became a growl of terror.

"Set. Set. No. Set!"

It went on and on. It was my fault that she was crying which made it worse for me. I wanted to hug her as I had done before when she had fallen. I wanted it to stop but I had no power. I couldn't bear to hear her in distress. I didn't know what to do. I began to cry. Mr. Shaefer took me and shoved me in the car. He drove off. My last vision of Bell County was through a wall of tears. For once, Lukas Shaefer said nothing. Even he knew it was all over.

The Great Depression had not only forced the Boldts out of their house, driven me to wander far and wide and invaded my daddy's home but it had also ruined our departing embraces, tearing at our faces with thorns as we tried to kiss our goodbyes with eyes closed. I knew there was no use attacking all of the exalted Cyclops that had risen up in our midst. Just one little bit would do me. Dang, that was it.

I was going to save enough money in New York so I could buy the Boldts' house off them brokers. That way, they could return home and I could get my daddy's house back.

We took a strange route, dictated by Mr. Shaefer's business, passing through Athens in Tennessee, Ulysses in Kentucky and Ithaca in Ohio. I had funny thoughts along the way: images of the black and white bald eagle feather that Ops held up to ward off the thunder and lightning; the blue and purple cover of the book about Troy, the one in Asia Minor, now stored in the outhouse; and my daddy's sadness because he didn't really have his own home anymore.

As we approached New York, I closed my eyes and imagined the smoke rising from our neighbors' houses outside Troy, the one in Texas, and thought how much I'd love to see them again. But I had left my home in the Central Plains between the Piney Woods and the Hill Country, and had traveled north east, to New York where my uncle lived. My uncle lived there. I did not know what the future hailed.

2

THE VOICE THAT MUST BE HEARD

A S THE BUILDINGS BECAME TALLER and taller my eyes became wider and wider. Lukas Shaefer didn't appear much interested in the high office blocks, though. He was more looking out for girls, pretty ones in particular. Mr. Shaefer started querying how rich folk could build all them skyscrapers one minute and then attack us folk the next but he put it another way.

"How can they go up so high and down so low?" he asked.

"They's dumb," Lukas said. "Putting that extra walk on themselves, having to go all the way up them stairs."

"They *do* have elevators, Lukas," Mr. Shaefer said.

"Yeah, but they don't always work, Daddy," Lukas argued. "Got to take that into account."

He always had an answer for everything, Lukas. Mr. Shaefer held my shoulders tightly as I stood for the first time on a New York sidewalk.

"It's around that corner, not so far," he said. "The Cyclops hotel, where your uncle lives. You remember? Got me some business to do but I'll be back here in this spot in an hour or so. I'll wait ten minutes, traffic willing. Just in case."

It was cold. I knocked on the window of the car but Lukas just kept looking away.

"What's wrong with him?" I asked.

"Can't you guess?" Mr. Shaefer said back.

As Mr. Shaefer drove off, Lukas looked back at me, tears streaming down his face. I put my hand up but didn't wave. Thought he'd stick his tongue out at me like he normally did but he just turned away.

I hugged my small suitcase and saw a sign – Broome Street. It looked like a real untidy yard. Reminded me of the one behind the General Store in Troy where there were rusty railings, an old "General Store" sign and plenty other things once prized, now trashed. I thought someone must have dumped all these bits of junk here on Broome Street just like that old yard in Troy. Funny name, Broome Street, because it was in need of a good sweeping, like what Mrs. Boldt might give it.

There was a man with a cloth cap standing at the doorway of a three-storey building across the street. His hands were in his pockets, legs apart. He looked like he was guarding the place but, to tell the truth, the place didn't look as if it was in need of much guarding.

I walked round the corner and found the Cyclops hotel easy enough. The man behind the reception desk was talking to a woman who was holding a small dog. Her perfume smelt like a greengrocer's shop. I waited quite a while. Then I got fed up, couldn't help myself interrupting. The man raised his hand: he wasn't ready. They kept on talking and talking. Eventually she left. Her dog looked at me as she carried it out.

"Well now, and what can I do for you, me boy?" the man asked.

When I told him my uncle's name, he said he hadn't ever heard tell of him. He checked the register and then he found he *did* remember him. This all took too long for my liking.

"Ah, you won't find him now," he said.

"Why not?" I asked.

"Well, you might," he said.

I told him I was in a hurry because Mr. Shaefer was coming back. He still took his time answering.

"Dead," he said. "Pauper's grave. Last week. Nice man."

"You sure?"

"Stone cold sure."

He laughed.

I ran out, leaving my suitcase behind me. I just plain forgot it. I found the place where Mr. Shaefer had dropped me off. I waited and waited but there was no sign of him. It must have been longer than an hour. My mind played tricks on me. Had it really been that long? The man I had seen earlier, guarding the building or whatever he was doing, was still there.

"Hey, mister, did you see a truck stopping by here about an hour ago?" I shouted.

"The one that dropped you off?" he asked.

"Yeah that's the one," I said.

"Yep," he replied. "Came back again, waited a few minutes and then drove off."

"Thanks, mister," I said.

"Don't thank people for giving you bad news in New York," he roared back at me as I walked off. "They'll make a habit of it."

I ran back to the Cyclops hotel. The man was still there, my suitcase wasn't.

"Where's my suitcase?" I asked.

He was on the telephone and put his hand up again to stop me talking. I had to wait again.

"What suitcase?" he asked when he hung up.

Well, I didn't stop to think about what to say. The words just came out. I was mad. Before I knew it, I was being grabbed from behind by a policeman.

"That's him," the man said. "A right young pup."

I didn't realize it then but later I did. When I had gone, the man must have hidden my suitcase and then telephoned the police telling them I was a thief or something, knowing that I'd come back and kick up a fuss.

"What's your name?" the policeman asked.

"He stole my suitcase," I told him.

"Tried to steal a woman's bag too," the man said. "Mrs. Carey's. Now he's accusing me."

Without thinking, I jumped up onto the reception desk and went to punch him in the face but he ducked. The officer pulled me back and dragged me out and all the way down to the police station. I was locked in a cell with some other boy. It was cold. He was dressed like me, about my age, wearing a cloth cap and collarless shirt too. In the silence that followed I stole a glance at him. He was sad and dreamy-looking but he seemed like he'd know which alley to run down if he was being chased.

"What's yer name, boy?" he asked me.

He was Irish.

I wasn't in the mood for small talk or being called boy by another boy. I kicked one of the cell bars. Ouch.

"Goddam it."

"Mine's Pen."

"Like, Benjamin?"

"No. Pen. P-E-N, as in penitentiary."

"Mine's Set."

"As in settler?"

"No. Just Set. They stole my suitcase."

"The cops?"

"No. That man. The man in the hotel."

"What hotel?"

"The Cyclops hotel?"

"Oh yeah. He's a right shite, that fella. Sullivan. Smoke?"

I declined.

"Put that cigarette out," the cop said.

Pen kept on smoking.

A big man had arrived with the policeman at the cell door. The big man was wearing a bowler hat and a long black coat.

The officer – the one who had pulled me out of the Cyclops hotel – opened the cell door and Pen went out. Pen whispered to the big man.

"Him too," the big man said, pointing at me.

"I don't think so," the cop said and locked the cell door. "He launched a boot at me when I was taking him in."

The big man stared at the policeman.

"Open it," the big man growled.

"Go on," the cop said, letting me out. "Off with yourself."

Pen started imitating the cop's accent and what he might say to us.

"I don't for to be wanting for to be seeing the pair of yiz about here again, in the name of God and his Holy Mother, for to be sure and all the saints preserve us from harm."

The big man pushed Pen. That stopped him talking.

"Come on," the big man said, and the three of us left the station.

We stopped on the sidewalk.

"He'll need somewhere to stay," Pen said.

"Can't he stay at yours?" the big man asked.

"No. Bring him to me parents' place," Pen said and walked off.

"Come on," the big man said.

I followed him down Broome Street. People tipped their hat to him or nodded their head. He stopped to talk to some people on the way down. Some were poor, others looked as if they were not so poor. He whispered to still more people.

We turned a corner a few blocks away, leaving Broome Street behind us and stopped outside tall houses with steps leading up to their front doors.

"What was in the suitcase?" the big man asked me.

"My suit," I said.

"Suppose that's why they call them suitcases. Anything else?"

"Change of underwear. Clean shirt. Pair of socks. Four dollars and my birth papers and…"

"And?"

"And two gramophone records. Mrs. Taylor gave them me. She's my neighbor. Was. Was."

"Who's singing on them?"

"Balfe and Caruso."

"Second floor," the big man said. "The door with a pane of glass in it. You can't see through it. Frozen, I think they call it or frosted. The Finnegans' place. Irish, like meself. Say I sent you: Haltigan."

Mr. Haltigan walked off.

"Mr. Haltigan," I said. "What about my suitcase?"

He didn't answer. I went up to the second floor and found the door with a pane of glass in it. Frozen, frosted, just like the weather. It was cold.

I heard the chugging of a small engine from behind the door. I waited until I heard it stop before knocking. A tall woman opened the door. She was holding pins between her lips and had a piece of cloth thrown over her shoulder.

"Come in out of the cold," she said like she had been expecting me. "We don't ever leave guests standing at the door."

"Sit down there on the bed," she said. "We'll have soup in a few minutes. I'll just finish this. Potato and carrot."

I reckoned she was just mistaking me for someone else. Every time I tried to explain to her what happened, she just kept talking about bread rolls, the theater and a set of china that she had been given as a wedding present. I wasn't really able to listen too careful after all that had happened to me. I tried but I couldn't get a word in edgeways. She sat behind a Singer sewing machine that was introduced to me like most other things in the place.

"1921," she explained. "The 99 model. Singer. A great old machine. And look at the box it came in. Isn't it great? A beautiful box."

The Singer sewing machine was bobbing away. The light was shining on the pins sticking out of her mouth.

"It's electric," she said, stopping the machine and looking at me.

It was her ace card for the Singer sewing machine.

"The boys'll be back shortly," she said. "Tom was it, you're looking for?"

I stared at her, fearing I was nearing the end of my stay.

"No, ma'am," I said. "Mr. Haltigan sent me. I should have said earlier, just that you didn't give me a chance."

"Haltigan," she said, stopping the sewing machine. "Why did he send you?"

"Well," I said, "I was to meet my uncle but he's dead. In the hotel. But this man, he stole my suitcase. I had all my things in it. My suit and other things, things I need and four dollars. And then I got arrested and they put me in jail and then Mr. Haltigan came along and sent me up here."

"They put you in jail?" she asked.

"Well, I was mad when the policeman wouldn't listen to me. So I kicked him. Wasn't no accident."

"The policeman made him kick you and then he had the gall to put you in jail?" she asked.

"And it's only my first day here, Mrs. Finnegan."

"You kicked a policeman and you were put in jail on your first day in New York?" she asked.

"Yes, ma'am," I said.

"You must be Irish," she said. "You can stay a night or two, of course."

"Thank you, Mrs. Finnegan. Promise I'll pay you once I get my suitcase back. There's four dollars in it."

"Why did Mr. Haltigan arrive in the police station?" she asked. "Was it to get someone else out?"

I couldn't say nothing.

"I know," she said. "Pen must have been there. She does that."

"She?"

"Tomboy. They all think we're a laughing stock. She stays with her Aunt Lil now. My sister. Not much room here or privacy for a girl her age. She needs that. They say she's left because of what she is. That's what they think. It's not true."

She went quiet and looked as if she was about to cry. I felt I had to say something to comfort her. My mind raced.

"Mrs. Finnegan, it's like what Mr. Boldt said, my neighbor. She's just a voice that should be heard. Being herself, that's all. Ain't no harm in that. Leastways, that's what I think."

She stared at me. "Did I just say you could stay a night or two? How stupid of me."

I didn't know if I had said the right thing or the wrong thing. The sound of heavy footsteps on the stairs saved me from having to figure it out.

"Like a herd of elephants," Mrs. Finnegan said.

Stephen, Finn and Tom burst in and stopped in their tracks when they saw me.

"This is Set," Mrs. Finnegan said. "He's staying with us."

They mumbled hellos. Tom was about my age. He was angry and kept to himself. Finn was a few years younger and real shy. Stephen was only about four or five. Tom got a newspaper, and lay on the bed behind me reading the funnies. I wanted to get to know them but thought my time with the Finnegans was coming to an end because of what I had said about Pen.

"How long's he staying?" Tom asked.

"Permanently," Mrs. Finnegan replied.

We had all sat down to eat when Mr. Finnegan came in.

"And who is this handsome young devil?" he asked.

"Set is his name," Mrs. Finnegan said. "Set Wright."

Mr. Finnegan clapped and then shook my hand. His eyebrows went up and he smiled at me like he was about to laugh.

"Good," he said. "We'll all have a grand old time."

As we were eating, I told my story again about what happened to me earlier. I was interrupted so much by the Finnegan brothers that I thought my story would last well into the night. I told them about Lukas Shaefer, Mrs. Taylor and Ops which led to more questions. Mrs. Finnegan tried to stop them but it was no use. They liked to talk just as much as she did.

At one point, Finn repeated what I had said, imitating my accent.

"*It weren't no eek-sah-dint,*" he said, "*keek-an daw poh-lees-main.*"

"Finn," Mrs. Finnegan said. "You do not insult a guest in this house. Get up and stand in the corner, facing the wall. Move it."

For all his shyness, Finn had the presence of mind to dig out a large chunk of his meal and fill his mouth before obeying his mother. When he had taken up his position, she gave him another order.

"When you've finished getting that mountain of food down your gullet, turn around and apologize to Set and then turn back to the wall again."

We listened as he chewed and chewed and gulped. Mrs. Finnegan began to smile. Finn turned round. "I'm sorry, Set," he said. "I'm sorry what I done. Didn't mean it. Honest."

He turned back to face the wall again.

"I didn't take no offense, Mrs. Finnegan," I said. "He told me he liked my accent earlier. He didn't mean no harm."

Finn was called back to the table. He didn't eat any more, just kept looking at me and smiling.

✝
✝

"You're over by the window, Set," Mrs. Finnegan said, handing me pajamas. "The three of ye, in the other bed. Be asleep by the time we get back. We're just going downstairs to Mr. and Mrs. Blois. Wedding anniversary. A little celebration. Set, as I said, you're staying here now. I don't take kindly to anyone stealing out before breakfast. And don't you worry, *I'll* deal with that horrible man in the hotel. I've seen him before; face that'd stop a clock."

I drifted off to sleep but, later on, I half-woke up when Mr. and Mrs. Finnegan returned. They were quiet but Mrs. Finnegan could not help whispering.

"Goodnight, boys. Goodnight, Pen."

"Set," Mr. Finnegan whispered, correcting her.

"Oh yes, Set."

They went into their bedroom and it became quiet again except for the strange sounds of New York outside and the footsteps of a late night worker or drinker coming up the stairs. I went back to sleep on my first night in New York: the day I had stumbled upon Pen Finnegan whose voice was being heard, who had sent me to her parents' home for shelter.

✝
✝

"What do you think of New York?" Mr. Finnegan asked me as all the other Finnegans were yakking over breakfast.

"Strange," I answered.

The Finnegans stopped talking. I needed to explain.

"When I got here yesterday, all the feelings I had in Texas, why, they came up with me. I thought they might stay in Texas."

"Feelings?" Mrs. Finnegan asked. "You mean missing your family? Of course you will, it's only natural."

"No, Mrs. Finnegan," I said, "not only that. Feelings. Feelings, like anger."

"What are you angry about?" Mr. Finnegan asked.

"What I told you all yesterday," I said. "Don't you remember? Our neighbors, the Boldts, evicted. Nowhere to go. We took them in. Ain't easy for my daddy. He's not there much. Him and Mrs. Boldt don't really get on. She don't like him drinking. So, I'm angry. It's not easy to tell. See, I'm angry that the Boldts lost their house but I'm also angry that my daddy has lost his house now as well. It's really not his anymore and I'm angry that I feel this way about the Boldts because they were good neighbors. I feel bad about it. And I'm angry that I had to leave. And I'm angry because I don't know who did it. And I'm angry because my suitcase is gone. And I'm angry that I don't have any money to pay you."

"Your breakfast is getting cold, Set," Mrs. Finnegan said. "Eat up."

Mr. Haltigan called that afternoon with my suitcase. I noticed that his knuckles were red. The four dollars were still in my suitcase. Mrs. Finnegan refused to take any money but put my four dollars in a tin. Mr. Haltigan told me he'd get me a job as a look-out for a speakeasy. Spotters, they called them. I wanted to ask him about it but we were interrupted by Finn who came over to ask me to help him with his math tables. He said he couldn't do them and so he started drawing with crayons expecting me to do his homework.

"Now you just hold on a minute," I said. "Ain't no use me doing your homework while you slouch off there. Now, put them crayons down."

Mrs. Taylor had taught me more than learning. She had taught me teaching too. I wrote out the answers in any case but he didn't seem pleased.

"I still can't do them, Set," Finn said. "Davy Springer can, though. He helps me."

"Course you can," I told him.

"I can't remember," he said and hung his head. "I'm stupid."

"Don't you ever say that to me again," I said. "Now give me them crayons."

I used the crayons to color the numbers; a yellow circle round all the fives, a purple square around all the ones and so on. There weren't enough colors so some had a yellow triangle or a blue star around them.

"Now, that'll make it easy to remember," I told him. "Coloring the numbers makes it easy to remember. That's what I find anyway. You need to know these. Do you hear me?"

"Yeah."

"So keep looking at them," I said. The colors'll help. Do this for the next set of tables too but learn these off first."

"Thanks, Set."

Mrs. Finnegan didn't correct my grammar like she did after any of her children spoke. For the first time, I had used my way of talking to get my point across. Finn paced up and down the room with his copy-book held behind him, looking at it every now and then.

"Set," Mrs. Finnegan said. "Come to the table now and write a letter to your father. We'll post it tomorrow or, as they say here, mail it."

I asked Mrs. Finnegan if I should tell my daddy that my uncle was dead or that his brother was dead.

"You're writing the letter," she replied. "He's your uncle. So, your uncle is dead."

When me and the Finnegan brothers went to bed, Mr. and Mrs. Finnegan spoke quietly at the table. They were laughing. She spoke about the Theatre Royal in Dublin. From what she said, I found out that she had been a dancer, a seamstress and an actress at the theater.

I was still tired by all that had happened. The last thought I think I had before I went to sleep was a conversation I had heard earlier in the day when Tom and me had gone out. Two women spotted us. We walked round a corner and stopped. We could hear them talking.

"That was him there. The young lad from Texas."

"With the Finnegan lad, is it?"

"Black as the Devil himself when he came up. Covered in dirt."

"Jaysus."

"Mr. Gargan says Texas is full of dirt."

"It must be an awful place."

"Two hours he was in the bath rubbing himself back to normal."

"Jaysus. Two hours?"

"And all his family were butchered and eaten by the Indians."

"Christ, it must be an awful place."

"They had to go to the later Mass because the whole lot of them took the morning scrubbing the dirt off him."

"Jaysus, there must be a great trade in soap down there in Texas with all that dirt flying about."

"Arrah, I don't think they mind washing at all down there. Savages."
"No wonder he left. They went to the later Mass, did they?"

✝
✝

In no time at all, Mr. Haltigan got me a job as a look-out at the 21 Club. I thought Mrs. Finnegan mightn't like me being a spotter but she raised no objection because she thought alcohol should be legal. Then, when Tom taught me a song about Prohibition, Mrs. Finnegan showed us a dance routine to accompany it. We spun around, banged our feet on the floor and stretched our arms out as we sang:

> *Mother's in the kitchen,*
> *Washing out the jugs.*
> *Sister's in the pantry,*
> *Bottling the suds.*
> *Father's in the cellar,*
> *Mixing up the hops.*
> *Johnny's on the front porch,*
> *Watching for the cops.*

Mrs. Finnegan pointed a knitting needle at us when we went out of step. Finally, we got it the way she wanted and did the routine almost every day, before, during and after meals, when we met on the street and when we arrived back after working.

When I received my first letter from home, I tore open the envelope. The letter was from Ops, not my daddy.

Dear Set,

> *I have written another letter to Mrs. Finnegan which is enclosed. You have landed on your feet and we know you are being well looked after despite the bad news about your uncle. Your daddy is taking a while to come to terms with it. Only natural.*

Speaking of your daddy and indeed the rest of us, we all send you our love. We think about you all the time. All your things are kept carefully in the outhouse for your return.

Lukas is always asking about you. He misses you a lot even though he doesn't admit it.

Everything is the same here. Look after yourself,

Love,
Ops.

P.S. Your daddy had a slight accident with the John Deere, hurt his hand so that's why I'm writing.

All the way through the letter, I kept wondering why my daddy hadn't written. I raced through it until I found the last line. I didn't know why I thought what I did. Maybe it was because it should have been the first thing Ops told me but it was the last, like she was trying to make it seem as if it wasn't anything important. I just felt that my daddy hadn't hurt his hand working on the tractor but that he had fallen when he was drunk and probably broken it.

The Finnegans helped me to forget about sad things. Mr. and Mrs. Finnegan took turns teaching me French. Mrs. Finnegan drilled good grammar into me left, right, upside down, inside out and all around. So much so, that I said to her one day as a joke, "Mrs. Finnegan, I think there ain't no harm knowing this good grammar so I can speaks it when I wants". She didn't think that was funny.

My favorite times were when I was alone with Mr. Finnegan. He rubbed his hands as he stood and looked out the window. He was real excited when he talked. There was a thrill in his voice and it made me feel real good. I felt at home talking to him, so that once I said something real stupid.

"Mr. Finnegan, you know when Mr. Haltigan takes me and the other spotters to the cinema? Well there was this film we went to, *Chasing Rainbows* it was called up at the Capitol."

"Ah yes, Broadway at 51st," Mr. Finnegan said.

"That's it. Well, I didn't really like it but the poster, it had colors on it. Purple and blue. See, I used those colors when I was helping Finn with his math and them's the color on the front of a book I read about Troy, the one in Asia Minor. Same colors. And then Ops – you remember I told you about her?"

"Yes."

"Well, she's afraid of thunder and lightning and she uses a feather to ward it off. It's, like, her way. Don't work too well. Anyway, it reminds me of when Mrs. Finnegan was teaching us the dance and she used a knitting needle like a conductor would, you know, to kind of conduct us, teach us."

"I see. Yes, yes," Mr. Finnegan said.

"And then there was Ira Young. He was a friend of my daddy and he was put in jail for eight years, you see? He was black and then my daddy told me about the Klan and the names they have like the Exalted Cyclops and then I come here and there's this Cyclops hotel. It's like when I arrived here first on Broome Street, I thought someone had got all the bits of trash I saw at home and put it all together for me. You know, Mr. Finnegan?"

I stopped talking for a few moments.

"That's stupid, Mr. Finnegan, what I'm saying."

"No, not at all. It's natural when you come to a new place to try to find connections with home. Nothing wrong with that. We all do it. You remind me of Joyce."

"Who's she?"

"James Joyce. His book, *Ulysses*, takes a lot from Homer's *Odyssey*. So people read one and refer to the other trying to find connections or where Joyce has reflected the story in *Ulysses*. That's if they can get their hands on a copy of *Ulysses*. You have found, Set, at an early age that life repeats itself in strange ways. I think you might have the mind of an artist."

"I don't know about that, Mr. Finnegan. What do you mean, if they can get their hands on a copy of *Ulysses*? Is it nearly sold out?"

"No," Mr. Finnegan answered. "It's banned."

"You mean, they won't let him talk?"

"I suppose that's one way of putting it. Wrote *Dubliners* too – book of short stories."

"Do you have it, Mr. Finnegan?" I asked. "I'd like to read it."

Mr. Finnegan went into his bedroom and came back with *Dubliners*. "Thanks Mr. Finnegan. I'll take good care of it."

"I know you're not the type to burn a book," he said.

Finn's birthday arrived and we all had to get up and do something so I recited *Doktrin* by Heinrich Heine. Finn did a recitation. He stood up and, for a moment, all his shyness went as he became an actor, under the direction of his mother holding a knitting needle. Finn bowed, we clapped and then he began:

"It's about Mr. Kelly," he told us, "who came to New York to find his relatives and it goes like this:

> *I went to the directory me uncle for to find*
> *But I found so many Kellys that I nearly lost me mind.*
> *So I went to ask directions from a friendly German Jew*
> *But he says, 'Please excuse me but me name is Kelly too.'*

When I went to bed that night, I couldn't help smiling every time I remembered how Finn had done his routine. Another thought crept into my mind. Mr. Finnegan had told me about Mr. Joyce, that his book was banned. He wasn't allowed to talk. I dreamt that some day his voice might be heard.

3

THE ROCK AND THE
DEEP BLUE SEA

THE BELL RANG FURIOUSLY. RAIN — belting, pelting rain — began battering the window beside my bed. Someone was anxious to get in out of the beginning storm. The wind rose, lightning struck and thunder clapped. Sirens blared and horns honked. It was around 7 o'clock on Friday evening, May 1st, 1930.

The bell rang furiously and then there was a rush of footsteps downstairs to rescue the caller who, I guess, was sheltering against the door. The bell stopped ringing and there were the sounds of more footsteps up the stairs, of an umbrella being shaken and of voices shivering and complaining about the downpour.

I kept reading the line. It was the first line of *Counterparts* in *Dubliners*, James Joyce's book of short stories. I had just opened the book somewhere around the middle and landed on the opening page of *Counterparts*. I read the first line, or rather, part of it. *The bell rang furiously*. No sooner had I read it, than the bell starting ringing furiously in real life. I felt I had no choice but to read on.

"Mr. Finnegan, can I ask you a question?" I said.

"Of course, Set," Mr. Finnegan replied as he put down his newspaper.

I got off the bed, went over and sat opposite Mr. Finnegan at the table.

"I just finished reading a story by Mr. Joyce. *Counterparts*. It's not the first story. I just opened the book on that page and started reading I guess. Is that all right?"

"Of course," Mr. Finnegan said. "Begin at whatever point you will."

"Well, Mr. Finnegan. I have another question. You see, it ends off in the middle of a sentence. This man is beating his son for no reason. He's drunk, I guess, the father, that is. And then the son is pleading with him to stop but it just ends. I don't know what happened. What happened?"

"It's up to you," Mr. Finnegan answered. "Joyce has given you power of attorney. You decide or wonder what happened. He has relinquished the power to round off the story and placed this in your hands. Aposiopesis."

"What's that, Mr. Finnegan?"

"Aposiopesis is when a writer ends abruptly, in the middle of something. It's a literary device. Joyce is fond of tricks. He produces them from his deep blue sea: word play, breaking the rules of writing, dismissing punctuation for example."

"Well, I agree with that," I said. "I don't hold no truck with pronunciation myself."

"You have something in common then."

"Mr. Finnegan, I'm just thinking."

"Yes, Set."

"If I ever write anything, I think I might use this, what is it, the device?"

"Aposiopesis."

"That's it, but I think I might kind of change it."

"Yes?"

"Yeah, instead of breaking off in the middle of something, I'm going to finish it. Complete it."

"Write whatever way you want," Mr. Finnegan said.

"What would that be called, if I did that?"

"Classical narrative conclusion, perhaps," he said.

"I like that better. I might go and read another story now, Mr. Finnegan."

"Did you like *Counterparts*?"

"It kind of disturbed me a little."

"What did you think of the title?" he asked. "What does it mean to you?"

"I'm not really sure," I said. "Hadn't thought about it."

"There are several Dublin pubs mentioned," Mr. Finnegan told me. "It could refer to parts of a counter in a pub. Then again, it could be someone who holds a position in life similar to the one you hold, a counterpart. Or, as you know, to counter something is to go against it, to challenge it. Parts could suggest that the characters are acting like parts or roles in a play or forced to act out of character. It could mean anything. Whatever you decide. Joyce holds out his stories half-way to us, inviting us and we must travel a half-distance to meet him, his stories, his mystery."

"I guess I better read *Counterparts* again, Mr. Finnegan."

I wanted to talk to Mr. Finnegan some more but his wife started clearing the table to do some sewing with that machine she liked so much so I went back to bed and lay down. Instead of reading *Counterparts* again, I decided to read another story, *After the Race*. It began, "The cars came scudding in towards Dublin, running evenly like pellets in the groove of the Naas Road". I closed my eyes and imagined this image. I heard the noise, the scudding. It frightened me because I could actually hear it. Life, at that moment, had torn down the wall between reality and make-believe. I opened my eyes. Mrs. Finnegan was sewing. It was the noise of the Singer sewing machine.

"He should be back by now," she said, referring to Finn who was visiting Aunt Lil and Pen.

"She'll have kept him in," Mr. Finnegan said. "He'll stay the night there."

The noise of the sewing machine stopped.

"What if he left, Vincent, before the downpour?" Mrs. Finnegan asked.

"Hope he doesn't take the quickest way back," Tom mumbled to himself.

"Why?" I whispered.

"It's not the safest," Tom replied. "There's a gang that hangs out there."

"Even in this rain?" I asked.

"Suppose you're right," Tom said. "No-one likes fighting in the rain."

Even though the storm raised its voice regularly, I was aware of the silence in the room and the anxiety that was causing it.

"Do you hear that?" I said.

"The rain?" Tom asked grumpily.

"No," I replied. "Can't you hear it?"

Mrs. Finnegan stood up. The lights flickered from the storm.

"Hear what, Set?" she asked.

I didn't answer because I heard it again. I ran out and downstairs. I found Finn drenched and lying on the steps outside. He had taken the quickest way back.

Finn was brought into his parents' bedroom. He left a trail on the floor: rain and blood. Mr. Finnegan went out to fetch a doctor. They came back quickly. Mrs. Finnegan led the doctor in to see Finn. A little later the doctor came out on his own and spoke to Mr. Finnegan.

"I've given him something for the pain," the doctor said. "It'll help him sleep. The mark extends from just below the eye-socket to the side of his mouth. I can't say much now. I'll come back later. Kick from a toe-cap, more than likely. The force of a rock. Unusual angle. He might have received it after they had knocked him to the ground. It could, of course, have been dealt when he was bent over, holding one nostril closed as he blew blood from the other. In other words, when he was off guard and when he thought, perhaps, that they had gone."

"Don't tell anyone about this," Mr. Finnegan said.

In the morning we were quiet as we ate our breakfast. Mrs. Finnegan left the table every now and then to check on Finn. Her husband went upstairs to the Taylors. They were trusted neighbors of the Finnegans just like what the other Mr. and Mrs. Taylor in Pendleton had been to us. I waited for the doctor to come back. He did, but not through the front door. He emerged from Mr. and Mrs. Finnegan's bedroom. He had slipped in the back way up the fire escape.

"He'll be fine," the doctor said. "A few days rest. I've given him something a little stronger."

Mrs. Taylor brought the doctor downstairs onto the street. It would appear to anyone watching that the doctor had visited the Taylors, not the Finnegans.

Mr. Finnegan went out to work as usual. Tom wanted to go out too but Mrs. Finnegan ordered him not to.

"Haltigan's calling round," Mr. Finnegan announced when he returned.

"Aren't we going to do anything?" Tom asked.

"We'll wait for Haltigan," Mr. Finnegan replied.

Tom got up. He was shaking with anger. "Why do we have to wait for him?" he demanded. "Why do we have to wait for him?" He grabbed his coat and made his way to the door.

"No-one goes out," Mr. Finnegan said.

Tom ignored him and turned the handle. Mr. Finnegan had locked the door.

"No-one goes out," he said in the same quiet tone.

"What are we?" Tom shouted. "Cowards?"

"Tom," Mrs. Finnegan shouted.

Tom tried to go to his parents' bedroom not to see Finn but, I suppose, to get out the back way. Mrs. Finnegan stood in his way.

"No," she said, putting her hand gently on Tom's shoulder. He jerked his body away and then stared at her.

"Sit down, Tom," she said calmly. "Your brother's trying to sleep."

Tom slammed his coat on the bed and sat facing the window, his back to us.

The silence was broken by the arrival of Mr. Haltigan who appeared surprised that the door had to be opened. It wasn't ever locked.

"Tom, come to the table," Mr. Finnegan said.

Tom reluctantly obeyed.

"Someone saw what happened or more correctly, half-saw," Mr. Haltigan said. "There's talk."

"There's always talk," Mrs. Finnegan said.

"It's more rumor," Mr. Haltigan said.

"What are they saying?" Mr. Finnegan asked.

"That there were four or five of them," Mr. Haltigan explained, "and that one of them kicked him when he was down."

"I see," Mr. Finnegan said.

Mr. Haltigan spoke quietly. "They were much older, about fourteen or so. Italian."

"Imagine, kicking him when he was on the ground," Tom said.

"They didn't set the precedent," Mr. Finnegan said.

"I suppose we did?" Tom asked.

"More than likely," Mr. Finnegan replied.

"Please," Mr. Haltigan said. "I've just spoken to La Guardia."

"Why's he getting involved?" Mr. Finnegan asked.

"He's knows this might get out of hand, spread," Mr. Haltigan replied. "He wants us all to sit down; the boy who attacked Finn, his father, you, me, La Guardia, too."

"La Guardia? The politician?" Tom asked.

"Yes," Mr. Haltigan answered.

Tom became unsettled and began to prowl. "Let them all come over here then. We'll be ready for them."

"Yes," Mr. Finnegan said. "Tom's right. Bring them over."

"They want to settle matters," Mr. Haltigan said, "not make things worse."

"Our thoughts as well," Mr. Finnegan said. "The sooner the better."

"Yes," Mr. Haltigan said and left to arrange the meeting.

As soon as he had gone, Mr. Finnegan brought Tom in to see Finn. It was impossible to hear the words, only the rhythm; loud at first, angry, then quiet and then a conversation. They came back out after about half an hour and we sat in silence for the rest of the morning and afternoon until Mr. Haltigan returned to tell us that the meeting was arranged for 8 o'clock that evening.

Four hours seemed like a long time to wait. Mr. Finnegan and Stevie went into the other room to sit with Finn. Tom and me played cards but our minds were not really on the game. Mrs. Finnegan returned to her Singer sewing machine. Then there was a knock. It was Mrs. Blois another neighbor of the Finnegans.

"Did you ever hear anything like that last night?" she said.

"No, Mrs. Blois," Mrs. Finnegan replied. "It was one of the worst."

"There's a man dead after it over across in Queens and another one mortally afflicted in Brooklyn."

"Isn't that dreadful?" Mrs. Finnegan said.

"There's roofs after falling off buildings all over New York. It's a sign. The end of the world."

"Oh, I doubt that, Mrs. Blois. Storms come and go."

"Not like this one, Mrs. Finnegan. It's a sign, I tell you. The light in the Statue of Liberty went out."

"I'm sure they have it back on by now, Mrs. Blois."

"It's a sign. Did the young lad get back all right?"

"Oh yes," Mrs. Finnegan replied. "Just in time to miss the worst of it."

"He's gone out then, is he?"

"I sent him up to his Aunt Lil. Thought she might be worried that he got drenched last night. Did you want him to do a message for you, Mrs. Blois?"

"No, no. He's all right then."

"Right as rain," Mrs. Finnegan said and laughed. "That's a funny thing to say isn't it, Mrs. Blois, after the rain we had."

"I saw Mr. Haltigan called."

"He normally comes round on a Saturday," Mrs. Finnegan said. "There'd be something wrong if he didn't call round."

"Yes. When will he be back, the young lad?"

"Shortly, I suppose unless his sister leads him astray." Mrs. Finnegan replied. "I'll send him down to you. What would you like him to do?"

"Oh nothing, I was just asking."

Mrs. Blois left.

We had our supper early. Finn was brought out and put into my bed. He was sleepy. The doctor said he'd be better off beside a window but that it should only be opened at the top so that he wouldn't be in a draft.

"You don't mind sharing a bed with him?" Mrs. Finnegan asked.

"Not at all, Mrs. Finnegan," I said. "Why, he's so small I won't even know he's there."

"He looks up to you," she said. "I know you'll take good care of him."

"Sure I will."

Mrs. Finnegan took Stevie up to visit her sister, Aunt Lil. Either she trusted her husband to be able to handle whatever was about to happen or she didn't trust herself to keep what she really wanted to say if she remained and met her son's attacker.

Mr. Finnegan told Tom to sit on his bed facing the meeting which was to be held round the dining table. He uncorked a bottle of wine and put it within easy reach of him in a cupboard. The table was cleared. Three chairs faced Mr. Finnegan and there was one at the top. He told me to sit beside Finn and read a book or pretend to read a book. I picked up *Dubliners* and pretended to read. I glanced at Finn who was asleep. The bruise on his face was now purple and blue, the two colors that seemed to be following me around New York.

"You know what to do?" Mr. Finnegan asked.

"Yeah," Tom replied.

"There's a crowd outside," I told them.

"Thought there would be," Mr. Finnegan said. "There's always a crowd in New York."

They arrived on time; the Italian man, his son, Mr. Haltigan, and Mr. La Guardia. Mr. Finnegan shook hands with them all.

"Sit down, sit down," Mr. Finnegan said.

Mr. Haltigan sat at the head of the table. Nearest to him was Mr. La Guardia. Next to him sat the Italian man, with his son occupying the remaining chair. Finn groaned but remained sleeping. The Italian man looked over.

"Well," Mr. Finnegan began cheerily. "There's not much to say."

We all remained silent.

The Italian man opened the conversation.

"We just want to say," he began.

"Oh there's no need for that," Mr. Finnegan interrupted and looked over at Tom.

Tom stood up and approached them quickly. He extended his hand to the Italian boy.

"Put it there, boss," Tom said. "Fair fight."

After a while, the Italian man nudged his son and then nudged him again. The boy stood up and shook Tom's hand.

"He's got a good right hook," Tom said. "Got me fair and square in the jaw. Must have Irish blood in him."

They released their hands from one another. Mr. Finnegan reached into the cupboard and took out the wine bottle and several glasses including one for Tom.

"A toast to peace," Mr. Finnegan said. "Thank you for coming over."

I was as confused as the Italians were.

When the glasses were empty, Mr. Haltigan stood up and addressed the Italian boy.

"Now, young man, if you walk out with Mr. Finnegan. Tom, you accompany his father."

They followed Mr. Haltigan's instructions so that all the people on the street saw that peace had been made. I looked down and saw Mr. Finnegan coaxing Tom and the Italian boy to shake hands in front of everyone. He then began joking with the crowd, asking one man about his lazy brother that raised a few laughs and asking another about his stolen bicycle that raised even more laughs.

Mr. La Guardia did not go down. He joined me at the window, opened it and looked out.

"Hey, Carthy," La Guardia shouted. "Yeah, you."

I heard people on the street saying La Guardia's name as they recognized him.

"Didn't I get you a place?" La Guardia roared.

"You did, indeed," Carthy shouted back. "Thanks, Mr. La Guardia."

"Well, I'm not like all those other corrupt politicians," La Guardia shouted. "They'd be looking to get paid for doing you a service, like twenty dollars. But you know me; I'm not corrupt so I'll just take nineteen dollars."

The crowd erupted in laughter.

"Now, let's get these two heavy-weights a drink before they turn on the lot of us," La Guardia roared and closed the window. The crowd cheered.

"How is he?" Mr. La Guardia asked me.

"Fine."

"La Guardia," Mr. La Guardia said as he held out his hand.

"I'm Set," I replied, and shook his hand.

He left and joined the lively crowd, roaring good-humored insults at them. They all now knew the rumors they heard were wrong. It had been a fight between an Italian boy and an Irish boy about the same age. Nothing unusual there. They had shaken hands. A fair fight. Everyone saw it. It was now over and La Guardia was bringing them all for a drink.

The crowd expected to hear another story but the one they heard was the one Mr. Finnegan wanted them to hear. He had succeeded in making his voice heard in a particular way; a civilized kind of feller, as Mr. Boldt might have put it.

They scudded off down the street to some speakeasy. The silence rang furiously. I felt alone even though Finn was with me. I took up *Dubliners* and read the first line of another story, *Eveline*: "She sat at the window watching the evening invade the avenue'.

I sat at the window and, like Eveline, I watched the evening invade the avenue.

4

MONUMENTS OF
MANHATTAN

THE DICE HOPPED, SKIPPED AND jumped before twirling to a stop. Vuoto, the alley where we played crap, resounded with boyish shrieks.

I had asked why this alley was called Vuoto, not the Vuoto or Vuoto alley, just Vuoto. The Italian kids told me it meant nothing or empty. I was filled with excitement in this empty alley as Tom and me delayed our return home with the bread that Mrs. Finnegan had asked us to fetch.

Crap was more than just a game to us. We formed the shape of a horse-shoe; those closest to the action huddled with elbows on their neighbor's shoulders, those behind crouched, their knees digging into the backs of their competitors. The wins and losses were reflected in our jumping or palm-punching. Alarm whistles injected panic. The cops were near. False alarms from mischievous look-outs were met with real assaults on them, lessons they never learned. There was too much fun for these prankster sentries in being calm, in the know, while everyone else was scattering. It was more than just a game.

In Vuoto nothing became everything. There was no past or present, only the future expectation of lucky victory as the dice rolled, their announcement signaling disappointment or delight, the result greeted with vulgarities, profanities, jubilation, triumph. We broke the rules of grammar: the dice not the die when one of the tumbling cubes went behind a trash can. However, the rules of the game themselves were never broken but enforced with ferocity.

Boylanzo never took part. He was Irish but because he looked Italian we gave him an Italian name. He wore clothes that were rags but they were clean rags. He always stood dreamily at the edge of the horseshoe, a self-discarded nail. His winning smile and exotic looks made him a favorite of the girls. No other boy liked him because of this. We were all unbridled from parental restrictions while playing crap. The real us emerged. This included Boylanzo. His reality was his remoteness. Crap forced out a shorthand of our natures. It was more than just a game.

From May to December, Prohibition fueled more and more organized crime, the Depression destroyed more and more lives, while the politicians – well most of them – told more and more lies. Ops sent a letter every month. I read them myself first and then to the Finnegans, always after tea, the meal that is. They all seemed interested in the people who were mentioned and in the life I had once lived. It all changed in early December when I finished reading the latest letter from home. This was no surprise. My daddy always said that things happened in December.

"Is that all?" Mrs. Finnegan said.

She was holding a stack of dinner plates but stopped short of putting them down. She was waiting for me to reply.

"Yeah. That's it, Mrs. Finnegan."

"She normally signs off by saying that everything is the same there and then something about looking after yourself," Mrs. Finnegan said, still holding the plates. They had become a guillotine.

"Yeah," I said. "She does normally."

"You don't have to read it all to us," Mrs. Finnegan said. "It's your letter."

I couldn't lie to Mrs. Finnegan.

"Well, she just said, you know, she just…"

They were all looking at me now.

"She just asked me if I enjoyed my birthday. That's all."

Mrs. Finnegan put the plates down with a crash but they didn't break.

"Your birthday?" she asked.

"Yeah," I mumbled.

"When was it?" she asked.

"Yesterday, Mrs. Finnegan."

"And you didn't tell us?" she asked.

"I didn't want to make a fuss," I replied. "It's only my birthday."

"How old are you?" Tom asked.

"Fifteen."

"We could've had a party," Finn said.

"Well, I never," Mrs. Finnegan said.

I knew by the way she was tidying up that her anger was going up, now down.

"Saturday," she said. "Saturday, we'll have the party. Mr. Finnegan will take you out and we'll have the party in the evening when you come back. He takes them out on their birthdays. Yes?"

"Yes," he replied. "We had been planning to take you out in any case, Set."

"We?" Mrs. Finnegan asked.

Mr. Finnegan did not answer. I felt sure this meant that Mr. Haltigan would be around on Saturday.

The readjusted birthday date arrived. As Mrs. Finnegan prepared breakfast, the Finnegan brothers put presents on my bed. That's the way they did things on birthdays.

"Aren't you going to open them?" Finn asked.

"After breakfast," Mrs. Finnegan announced.

"Mammy," Finn said. "Can I go out with Set and Daddy?"

"No," she replied.

"Mrs. Finnegan," I said, "I was just wondering if I could take some of my money when I go out? I'd like to get a few things."

"You may take your money anytime, Set," she said. "It's yours but today is your birthday and today you get presents, not the other way round."

As usual, she knew what was in my head. I looked up at the tin which held all my savings, the four dollars I brought with me from Texas and the tips I got from being a spotter. It was building up real good. I decided to obey Mrs. Finnegan. Finn spoke up again.

"Tom said if he had all of Set's money, he'd go to Betsy's."

"Betsy's?" Mrs. Finnegan inquired.

"It's a candy store," Mr. Finnegan explained, without looking up from his newspaper. He turned a page.

"A candy store?" she asked.

No-one responded. Tom kept his head down. Mrs. Finnegan repeated her question.

"Yes," Mr. Finnegan replied and turned another page of the newspaper.

"And where is this Betsy's candy store?" she asked.

"Mid-town, I think," Mr. Finnegan said dismissively. "Now, Set, are you looking forward to today?"

He was not off the hook. Mrs. Finnegan persisted.

"Have *you* been in this candy store, Mr. Finnegan?"

"No."

"I see," she said. "That's something, at least."

When breakfast was over, we gathered round my bed and I began opening my presents: a pair of socks from Mrs. Finnegan, a shirt from Tom, an apple from Stevie, another apple from Finn and two books by James Joyce from Mr. Finnegan, *A Portrait of the Artist as a Young Man* and the banned *Ulysses* which must have made its way through customs some way or other. There was another present, a note-book and a fountain pen.

"Who's this from?" I asked.

"It's a pen from Pen. The clue's in the present," Tom explained.

"Dang, I don't know what to say. Thanks. Thanks for all the presents."

Mr. Finnegan clapped his hands. "Come on Finnegans. Plenty to do. Help your mother. We'll be off in a minute, Set. It's a fine day."

The Finnegans busied themselves. Mrs. Finnegan started rattling pots and pans in the kitchen. I presumed they'd all be used for the purpose of making a birthday cake. Stevie crawled under one of the beds as he did anytime he felt there was work to be done. Tom sat on the bed, his back bolt upright waiting for orders from his mother. It appeared he had already been told that he would be helping in the kitchen. Finn came up beside me and leaned on me like I was a wall. Mr. Haltigan arrived.

"You go down, Set," Mr. Haltigan said. "She's waiting. I want to have a word with Mr. Finnegan."

"Who's waiting?" I asked.

"You'll find out soon enough," Mr. Haltigan replied. "We'll be down shortly."

There was a Bentley 8 liter chugging away on the street just outside. I went over to it and saw a woman in the driving seat. She was smoking a cigarette with a long filter and she had on the reddest lipstick that I ever did see.

"Get in," she said. "Front seat."

I got in.

"You got my husband a job," she told me.

"I did?"

"Mr. Janosik," she explained.

"Mr. Janosik?" I asked. "Where?"

"The Cyclops hotel," she said. "Mr Sullivan's employment there has terminated thanks to you and your suitcase. They're bringing you to meet someone today but first we have to find him. He likes to walk around Central Park. We'll start there."

Mr. Finnegan and Mr. Haltigan got into the back seat. They were in deep conversation about politics.

"Quiet," Mrs. Janosik snapped. "It's not *your* day. Mr. Finnegan tells me you're a reader. Do you know about alliteration, Set?"

She saved me from having to answer.

"It's when the initial letters are generally the same such as 'Peter Piper picked a peck of pickled peppers'. That kind of thing."

"Oh," I said. "I didn't know that."

"Let's make a sentence about today with alliteration," she announced. "Mr. Haltigan, have you any suggestions?"

"Well, we're on the Avenue of the Americas," he said. "So, that's a start."

"No, it's not," she said. "The locals call it Sixth Avenue. I don't think we should put what the map says over what the people say."

As she drove us through Manhattan, Mrs. Janosik pointed out many things; the beginnings of the Empire State building, Carnegie Hall, around Central Park, Jack and Charlie's 21 club where I worked as a spotter and Tammany Hall, the place where the Democrats decided most things that went on. There was no sign of the person we were supposed to meet.

The car stopped at Macdougal Street where, apart from Mrs. Janosik, we all got out.

"You'll see him here," she said. "He'll definitely be here. Enjoy the coffee."

She drove off and we took our seats, facing east, outside Caffè Reggio.

"The owner here," Mr. Finnegan told me, "is Domenico Parisi. He was the first to start selling cappuccino in New York. He brought over an espresso machine from Italy. It's some machine. You'll have a cup?"

"I'd like to try it, Mr. Finnegan," I said.

"Mr. Parisi doesn't take his hat off," Mr. Haltigan told me. "He says it makes him sneeze."

"Finnegan," a man shouted. He was sitting a few seats up. As soon as he shouted Mr. Finnegan's name, he hit the table with a tuning fork. His eyes danced from side to side. It was like he just wanted to announce Mr. Finnegan's name.

"I might have one too," Mr. Haltigan said.

"Haltigan," the man announced.

Pronggggg went the metal.

"Who's he?" I asked.

"The blind piano tuner," Mr. Finnegan replied. "Now, we'll have a little debate as they do in New York coffee houses. Yes, a debate. A debate at Caffè Reggio."

"Can he see the sunshine still?" I asked.

"I'm sure he can feel the warmth of it," Mr. Haltigan replied.

A man sat down in front of us. He took out a note-book and pen. I wondered was this the man we were supposed to be meeting, a thought reinforced by the number of coffees ordered. The piano tuner did not announce this man's name so I guessed he was a stranger to the Caffè Reggio.

I noticed a rainbow appearing. The coffees arrived. The waiter gave one to the piano tuner and one to the man with the note-book who raised his hand without looking round. It was a kind of thank-you. Mr. Haltigan produced a hip flask, unscrewed the top and poured some of the contents into Mr. Finnegan's coffee and then some into his own cup. The coffee was hot. I waited for it to cool down.

"That's mighty," Mr. Haltigan said, referring to the coffee and whatever he had poured into it. "Mighty. Mighty. Mighty."

"Why did you come to the United States, Mr. Finnegan?" I asked.

"Many reasons," Mr. Finnegan replied. "I was tired, annoyed. We had a revolution in Ireland, the Rising, 1916. Then we had a war of independence, a treaty and then, to top it all off, a civil war. We managed to do all this in less than a decade. I wasn't pleased with the result. So I came over here, we came over here, to see the future. They did all those things here in the United States years ago and I wanted to see how it had all settled down. What had it become? Well, as you see, it has become a Depression, Prohibition and corruption. Some future."

"Mr. Finnegan is not one to give up," Mr. Haltigan said.

"No, indeed," Mr. Finnegan continued. "Battles await. We have to get Roosevelt into the White House and La Guardia elected as mayor."

"Why?" I asked.

"So they can fix it," Mr. Finnegan replied.

"How d'you know they will?" I asked.

"Because I've met Mr. Roosevelt," Mr. Finnegan said. "He told me he would change things."

"How do you know he's telling the truth?" I asked. "He's a politician. My daddy don't trust politicians. Are you saying my daddy was wrong?"

"No, he was nearly right," Mr. Finnegan replied. "Some politicians can't be trusted. We have Roosevelt now."

"And why La Guardia?" I asked. "Is it because he came to the apartment the night we were sorting out things with the Italians? Maybe he did that and other things just so he'll get elected mayor."

"Walker," the piano tuner shouted as Mayor Walker arrived.

He was a regular at the 21 Club. They called him Beau James.

"Well, gentlemen, a leisurely day for you," Mr. Walker said.

"Yes, Mr. Mayor," Mr. Finnegan said. "You have many leisurely days, yourself, I understand."

The mayor laughed.

"How's the inquiry going?" Mr. Haltigan asked him.

"Well, I'll tell you," Mr. Walker said. "I'm going to steal a line that Al Smith used. I've heard on good authority that the prosecutor is going to try to make fun of me."

"He's not a prosecutor," Mr. Haltigan said. "I doubt he'll have much difficulty making fun of you. In fact, you can do that quite well all on your own."

Mr. Walker laughed.

"He's a prosecutor to me," he said. "Anyway, he's going to say that if they got my brain and put it on a scale, that it wouldn't weigh anything. So I'm going to wait for the laughter to die down and then I'm going to say that if they left my brain on the scale and added the prosecutor's brain to it, they would weigh less than nothing. Good-day boys."

He laughed and left.

"There he goes," Mr. Finnegan said. "We're all supposed to relate his funny tales to other people in New York and then they're supposed to say what a funny man he is, our mayor. Mr. Walker is a royal family rolled into one man. He hardly ever goes into the office. He has a suit for every day of the year, even a leap year. He's corrupt but, despite all this, the people of New York, in this Depression, are glad to have something to laugh at. They think that maybe some day, they, too, could be mayor and live like him, like a king. He's all spats stirred with a cane."

"He defeated La Guardia at the last election," Mr. Haltigan said. "Pity."

"I don't know about any of this, Mr. Haltigan," I said. "Coffee's nice."

"But you know enough to doubt La Guardia and Roosevelt?" Mr. Finnegan asked.

"Suppose."

"I trust them," Mr. Finnegan said, "because I just do. Is that enough? I know they'll sort things out. They'll leave an elegant legacy."

"And there it is," the man with the note-book said. "You see, I knew you Irish would give me some phrase today. Elegant legacy. I like that."

He wrote it down in his note-book.

"Harburg," the piano tuner shouted and tapped the table with the tuning fork.

"I've been recognized," Mr. Harburg said. "Something I wish would happen a bit more in New York."

"Yip is a musician or lyricist," Mr. Haltigan informed me. "Same thing I suppose."

Mr. Harburg got up and put his note-book into one of his coat pockets.

"I'm trying to find Varick Place," he said. "Meeting a friend there."

"Just walk towards the rainbow," Mr. Haltigan said. "The name's gone. It's now part of Sullivan Street. Strange that someone is still calling it Varick Place."

"Old street names die hard," Mr. Harburg said.

He took out his note-book again and started writing.

"Do you have to write everything down?" Mr. Haltigan asked. "Is Sullivan Street that hard to remember?"

"I need to write down that line, 'towards the rainbow'."

When Mr. Harburg left, Mr. Haltigan told me about him. "Like many people, he lost a lot of money in the Crash. He's paying it all back. He's New York."

Mr. Finnegan restarted the debate.

"We can elect who we want here despite what Tammany Hall does. Other countries don't have this freedom. That film, what was it? *All Quiet on the Western Front*. They tried to show it in Germany and these people broke up the cinema. Wouldn't allow it."

"What people?" I asked.

"*Nationalsozialistische Deutsche Arbeiterpartei* or Nazi for short," Mr. Haltigan explained.

"That wouldn't happen here," I said.

"Oh, but it has," Mr. Finnegan said. "When they were printing extracts from *Ulysses* in the magazine *The Little Review*, some people here burned it."

Mr. Haltigan addressed the piano tuner in German. I couldn't catch it. The piano tuner replied, Mr. Haltigan thanked him and then turned to me.

"I was looking for a phrase. It's *Das war ein Vorspiel nur, dort wo man Bücher verbrennt, verbrennt man auch am Ende Menschen.*'"

"What's that mean?" I asked.

"Wherever they burn books, they'll eventually burn people."

"Heine," the piano tuner shouted.

"Heinrich Heine?" I asked.

"The very one," Mr. Finnegan replied.

Another man approached and started talking to a newspaper seller.

"Klopfer," the piano tuner shouted. Another *pronggg* followed.

"The man we're supposed to meet will be here shortly," Mr. Finnegan told me. "That man Klopfer there is his business partner. The two of them meet and have a coffee here sometimes. I knew we'd find him."

"Why does he shout out everyone's name?" I asked.

"Because," Mr. Haltigan explained, "it's cheaper than taking out one of the classifieds in *The New York Times*. Everyone knows him in New York but more than that, they know where to find him. He uses his ear to identify voices and his mouth to shout the names and his brain to know that this will get him noticed. Here he is. The man we've been waiting for all day."

The man came over to us and greeted Mr. Finnegan and Mr. Haltigan. I half-recognized him from Jack and Charlie's. Even though I knew some of the other publishers there, I didn't know him. They called him Bennett.

"This is the young man," Mr. Finnegan said.

"Howdy," I said. "I'm Set Wright. That's my name."

We were all standing up.

"Hello, Set," the man said. "They probably haven't told you, these two. Men of mystery, as you will have gathered. Anyway, I'm here to interview you for a job, in an office. We're going to try to publish *Ulysses*. Mr. Finnegan has told you about it. It'll mean more work, paperwork. That's where you might step in."

"I don't think I'd really be able to do that," I said.

"Don't be so meek," Mr. Bennett said.

I didn't know what meek meant; I looked at Mr. Haltigan for help.

"Humble," he said.

"Oh," I said and collected my thoughts. "Thanks, but see, I get a lot of tips now. I do a bit of spotting. I don't think I'd get as much in an office."

"No, you wouldn't," Mr. Bennett said.

"Thought so," I said. "Anyway, I need to earn as much as I can because I have to get back our house, my daddy's home. It's in Texas. That's where I'm from. Them brokers gone and took it. Sort of. Sorry."

"I understand," Mr. Bennett said.

I felt a little ashamed and hung my head.

"Gentlemen," Mr. Bennett said, wishing us goodbye, before walking away with his business partner, Mr. Klopfer.

"Sorry," I said.

"We understand too," Mr. Haltigan replied. "It's up to you."

"Cerf," the piano tuner shouted.

I didn't hear the tuning fork resonate although I'm sure he hit the table with it.

"What's he saying now?" I asked. "Surf?"

"Cerf," Mr. Haltigan explained. "C-E-R-F. That's his name."

"Whose name?" I asked.

"The man you've just been talking to," Mr. Haltigan said.

"I thought his name was Bennett," I said.

"It is," Mr. Haltigan explained. "Bennett Cerf."

I looked at the rainbow and saw the colors blue and purple or was it violet? I thought of the tuning fork, the feather that Ops carried, the knitting needle that Mrs. Finnegan used to direct the stupid dance Tom and me did. I thought of Heine, banging the drum and now reappearing to warn about the burning of books and what it could lead to. Then I thought of the deer at Deer Creek and then of Mr. Cerf.

We got up to walk away but I became stuck to the sidewalk.

"Dang," I said.

"What's wrong?" Mr. Finnegan asked.

"I should have gone for that job," I said.

"Why the sudden change of heart?" Mr. Haltigan asked.

"Cerf," I said. "It means deer in French."

"Wright," the piano tuner shouted as we walked home towards Broome Street, towards the rainbow.

✝
✝

Mr. Haltigan couldn't join my birthday party immediately because he had something to do. He was always up to something but he promised to drop by later. All the Finnegans were in their best clothes even Pen, dressed as a girl. Boylanzo was there too, sitting beside her. They seemed to be together. He had a sweater on but it had a hole in it. It was the best he or his mother could do. He was quiet but managed several courteous replies to Mrs. Finnegan when handed the succession of courses.

"What did you get Set for his birthday?" Finn asked.

Boylanzo blushed and lowered his head. He hadn't got me anything.

"An apple," I said matter-of-factly, the way Mr. Finnegan would have spoken. "Gave it to me the other day when me and Tom were coming back with the bread. And it was just as good as the one you gave me."

"But you haven't eaten mine," Finn persisted.

"I was talking about the gesture, not the flavor," I said. "Now eat up and stop yakking."

I wasn't too keen on Boylanzo but it went against my grain to see him humiliated because of his family's poverty. Anyway, he was part of our crap game. Even though we spent most of the time trying to defeat one another, we banded together when anyone outside challenged one of us.

I looked over at Boylanzo. My intervention hadn't helped. He was chewing his food like it was a chore. He was trying not to cry. Mr. Finnegan noticed this too and then looked at me. Mr. Finnegan drank some tea, held his head up and began to gargle – or was it gurgle?

"What are you doing?" his wife asked.

"Gargling or gurgling," Mr. Finnegan replied. "I never know which word to use. There's no law against it. Tom, I bet you can't do it."

Tom began to gurgle or gargle and before long we were all at it.

"Well," Mrs. Finnegan said, starting to clear the plates. "You seem to have had a little more than coffee today, Mr. Finnegan."

She brought some plates over to wash them. While her back was turned, Mr. Finnegan began to gargle or gurgle again. He stopped when she looked round.

He blamed Pen for making the noise, telling her to stop. She started laughing. Mrs. Finnegan shook her head and turned away to wash the plates. We all began to laugh with a little bit more gurgling or gargling thrown in. Boylanzo was still finding it difficult to chew his food, but this time it was because he was laughing.

They sang 'Happy Birthday'. I did a tongue twister: Peter Piper picked a peck of pickled peppers. Then I told them that when all the words start with the same letter, that's alliteration.

"That's really, really interesting," Tom said, meaning the opposite.

I let Stevie help to blow out the candles. I made a wish. We ate cake. Mr. Finnegan asked me if he could play my gramophone records. He fetched a gramophone player from Mrs. Blois. We listened to 'Marble Halls', 'Through the world wilt thou fly, love' and "Tis gone – the past was all a dream'. Then we listened to 'Santa Lucia'. Caruso.

Mr. Haltigan dropped by, as he had promised, and told me he had just seen Mr. Cerf again.

"I thought," Mr. Haltigan said, "Mr. Cerf might not be too im-pressed with someone who changes their mind. He didn't agree. He reminded me of the reason you gave for not wanting to work for him; to save up so you could get your father's house back. He said that whatever changed your mind must have been one hell of a reason. I was wondering too. What did change your mind? And don't tell me it was because of a deer."

"Not only that, Mr. Haltigan. See, Mr. Boldt, he's our neighbor in Texas, he told me to find someone they were trying to shut up. Told me I had to make sure they'd get a voice, be allowed to speak. They're trying to shut Mr. Joyce up ain't they, banning his book and all? Ain't they? He never put me wrong, Mr. Boldt. Never. Never once. He's my neighbor. I'll just have to try and save a little bit more that's all. And Ops said important things are decided over a cup of coffee."

"So, you're now trying to reclaim a house and, at the same time, fighting for a book to breathe," Mr. Haltigan said.

"I reckon all them fellers is the same; the one who took the Boldts' house and the one trying to muzzle Mr. Joyce. Same breeding. Wipe the smirk off of one of their faces, the other one'll wise up too."

"Do you think you can ride two saddles?"

"Mr. Haltigan, I'm from Texas. Besides, I just see it as one saddle."

Mr. Haltigan shook his head. "Well, that makes it all very clear. Eight o'clock Monday morning. Mrs. Janosik will pick you up. Seven-thirty. Sharp."

I lay awake for a long time. Finn was sleeping off all the food he had eaten.

I got the note-book and pen that Pen had given me. I thought I would write a bit of alliteration before I went to sleep but I didn't know what. Then it came to me and I wrote down a sentence that I had been mulling over most of the day. When I read it back, I thought that Mrs. Janosik might be proud of me. I left the pen and the note-book under the bed and lay back thinking of all the things that had happened during the day, a day when we had motored through the meek and mighty monuments of Manhattan.

5

GUEST FRIENDSHIP

I HEARD MY NAME. I was asleep. Set. Set? I woke up. I heard something else, a sound that had traveled from far away, a sound I knew; the wind again, carrying this sound to me. I got my teddy bear and went to my mother's room. It was hot. She was hotter. There was another sound, a child crying at the door.

"Set?"

My mother was pointing at the little girl who was crying.

"Set?" Mr. Finnegan said.

"Sorry, Mr. Finnegan. I was miles away."

"Texas?"

"Yeah."

"I've just got him to sleep. There's an art in it."

"That was it. You putting Stevie to bed. It reminded me of when I was in bed once when I was real young. I was thinking about that."

"The past has a way of intruding."

"Yeah."

"A good memory, I hope?"

"I don't know."

"I'm all yours."

"Sorry?"

"You said you had a question."

"Oh yeah. That's right. Sorry."

"Well?"

"It's this word I keep seeing. I saw it in the newspaper the other day. It was … I can't say it. I can spell it though."

"Yes?"

"X-E-N-I-A."

"Ah, Xenia."

"The X sounds like a zee?"

"That's it, like xylophone."

"What is it, this Xenia? There's a Princess Xenia, I read about her, and then there's Xenia in Ohio. That was in the newspaper too."

"Ah yes. Good horse-breeding there, the one in Ohio I mean. The other one, Princess Xenia, is from Russia. She's what you might call a society figure."

"Oh, I see. What's it mean, Xenia?"

"It's from the Greek. It means guest friendship. It's a theme that's used in a lot of the old stories, the epics."

"So, someone has to guess if a person is their friend?"

"No, not guessed like to estimate. Guest, as in someone who stays for a time in your home. Hospitality you might call it. Like what your father has done for those neighbors you keep talking about, the Boldts."

"I get that but, you see, things keep on cropping up all the time with me. This word, Xenia, it cropped up twice and who knows where I'll see it again. Then there's colors that keep like, I don't know, I keep seeing them too."

"Is it your eyes?"

"No, it's not like that. It's like. I see them. You see, I can't explain it. It's just that, like deer, you know. There was the John Deere, the tractor, and then Deer Creek and then there's Mr. Cerf. His name means deer in French. I don't know."

"Words will appear and reappear, keep reappearing. Of course they will. As I said to you before, you're just making connections. It's nothing to worry about."

"But I do worry about it."

"You think it's a message? That there's some force, a God maybe, bringing these words and colors to your attention for some reason?"

"Oh no, Mr. Finnegan. I don't think that at all. It's me, just me, making connections or seeing them and wondering about them. That's all."

"You're blessed with an inquisitive mind. You've answered your own question."

"I guess I have, Mr. Finnegan."

"We all do that. Maybe what you're talking about is to do with coincidences. You know what they are?"

"Yeah."

"These happen in life. Someone you haven't seen for years, you suddenly start thinking about them and then all of a sudden they turn up. It just happens. People try to read something into it that's not there. Am I making sense?"

"Sure."

"Some things are difficult to define, like Xenia."

"You explained it real well."

"Not sure I did. You see, it might not be a person who visits and who is treated kindly. It could also be a memory from the past, one from Texas for example, one that takes you back to a particular moment. The memory is a guest, and it's visiting your mind which is your home. It's best to offer it friendship and not to close the door to it, even if the visitor gives rise to sadness. The past is what we are."

"I see, Mr. Finnegan."

"Beethoven went deaf but wrote sublime music," he said. "I often wonder how this ailment, which should be more catastrophic to a composer than the rest of us, helped rather than hindered him. James Joyce, blind, or near-blind, has an affliction that should damn his power as a spectacular and alert craftsman. Yet he delves into a dream-like state, further down than any of us. He flies higher as well. In *Ulysses*, we are allowed to walk on deep sea-beds and shoot across the heavens, experiencing more and attaining the power to look more closely at ourselves. Deafness, blindness and other limiting forces not only fail to halt the creative spirit but become guests that allow us to savor more friendship."

"Thanks, Mr. Finnegan."

"So, Set, Xenia can be a person or people. It can be a memory or indeed it might be something else altogether that enters your life. The effect is at all times positive. Now that you've learned what Xenia is, it might drop by unexpectedly if you're lucky and keep knocking at your door. That wouldn't be so bad now, would it?"

"No."

I really liked talking to Mr. Finnegan.

✝
✝

I decided to keep a look out for this Xenia thing but I didn't have to look far on account of two people who came visiting the day before I was to start working for Mr. Cerf. The Finnegans told me to expect a surprise. They all knew, even Finn. He waited at the door and announced their arrival. "Here comes Elijah, Davy Springer's brother."

Elijah's daddy, Rabbi Springer, arrived shortly after.

"I don't know what happened to it," I told Rabbi Springer, with all the Finnegans and Mr. Haltigan looking on. "It fitted me fine when I put it on back in Texas. Guess it shrunk."

"Nah," Rabbi Springer said. "You've grown. I can't do anything with this which is a pity. It's a fine suit. Tweed. Maybe, your brother here could wear it when he grows up a bit."

"Finn ain't my brother."

"We are all brothers," Rabbi Springer said. "Mrs. Finnegan, you were right. He's about the same height as Elijah here. Now, I need to know what this job is?"

"It's a publisher," Mr. Haltigan said.

"Gray, then," Rabbi Springer said. "It is an underrated color. Get the gray ones."

Elijah fetched the gray suits from their van. Rabbi Springer examined them carefully. They all looked the same to me but he seemed to think one was much better than the rest so he told me to put it on.

"A fine fit," he said. "I need to take it in a little. Don't slouch."

I stood as straight as I could. Rabbi Springer took a wafer of chalk from his pocket and made marks here and there, turned me around, stood back and looked at me, pulled the jacket down, smoothed the sleeves and stood back again.

"Take it off."

He took the suit and went to Mrs. Finnegan's sewing machine, ripping, examining, folding, unfolding, sewing, putting pins in his mouth and taking them out again. I had to put the suit on and take it off again several times.

"All right. Tie. Get the blue ties. Thin ones."

Elijah fetched the ties. Rabbi Springer spent another long time choosing the right one.

"This one," he said eventually.

He told me to bend down so he could put the tie on.

"I can do it," I said.

"Are you a tailor?"

I bent down.

"I wouldn't say no to a coffee, Mrs. Finnegan. Coat?"

"Nothing suitable I think," Mr. Finnegan said.

Rabbi Springer looked at Elijah and then addressed him.

"What do you think?"

"Yes, Father. It will go well with the suit."

"I agree," Rabbi Springer said.

I had no idea what they were talking about but then Elijah took his coat off and gave it to me.

"Well, put it on," Rabbi Springer said, sipping his coffee.

I put on the coat.

Mrs. Finnegan went to her handbag.

"No. I'll pay for it," I said as I went to get my money tin.

"Stop," Rabbi Springer shouted. "No!"

"But I have to pay. I can't..." I pleaded.

Rabbi Springer ignored me and went towards the door.

"You just hold on there," I said, taking my tin down from the shelf.

"*Shtum*," Rabbi Springer whispered and left with Elijah following close behind.

"What does that mean?" I asked.

"Quiet," Mr. Haltigan said.

✝
✝

There was one voice and, boy, was it loud. I waited at the door, not wanting to enter because of the mother and father of all arguments that was going on. Next thing, the door swung open and Mr. Cerf stormed out. He didn't even see me. I had to think. I thought it best not to go after him when he was in a mood like that. He might fire me on my first day. I knocked.

"Back already?"

I went in.

"Hi Mr. Klopfer."

He looked at a woman who was collecting papers from a desk.

"You knew it wasn't him," she said to Mr. Klopfer, then turned to me. "I'm Miss Kreiswirth. Pauline. How do you do?"

"Fine, ma'am. And you?"

"Are you from Simon & Schuster?" Mr. Klopfer asked me.

"No. From Mr. Finnegan, well, Mr. Haltigan too."

"Ah, Finnegan and Haltigan," he said. "Never heard of them. We have more competition, Miss Kreiswirth. So, where are you from young man? Originally, that is?"

"Texas."

"And what are you doing here?"

"Mr. Cerf said, well, he told Mr. Haltigan that I could start working here today at eight o'clock. It's eight o'clock."

"First I've heard of it."

"It comes an hour before nine o'clock," Miss Kreiswirth said to Mr. Klopfer. "I'm sure you've heard of nine o'clock."

"Best go after him," Mr. Klopfer said.

"You sure?" I asked.

"Yes," Miss Kreiswirth said. "You might have heard. There was an argument but the blood goes back down to his toes soon enough."

"Head down Madison Avenue," Mr. Klopfer said. "Turn right on West 52nd Street, number twenty-one."

"He's gone to Jack and Charlie's?" I asked.

"Yeah."

"I think it'd be quicker to take Fifth Avenue," I said.

"Not so sure about that," Mr. Klopfer replied, chewing one of the legs or arms of his glasses.

"*I* am," I said.

"Well, go whatever way you want."

"What'll I say to him?"

"Tell him that was the most cockeyed scheme he's ever come up with," Mr. Klopfer said.

"To hire me?"

"That as well."

"Don't mind him," Miss Kreiswirth said. "Go find him. He'll be cooled down by the time you catch up with him."

"Thanks, Miss Kreiswirth, Mr. Klopfer."

"It'll be quicker the other way, I reckon," Mr. Klopfer shouted at me as I went out.

I took my own route, hoping that I might see Mr. Cerf on the way down. I reckoned that he was probably walking quickly because that's what people do after an argument.

The night-time customers were clearing out of Jack and Charlie's but there were a few stragglers inside.

"Can I go in, Mr. Jack? I just want to see Mr. Cerf."

It took a while for Mr. Jack to recognize me.

"Hey. So what bank did you rob?"

"I didn't rob no bank."

"Looks as if you did."

"I got a job."

"Good for you. He's over there."

Mr. Cerf was sitting at a table with a lot of other people in the corner to the right of the bar. I knew them all. There was the writer, Robert Benchley; he was a good tipper. If it was raining, he'd tell me at the door that he couldn't wait to get out of his wet coat and into a dry Martini. He normally drank or dined at a little table on his own.

The others were publishers: Mr. Guinzberg, Mr. Huebsch and Mr. Oppenheimer of Viking Press, Mr. Knopf and two other publishers, Mr.

Simon and Mr. Schuster. Sitting away from them was the theater owner, Baa Baa Grenado, with his two assistants. One was built like an ox, the other like the ox's brother. Mr. Grenado was the type of man people stared at. He wore a brown-colored coat with a black-colored collar. His hat, a blue-colored panama, was angled to one side. He wore a cravat too, never a tie or bow-tie and then there was his cane with a silver handle gripped by his right hand. He wore a ring with a dark-colored jewel on his little finger. You could see your face in the shine of his shoes. Mr. Pete, who worked with Mr. Charlie and Mr. Jack at the 21 Club, said to me once that he reckoned someone must have taken Mr. Grenado's larynx out, rubbed it against a pebble-dashed wall and put it back in again.

Mr. Benchley invited me to sit down. The conversation was very loud.

"We're just going," Mr. Benchley said.

"Well, I don't believe that for a second," I said, knowing that he liked to be teased in conversation.

"Neither do I. Any trouble tonight?"

"Well, it's the morning and I wasn't working here last night."

"Mr. Benchley cannot distinguish between the night and the day," Mr. Cerf said.

I found this very strange because Mr. Cerf was sitting way up at the other end. He looked as if he was lost in thought. On top of this he managed to hear what Mr. Benchley had said through several loud conversations.

"But you're all dressed up," Mr. Benchley said. "Promotion?"

"Kind of. I think."

Our conversation was interrupted by a man who sat down in Mr. Benchley's usual place. He started banging the table. We all stopped talking.

"Benchley, with all his Jewish friends," the man said. "The publishing world now has one thing in common with itself. Jews."

"Out," Mr. Jack said to the man.

He didn't move.

"Boys," Mr. Jack said, not taking his eyes off the man.

Mr. Grenado made his way, real slow, over to the table where he stood, looking up at the ceiling. His two assistants followed, their steps adjusted to take account of Mr. Grenado's.

"I could give all of you a hiding you'll never forget," the man said, taking his time to get up.

"Tell me," Mr. Grenado said. "You being a publisher and all that, are you more upset that you're being whipped in the marketplace by better publishers or that you're being whipped in the marketplace by Jews who are better publishers?"

"Two-bit ringmaster," the man said.

Mr. Grenado signaled to the two oxen to remove the man so they frog-marched him off the premises.

"Who is that?" Mr. Cerf asked.

"He's Mr. Grenado, theater owner," I explained.

"Hence, the rather poor put down of two-bit ringmaster from our dear departed friend," Mr. Benchley said. "Grenado used to be in vaudeville. Is a better impresario than he was a comedian. He exudes a wonderful sense of terror does he not, with the aid of the two looming Lucifers he keeps in tow?"

The conversation broke up into groups again and everyone dwindled away, even Mr. Benchley. I found myself sitting on my own at one table with Mr. Cerf way down at the other end. I went and sat beside him.

"Is that a Texan accent I detected?" Mr. Cerf asked.

"Yes Mr. Cerf. I'm from —"

"I knew Elliot Sanger when we lived at The Riviera, 157th Street. Long time ago. You know them? The family owns the store in Dallas."

"Heard of it but I —"

Mr. Cerf interrupted me again. He liked to talk. I decided to interrupt him.

"Are you from New York?"

It was a stupid question. Mr. Cerf 'New-Yorked' his sentences, gnawing his words as he said them.

"All my grand-parents were born on the island of Manhattan."

"I'm from Pendleton."

"Where's that?" he asked.

He hadn't been listening to a word I said, probably thinking about the row he had with Mr. Klopfer. I told him again where I was from.

"Your parents are there?"

"Well, my daddy is. My mother died when I was young and then my sister. She had given birth, you see, to my sister, and she died too."

"Really? My mother died just before my sixteenth birthday and my little sister after that."

"I'm sorry."

"So, you work here?" Mr. Cerf asked.

Hell, now I found out he had forgotten that he had offered me a job. He just didn't listen to anything, this man.

"I used to work here," I said.

"Used to? Oh, so you work with Mr. Benchley then at *The New Yorker?*"

"No, Mr. Cerf. I work for you."

"For me?"

"Didn't you say to Mr. Haltigan that I could start today?"

"Oh. Haltigan, yes. I remember. I've been a bit distracted. Come on, let's get back to the office."

We got up and Mr. Cerf went to pay but Mr. Jack told him that Mr. Grenado had taken care of it.

"See," Mr. Cerf said to me. "Distracted."

As we walked up Fifth Avenue, Mr. Cerf started talking about Mr. Haltigan.

"He wants me to publish *Ulysses*. Ben Huebsch has it now. He's working on it. You know Mr. Huebsch?"

"Yeah, he was at the table."

"That's right, yes. Viking Press."

"What's it about, Mr. Cerf, *Ulysses* that is? I haven't read it. You see, I kept reading one book and before I'd finish it I'd start reading another so I had to stop doing that. I got a note-book for my birthday, you see, and I wrote down all the books I was going to read and I'm sticking to it. Only I forgot about *Ulysses* so I put that at the end."

He didn't say anything.

"Mr. Cerf? What's it about?"

"What's what about?"

There he went again, not listening.

"*Ulysses.*"

"Oh. It's about these people. There's Leopold Bloom. He's a Jew of Hungarian extraction."

"Is that an Irish name, Bloom?"

"I don't know," Mr. Cerf said. "It's about us."

"That's a coincidence, Mr. Cerf," I said, "don't you think, our mothers and sisters gone like that?"

He didn't answer. He wasn't listening. I decided to keep on talking anyway.

"See, I find things are happening like, coincidences. I was telling Mr. Finnegan about it the other day. You know Mr. Finnegan. We met at the Caffè Reggio. Anyway…"

I went on and on but Mr. Cerf was in another world. I gave up. He didn't even notice that I had stopped talking. He wasn't much interested in coincidences. We spent the rest of the journey not saying anything to each other. We arrived at the door of Random House. Mr. Cerf started up again.

"In my opinion, Leopold Bloom is the most well-drawn character in all literature."

When we went into the office, Miss Kreiswirth was filing papers and Mr. Klopfer was at his desk. There was another man there.

"Look who I found," Mr. Cerf said as we walked in.

"Didn't he find you?" Mr. Klopfer replied.

"Are we in trouble, Donald?" Mr. Cerf inquired, pointing to the stranger.

"Am I working here or not?" I demanded.

"Don't we get an introduction?" Miss Kreiswirth asked.

"Set, this is Miss Kreiswirth," Mr. Cerf said.

"You can call me Pauline."

"Thank you, ma'am," I replied.

I shook hands with Miss Kreiswirth.

"You're polite," she said. "Won't last a day here."

"And, my long-suffering business partner, Mr. Klopfer," Mr. Cerf said.

I shook hands with Mr. Klopfer.

"And this is the distinguished attorney, Mr. Ernst," Mr. Cerf said.

I shook hands with Mr. Ernst.

"Morris L. Ernst, for your information," Mr. Ernst said.

"What does the 'L' stand for," I asked.

"Leopold," Mr. Ernst replied.

"Leopold," Mr. Cerf said, laughing, and then turned to me. "You were right. Coincidences."

He had, after all, been listening to everything I had said.

I did chores for Mr. Cerf and Mr. Klopfer. Sometimes Miss Kreiswirth even let me answer the phone. Writers came in. Some were drunk. Some were sober. Most were drunk. When it was quiet once, I asked Mr. Klopfer about *Ulysses* and he told me that no-one had ever written a book like it.

This set me thinking that maybe I should bend my rule of not reading two books at the one time and maybe just have a peek inside *Ulysses*. I got a day off because they were opening the Empire State Building. That Friday morning, I left the Finnegans' place with my copy of *Ulysses* and went around the corner to Mulberry Street where I sat on some steps and began flicking through it. I was still hell-bent on sticking to my rule of reading all the other books on my list first but I felt I was cheating a little.

"What you reading?" Boylanzo asked as he sat on the step beside me.

"I'm not. Just flicking."

"Read us a bit of it anyways," he demanded.

I was a bit annoyed, him invading my time like that and then ordering me to read. I thought that maybe he couldn't read so I turned a few pages and started reading. It was a letter Mr. Bloom had gotten from some lady-friend of his. She called him Henry even though his name was Leopold. I think it was a kind of secret love letter. She was complaining to him about not including stamps in the last letter he sent, saying she was angry with him. She signed the letter, Martha. I stopped reading.

"What's it about?" Boylanzo asked.

I told him all the things that people had said to me about the way Mr. Joyce used clever tricks when he was writing and played on words; all that kind of thing.

"Sure, I could do that," he said.

"Well, why don't you go and do it then?" I shot back.

I had spoken too harshly. His head went down. I put my hand in my pocket and gave him what was in it.

"Here," I said, and then went back onto Broome Street again with *Ulysses* under my arm, wondering whether Boylanzo's appearance was another form of Xenia.

That Friday afternoon, I met Mr. Benchley in Jack and Charlie's. I asked him about Xenia and told him that Mr. Finnegan said it could take many forms. Most other people might have been confused by this or maybe might have pushed the conversation onto something else. Not Mr. Benchley. He pulled a manuscript from his bag and gave it to me. Said it was a film script he was working on. He had another copy. I didn't understand.

"It's another form of writing," he told me. "Another form of Xenia. People go into a cinema and sit down to watch what I have written being brought to life in moving images. While they sit in the dark picture-house, they are my guests and I hope they see the friendship I have created, the film script enlivened by carpenters, actors, musicians; the ultimate in collaboration. You might give it a go yourself. Do your own script about Xenia."

THE THING SPEAKS FOR ITSELF

The 21 Club, also known as Jack and Charlie's, 21 West 52nd Street, that Friday evening, May 1st, 1931. Me and Mr. Haltigan are having a meal. The steak is real tender. Potatoes tasty too. They're opening the Empire State building today.

ME

Mr. Haltigan?

MR. HALTIGAN

Yep.

ME

What does that say on the menu? *Res ipsa loquitur.*

MR. HALTIGAN

It's Latin. It means 'The thing speaks for itself'.

ME

Oh. Remember that film we were talking about? *All Quiet on the Western Front* back in December in the Caffè Reggio? Things happen in December. That's what my daddy says. Well, I read the book and then I went to the film. They were different, see, so I asked Mr. Finnegan about it and Mr. Benchley too. He writes films, Mr. Benchley. And Mr. Benchley said that's because they're different.

MR. HALTIGAN

Not one of Mr. Benchley's more memorable observations.

ME

So he told me, like he showed me, the way to write a script for a film. Even gave me a copy of one he was working on.

MR. HALTIGAN

You're going to write a film?

ME

(*Loudly*) Hell no.

MR. HALTIGAN

You want to be a writer then?

ME

No. I just want to write.

MR. HALTIGAN

I see. Are you all right?

ME

(*Confused*) Don't know.

MR. HALTIGAN

They seem to find us funny, those two over there.

ME

Aw, they're all right. Called me over to their table
when I comes in, while I was waiting for you. Gave
me water.

(*To the two men*)

Hi.

(*To Baa Baa Grenado, sitting
at the other end of the restaurant with his two assistants*)

Hi.

I drop a fork and nearly fall off the chair when I lean down to pick it up. Mr. Hal-
tigan takes my glass of water, smells it and takes a sip.

MR. HALTIGAN

(*Calling*) Charlie.

Mr. Charlie comes over and Mr. Haltigan whispers to him. Mr. Charlie takes a sip of my water, goes over to Mr. Grenado and whispers to him. Mr. Grenado and his two assistants walk over to the table where the two men are sitting. Mr. Grenado talks quietly to them and the two men leave.

MR. HALTIGAN

A Mickey Finn. Wasn't just water. You feel all right?

ME

(*Unsurely*) Sure.

Mr. Grenado approaches our table.

MR. GRENADO

Is he all right?

MR. HALTIGAN

Think so.

MR. GRENADO

Strong?

MR. HALTIGAN

Yeah. Spiked.

Mr. Grenado goes back to his table. Mr. Charlie brings me a jug of water and a new glass.

MR. CHARLIE

Château New York. Left bank of the Hudson. 1931,
a good year.

MR. HALTIGAN

Water, in other words.

MR. CHARLIE

No harm in a little sales talk.

Mr. Charlie attends to other customers.

MR. HALTIGAN

Drink some water.

ME

Why did they do that? I never done nothing to them.

MR. HALTIGAN

Maybe it's because you work for Cerf. Come on, eat up. What were you saying?

ME

Oh yeah. Well, I was wondering could I write down what we're talking about now?

MR. HALTIGAN

Sure. Will you be able to manage it when you're eating?

ME

(*Loudly*) No, I'm not going to write it now. I'll write it later. I just want to write what we're talking about now but write about it later. I made me out a few questions to ask so I'll remember what we're talking about.

MR. HALTIGAN

I'm sitting in front of you. You don't have to shout.

ME

Sorry.

MR. HALTIGAN

I like that. You don't want to be a writer but you
want to write.

ME

Well? Can I?

MR. HALTIGAN

Sure, but just before we begin, how's Jamie getting
on?

ME

Jamie?

MR. HALTIGAN

The boy who took over from you here. You know?

ME

Oh. Boylanzo you mean?

MR. HALTIGAN

No, I meant Jamie. It's hard enough trying to remember the names of 300 spotters without having
to learn another 300 nicknames.

ME

Yeah. Suppose. I never knew that was his name.

MR. HALTIGAN

Well?

ME

Yeah. I don't know. I don't come in here at night.
He's a good spotter. Don't go asleep on the job like
some of them.

MR. HALTIGAN

You just come in during the day?

ME

Sometimes. Mr. Cerf does a lot of business here.

MR. HALTIGAN

I should have been a publisher.

ME

So can I start?

MR. HALTIGAN

Yes. Yes.

I take out a sheet of paper with all the questions I want to ask on it. I smooth out the paper and leave it on my side-plate.

ME

See, Mr. Haltigan, Mr. Cerf said he don't think he's going to get to publish *Ulysses* because Mr. Huebsch has it. He's Viking Press. Anyway, I think you got me this job so I could help with publishing it, right? So, maybe Mr. Cerf will get it but how did you think I could help with it if he does get it?

MR. HALTIGAN

Because you help Finn with his homework.

ME

What has that go to do with it?

MR. HALTIGAN

We are all Finn. We need someone to help us.

ME

I don't understand.

MR. HALTIGAN

You're clever and high-spirited, determined,
humane and you can be a real pest when you want
to be. There you have it, all the qualities necessary
to get *Ulysses* published.

ME

Still don't make no sense to me. Anyway, you see, I
wrote down all the books I wanted to read, the ones
on Mr. Finnegan's bookshelves. See, I was half-way
through one book and then I'd start reading another and it got confusing. So anyway, I forgot about
Ulysses and I put it at the end. I haven't read it but
I flicked through it but I haven't read it. I promised
myself that I'd get through the other books first.

MR. HALTIGAN

There's no rush. You don't have to read *Ulysses* to
help get it published, you know? Like, you don't
have to drink whiskey to sell alcohol.

ME

Could you tell me something about it, Mr. Haltigan? I know it's about Leopold Bloom and Stephen
Dedalus and Dublin.

MR. HALTIGAN

Now there's a question.

ME

Well, could you Mr. Finnegan?

MR. HALTIGAN

Haltigan, my name is Haltigan.

ME

Aw, sorry.

MR. HALTIGAN

Want to get some air?

ME

No. I'll be all right. Keeps talking.

MR. HALTIGAN

Keep talking, you mean. It's about one day, just one
day, all the actions of the characters in one day. A
fascinating idea, don't you think? At the beginning,
the language is clear, precise. When you reach the
end, the characters, Bloom and Stephen, are tired.
They arrive back at Bloom's house at two o'clock
in the morning. The descriptions become tired too,
reflecting the exhaustion of the characters. They're
worn out and so is the language used to describe
them.

ME

I see. What else?

MR. HALTIGAN

The sound a cat makes is written as 'Mkgnao'. Joyce
must have listened to the cat. That's how they sound,
not 'Miaowww' that writers normally use. But the
cat makes another sound a few moments later. Joyce
records it as 'Mrkgnao'. Different. He must have
listened to the cat a second time.

ME

I see.

MR. HALTIGAN

Then there's a young child asking for a glass of
water. 'A jink a jink a jawbo'. There's a sneeze. How
does he render it? 'Chow'.

ME

What else?

MR. HALTIGAN

I was reading it many years ago. It had just been
published. I was in a hotel, here, in New York. This
Italian woman sat down near me and she spotted
the blue cover and the title I suppose. Anyway, she
started talking but she had no English really. I
answered her in Italian, told her who wrote the
book. She asked me if I might read some of it to
her. I asked her if she understood English. She told
me she didn't have a word and couldn't understand
it but she just wanted to hear what *Ulysses* sounded
like. So I began reading it.

ME

What did she say?

MR. HALTIGAN

I read the opening to one of the chapters. It begins,
this chapter, with a summary of what is to follow.
Like a chorus, perhaps, or the overture to an opera
which is a medley of all the songs. So this summary
at the beginning of this chapter is only about a page
long. I read that page to her, just that page and then
I asked her if she had understood any of it.

ME

What did she say?

MR. HALTIGAN

"*Musica*," she said. It's Italian for music. She understood it just from the sound.

ME

Just like Heinrich Heine. He wrote a poem about a
drum and it sounds like a drum. What else?

MR. HALTIGAN

Well, there are some chapters written like questions
and answers, other chapters run on and on with no
periods, commas or paragraphs, just flowing like
a river. In other books a writer might write something like, "Set would have another sip of water in
a few moments. He felt good about that because his
mouth was dry." Joyce doesn't do this. His actual
description is how you, Set, are thinking. So he
would write instead, "Glass of water soon. Good.
Mouth dry." He brings the reader into the mind of
the characters.

ME

I was flicking through it, as I said, and I saw a name,
Caruso.

MR. HALTIGAN

Yes.

ME

The singer?

MR. HALTIGAN

Tenor.

ME

Did it take him a long time to write it?

MR. HALTIGAN

About six years or so. I suppose writers take all their
lives to write a book. I met Ezra Pound in New York a
few years ago. He's helped Joyce. He told me that Joyce
used small purple-colored note-books to write in. He
had a scheme, a plan for each chapter where they represent a color, an element of the human body, a theme.

ME

What's it about, Mr. Haltigan?

MR. HALTIGAN

It's a mirror. We look into it and see ourselves. It's
about wandering, life. Joyce challenges us to hold
out our hand. He grips and shakes our hand as a
friend, a companion, another human being. The
book is very much a part of him, of his life. We
should not stand back aloof but hug the covers, give
it a grand old welcome and realize a friend is in our
home, in our hands. That's it. That's what it's about.
It's human. There's no mystery to it. *Res ipsa loquitur.*
The thing speaks for itself.

ME

Why are they burning it and banning it?

MR. HALTIGAN

Well, if you write about everything men and women
do in a single day, their thoughts, their desires, it's

too much for some people. I just think, and this is my own opinion, that Joyce has made heroes and heroines of ordinary people. People like us. And they don't like it.

ME

Who are they?

MR. HALTIGAN

Idiots. Idiots who abuse their power. People who spike drinks.

ME

Thanks, Mr. Haltigan.

MR. HALTIGAN

You didn't seem too interested in Boylanzo when I asked. We have to look after people. Don't forget them. They're depending on us. They don't have anyone else to depend on.

ME

Sure. I'm sorry…

I rush outside and lose my meal on the sidewalk. Boylanzo, who's wearing a blue sweater, comes over and puts his hand on my back. Mr. Haltigan arrives outside.

MR. HALTIGAN

You'll feel better in a moment.

ME

Yeah.

Mr. Haltigan and me walk off.

BOYLANZO

Hey, Set, thanks.

My legs feel weak and I bend down, put my hands on my knees.

MR. HALTIGAN

Thanks for what?

BOYLANZO

Didn't he give me some candy this morning, Mr. Haltigan, and a dollar too.

6

WANDERING CLOCKS

I T WAS QUIET IN THE Finnegans' place, so quiet I could hear the wall-clock ticking. All the Finnegans were out. I opened the letter from home.

Herman Shaefer,
Deliveries
Pendleton,
Bell County,
Texas

Dear Set,

Got me this headed note-paper printed as you can see. No use doing it less I can show it off to someone. Who better than the up-and-coming Set Wright blazing a fine old trail in New York city. Why, I never thought I'd see the day you'd be getting so worked up over a book. Rest of the world seems to be following your lead. Only yesterday some feller offered to sell me a copy for ten dollars. You said last time that Mr. Cerf was hoping to publish it. Good for him.

Well, no use beating around the bush. Your daddy's staying over at Mr. Nestor's all the time now. Don't talk about you much. That don't mean nothing. Feels a bit bad, I reckon, about you having to leave but don't you worry. We're all keeping an eye on him.

They still haven't got anyone to buy the Boldts' house. There are these fellers looking after the place. At least they say they are. They come every Friday night, spend the week-end. Lately, they've taken to drinking and lighting a camp fire outside, making a lot of noise. It's bad enough for the Boldts having their house taken away but when you see folk doing that kind of thing it makes it worse.

Mrs. Boldt is always busy at her sewing. She's making curtains. Last week, she took them up to her house and woke up those fellers who had been making all the racket. Showed them the curtains. Said by the time she's finished them the house would be back in her possession. They told her she was trespassing. They started cussing at her.

When Mrs. Boldt finishes the curtains, she rips out the stitching and starts again. Mr. Boldt keeps himself busy too. You might have heard we had one hell of a dust storm down here. Couldn't see two feet in front of you. The outhouse near blew away. All your things are still there though. Your school-books and things. Anyway, Mr. Boldt went out afterwards and hammered a few more nails into the shed to make it more secure. He was real happy he had something to do.

We all sit around when your letters arrive. Ops waits until we're all there before she opens the letter. We're real happy you're working in an office now. And we all like to hear the stories about that man you keep talking about, Mr. Grenado.

Lukas has grown up. Gangly and ogling after all the girls. He asks about you a lot. We all miss you a lot. Mr. Boldt wants to know if you've been to the Heine memorial.

My daddy used to say all of us is just wandering clocks going around and around and coming back to the same time. Told me the best we can do is make sure that when we're chiming, the rest of the world'll hear. Talking about time, it's half past four now, so I better get a move on up to Troy. Deliveries to do. Just thought I'd say hello,

Mr. Shaefer.

After that letter arrived, changes just kept on chiming. Viking Press gave up on trying to publish *Ulysses* so it changed hands to Random

House. Mr. Cerf went over to Paris and shook hands on a deal with James Joyce. Things were moving real quick. Mr. Cerf said I'd be more use to Mr. Ernst than to Random House. So, I changed from working for a publisher to working for an attorney.

Mr. Ernst had his office around the corner from Random House at 285 Madison Avenue. It was just a twenty minute walk. I looked at the brass plate: Greenbaum, Wolff & Ernst. I imagined an earnest green wolf.

"Who are the others?" I asked Mr. Ernst when I sat down in the chair facing his desk.

He shook his head, not understanding.

"Mr. Greenbaum and Mr. Wolff?" I explained.

"Ah. Mr. Edward S. Greenbaum and his older brother, Lawrence, Mr. Herbert A. Wolff and little old me."

"Why are you at the end: Greenbaum, Wolff & Ernst? It's not in alphabetical order. And shouldn't it be Greenbaums? There's two of them."

"We like to confuse people."

"Why?"

"We're attorneys."

I thought I'd try to suss out Mr. Ernst when I had the chance.

"Who are you voting for, Roosevelt or Hoover?"

Mr. Ernst looked surprised.

"Neither."

He sat back in his chair, thought for a while and then leaned forward. We stared at each other. He had a kind face, nestled above his bow-tie. He looked like someone who had been the best boy in the class but who would have helped you with your homework instead of laughing with the others when the teacher tried to make a fool of you.

"Roosevelt is financially secure," he began. "This frees him from envy and bitterness. He's ill. Constantly ill, not being able to walk or to be able to walk well, a daily difficulty that struck him in adult life making it all the more apparent. This is what makes him different. This is what makes him great. Have you ever been in pain, I mean real pain?"

"Once, when I was playing with Lukas Shaefer, I kicked my toe off of a rock. Stubbed it. Boy was it sore."

"Imagine having that constantly. He can relate to every pain anyone has and he has risen above self-pity and anger to the mantelpiece of understanding, hard work and empathy. He has an able mind into the bargain and, perhaps most important of all, his wife, Eleanor, feels people's needs as much as he does and lets him know in no uncertain terms what must be done. So, I'm not voting for Roosevelt. I'm voting for the Roosevelts."

"I see," I said.

"So, do I get the job?" Mr. Ernst asked.

"Oh, I'm sorry. I'm like that you see. Asking questions. It's my way."

"Curious?"

"Suppose. I don't know about the law, Mr. Ernst."

"That's my job. I want you to look after the correspondence from the *Ulysses* case. I'll show you how to file the papers away so they can be retrieved at a moment's asking."

"Couldn't your secretary do that?"

"Don't talk yourself out of a job. Any questions?"

"Can you explain it to me Mr. Ernst? All I know is that *Ulysses* is banned and that people have been burning it?"

He sat back in the chair again and thought for a little while and then sat forward. He was a real attorney.

"This case is full of contradictions. There is no overall, and I mean overall, ban on publishing *Ulysses* in the United States. Some of it was deemed obscene by a court eleven years ago but more important, four years ago, seven copies of the book were impounded in Minneapolis. This seizure was upheld by the US Customs Court so there is, what you might call, an import ban. That is, it's illegal, or it may be, to import the book into the United States. However, it may not be illegal to publish it here. That's where we're at."

"That sounds complicated."

"We're going to force the issue. Random House would be stupid to start publishing *Ulysses* only to find out later that they're in breach of the law. So, we're going to have to arrange for a copy of the book to be sent by mail into the United States and then make sure it is impounded. Then we go to court. However, even if we win there'll be another hurdle."

"What?"

"You see, *Ulysses* is not copyright. When it was first published, in 1922, the procedure to protect it under copyright in the United States was not followed. A book published in the English language anywhere in the world must be republished in the United States within six months to secure copyright here. That wasn't done so anyone can publish it in the United States if they wish."

"What's stopping them?"

"It has a reputation, undeserved in my opinion, among American publishers for being obscene so they are afraid to go near it. As I said, Random House would be taking one hell of a risk if it went to all the expense of publishing only to have a court deciding later that it must be withdrawn from the shelves. Of course, the import ban is also making publishers wary of going near it."

"Yeah but if you get the ban, this import ban, lifted, what you're saying is that any publisher can bring the book out."

"Correct."

"So you're fighting the case for all publishers?"

"No, just for Random House. If we win, Random House will publish the book. Other reputable publishers, who know that they can publish it, will not because there is honor among publishers. However, you make a valid point. There are publishers who are not so honorable. They've already issued pirated editions of *Ulysses* in the US without Mr. Joyce's permission. The most famous or infamous is Samuel Roth. He used to write himself, poetry. Some people thought it was good but I just thought it was purple prose. Anyway, these pirates, we like to call them bookleggers, may bring out a copy of *Ulysses* once the fear of prosecution is lifted by us."

"So Random House could lose out? They do all the work to get the book made legal and these pirates can move on in and get the benefit."

"Yes."

"How you going to stop them? You are going to try to stop them, ain't you?"

"Mr. Cerf and Mr. Klopfer will stop them."

"How?"

"We'll wait and see. I wouldn't mention it to Cerf. He's a bit nervous about it. Rightly so."

"There's one thing though, Mr. Ernst, that I got to tell you. You see, you see, I've kind of flicked through it, read bits of it, *Ulysses*. You know? Mr. Ernst, I haven't read it. I haven't read *Ulysses*."

Mr. Ernst leaned forward and adopted a learned tone like he might have used in court, I reckoned.

"There's no law saying you have to read it. There is, however, one saying you can't. That's why we're here."

"Mr. Ernst, you explained all that to me real good. I think you'll be good at this."

Mr. Ernst smiled.

"Thank you. Cerf and Klopfer want a meeting with us. They're our clients now. Ten o'clock tomorrow morning."

"Will Miss Kreiswirth be there?"

"Yes."

"Anyone else?"

"Alexander Lindey, works here, born in Budapest and a Mr. Waugh."

"Who's he?"

"He's what you might call an apprentice attorney, works at Slater and Penzance. Staten Island. He's doing the rounds. That's what we do. We send our trainees or apprentices around to each other's offices so they can get a feel for more than one style of attorneying, as you might say in Texas."

"Well, that'll be a big meeting. Six people."

Mr. Ernst sat back and started counting in his head.

"Seven," he said.

"Me?"

"Guess so. Now take the rest of the day off."

"I don't mind working."

"Random House has fully apprised me of your work ethic. Take the advice of an attorney and it's free. Go tell Mr. Haltigan that we're at the starting gate. It'll raise his spirits."

"Sure," I said, but wondered why he felt that Mr. Haltigan needed cheering up.

"Are you from New York, Mr. Ernst?"

"I grew up here but I was born in Uniontown, Alabama. My spiritual home is Nantucket. You see, typical attorney; three answers to one question."

"You do a bit of farming?"

"The garden is not my cup of tea but I like it in July especially when it's all lush with roses and full of blue, the greatest garden color."

✝
✝

I found Mr. Haltigan at the Caffè Reggio. He was always there mid-morning.

"Howdy, Mr. Haltigan. Guess what? Mr. Cerf and Mr. Klopfer have only gone and got *Ulysses*, like, they're going to try and get it published. And Mr. Ernst is going to help. He's an attorney and I'm working with him now. He wants me to put all the papers, letters, I don't know, into some kind of order. He's going to show me how to do it. He even gave me the day off."

Mr. Haltigan was sitting forward, his hands clasped between his knees. He lifted his head when I arrived but looked over my left shoulder and then lowered his head again. I sat down.

"So who spilt your grape juice?" I asked but got no answer. "Coffee?"

Mr. Haltigan shook his head. He looked down at his right foot and began tapping it on the ground, slowly.

"You need to know what you're up against," he said.

"Mr. Ernst explained it all to me."

He stopped tapping.

"Not all of it."

The waiter came out.

"Coffee, please," I asked.

"Wright," the blind piano tuner shouted.

"Hi Mr. Piano Tuner."

"Didn't you see that man?" Mr. Haltigan asked.

"Where?"

"When you arrived here and sat down, a man walked by. He had been walking behind you."

"I don't have eyes in the back of my head like Mrs. Finnegan."

"He was wearing a macintosh, the loudest coat on earth."

"I didn't see him. Why would anyone be following me? Ain't you pleased about *Ulysses*?"

He sighed.

"There you go," the waiter said as he left the coffee on the table in front of me.

"See this?" Mr. Haltigan asked.

He was acting very strangely. When he took the pamphlet or journal out of his side-pocket he held it up but kept staring at the ground. He reminded me of a magician pulling a rabbit out of a hat but not looking at the rabbit or even the hat.

"It's *The Catholic World*," he explained. "March edition. They're writing about Joyce so you'd expect them to attack *Ulysses*, wouldn't you?"

He began reading through it. I sipped my coffee.

"This writer, his name is Michael J. Lennon, a friend of Joyce or so we thought. He talks about Joyce's birthplace in Dublin fifty years ago in Ontario Terrace, Rathmines. He writes, '*Ontario Terrace consists of some twenty pretentious houses each of which is approached by a useless and highly ornate flight of steps*'. Pretentious? He says the terrace is somewhat gloomy and overlooks a still gloomier canal. He goes on to talk about Joyce's surname, says it's Norman–French and, '*that in Ireland the possession of a Norman name really means nothing*'. He attacks Joyce's father, calling him careless and indifferent. He accepts that Joyce can speak many languages but can't resist telling readers that all the language-learning is diminished because of Joyce's Dublin accent and pronunciation."

"What has this got to do with anything?" I asked.

"Everything. Lennon goes on to claim that Joyce worked as a spy for the British Government in Rome and that he was well-paid for this. This is wrong. Lies. He calls Joyce's writing mediocre, wretched and says he'll always fail as a writer. And how about this, '*Were the mood to seize him, he might be able, some day or other, to give us fine strong prose, in which Catholics could take pride*'. About *Ulysses*, he says Joyce has opened the sewers of the mind."

"Well, what's so surprising?" I asked. "You said yourself that they wouldn't like the book."

"It's not that," Mr. Haltigan replied. "Don't you see, they're attacking the canal beside where he was born, they're attacking the architecture of the house he was born in, the steps. They're attacking his surname, his father, lying about him being a spy. Don't you see?"

"Let them. Don't bother me."

"It should. To them, you're Joyce's architecture now. They see you as his front door. You're his surname. That's why they're following you."

"Who's following me?"

"The New York Society for the Suppression of Vice."

"The one with the macintosh?"

"He followed you down from Ernst's office."

"And just how do you know that?"

"Because my people are following him. I told Ernst to give you the day off. I told Ernst to suggest that you come down here. I knew Mr. Macintosh would follow you."

"Oh."

I thought for a few seconds.

"They ain't going to find anything out from me."

"They just did. When he followed you here, he found out where I was."

"Well, you arranged it. Don't blame it on me."

"I just wanted you to know that they're following you."

"Well, now I know."

"He does the same thing every day, Mr. Macintosh. He follows people around and then, at four o'clock, he has a meal in Jack and Charlie's."

"Why?"

"Because he's hungry."

"Yeah but why does he go to Jack and Charlie's."

"So he can eavesdrop. Mr. Cerf might say something about *Ulysses*, the court case."

"Oh."

"He's a spy. Imagine that. Every day he does that; follows people around, takes notes, for example, quote, 'Texas yokel meets Haltigan at Caffè Reggio'. Then he goes for his meal at Jack and Charlie's."

"He calls me a yokel?"

"Maybe. They call Jack and Charlie's the synagogue of hell; all those

Jews, illegal sale of alcohol, liberals and of course, Benchley. They see themselves as Jesus going into a brothel. They can't resist that but they don't preach when they're on foreign territory. They spy."

"What do these people want?"

"To defeat *Ulysses* and all who sail in her. The book is the ultimate vice to them."

"Where is he now, this man who's following me?

"Around the corner to the right, possibly hiding behind a newspaper and popping his head over it every now and then, checking that you haven't moved."

"What you going to do about him?"

"Nothing."

"Well, thanks to you, Mr. Haltigan, he knows you're connected to me and he knows I'm connected to Mr. Ernst and Mr. Ernst is connected to Random House which is trying to publish *Ulysses*. So now he'll probably be following you. Ain't that right?"

"It doesn't matter."

"You mean this vice society ain't powerful?"

"Oh, it's very powerful. They have judges and politicians in their pocket, policemen dedicated to their cause, attorneys who work for nothing for them. They're very powerful."

"Ain't you worried then?"

"No."

"Why not?"

"Because they're up against me."

"Harburg," the piano tuner shouted.

"You certainly have a high opinion of yourself, Mr. Haltigan."

"Deservedly so," he replied.

"What do I do now?"

"You have the day off. The day is yours."

I went over to the piano tuner and asked him a question. He knew the answer.

"What was that about?" Mr. Haltigan asked.

"I thought I might go up to the Heine Memorial. It's in The Bronx. Mr. Piano Tuner knows exactly where it is, says he'll come along with me. Is that all right with you, Mr. Haltigan?"

"You're in luck," Mr. Haltigan said after checking his pocket-watch. "Clancy, the book-maker round the corner, normally sends a truck up there around this time. He's not only a book-maker. Hooch, too. You might be able to hitch a ride."

"We can make our own way up."

"Why make it easy for them?" Mr. Haltigan asked, referring to the fellow on my tail. "Here, put five dollars on a horse in the George Washington bicentennial trophy."

"Which one?" I asked, taking the five dollars.

"The one that'll win."

I went around to Clancy.

"Haltigan sent me."

"Race? Horse?"

"George Washington bicentennial trophy."

"The horse, the horse."

"Well, what's running?"

"Pigeon-hole, Blimp, Soupcon, Chestnut Oak, Avalon."

"Chestnut Oak, I like the sound of that."

"Is that the one Haltigan told you to bet on?"

"He asked me to put it on the horse that'll win."

"Well that'd most likely be the favorite, Avalon."

"Mr. Haltigan asked me to put it on the horse that *I* think will win so I think Chestnut Oak'll win. Put it on that."

Clancy wrote the bet out on a piece of paper and gave it to me.

"Mr. Haltigan said you might be able to give me and a friend a ride up to The Bronx. Can you?"

"You at the café?"

"Yeah."

"Five minutes."

"He won't be able to follow us in the car," I said to Mr. Haltigan when I returned.

"They have a car as well, the one across the road. It creeps along with Mr. Macintosh, calling the attention of the world to it. Make sure to be at Jack and Charlie's at four o'clock."

"Why, to start spying back on Mr. Macintosh?"

"No, because your friend, Boylanzo, will be there. I said I'd get him a meal after what happened but I can't make it so you might fill in for me."

"After what happened?"

"He was beaten up."

"Is he all right?"

"He's Irish."

"Who beat him up?"

"He won't talk. Afraid. Maybe, someone who followed him home from Jack and Charlie's or just a random assault. I don't know. Be kind to him, won't you?"

"Sure."

Mr. Haltigan became angry all of a sudden. "They accused Joyce of being a spy. He's not. They're incapable of keeping their prejudices to themselves. I wonder how they would like it if they were accused of doing something that they hadn't done?"

"Calm down, will you?" I said.

"I wonder how they'd like it," he said after calming down. "There's a section in *Ulysses*; Hades, the Underworld. I wonder how they'd like to visit the Underworld."

I led the piano tuner from Caffè Reggio to Clancy's car when it arrived.

"Enjoy the meal at Jack and Charlie's," Mr. Haltigan said before we got in. "Order steak."

We couldn't move off immediately because there was another truck in the way and the piano tuner had to take his time. Meantime, a car pulled up behind us. A man got in.

"Macintosh," the piano tuner whispered to me.

I didn't look around. I didn't need too. The piano tuner could hear the loudest coat.

We stood facing the Heine Memorial near the Grand Concourse at 161st Street.

"I won't run away," the piano tuner said.

I released my grip from his arm.

"Mr. Boldt told me about this. I can tell him I was here now. He'll be happy with that."

"You know about censorship?"

"I should do," I replied. "I'm working for Mr. Ernst."

"Heine hated them – the censors. He wrote something once, a few lines. Try to imagine how it looks. There's this square block of dashes with only three words at the beginning, '*Die deutschen Zensoren*' meaning 'The German censors' but somewhere, a few lines down, only one other word appears, '*dummköpfe*' meaning 'idiots' and then the dashes reappear and conclude the square. Can you imagine that?"

"Sure."

The German censors − − − − − − − − − − − − −
− − − − − − − − − − − − − − − − − − −
− − − − − − − − − − − − − − − − − − −
− − − − − − − − − − − − − − − − − − −
− − − − − − − − − − − − − − − − − − -
− − − − − − − − − − − − − − − − − − −
− − − − − − − − − − − − − − − − − − -
− − − − − − − − − *idiots* − − − − − − − −
− − − − − − − − − − − − − − − − − − -
− − − − − − − − − − − − − − − − − − −
− − − − − − − − − − − − − − − − − − −

"Imagine also how angry the censors were and how they might have complained to Heine. Of course, his argument might have been that he was not calling them idiots. He could have been calling their opponents idiots. He could have been calling anyone idiots or even saying they're not idiots. In other words, he stifled the censors with the very method they had used to stifle him, forcing them to a conclusion made by themselves."

The piano tuner sat on the ground and hugged his knees. I followed his lead.

"I remember tuning a piano at the Met," he said. "I heard the aria, 'Rachel, quand du Seigneur', and I stopped. I had never heard a voice like it before. It was Caruso."

"What's that got to do with censorship?" I asked.

"Death is the greatest censor. He died shortly afterwards, after I heard him. He went back to Italy and he died there."

"People still remember him," I said.

"More than that. I wake up every morning with a tune in my head. I've been dreaming about it. I know many tunes. I can identify them all. This one, I can't. You see, I met a woman who was working in a hotel where Caruso stayed. It was either the Hotel Vittorio or the Hotel Vesuvio where he died. I can't remember which one it was. She said he sang to his wife even though he was dying – fought it up to the last moment. Telling her how much he loved her."

"What song was he singing?" I asked.

"I don't know. The song I hear in my dreams has not been written yet. I can only hear snatches of it. When I wake up and try to think of it, it runs away from me."

"So you're going to write this song?"

"No. I'm a piano tuner. This song will be written in the future. I just find it fascinating that someone will write a song about Caruso. Whoever it is, will know that justice must be done to this great singer in this song. It will be an enormous task."

"Do you think they'll do it?"

"The challenge will be met beautifully."

"What will it be called, this song?"

"'Caruso'."

"How do you know you're right?"

"I'm a piano tuner. When I adjust the tensions of the strings I know how the notes will sound when they're played in the future because of my sense of hearing. When I dream of a song that is not yet written, I know how it will sound in the future because of my sense of feeling. We must get back. One of the advantages of being blind is that you can always hitch a ride – even in New York."

He was right. A man in a pick-up truck pulled up and asked us where we were headed. As we made our way back, the piano tuner asked the driver to take a detour. The truck stopped on West 52nd Street outside the 21 Club.

"I didn't want you to be late for your appointment," the piano tuner said. "The overture is complete. The grand opera begins."

The time was wandering towards four o'clock.

✢
✢

After a short time, I saw Boylanzo limping towards me. The middle and index fingers of his right hand were bandaged together. There were dark arcs under his eyes and, when he spoke, his swollen jaw made him sound drunk.

"So what war were you in?" I asked.

"Hiya, Set. Is Mr. Haltigan coming?"

"Just me. How are you?"

"Ah, sure, battered and bruised."

"They gave you a right going over."

"He landed a dirty kick into me too, Set. There was no need for that, like."

"There was no need for any of it."

"Table thirty-one," Mr. Jack said when we arrived.

"Sure a bit of bread and soup in the kitchen'll do me," Boylanzo muttered.

"Come on," I said as I ushered him over to the table in the center of the bar room.

"Hi, Mr. Benchley," I said.

"Quiet. This afternoon," Mr. Benchley replied.

It sounded more like a suggestion than an observation.

We sat facing each other, the bar to my right, the recess accommodating eleven tables to my left and, just behind me, round the corner in the first section was Mr. Benchley.

There were two cops with napkins stuffed into their collars, chewing on steak at the table just behind Boylanzo in the third section.

"I wrote a letter," Boylanzo whispered to me as he leaned forward.

"Yeah?"

"To Pen."

"Has she left New York?"

"No, it's a love letter."

"Oh."

Boylanzo looked around. He didn't want anyone else to hear.

"Do you remember the letter you read out from the book?"

"*Ulysses?*"

"And then you told me all the clever things that the man was writing, like the way he was writing?"

"Yeah?"

"Well, I said I'd try me hand at it meself."

"Oh."

"Anyway, here it is."

He used his injured hand to take out a piece of paper gingerly from his trouser pocket. He laid the letter on the table and then folded back the bottom third of it.

"Have a read of that and see what you think but don't read the bit I've folded over."

"I don't know if I should read it. It's private."

"Sure I know you won't tell anyone."

I remembered what Mr. Haltigan had said: "Be kind to him".

I took the piece of paper and read it.

To Pen from James

Sure didn't I tell you that the love I have for you
is just a silly bit of a joke and my anger
goes up every day. The more I see of you the more
you makes me want to be alone with meself
I feel convinced in meself to be determined
to get away from you. It was never my intention
to shack up together. The last talk we had has
left me fed up altogether and
given me a fair idea about what you're like

I looked up.

"Well, what do you think?" he asked.

I thought that he needed a German censor.

"Go on, read the last bit, the bit I turned over," he said.

I unfolded the paper and read.

> *P.S. To find out how I really feel about ya, read the first line, and then the third, fifth, seventh and ninth leaving out all the ones in between. I love you very, very much you know, James.*

I read the first and every alternate line and saw that the letter changed its meaning.

> *Sure didn't I tell you that the love I have for you*
> *goes up every day. The more I see of you the more*
> *I feel convinced in meself to be determined*
> *to shack up together. The last talk we had has*
> *given me a fair idea about what you're like*

"That's clever," I said.

"Do you think she'll like it?"

"Well, what's this?"

A man snapped the letter out of my hand but I grabbed it back again. "Give me that."

"Angry little man," he sneered.

I put the letter in my trouser pocket. The man had a glass of water. He started drinking it and, as he did so, he put his free hand round Boylanzo's head and caressed his cheek. I got a sick feeling. When he had finished drinking, he left the empty glass down in front of me and then sat at the table in the recess nearest to us, facing us. He disappeared behind a newspaper. It was 4 o'clock and there was a macintosh hanging on the coat rack. I looked at Boylanzo. He looked like he was about to die. I put my hand round the empty glass and was about to stand up but Mr. Jack arrived, put his hand on my shoulder and pushed me back down.

"Quiet this afternoon," he said before turning to the man behind the newspaper, Mr. Macintosh.

"Now, sir, usual is it?"

I felt safe when Mr. Jack was there but then he went off to put the order in and I felt we were in danger again. I tried to make out things were back to normal.

"What are you going to have?" I asked.

Boylanzo looked at me with a pained expression.

"I think I might go, Set," he whispered.

"Hey, Jack, more tomato sauce," one of the cops shouted.

"You can't. Mr. Haltigan'll kill me," I pleaded.

"Sure I'll just have the bowl of soup then and a bit of bread, if that's all right."

From behind the newspaper, the macintosh man jeered and mocked Boylanzo's Irish accent. I remembered what Mr. Haltigan had said: "They cannot keep their prejudices to themselves".

"Shoor, isn't me name Mick and won't I bay heaving, da bowl o' dah soup and da bit o' da bread."

Boylanzo blushed and lowered his head. I could hear myself breathing deeply through my nose.

"Jack, tomato sauce," one of the cops shouted again.

Some of the lights went out but our table, and the one Mr. Macintosh was sitting at, remained illuminated. My anger was growing but I became distracted by a noise, the noise of a tap and then, a few moments later, another tap. It was the sound of the base of a cane hitting the floor. It could also have been the ticking of a loud clock. It felt like we had all descended into the Underworld.

Three figures appeared in silhouette behind me. The one in the middle stepped forward into the light. It was Mr. Grenado. It was like as if a corpse had emerged from its coffin to make all the world shiver. He looked straight at Mr. Macintosh who, by now, had lowered his newspaper and was returning the stare.

"Swanny Bean said you'd be here at four o'clock," Mr. Grenado said. "I have to say I didn't think you'd have the courage. Boys."

Mr. Grenado's associates walked over to Mr. Macintosh's table and sat on either side of him.

"Excuse me," Mr. Macintosh said. "I'm sorry. I don't know who you are. I don't know any Swanny Bean."

Mr. Grenado began to wave his hands from side to side in front of him.

"No, no. Don't start that now. That's...I don't like that," he said.

Mr. Macintosh tried to stand up but was impeded by the table. Mr. Grenado's men put their hands on his shoulders and forced him back down.

"Officer! Officers! Officers!" Mr. Macintosh shouted.

In the half light, I saw the two cops looking over. Mr. Grenado slowly turned his head and looked back at them.

"Hell," one of the cops roared as he jerked the napkin from his collar and ran out. His colleague followed close behind.

"I'll pay for that later, Jack," Mr. Benchley said nervously as he stumbled out of his chair. "There's something … something I forgot to do."

He, too, ran out.

"You know who I am. Let's not dally around," Mr. Grenado said.

"I don't," Mr. Macintosh replied. "I have no idea who you are."

"I've had enough of this. Napkin."

One of Mr. Grenado's men tried to stuff a napkin into Mr. Macintosh's mouth but he fought against him.

"Now look here," Mr. Macintosh shouted.

"Quiet," Mr. Grenado croaked. "Napkin. Steak-knives."

Within seconds, Mr. Macintosh found himself holding the blades of steak-knives in either hand. His captors grasped the handles and used their other hands to keep the blades secure in his palms. His protests continued.

"What *is* this? I said that I don't know any Swanny Bean."

Mr. Grenado approached the table and picked up the napkin.

"You know the most dangerous word for you at this moment? Pull. If I have to say that word again you're going to be pissing in your pants for the rest of your life. Now. Open your mouth. Wide."

Mr. Macintosh looked from side to side and then at Mr. Grenado. He flinched as his hands were gripped tighter by the men on either side of him. He opened his mouth slowly. Mr. Grenado stuffed the napkin into it.

"That's a good boy," Mr. Grenado said. "I'm the one who does this bit. These two, they're a bit zealous and even, over-zealous. Wouldn't want this Irish linen going all the way down your gloomy alimentary canal, would we? Now, I want you to turn your head and look at my friend on your right. Go on. Don't be afraid."

Mr. Macintosh did as he was told.

"Good. Now turn your head to the left and look at my other friend."

Mr. Macintosh obeyed.

"Good. Now look at me. That means no; shaking your head like that. Now look up at the ceiling and then look down at the floor."

"Good. That means yes. You understand?"

Ceiling. Floor.

Mr. Grenado stepped out of the light and became a silhouette again. There was silence and then he roared as best he could with his croaky voice.

"Jack!"

Mr. Macintosh jumped in his seat. Mr. Jack rushed to Mr. Grenado and began bowing.

"Yes, Mr. Grenado."

Mr. Grenado's cane appeared in the light pointing at the table between us and Mr. Macintosh.

"The table," Mr. Grenado said.

Mr. Jack started clearing the table of plates and glasses.

"Quicker!" Mr. Grenado shouted.

Mr. Jack put all the plates and glasses he had picked up back down on the table and then used the table-cloth as a kind of sack to take everything up all at once before rushing off.

Mr. Macintosh stared at the decluttered table which had been transformed into a naked but unknown threat.

We heard Mr. Grenado talking in the darkness. He seemed to be travelling around the restaurant; a voice without a body.

"That wasn't a good move, saying you don't know any Swanny Bean. He's not any Swanny Bean. He's *the* Swanny Bean. I won't tell him what you said."

We all stared into the darkness to where the voice was coming from but then we all jumped (I think all of us) when Mr. Grenado appeared from the opposite part of the room into which he had walked.

"Charles Dickens used to write under the name Boz. Then he got a cartoonist and he was called Phizz. Boz and Phizz. They go together. I have a dog, Shih Tzu; a real good bitch – or least I did. I did have a bitch. She was called Go Go. My name is Baa Baa. Go Go and Baa Baa. They go together."

Mr. Grenado circled us as he spoke and then leaned against the bar.

"The Mulligan boys came round to my house last week. Irish. Social call, they said. The three of them. You know them: pram-burner Gerry, granny-blinder Joe and groin-grabbing Willie. Nice boys. So they came round to the house. It's a small house with steps in front. Some people think it's pretentious. Poker. You know poker? You know poker?"

Ceiling. Floor. Ceiling. Floor.

Mr. Grenado approached Mr. Macintosh and wrenched the napkin out of his mouth.

"I asked you if you know what I'm talking about. Poker. Poker."

"Yes. Yes. I know but I don't play it."

"You don't play it?" Mr. Grenado asked. "You don't play it? I'm talking about a poker; a poker for stoking up the fire. Not the game. You don't get fresh with me."

Mr. Grenado threw the napkin at Mr. Macintosh. It covered his face.

"Put it back in," Mr. Grenado ordered one of his associates who obliged. "So, while we was all sitting down, groin-grabbing Willie went to the john. We kept talking, friendly chat. He was gone a long time. With a name like that, I didn't know what he might be doing in the john, so I asked one of the others to check on him. Pram-burner went out, came back in, said groin-grabber had taken a turn, needed to go home. I said I was sorry to hear that. We said our goodbyes.

"Well they hadn't gone a minute when I realized something. Go Go was gone. Now there's no way on earth anyone could have taken her out of the house without her barking. Poker. Groin-grabbing Willie had taken the poker and bashed her head in before sneaking her body out of my house, down the pretentious steps. Imagine that, they were too mean, even, to buy the murder weapon.

"So I went down to our friend, Swanny Bean. He always hangs around there at the Empire Exterminating Company. You know it. I said, you know it."

Mr. Macintosh shook his head.

"You must know it," Mr. Grenado said, the anger rising in his voice. "330 Fifth Avenue at 32nd Street?"

Mr. Macintosh did not respond.

"Everyone knows this place," Mr. Grenado continued, his anger now mixed with disbelief. "You have to know it. Do you know it? The Empire Exterminating Company 330 Fifth Avenue at 32nd Street?"

Mr. Macintosh nodded. Floor. Ceiling. Floor. Ceiling.

"I thought it was on Fifth Avenue at 33rd Street, not 32nd Street," said one of Mr. Grenado's men.

"You know what?" Mr. Grenado said after thinking for a second. "You're right. It is on Fifth Avenue at 33rd Street."

Mr. Grenado turned on Mr. Macintosh again.

"Why did you say it was at 32nd Street? You trying to make a fool out of me?"

Mr. Grenado waved a finger in front of Mr. Macintosh

"I don't like that. Don't try that again. What's that badge there?"

Mr. Macintosh looked down at the badge on his lapel.

"Take it out," Mr. Grenado said, and one of his men removed the napkin.

"Well, what is it?" Mr. Grenado asked.

"It's the New York Society for the Suppression of Vice."

"What the hell is that?" Mr. Grenado scoffed. "Why don't you just leave those little creatures alone. All they're doing is scurrying around looking for cheese."

"It's vice, not mice," Mr. Macintosh explained.

"Shut him up again. I can't listen to anymore of this."

Mr. Macintosh's mouth was reloaded with napkin.

"Anyway," Mr. Grenado continued, "that's where Swanny Bean hangs out. So I asked him if he heard what had happened to Go Go. He had. I told him that all I wanted to know was where they'd buried Go Go. That's all. He told me he'd look into it."

Mr. Grenado disappeared again into the darkness and reappeared behind me. He lifted up the glass that Mr. Macintosh had left on our table and resumed his story.

"So, yesterday, Swanny Bean came round to the house. He told me that he didn't know where they had buried Go Go but, he said, he had spoken to the man who did it. It wasn't one of the Mulligans. They got someone else to do their dirty work. So, Swanny said that the man who buried Go Go, who knows where her little body is, will be in Jack and Charlie's tomorrow, that's today, at four o'clock, that's now, sitting where you are, that's there. Now, I have one question for you."

Mr. Grenado approached Mr. Macintosh and banged the glass down on the table in front of him.

"Where did you bury my bitch?"

Mr. Grenado began his walk around the restaurant again appearing and disappearing in the shadows.

"They call me Scarface. I got the name when I was at school. I was only seven. As you can see, I don't have a scar on my face. So I'll leave it up to you to figure out why they call me Scarface. Take the napkin out of his mouth."

Free to speak, Mr. Macintosh did not say anything.

"When you tell me," Mr. Grenado explained, "we'll go there and dig up the body. I have a plentiful supply of shovels. I always do. Find they come in handy."

Mr. Macintosh still didn't say anything. His eyes darted around the room.

"I'll tell you what I'll do," Mr. Grenado said. "Because you had the gumption to come here, I'm going to trust you. So, what I want you to do is to go out, take a walk around the block, on your own. Fresh air, I find, is good for waking up common sense. So you go out, on your own. Walk around the block. Come back here and then, we'll go and dig up the body."

Mr. Grenado's men released their grip and removed the threat of the steak-knives.

"I can't get out," Mr. Macintosh said gesturing to the men on either side who were blocking his exit.

"Try crawling under the fucking table," Mr. Grenado suggested.

Mr. Macintosh made his way clumsily under the table and stood up.

"Don't forget your coat," Mr. Grenado said. "It's cold out there."

Mr. Macintosh walked slowly over to the coat rack and took his coat.

"Put it away," Mr. Grenado said to one of his men. "No need to plug him."

Mr. Macintosh froze, his back to us.

"I said put it away," Mr. Grenado said again.

Just as Mr. Macintosh was about to go out, Mr. Grenado lifted his cane and whacked it on the table that Mr. Jack had cleared earlier. Bells rang in our ears. Mr. Macintosh bolted out of the premises. Lights came up.

"That took a while," Mr. Jack said.

"For God's sake," said one of the cops, making his way back to his seat. "Why don't you just throw these crazies out and be done with it?"

"Hey, Jack," the other cop shouted as he took his seat. "This steak is arctic."

"Which one was it?" Mr. Benchley asked as he returned.

"The Go Go story," Mr. Grenado replied.

"I'll get you another. Keep your hair on," Mr. Jack shouted back at the cop as he stood by our table waiting for us to order.

Boylanzo had his mouth open. His face was locked in an expression of surprise or shock. He looked from Mr. Jack to me, back to Mr. Jack and then to me again, still bright-eyed and open-mouthed. I couldn't think of anything else to say.

"Soup?"

"Ah yes, I've heard of him," Mr. Finnegan said when I told him I was working for Mr. Ernst.

His wife interrupted the conversation. "Time for French."

I opened my lesson book at one end of the dining table while Mr. Finnegan concentrated on painting an election campaign poster for Roosevelt at the other.

"Cerf sacked you?" he joked.

"It's like a promotion, I think. Mr. Ernst is going to try and get *Ulysses* published in the United States. I'm sure they'll be real good attorneys up against us, though."

"Oh, I'm sure of that as well," he said, "but they won't have a hope against Ernst."

"Why not?" I asked.

"He's lucky."

I was too excited thinking about my new job to concentrate on the lesson. After a while, Mrs. Finnegan gave up.

"You must start dreaming in French," she said, as she tidied up the books.

"I will. I promise, Mrs. Finnegan."

Mr. Haltigan came in and began chatting. It was all about Roosevelt and the nasty things President Hoover was saying about him. Eventually, Mr. Haltigan turned to me.

"How was the meal?"

"Stirring," I said.

"Didn't ask about the spoon. How's your new job?"

"Exciting. We have a meeting tomorrow, about the case, *Ulysses*, with Mr. Cerf and Mr. Klopfer."

"I see," Mr. Haltigan said.

"And Miss Krieswirth'll be there too. And then there's Mr. Lindey, Alexander Lindey. I haven't met him."

"Works with Ernst," Mr. Haltigan explained to Mr. Finnegan. "Hope you have enough chairs."

"I'm sure they'll have seven chairs," I said. "If not, I don't mind standing."

"Why seven chairs?" Mr. Haltigan asked. "By my reckoning, you should only need six."

"I'll be at the meeting too."

"I had included you and Mr. Ernst. Who else?"

Mr. Haltigan had a quick mind.

"There's a Mr. Waugh. He's learning to be an attorney and he's from Slater and Penzance in Staten Island. They all got funny names these attorneys."

"I see," Mr. Haltigan said. "Didn't win, by the way. Avalon, the favorite, the horse I asked you to put the bet on."

"What won?"

"Chestnut Oak, by a nose."

"I thought you asked me to put a bet on the horse that *I* thought would win?"

I took Clancy's note out of my pocket and handed it to Mr. Haltigan. He unfolded it and saw that I had put the bet on Chestnut Oak. He looked up at me.

"You're lucky," he said.

+
+

During the night, I was woken up by the sound of women's voices on the street.

"I don't believe it," one of them said.

The other was quick to respond. "True as God. Earlier. This evening. He'd been with the savage. The one from Texas. Laughing, the two of them were, and then the savage went off. I followed the other one. The young lad they call Boylanzo. You know the one. Small, about as high as a trash can with half another one put on top of it and the young Finnegan girl; the tomboy, a right trollop. Up against the wall. Sucking the tonsils out of each other they were."

"Merciful hour."

"And the hands going everywhere."

"His?"

"The four of them. Grunting like a brace of pigs. All black and blue he was."

"Black and blue. From a fight, was it?"

"Must've been. Probably by the father of some other girl he'd hopped on this morning."

"Maybe she's not a girl at all but a boy."

"Wouldn't surprise me. The very thought of it; two boys together using their filthy paws to flush God's design down the toilet."

The women moved off. Their conversation drifted with them. I tried to think of the phrase in French, the one about absolute silence arriving and it came to me.

"*Il s'est alors produit un silence absolu,*" I whispered.

"Are you dreaming in French?" Tom asked from the other bed.

"Nightmaring in English," I replied, and then it was time to sleep.

7

ACHILLES HEALED

The offices of Greenbaum, Wolff & Ernst on Madison Avenue, number 285 that is, in New York with me and a lot of other people on April twelfth, 1932. It's Tuesday.

I HEARD HER. TOO WEAK to moan. Trying to moan. Sharply aching. Automatically, I got out of bed and began walking to her room. I stopped after a few steps, turned back and half-mounted my bed, pretending it was a horse, one knee up on the warmth of where I had been sleeping. I grabbed my teddy bear. He went everywhere with me.

Even though Mom was uncomfortable because of her bed, in pain because of the illness and exhausted because of the heat, she smiled because of me. I was standing beside her, biting my teddy bear's ear. There you are. Another weak sound of distress. She shouldn't have smiled.

"Set."

Takes my hand. Look after your daddy. There was a message in there. She was dying. More than a fact, a feeling I couldn't put into words, making it more terrifying, scrunching my belly and draining electricity from my legs with a silent buzzing. Look after your daddy? Yeah. And look after your baby sister. Silence. I was distracted by her shivering. Won't you? Quickly. Yeah. I looked over at my baby sister lying in the cot, her arms up, her hands trying to grasp an invisible ball, kicking with excitement.

One of the Mexican children, Alejandra, and her friend were sitting in the doorway.

"Set."

Alejandra began to cry. Her brother had left her there for a while with her playmate. He was outside home-running with the others. I could hear them. Go. Look after the little ones. Won't you? Yeah. I shook my teddy bear in front of Alejandra. She grabbed it and stopped crying. I went back to Mom. Did you look after the little ones? Yes, Mom. I did. Then she drifted away from me and from everything in life. I had nothing to bite on. I couldn't ask for it back. I had told Mom I would look after the little ones.

"Set."

"Yeah."

"Are you all right?"

"Yes, Miss Kreiswirth."

"Thinking about a girl?"

"No."

"I used to daydream at your age too."

"What do you do now, Miss Kreiswirth, have nightmares?"

"I try not to."

"When's this meeting getting started, Miss Kreiswirth?"

"Shortly. Have you read it yet? *Ulysses*?"

"Got started on it. See, I had to read all these other books first —"

"Yes. You told me. You might be better off reading his other books first. Mr. Joyce's."

"I have. I know about aposiopesis."

"About what?"

"Aposiopesis, it's when you nick the butt end of a sentence off so no-one knows if they all lived happy ever after or not."

"I never heard of that."

"I'm not boasting about it. Don't get me wrong."

"Oh, I'm sure you're not."

"What'll I be doing here?"

Miss Kreiswirth explained the ins and outs of filing. I didn't really understand much of it.

"Morning, Set," Mr. Ernst said from the door of the conference room. "Miss Kreiswirth, when you're ready."

I was left on my own. Nothing to bite on. They didn't want me at the meeting.

And then…

Aposiopesis.

†
†

"Mr. Haltigan. I can't bunk off work like this every time you come round. I got to get back."

"Sorry to disturb your very important life."

"You don't look too good, Mr. Haltigan."

"Been up all night," he explained, and then introduced me to the man standing on the sidewalk beside him. He looked like an attorney. He was. Mr. Haltigan put something in my hand and left…

Aposiopesis again.

I stood at the door of the conference room with Mr. Haltigan's friend. I could hear them chatting and laughing. The meeting hadn't begun. Good.

"Aren't we going in?" Mr. Haltigan's friend asked me.

"In a minute," I said.

I heard one voice. It was Mr. Ernst talking. No interruption. The meeting had begun. I looked up at Mr. Haltigan's friend.

"Now's the time," I said. "Follow me."

I swung the door open and breezed in like a hurricane.

"Howdy. Sorry I'm late. Miss Kreiswirth, this is a friend of mine. Well, go on, shake his hand."

"Set, what are you –?" Mr. Ernst said or half-said or maybe quarter-said. He didn't get to finish it, see. Aposiopesis.

"And this is Mr. Cerf."

"Set," Mr. Ernst said.

"And this is Mr. Ernst. He's the boss."

The reluctant hand-shakes continued. Mr. Ernst tried to speak to me again.

"Set. This is not the time..."

I barked back at him. "Now you just hold on there. I ain't through with the introductions yet. This is Mr. Klopfer. He works at Random House with Mr. Cerf. They're publishers. And I don't know what you do."

"Well I don't know what you do," the man said as he, too, shook the hand of Mr. Haltigan's friend.

"I do filing. That's what I do," I informed him.

"Well I'm glad to hear it. I'm Alexander Lindey, Mr. Ernst's associate."

"Set, could I see you outside for a moment, please?" Mr. Ernst said, half-getting up.

"No," I replied and he completely sat down.

There was only one person left, a stranger. He was just a few years older than I was, I guess.

"And where are you from?" I asked.

"I think Mr. Ernst wants to have a word with you," the stranger said.

"It can wait. Where are you from?" I persisted.

"Where are *you* from?" the stranger retorted.

"I asked you first."

"Set," Miss Kreiswirth said.

"Hold on Miss Kreiswirth."

"He's from Staten Island, I think," Mr. Lindey put in, trying to hasten matters.

I ignored his response.

"Where are you from?" I asked again.

"Mr. Lindey told you, Staten Island."

"Yeah but *where* are you from?"

"Oh for God's sake," Mr. Cerf said, losing his patience.

"Don't anyone know?" I asked.

"He's from Slater and Penzance, attorneys," Mr. Lindey explained. "Doing the rounds. Mr. Waugh is his name. Here to learn about attorneying. Anything else you'd like to know?"

"Well, Mr. Waugh, this is my friend," I said. "He's Mr. Penzance of Slater and Penzance, the attorneys from Staten Island."

"I've never seen you before," Mr. Penzance said to Mr. Waugh. "I don't know who you are. Who are you? Where are you from?"

"I found this on the floor beside the coats outside," I said as I placed what Mr. Haltigan had given me on the mahogany table in front of Mr. Waugh. "It's a badge; the New York Society for the Suppression of Vice."

"It's not mine," Mr. Waugh mumbled.

"Well, it sure as hell don't belong to any of us," I said.

Mr. Waugh couldn't look at anyone.

"You're all hat and no cattle," I said, my Texas accent surfacing a little bit more above the water line than it normally did. "Dumbass. Now. You. Go on, get outta here. Go on. Git."

Mr. Waugh stood up quickly and glared at me. I thought he was going to hit me but he just went out.

"What the…" was all Mr. Cerf could manage. More aposiopesis, I guess.

"Is that it?" Mr. Penzance asked me.

"Yeah," I said.

"Looks like you people have your work cut out," Mr. Penzance said before he left as well.

I began explaining.

"Last night, I kind of told Mr. Haltigan that we'd be having a meeting this morning and who'd be at it. It was late so he went to Staten Island and searched all night for Mr. Slater or Mr. Penzance and found Mr. Penzance who said he didn't know anything about a man from his office coming here. So he rang Mr. Slater who was in bed asleep. It was late. He didn't know nothing neither."

"I don't understand," Mr. Lindey said. "Why did Haltigan…what raised his suspicion?"

"Funny, I asked him that too this morning when he brought Mr. Penzance along. Mr. Haltigan's on high alert, you see. High alert for attacks on us, that is. On top of that, he told me that before he plays poker, he finds out who the other players are, where they're from. He never starts a poker game without knowing who everyone around the table is."

I wanted to explain the rest of it but Mr. Cerf stood up and got real angry. He started pointing at the chair that Mr. Waugh had been sitting in.

"He was sitting there. He was sitting there! Morris. He was sitting there. How did he get in here?"

"I don't know," Mr. Ernst said, shaking his head.

"He was sitting there. Among us. And you don't know? You don't know?" Mr. Cerf asked as he began to leave the room.

"Bennett?" Mr. Ernst pleaded.

Mr. Cerf turned round real quick and pointed at the chair again.

"He was sitting there. There."

Mr. Cerf left us.

"There was another man who should have come here today to learn about attorneying," I explained. "Mr. Haltigan said they must have found out who it was, rang up here and cancelled his placement, suggesting someone else, Mr. Waugh. It wouldn't have been hard to do. Why would anyone check it? Then they put the other feller with another attorney. There's plenty of them who are members of the New York Society for the Suppression of Vice. That's what Mr. Haltigan thinks."

"Forgot his badge," Mr. Lindey said.

"It's not his badge," I explained. "Mr. Haltigan gave it to me. When Mr. Waugh goes back to his people they'll ask him how we knew he was spying on us. Of course, he won't say that we found his badge because it's not his badge and, even if it was, he's not likely to tell them he was so careless."

"What's the point of all this?" Mr. Lindey asked.

"Mr. Haltigan says he's learned a lot from all the wars and risings he's been in and that the best way to deal with the enemy is to confuse them," I explained. "He said we might write a letter to Mr. Sumner, he's the head of this Vice society, telling him that one of his people left this enclosed badge at our office and that he might like to have it back."

"What happens now?" Mr. Ernst asked Mr. Klopfer.

"Ten minutes?" Miss Kreiswirth suggested.

"I'd say maybe twenty or half an hour," Mr. Klopfer replied.

"What?" Mr. Ernst inquired.

"The length of time it'll take before he comes back," I explained. "It's what Mr. Cerf does. Blows up and then cools down."

"I'll go after him," Mr. Klopfer said. "Meet again after lunch, if that's all right."

"You're going back to Random House?" Mr. Ernst asked.

"No," Mr. Klopfer said as he reached the door. "I'll go around the park. It's our walk. Very specific. Nothing random about it."

‡
‡

The offices of Greenbaum, Wolff & Ernst on Madison Avenue, number 285 that is, in New York with me and Mr. Ernst in Mr. Ernst's office on April twelfth, 1932. It's Tuesday but a little later.

"Mr. Ernst, I'll tell you, there's some amount of filing to be done here," I said as I put boxes of documents on top of each other. "I can't understand it. This case hasn't even begun yet and look at it. You attorneys like papers. I'll say that."

Mr. Ernst was unsettled, standing behind his desk and looking at his watch every now and then.

"I cleared my diary for today, for this," he said.

"Don't worry about that. Mr. Cerf'll come back. If I had a diary, Mr. Ernst, it would've been cleared as well except for this filing. Mrs. Finnegan made me bacon sandwiches and I got a bottle of milk too. You want some?"

"No. No, thank you. Set, when you come into my office, it's best to knock, you know?"

"Why?"

"I might be with a client."

"You don't worry about that, Mr. Ernst. I won't say nothing even if I hear anything. You know that."

"Yes, but –"

"Mr. Ernst. I'm going to do a good job here. Miss Kreiswirth told me about filing. There's alphabetic, chronologic and by subject. Now, I reckon I'd be best going with chronologic but then you might ask me for a letter from such-and-such so maybe I should go alphabetic.

"Set?"

"And I don't know about the subject thing. What if there's a letter and it's about obscenity and aposiopesis. Where in hell's name am I going to file that? Under 'A' or under 'O'?"

"Set?"

"You know what I could do? Miss Kreiswirth said we can do a photostatic. That's a copy. So I could have three filing systems: alphabetic, chronologic and by subject. Is it chronologic or chronological?"

"Set. Set, please."

"You think there's another way?"

"Set!" Mr. Ernst shouted.

"I'm sorry. Am I doing something wrong? I'm doing my best Mr. Ernst."

Mr. Ernst closed his eyes and sat down. He opened his eyes.

"Set."

"Do you want me to go?"

"Sit down."

I sat down.

"I just realized something when you were talking," Mr. Ernst said. "What you're doing is crucial. Really important to us. You need an office on your own where I won't distract you, with a desk."

"Well, you don't have to do that."

"Oh yes I do. How stupid of me not to realize how important your work is, will be."

"Well, when will I get my office?"

"Immediately. I insist."

"Will I have my name on the door?"

"Anything you want."

"Mr. Ernst, can I ask you a question?"

"Yes."

"What's that thing called, you know, the thing between you and Mr. Wolff?"

"The what?"

"The thing. This thing."

I got one of the documents out of one of the boxes and showed him: Greenbaum, Wolff & Ernst.

"That thing there," I said pointing to the & between Mr. Wolff and Mr. Ernst.

"*And*. It means *and*."

"I know that but what's it called?"

"It's an ampersand."

"Why don't you just use *and*. A-N-D?"

"Saves on ink."

"Well, I'll tell you, Mr. Ernst, we could save even more money on paper if you didn't write so many letters. We might have a chat about that when this case is over. What do you think?"

"I think that would be a very good idea, Set."

Outside Mr. Ernst's office on Madison Avenue, number 285 that is, in New York on April twelfth, 1932. It's Tuesday. Lunchtime.

There weren't no steps outside Mr. Ernst's office to sit on so I sat on the sidewalk and had me my lunch – bacon sandwiches and milk. Mr. Klopfer and Mr. Cerf returned shortly after I'd started eating. They didn't say anything to me. I don't think they saw me. Mr. Cerf still seemed a little sore. Miss Kreiswirth came out a short time later. She seemed to be short of breath.

"You can eat inside. I'm sure Mr. Ernst wouldn't mind."

"Needed fresh air."

"Me too."

"The argument?"

"No. I've been moving files."

"I could've done that, Miss Kreiswirth."

"*I* was asked to do it. I wouldn't worry about the row. He's back to himself now."

"That's good. Bacon sandwich?"

"No. Thank you. It's not only that it means a lot to him, this case. There are other things."

"Like what?" I said, munching on my sandwich.

"Well, Mr. Cerf is worried that if he wins the case, another publisher will try to publish *Ulysses*. You see, it doesn't appear to have copyright."

"Yeah, I know but there's trade courtesy between publishers."

"How do you know about that?"

"Mr. Ernst told me."

"Well it's not the reputable ones we're worried about."

"The pirates?"

"You seem to know all about this."

"You said Mr. Cerf was worried about other things, like apart from copyright."

"Yes. Random House is not the biggest publishing house in New York. Far from it. We're only five years old. We even had to negotiate a deal with Mr. Ernst. He doesn't come cheap. We've agreed a fee of $50 a day when it goes to court and that's a reduced rate. Then there's his retainer fee which comes to $500. The real payment to him will be made out of royalties from the book. That's if we win the case. If we don't, Mr. Ernst will be out of pocket. Depending on how it goes, he may also be out of reputation. This is a city that likes to see people win. Then there's what people will say about Random House, that it's publishing or trying to publish a dirty book. It's not really what people will say but the public might turn against us. Writers might turn against us just as clients might turn against Mr. Ernst. Mr. Cerf has to think about the people who work for him. They may lose their jobs, me included."

"Well, I wouldn't worry about that," I said as I stood up and whacked the street dust off my pants.

"Why ever not?"

"Well, as I see it, Miss Kreiswirth," I said just before wiping my mouth with my sleeve, "we're all going to do our best and that'll be good enough. You coming inside?"

Mr. Ernst's office building. A few seconds later, I guess.

Miss Kreiswirth grabbed a notebook and pencil from the reception desk and went into the conference room closing the door after her. I started thinking about how I was going to do the next bit of filing, remembering that I should really knock on Mr. Ernst's door even though he probably wouldn't be there anyways because he was in the conference room for the afternoon meeting.

"Set," Mr. Cerf said from the entrance to the conference room.

"Yeah?"

"We're ready."

I made my way to the conference room.

I had been invited in.

Conference room.

"I hope you don't mind us using your office," Mr. Ernst said to me.

"My office?"

"Yes," Mr. Ernst said as he gestured to heaps of files and filing cabinets that had been set against the wall. "You'll need this amount of space and of course the long table."

"Oh," I said.

"He's thinking about it," Mr. Klopfer said.

"Sure," I answered.

"If we're all ready?" Mr. Ernst began.

"Where'll I sit?"

"At the other end of the table to Mr. Ernst, our trusted attorney," Mr. Cerf said.

My office that is also the conference room.

Mr. Cerf began reading through some papers while we were talking. They looked like letters. His mood towards Mr. Ernst had softened. Still, he became quiet and isolated again but I knew him well enough to know he would be listening to everything.

"*Ulysses* has been damned by the US Government and various prudes for a decade," Mr. Ernst said. "Chief among these prudes was a dirty-minded man called Anthony Comstock, the founder of the New York Society for the Suppression of Vice. He has since gone to his eternal reward or punishment only to be replaced by John Saxton Sumner. His middle name strives to sound like sex, his surname almost like summer but all his name conjures up suffocation of the freedom of speech and thought. Sumner was indirectly responsible for the last big case against *Ulysses*, ten years ago. Mr. Lindey will outline, briefly, what happened then."

"I like the word 'briefly'," Mr. Klopfer said.

"The case Mr. Ernst referred to concerned the publication of one episode of the, as yet, unfinished book in a magazine, *The Little Review*," Mr. Lindey explained. "The publishers, Margaret Anderson and Jane Heap, included about half the contents of *Ulysses* in their publication with Joyce's approval. In any case, they were brought to court on charges of obscenity in 1921. They were defended by John Quinn. He had at least one moment of brilliance during the trial. The prosecutor, Joseph Forrester, read out what, to his mind, were the dirty bits and did so, it's said, in a rage. When he had finished, Quinn got up to defend the case and offered Mr. Forrester to the judges as his best exhibit. 'Look at him,' Quinn said and argued that Forrester was proof that *Ulysses* did not corrupt but instead made people mad."

"He lost the case, though?" Miss Kreiswirth asked.

"He did," Mr. Ernst replied.

"What'll be different this time?" Mr. Cerf asked as he continued reading the letters before him.

"The law," Mr. Ernst explained. "We will have a copy of *Ulysses* imported and then seized by customs. It will then go to the Federal

Court and the Government will have to put forward a case as to why it seized the book. Previously, seizure was made at the discretion of the customs officer. The person who was to have received the book had to make a case that it was not objectionable. This new law strips over-zealous Government officials of being a law unto themselves."

"If I might," Mr. Lindey interrupted. "The new law is an amendment introduced by Senator Bronson Cutting to the Tariff Act of 1930. The amendment was formulated on the advice of one Morris Ernst, here present."

"Why is this important?" Mr. Cerf asked.

"Because," Mr. Lindey replied, "under this redrafted law, the Government cannot bring either the sender of the supposed obscene publication or the person to whom it is addressed to court."

"Well who can it bring to court? The author?" I asked.

"No," Mr. Ernst replied. "It brings the book to court. The book becomes, in effect, the defendant and the evidence. It will be up to the Government to fight its case that the publication is obscene. We, as attorneys, will intervene on behalf of the book."

"That will only help a little," Miss Kreiswirth said. "I mean the last case you mentioned, the one ten years ago, was lost and it was all about obscenity. Won't it be the same this time?"

"Partly," Mr. Lindey explained. "Quinn had to fight charges against one portion of the book, we will be fighting charges against the entire book. Imagine that you're looking at a film and it's a scene of a house on a mountain but it's in close-up. We only see the house. Then the camera pans back and stops, showing the entire mountain and the house as a detail. It's easier now to argue that this image, that of the entire mountain, is of a mountain and not of a house. We will be able to argue the merits of *Ulysses* in its entirety and not be confined to a passage, a detail, that on its own magnifies one of thousands of themes."

"What part of the book did Quinn have to defend?" Miss Kreiswirth asked.

"The bit," Mr. Ernst responded, "where Leopold Bloom, as the judge put it, 'went off in his pants'."

"Was he ill?" I asked. "Why couldn't he have gone to the washroom?"

"He was looking at a woman on the beach some distance away and she lifted up her skirt," Miss Kreiswirth explained. "He became excited, masturbated and ejaculated in his trousers."

"And just when I was losing the will to live with all this talk about the law," Mr. Klopfer said.

Mr. Ernst resumed the conversation.

"Just one other point. We have the benefit of changing times, a more open view in society. This will work in our favor."

"I'm not so sure," Mr. Cerf said. "Look at these. Letters from people I wrote to asking if they would be the ones we could address the book to. Last month, I sent such a request to the Honorable Oliver Wendell Holmes. His secretary wrote back. No. Then I sent another letter to the president of Columbia University. Same reply. I sent out another letter to the Scripps Howard newspaper chain. Again, no. Where's the change, Morris?"

"It doesn't matter who receives the book, Bennett. All that matters is that it's sent to an address. What about Random House?"

"Who's sending the book," I asked.

"Paul Léon," Mr. Lindey replied, "a friend of Mr. Joyce in Paris."

"Apart from that," Mr. Ernst continued, "we'll send out letters to libraries asking them if they would take the book, get testimonials from universities, respected institutions, from writers."

"Not sure that's a good idea," I said. "When I was doing the filing, I read some of the stuff from writers. George Bernard Shaw said it was revolting, foul-mouthed and foul-minded. Virginia Woolf said it was nauseating, written by a self-taught working-man and Arnold Bennett described it as low-minded and inartistic."

"There are other writers," Mr. Lindey said. "However, there is a problem with this. We can get established authors and academics to vouch for *Ulysses* but the courts are reluctant to allow these or even reviews as evidence. The view of some, if not most, judges is that by allowing an expert witness to give evidence about a publication that is alleged to corrupt or to tend to corrupt, that expert witness would then become the jury."

"So we won't be able to put forward expert witnesses or authors or even positive reviews to show that this is a great book, that it's not obscene?" Mr. Cerf asked.

"It's very unlikely," Mr. Ernst replied. "This will weaken our case whether it comes before a judge or before a judge and jury."

"I think we should have a break. Ten minutes," Mr. Cerf said and left the room.

╈

My office that is also the conference room a quarter of an hour later because Mr. Cerf took five more minutes than he said he would.

"Mr. Ernst, should I file George Bernard Shaw under B or under S?" I asked as Mr. Cerf returned.

"You could file him under B and under S," Mr. Klopfer suggested.

"Then I'd have to make a copy," I protested.

"Not if you have a file called BullShit," Mr. Klopfer said.

"What's that doing there?" Mr. Cerf asked.

He was referring to the copy of *Ulysses* in the middle of the table.

"I put it there," I said. "Got it from one of the filing cabinets. I reckon, if it's the defendant, it should be here in front of us."

Mr. Cerf sighed and shook his head. Miss Kreiswirth surprised us all with a question. I think she did it to lighten the mood. It was getting dark again.

"Why are we all here? I mean by that, why do we want to have this book published? Mr. Ernst?"

"Aw, he's only in it for the money," Mr. Klopfer said.

Mr. Ernst smiled and put the question to Mr. Lindey.

"Well, I feel very keenly that this would be the grandest obscenity case in the history of law and literature, and I am ready to do anything in the world to see it through. Miss Kreiswirth?"

"How gratifying it is to see so many men seek a woman's opinion. It's more than a book. It's a consistently monumental event."

We all looked at each other. I decided to go next.

"Well, I'm working to get some money so I can help my neighbors, Mr. and Mrs. Boldt, and get my daddy's house back too. Besides, Mr. Finnegan said it's a good book so that's why I'm here. Mr. Ernst?"

"It's to do with censorship. Plays, books, films, stories, works of art, whatever, have been stifled by censorship. People telling us what to do. We've not been able to read them or see them or experience them because of some unidentified myopic bureaucrat deciding what we should or should not do. But more than that. Censorship has another effect. There are also people out there who, because they know about the stifling constraints that are imposed, do not seek to bring their great works to fruition. I want to live in a world where we can express ourselves. We've already seen how people who know it all, those on Wall Street, have bankrupted our friends and families, their children and their neighbors' children. Bankrupted not only their accounts but their hopes and dreams. The same can be said of censors. They try to choke us in so many ways. If *Ulysses* is about sexuality or sexualities then I believe no-one should have the right to control our sexual self-government."

"That was not brief," Mr. Klopfer said. "Like you Mr. Ernst, I'm here for the money too. Bennett?"

We had all been waiting for Mr. Cerf's view. Mr. Klopfer had done his best to inject some humor into the conversation before calling him in.

"I'm a publisher," Mr. Cerf replied, "and I want to defeat the smut-hounds but I fear that not having great writers testify with their testimonials or reviews about *Ulysses* in this case will, as you say Morris, reduce our ammunition to bows and arrows. It's our Achilles' heel."

It became dark again. Mr. Klopfer stood up and addressed the copy of *Ulysses* in the middle of the table.

"And what do you think?" he said, putting his hand behind one ear as if trying to hear what the book was trying to say.

"I think it's pleading the Fifth," Mr. Klopfer said as he sat down.

"Smart book," Mr. Lindey observed.

"Mr. Ernst, can I say something?" I asked.

Mr. Ernst nodded but Mr. Klopfer started talking again.

"If you want to know where to file Bennett Cerf, it's not under 'B'. I think he should be put undersea. The Atlantic Ocean would be my preference. I hear it's very deep with lots of hungry sharks."

We laughed. Even Mr. Cerf laughed.

"What did you want to say, Set?" Mr. Ernst asked.

"Well, what I wanted to ask was about *Ulysses*. You said it was the defendant and the evidence. Is that right?"

"Yes, Set," Mr. Ernst replied.

"Well, the way I see it. When Mr. Joyce's friend, Mr. Léon, sends the book over and it gets taken…"

"Impounded," Mr. Lindey said.

"Impounded. Well, that'll be allowed into court won't it?"

"Yes," Mr. Ernst answered.

"And you said the judge would more than likely not allow all the good reviews or articles about *Ulysses* into court because they're not evidence."

"Yes," Mr. Lindey said.

"Well, I'm from Bell County in Texas."

"So?" Mr. Cerf asked.

"From Pendleton. It's near Troy. Ain't you never heard of a Trojan horse?"

My office that is also the conference room. Later.

I was beginning to make some headway with the filing when the door opened and a cop came in.

"Caught red-handed," he said to me.

Mr. Ernst appeared behind him dressed in a tuxedo.

"It's all right officer. He works here," Mr. Ernst said.

"You sure?" the cop said, not taking his eyes off me.

"Yes. I'm sorry for disturbing you," Mr. Ernst said and the cop left.

"What are you doing?" Mr. Ernst asked.

"Filing. Still got a ways to go."

"It's half past one in the morning."

"Oh."

Mr. Ernst brought me home in his cab and told me he had been at a party. When we arrived outside my home, my New York home, I saw Mrs. Finnegan outside.

"Mr. Ernst, I presume?"

"This is Mrs. Finnegan," I said.

"Mr. Ernst, being an attorney you should know by now that slavery is well abolished. Look at the time."

"I'm sorry, Mrs. Finnegan. It won't happen again," Mr. Ernst said and got back into the cab.

"His brothers were worried sick about him," Mrs. Finnegan shouted as the cab moved off.

When I got into the apartment, Finn was sitting up in the bed all upset. He ran over and hugged me.

"I don't know what this dinner will be like," Mrs. Finnegan said.

She had the plate heating on top of a saucepan part-filled with simmering water.

I ate up my dinner as Finn sat on my knee. I gave him some potato to eat when Mrs. Finnegan's back was turned but she probably knew I was doing that anyway.

"Sorry for keeping you all up," I said.

"Don't worry," Mrs. Finnegan said, still sounding a bit put out. "We'll go to the late Mass tomorrow, or should I say today."

I finished my dinner, prepared for sleep and got into bed. It was two o'clock in the morning. The images of the day were flicking past my eyes. I was overtired. Two o'clock in the morning. What had Mr. Haltigan said about *Ulysses*? Ah yes, that was the time that Leopold Bloom and Stephen Dedalus went back to Mr. Bloom's house and, because it was so late, Mr. Joyce made the language tired. That was it. That was why Mrs. Finnegan told Mr. Ernst that Tom, Finn and Stevie were my brothers and why she thought tomorrow or today was Sunday. Should have said Wednesday. She must've been tired, too, staying up, worrying and trying to assure Finn that nothing had happened to me. I saw my name on the door of the conference room. Finn started a nightmare fed by me coming home so late.

"Set?"

I thought of the forces ranged against us: the judges, the New York Society for the Suppression of Vice, the law. All that filing to do. There he was, there was Mr. Lindey, little people against a big mountain. Where was the house on the mountain?

"Set?"

"Ssshh," I said to Finn. "I'm here. It's all right. Go back to sleep."

"Set?"

I thought of what Miss Kreiswirth had said about people losing their jobs, losing her job. Random House on a mountain. Abandoned house on a mountain. All that filing. Lilliput against the mountain. And *The Little Review*. The little ones. They lost.

"Set?"

"I'm here."

"You'll look after the little ones, won't you?"

"Yes Mom," I muttered and filed myself under 'Z' at the end for zleep. All that filing to do.

8

STARTLING
DISLOCATION

"You've been asking everyone else," Mrs. Janosik said. "Now, it's my turn to ask you. Tell me something you liked about it. Just one part."

"The hats," I replied.

"I haven't read *Ulysses* in a long time. Remind me."

"There's these men, the men with sandwich boards. They're advertising a shop. Hely's. They're wearing tall white hats. On each hat is a letter in scarlet. H-E-L-Y-S. One of them lags behind; the Y starts eating bread and, for a short time, they become H-E-L-S."

"Why that?"

"The word, the letters are walking around the city. They're alive and changing."

"You should record this court case, whenever it starts."

"I'd like to. I hope I won't be recording defeat."

"I know that you're all under attack from puritanical organizations. The more they chip away, the stronger you should become."

"Yeah."

"A little more enthusiasm, please. Convince yourself that you will be stronger the more they take away from you."

"Easy to say."

"Prove me right. Astonish me. Show me and show yourself that you have confidence."

"How?"

"Write something, something that will make me say 'Lordy me', something that will surprise me and something that will surprise you."

"Ain't easy to write, especially about something that gets stronger the more you take away from it."

"Exactly. One item, one element can be greater than the sum of its parts."

"I doubt it."

"If you take ink, bit by bit, away from the ribbon of the typewriter, look at the page you've been writing on – it'll be above the ribbon – and see what you've created. It should be greater than the sum of the ink dispensed. Something human, something moving. Unique. Eureka! Go on, drain the ribbon of ink and increase its volume. Archimedes."

"You want me to write about math?"

"Hats."

9

STARTLING

*D*EAR MRS. JANOSIK,
You asked me to write this. It comes from me which means it comes from Texas. Something astonishing, you said. I thought of another word like it. <u>Startling</u>. See, I've underlined it! You can strip away one letter at a time from this word and you have another word and then another. It goes like this: Startling, Starting, Staring, String, Sting, Sing, Sin, In, I.

I doubt I could get nine fellers to walk around New York with these nine letters on each of their tall hats. Instead, I'll record what comes next using these nine words as headings. We begin with 'startling' and end with just one letter, 'I'. It's not just one letter. I is me and me comes from Texas, greater than the sum of all the parts.

Mrs. Taylor, my teacher in Pendleton, told me once to underline important words, words my daddy used. My daddy doesn't talk the way words are written. He has an accent. So have I. I just found out that Mr. Joyce likes to write the way people talk. Mrs. Taylor didn't teach him. He even lets the words walk around his city and break up, reunite. There is no rule.

Still, I liked Mrs. Taylor. She was a good teacher. We never got to say goodbye. I think I just might underline all these words from 'startling' to 'I' as a tribute to her. After all, she was from Texas too.

What's that I hear, Mrs. Janosik?

Lordy me?

10

STARTING

O N May 1st 1932, Mr. Joyce's friend in Paris, Paul Léon, got a copy of *Ulysses* to send over to Mr. Cerf at Random House because Mr. Cerf had asked him to do that and something else as well. On Mr. Cerf's instructions, Mr. Léon got all the good reviews from famous writers and prominent people who had praised *Ulysses* and Mr. Joyce. He pasted all these reviews into the book and sent it over to the United States on the *SS Bremen*. It arrived a little more than a week later. In the meantime, Mr. Lindey told the Collector of Customs that the book was on its way and what ship it was travelling on. When the *SS Bremen* arrived, the Collector of Customs impounded the book. And so, that particular copy of *Ulysses* immediately became a defendant. What the customs man didn't know was that all these good reviews of *Ulysses* and Mr. Joyce had been glued into the book. We could now use the reviews to defend the book because they had become part of it, part of the defendant. We were just <u>starting</u> but it was a good start. Our Trojan horse had entered the citadel.

11

STARING

I WAS SITTING OUTSIDE CAFFÈ Reggio trying to figure out what I would do with all the new files that came in, ones from the previous case against *Ulysses*. Should I file them under Quinn for the man who defended the book or should I keep them in a separate locker because they were really a subject all on their own? Should I file *The Little Review* under 'T' for 'The' or under 'L' for *Little Review*? I shook my head trying to forget about it all. That's when I noticed a man <u>staring</u> at me. It was Mr. Waugh. He came over and sat down beside me.

"Just hear me out."

"Why should I?"

"Please," he said.

I decided I'd let him say his piece.

"I was wrong to do what I did, pretending to be someone I'm not but I believe in what I'm doing and, sometimes, that means you do things that go against your normal way.

"There are things you might not know. People, who have been campaigning for this book, are not like you. There was Margaret Anderson and Jane Heap. Do you know who they are?"

"Yep."

"I knew you were a clever boy. Then there's Sylvia Beach who published *Ulysses* in Paris. These are sinful women. They go against the natural order and against the will of God. Your school-friends in

Texas, where you're from, what do you think they would say to you if they knew you were on the same side as these evil women? Then there's the Jews. Ernst, Klopfer and Cerf. They stand to make a lot of money from this. That's the only reason they're doing it. You, on the other hand, what are you earning? Have they offered you a bonus if they win? I'll bet not. They're using you. And they'll drop you like a hot plate at their whim.

"This man who wrote the book, Joyce, is a pornographer. He's contaminating people's minds, trying to create a society drenched in sin and lust. He's a dirty man, a filthy man, a disgusting man, a drunk. He says Black Mass. He murdered his mother. These are all facts. And he's Irish, a race of street-fighters and slobbering drunks. What do you think your parents would say if they knew you were involved with these people? Do you think your parents raised you so you could help to destroy innocent people, to make our society another Sodom and Gomorrah?

"Perhaps you think that getting writers to say *Ulysses* is not a work of Satan will influence people. This argument can never be won. It is vomited out from the very soul of the Devil himself through one of his agents on earth. These writers, F. Scott Fitzgerald or Theodore Dreiser for example, won't have anything to do with this. Even if they do, their own lives will be exposed and any support they give will actually damage your cause.

"I know that you didn't know these things. The definition of being a man is to walk away from those who are trying to corrupt you and your family. Have you asked you parents if they think what you're doing is right? Why not? What do you think they'll say when they find out? All your names are going to be printed in the newspapers. You will all be brought to court and tried for trying to destroy America. You will be convicted and you will be hanged. You will bring disgrace on your family.

"I know you're a good boy. Be brave. Walk away from them. We will look after you and your father's house. God is speaking through me to you. Think about what I've said. God is kind but God will bring down His wrath upon those who savage the innocent."

He left me but not before patting my shoulder. I didn't say anything.

"Wright. Response?" the blind piano tuner shouted or perhaps it was, "Right response."

I could not go back to thinking about filing. I had become deeply troubled.

✝
✝

"And who's this reprobate?" Mr. Klopfer asked.

"Tom Finnegan," I said. "Works in McSorleys. He said he'd like to see where I work. You don't mind him being at the meeting do you?"

"No," Mr. Ernst said.

"Now that we know you, Mr. Finnegan," Mr. Klopfer said, "might we get a free drink in McSorleys if we happen to go in? Maybe about seven o'clock this evening, for example?"

"If the boss isn't around but that's unlikely," Tom replied.

"Guess we'll have to get to know your boss then," Mr. Klopfer said.

"Who's this?" Mr. Cerf asked when he arrived and sat at the table.

"Mr. Wright's assistant, Mr. Finnegan," Mr. Klopfer explained. "This is Mr. Cerf. He's my assistant."

"That's Mr. Klopfer over there," Mr. Cerf said. "He's deluded."

I hadn't been contributing too much at the meetings after what Mr. Waugh had said to me at the Caffè Reggio the previous week. I certainly didn't want to say anything when Tom was there because he might think I was showing off.

"What are they?" Miss Kreiswirth asked me.

"Nothing much, just a few files," I answered and then turned to Tom. "I just do the filing here, that's all."

"What's wrong?" Miss Kreiswirth asked me.

"Nothing. Ain't we going to start the meeting?"

"We have," Mr. Ernst said. "What's wrong? You haven't been yourself."

"These files, they're from the last case against *The Little Review*. I found these cuttings from the *Brooklyn Daily Eagle*. One of them talks about Mr. Joyce. It says, 'His book reeks of lust and filth'. Another one, this one, says,

'It's full of outspoken obscenities which give sufficient cause for keeping it out of the hands of ordinary people'. There's more."

"That's because he's Irish," Tom said.

Mr. Cerf started shaking his head like he didn't want to hear anymore.

"So you've told us what's in the files," Mr. Lindey said. "Now tell us what's wrong."

I told them about Mr. Waugh and what he had said to me.

"I wouldn't take any notice of him, Set," Mr. Klopfer said being, for once, serious.

"Well, I would," I replied.

"Why?" Miss Kreiswirth said.

"Mr. Waugh could have mentioned any writers but he didn't," I replied. "He mentioned Theodore Dreiser and F. Scott Fitzgerald."

"You need to explain this to us, Set," Mr. Ernst said.

"Well, the day I met this Mr. Waugh, that was the day I sent out just two letters; one to Theodore Dreiser and one to F. Scott Fitzgerald. Posted them at noon. No-one else knew. You see, I typed the letters. I'm trying to learn. They were the two writers he just happened to mention. Some coincidence! So I asked myself how he knew. I couldn't figure it out, so I asked Mr. Haltigan about it."

"Good idea," Mr. Klopfer said.

"Well," I continued. "Mr. Haltigan asked me over and over again if I had told anyone I was sending those particular letters out that day and I told him, no-one. Then he asked me again about it. I told him again, that I typed the letters, because I was trying to learn how to type and that's when it hit him."

"What?" Mr. Klopfer asked.

"Mr. Haltigan asked me if I made a mistake when I was typing," I explained. "I told him that sure I did. It's not easy, typing, you know. He asked me what I did with the letters, the ones with the mistakes. I told him I threw them in the waste-paper basket."

I stopped and looked around at everyone.

"They've been going through our trash cans," Mr. Cerf said, realizing this before the others. He sighed and put the palm of his right hand across his forehead.

"What'll we do about this?" Mr. Ernst asked Mr. Lindey.

"It's been taken care of, Mr. Ernst," I said. "We got Squeaky Molloy to deal with it."

"And he is?" Mr. Klopfer asked.

"The rat-catcher," Tom replied. "He's only about nine or ten but he can smell a rat."

"Well at least you employed the right person," Mr. Klopfer said. "So he takes our trash and burns it or something like that?"

"He does now," I explained. "But on the first day, the first day we knew about it, Mr. Haltigan left out the trash cans in front of the building, out there, and when one those fellers looked into it all he could see was ash. That's when Squeaky stood up. He was buried under the ash, you see. Used a straw to breathe. So he handed the man a letter. Blew the ash off the envelope so he could see who it was addressed to. I think the man sneezed. Anyways, it was addressed to Mr. Sumner, the head of the New York Society for the Suppression of Vice. Wrote it up myself."

"I really am dying to know," Mr. Klopfer said.

"Well, it said, *Dear Mr. Sumner, Please thank Mr. Waugh for telling us that people have been poking their noses into our trash cans, Yours Sincerely, Set Wright, Chief Filing Officer, Greenbaum, Wolff & Ernst'.*"

"Is there no level to which these people will not stoop?" Mr. Cerf asked.

"Whatever's below a trash can, I guess," Mr. Klopfer replied.

"I can't wait for the summer to be over, at least this will be all behind us," Mr. Cerf said.

Mr. Lindey and Mr. Ernst looked at each other like they didn't think the case would be over that quick.

"We'll have to change tack," Mr. Cerf said. "I was going to make this all very public. You know, fight it in the newspapers and on radio, get people on our side, but when you read what they're writing about *Ulysses*, I don't think that's such a good idea. Best to keep our heads down."

"I agree," Miss Kreiswirth said. "And then there's another reason. People out there are starving. They're more interested in finding the next meal than, well, with all respect, reading about a book like this."

"Aw, come on," Tom said, standing up. "You're completely wrong, the lot of yiz. Them people out there, they've been shit on for the past three years. It's no use getting into the boxing ring and sitting on your arse in the corner all the time. They're after ringing the bell."

Most of us sat up in our chairs, a bit nervous. Tom was shaking. He might've been used to facing a lot of people behind a bar but he wasn't used to this. His thumbs and knuckles were resting on the table. They were shaking too. We couldn't stop looking at his shaking.

"Everyone's telling them lies," he continued. "No-one'll do anything for them. Who's responsible? Ha? Who's responsible for the Crash? No-one? Who's responsible for the dust storms? Ha? No-one. They don't have anyone to kick because they're all after hiding. The whole lot of them. And here, you've smoked them out. The ones telling them what to read and what not to read. We mightn't have anything to eat, that doesn't mean we can't read. We need to see someone been brought down. Someone who's like the rest of them. The only flag we have now is a piss-stained mattress hanging on the line over the street where everyone can see. That's what they've done to us. We can't choose our food any-more, even we if get any and we can't choose our jobs anymore even if we have one but we can choose what we want to read when we goes to the library and no-one should take that from us. Yiz have got to get up onto the canvas and beat the living fuck out of them."

Tom stopped. The silence was underlined by the ticking wall-clock. Tom looked up at it.

"Shite. Look at the time. Got to get back to work."

Tom ran out and left the door open. I felt I better close it because, after all, I was the one who had brought him into the meeting. I noticed that no-one was saying anything even after I had closed the door and sat down. After a while, we all stared at Mr. Klopfer. I don't know why. Maybe we were expecting him to say something funny.

"Well," Mr. Klopfer said. "I guess that answers that question."

1 2

STRING

ERE'S SOME DIRT FOR YOU to put with the rest of your stash.
I looked in the envelope but there wasn't any dirt. Maybe Mr. Shaefer had forgot to put it in. The dirt couldn't have fallen out because the envelope was well sealed. The way he wrote, Mr. Shaefer, that is, made me think he had been drinking.

> *They call them dust storms. I call them dirt storms. There's dirt between my toes. There's dirt in my house. There's dirt in my engine. It makes my car stop. There's dirt in my son's hair. There's dirt in my hair. There's even dirt in the dirt. There's dirt in the outhouses. When folks want to think of better times or be reminded of them, they go to their cabinets, bottom drawers, and open them and then take out the boxes of treasured memories. Funny thing about those boxes. We keep them in the drawers and hardly ever open them. When we do, we can smell the comfort and joy of the past. We take the blankets off the boxes because we've wrapped them in blankets. They're like our children. We want them to be warm and protected. Then we open the lid of the box expecting to find that watch or necklace or toy. Sure, we find them. They've been there all along. We also find something else. Dirt. It's made its way into our precious memories, staining them with the present disasters that have befallen us.*

He made no mention of my daddy.

I am a religious man. Suppose that's why you wrote to me. You seem to think your empire stretches all the way down here to Texas. You say you're a religious man as well, so you might know this phrase. It's from the Book of Matthew, 'What you do to the least of my brothers and sisters, you to do me'. So, for the record, when you write a letter to me, sign it. I know your name, Mr. Waugh. I found out. I know people in New York. My empire stretches all the way up there. That's how I got your address. A Mr. Haltigan gave it to me. He seems to be like us folk down here. No hiding behind false bushes. So, for the future, you can save a lot of ink and paper because you will never convince me that my neighbor's child is what you say he is. I read your letter to the folks around here and we all laughed. However, we are not nasty people despite what you might think. And so, to prove this, I am enclosing some of the dirt that's been flying around here for some time now. You are a man who likes collecting dirt. So here's some dirt for you to put with the rest of your stash. You might notice, it's much better quality than what you've been trying to spread around.

Mr. Shaefer signed off his letter explaining what this was all about.

Well that's the letter I sent him, Set. Copied it out for you exactly as I wrote it. That'll fix him good. No reply. Il s'est alors produit un silence absolu, as we might say down here in Texas. We're very proud of you.

No mention of my daddy.

"You've gone into the ring, Bennett," Mr. Lindey said as we sat around the table in the conference room.

He was talking about a story in the *Brooklyn Daily Eagle*. I decided to read the first paragraph aloud.

Bennett A. Cerf, chief of Random House, has just hired Morris L. Ernst, the attorney, to wage war on the ban against James Joyce's Ulysses.

"This fellow knows what he's talking about," Mr. Klopfer said. "I see he had to tell everyone you are an attorney, Morris, although I'm not convinced. No mention of me, I see."

They are enlisting editors, critics, authors, members of the Bar, cler-gymen, psychoanalysts, teachers and librarians.

"I hope that they spelt 'bar' with a small 'b'," Mr. Klopfer continued. "Otherwise your assistant, Tom Finnegan, of McSorleys bar with a small 'b', won't have his say."

It has done more to alter modern rhetoric than any other single thing.

"That's the first time I've read anyone writing something good about it," I said.

"And maybe the last," Mr. Klopfer added.

"What if Joyce starts talking, complaining about the judges or the legal system?" Mr. Cerf asked. "We should send someone over to keep an eye on him. Writers are impossible."

"Joyce is with us," Mr. Ernst said. "He's not foolish."

"He's a writer," Mr. Cerf said. "I know what they're like. And this campaign, this publicity campaign won't be worth a damn if this drags on and on. We need to get to court quickly. People will get tired hearing about it."

"It will build up, the publicity," Mr. Ernst replied. "Maybe the longer it goes on, the better."

"No," Mr. Cerf said. "The longer it goes on, the more time they will have to attack us. We've beaten them off so far. They only have to shoot one pool ball into a pocket and they've won the game. We should send someone over."

I opened my eyes and looked at the ceiling. I moved a little. The bed didn't creak. It wasn't my bed. I remembered standing on my bed with someone on my shoulders. Who? I was afraid I'd go through the bed and even more afraid of how I'd explain the damage. The extra weight and the unstable bed put me in constant corrective movement. This was made even more difficult as the person on my shoulders attempted to draw a smiling face on the ceiling. My passenger complained to me that I was moving too much and that he wasn't able to draw it. I did my best and the face was drawn. He had wanted to see something happy before he went to sleep so I had come up with this crazy idea. Hadn't I?

"I done it," he said.

We collapsed on the bed and looked up. There it was, the smiling face. I thought about this as I moved again. The bed didn't creak. It wasn't the same bed. I continued to stare at the ceiling. There was no smiling face. It wasn't the same ceiling.

"Welcome back," a nurse said.

"Where am I?"

"Presbyterian hospital."

"I ain't Presbyterian. Am I sick?"

"That's normally why people come to hospital. How do you feel?"

"All right, I guess. What happened?"

"Accident. You'll be fine."

"What kind of accident. Did I fall on the bed?"

"No," she laughed. "I'll get the doctor."

"You don't look like a doctor," I said.

"I'm not a doctor. I'm your friend."

"I don't know you."

"They said you mightn't remember things."

"Where's my daddy?"

"At home I suppose."

"Can't you get him?"

"Where does he live?"

"Not far. Pendleton."

"Oh yeah, Texas."

"Yeah, Texas."

"You're in New York."

"Why am I in New York? Where's my daddy?"

"Sshhh. Sshhh. Sit back. That's it. Relax. Listen. Listen. You've fallen in with bad people. The Jews. The Irish. I'll protect you. That's why I'm here. Are you gone asleep?"

"I can't remember getting dressed. I can't even remember coming into this room. Who are you?"

"A doctor. Your doctor."

"I can't remember coming in here."

"You were injured. This is a hospital. You're getting better."

"I can't remember. What happened?"

"You were attacked. Blow to the head. That's why you're a little out of sorts. What's your name?"

"Set Wright."

"Good. Who am I?"

"I don't know."

"What's my job?"

"I don't know."

"I'm a doctor. Your doctor."

"Hey Mister, what's wrong? Mister?"

"Mister?"

"Yeah you. Don't worry. I'm not dangerous. She tied me to this chair 'cause I kept wandering off but I like to sit here in the corridor. It's busy. I don't know who it was?"

"You don't know who it was what?"

"I don't know who tied me to the chair."

"It was the nurse. A few minutes ago."

"Oh. Yeah. The nurse. Why you crying, Mister? You know someone here?"

"Yeah."

"They'll be all right, Mister. Your wife?"

"No. A friend."

"Oh. I'm Set."

"Pleased to meet you."

"What's your name, Mister?"

"Haltigan."

"Nice to meet you Mr. Haltigan. I'm Set. Why am I tied to the chair, Mister? Do you know?"

✝
✝

"Why am I here?"

"We invited you for a meal."

"Is this mine?"

"Yes. Yes. That's your suitcase."

"My suitcase?"

"It's all right. I'll take it. Here, sit down."

"Who are you?"

"I'm Mr. Finnegan and these are my sons: Tom, Finn and Stevie."

"Why's Finn afraid of me? Why's he afraid of me?"

"He's not. He's just a bit shy."

"Did I hit him?"

"No."

"He's real scared of me. Why?"

"He's just a little shy. Come and eat. Mrs. Finnegan is away in Ireland with her sister, Aunt Lil and Pen. They're gone for a few months. You can let go of the suitcase."

"Finn? That's his name? Why's he crying?"

"Why am I sleeping here? Mr. Finnegan, ain't it? That's your name. Why ain't I at home? Where's my daddy? The bed's creaking. I remember that. That's your name, ain't it? Mr. Finnegan?"

"Yes, that's me. Go to sleep now. Hey, Finn, don't you want to sleep beside Set?"

"No."

"Hi Mr. Haltigan."

"You remember me. That's good."

"Sure. You were in the hospital. Do you know these people?"

"These people? These fucking people?"

"Tom. Stop."

"We took you in off the fucking street and you don't know who we are?"

"Tom. That's enough. He needs understanding, not anger. Get out. Get out."

"Fuck you."

"What's wrong. What did I do to him?"

"It's all right, Set. Don't worry. Tom's just upset. Mr. Haltigan wants to bring you for a walk."

"Are you going to kill me?"

"No."

"What's this place, Mr. Haltigan?"

"The 21 Club, Jack and Charlie's. There's someone who wants to meet you."

"Do you know who I am?"

"No."

"I'm Baa Baa Grenado. Follow me."

"Why are we in the cellar, Mr. Grenado?"

"So I can tell you a story. About two years ago, this bum, his name is Walter Winchell, wrote a story in the papers about here, Jack and Charlie's. He was upset, you see, because he wasn't let in here. He's a muck-raker, gossip-merchant. Used to be a hoofer. Now he wants people to dance to *his* tune.

"Because of that article he wrote in the papers, the Feds raided the place. They found liquor. They also found that all their cars had been ticketed for illegal parking. Jack and Charlie got off light but they couldn't take no more chances so they got Soll and Ernie Roehner, they're brothers, Joe Whitney and Ben Crow to sort it out. They did a few things upstairs, very clever, and they did this. It don't look like a door but it is. Leads to number nineteen. That's next door. Jack and Charlie own it but it ain't in their names. Just looks like one of the other alcoves here but it's not. It's a two-ton door. If you blow smoke at the edges the smoke'll come back. If you use a hammer to tap it, don't sound hollow. And then there are all these holes. If you take this long meat skewer and push it into one of the holes, you'll hear a click and then you can open the door. They raided the place last week again. Didn't find nothing. Do you know which hole it is?"

"No."

"This one. See."

Click.

"Gee, that's great."

"That's what you said yesterday."

"I was here yesterday?"

"You said that too."

"Maybe I could come tomorrow. I'll remember. Did I say that as well yesterday?"

"Maybe you won't say it tomorrow."

"Do you know who I am?"

"You're Tom."

"Do you know where you are?"

"This is your place; the Finnegan's."

"That's right. Good. What's happening today."

"I don't know."

"I just told you."

"I can't remember. Why can't I remember?"

"It's nomination day for the Democrats."

"Yeah, that's right. Roosevelt."

"Da says there's a current going through the country. Like electricity. Sparks. Roosevelt is our man. He'll help us, if he can win the nomination, that is. They say the bookies in Chicago are giving five-to-one odds that Hoover will get back, when there's the election that is."

"When'll we know?"

"Later. Sometime. He won't let me turn on the radio. Just sitting there at the table. Haltigan said he'll stop by when he knows. Do you remember Haltigan?"

"Yeah."

"That's good, Set. You're doing real well so you are."

"Why is he afraid of me?"

"He'll come round. Finn, go back to sleep."

"Out last night he was, that lad from Texas, wandering again like a lone wolf."

"In that rain?"

"Aye, and not decent either. I hear they have him chained up but sure didn't he eat through them."

"No."

"Savage. He came down after him. Finnegan. The wife is away. Funny farm, they say."

"Why does he come out at night?"

"Didn't I tell ya. There's wolf's blood in him. Off to snatch a new-born and eat it raw. That's what they do."

☦

"Set, Set, wake up. Do you hear the footsteps?"

"Yeah."

"Haltigan's."

"Tom. Tom, I think something's happened."

"Yeah, the nomination."

"No. Something else."

"What?"

"It was like a click, like the door in Jack and Charlie's."

"It's all right, Set. It's all right. Go back to sleep."

"I see you're all up. Thought you might be."

"Did he win?"

"He got the nomination."

"Roosevelt?"

"Yes, Roosevelt."

"Mr. Finnegan?"

"Yes, Set."

"I want to go to Jack and Charlie's."

"Now?"

"Yes, now."

"What do you think, Mr. Haltigan?"

"It might be a little crowded given the news."

"Let's go."

☦

"Quiet. This is a speakeasy not a shout-loud. That's better. Well, Set, have you come to celebrate with us?"

"Why are all these people so quiet now?"

"We thought you were someone else."

"I want to go downstairs, Mr. Grenado."

"Why not?"

"It's this door, Mr. Grenado."

"Yes."

"Why are all these people waiting for me?"

"Has he opened it? Did he remember?"

"Quiet up there. Go on, Set."

"Looks like a knitting needle, Mr. Grenado, or a feather."

"Well it's just a plain old meat skewer."

Click.

"He's done it. He's remembered."

It was only when I lost my memory that I realized how important it was. The time from before the attack on me to the point before I woke up in the hospital was scissored, the fragment condemned to an abyss; down the plug-hole, you might say. Mr. Finnegan assured me that I'd be fine, though sometimes he'd ask me about a book I'd be reading. "Haven't you read that before?" he'd say. Probably had. Getting twice the money I paid for it seeing as I was able to read it again. My blanked memory belonged to the past. Its effects, however, made themselves known in strange and sometimes comic ways.

One night, I felt someone crawling over me into the bed and settling in beside me.

"Are you awake, Set?" Finn asked.

"Why wouldn't I be after a herd of cattle stampeding over me."

He laughed.

"Where's the face?" I asked him.

"What face?"

"The one up there on the ceiling. The one you drew. I had to lift you up."

"Don't you remember?" he said. "I never got to draw it because we fell down. You kept moving."

"You never drew it?"

"No. I hoped I might but I didn't."

I had remembered hope.

Soon I returned to work at Greenbaum, Wolff & Ernst. After all the hand-shaking and kissing (Miss Kreiswirth) we settled down at the long table in the conference room. I never got my name on the door. They were all a little nervous case I fainted or started talking nonsense. The usual hum of conversation subsided so I decided to ask a question.

"Well, is all the cotton nearly in?"

It was like I had cussed or something.

"Set," Miss Kreiswirth said eventually. "You're not in Texas."

"Well that don't stop me talking Texas-like. That's what we says when we wants to find out if something's done. Like, if I was doing my homework, my daddy'd say to me 'Well, son, is all the cotton in?' He wasn't talking about the cotton. Talking about my homework. I just want to know how far we've got. You didn't really think I was asking about cotton now, did you? You did? Hell, I reckon ya'll must've gotten a bang on the head to think that."

"The crop is still all out in the field," Mr. Cerf said, looking at Mr. Ernst. "Nothing has been harvested."

"I wouldn't say that," Mr. Ernst said.

"I would," Mr. Cerf replied.

The gloom cast by Mr. Cerf at meetings didn't so much get us down as remind us how difficult winning the *Ulysses* case was and would be.

There were moments of joy when I showed Mr. Ernst the big sacks of mail from academics and writers supporting the publication of *Ulysses*. Among them were testimonials from Theodore Dreiser, who said *Ulysses* was amazing and from F. Scott Fitzgerald, who said that *Ulysses* should, of course, be published legally in the United States. My personal favorite was from Mrs. Ruth E. Delzell who described the book as a masterpiece. She was the head librarian at the Free Public Library in Amarillo, Texas.

"You're very proud of where you're from?" Mr. Ernst asked me.

"Sure. Why shouldn't I be?"

"I didn't go to any of the fancy law schools, you know, not like my partners here."

"Yeah but you're better than them."

"I wouldn't say that, Set. Just lucky. My father came to the United States from Bohemia. Settled in Uniontown, Alabama. He was only fifteen. He told me he arrived with a mattress, a spoon and an address tag with the words 'Union Tauber' on it. That means Uniontown. That's all he had when he was fifteen, when he arrived."

"A tag. What do you mean a tag, like a note?

"No, a tag, an address tag. It was around his neck, held there by <u>string</u>."

13

STING

"Mrs. Janosik," I said, "that Mr. Waugh visited me in the hospital. I remember. Why is he trying to harm me? I'm just the office boy."

She smiled. "It's to do with the stack of playing cards built up on a table in a triangle to the top where *Ulysses* rests in majesty. Directly below it, you could say, there's Random House and further down again all the people who support our cause. At the base, there's you and me and others. They try to pull out your card in the hope that the triangle will be collapsed because the people at Random House might say it's not worth it. They're hoping that Mr. Cerf and Mr. Ernst will decide that your happiness or indeed your life is more important than *Ulysses* and give up. It's an old card trick. You can do the same with a great edifice if you find the supporting beam and sledge-hammer it out of its socket."

"Why did you smile when I asked you that question?"

"Because I arrived at your bedside one day and found that Mr. Waugh. Apart from an aptitude for languages, I know where to kick. I know how to <u>sting</u>. He didn't return to your bedside."

"When I was in hospital did Mr. Cerf or Mr. Ernst ever think about that, about giving up?"

"Perhaps, but they knew you would have been very angry with them if they had. Were they right?"

"Damn sure they were."

"Anything else?"

"There was just one other thing."

"Yes."

"I remember the French books Mrs. Taylor had; Mrs. Taylor in Pendleton. They were all grammar books. Then I looked at the French books Mrs. Finnegan had given me; novels and essays. I read them all again but there's a phrase that's in my head. I don't know where it comes from. *On verra bien si l'on ne vient pas de préparer, pour plus tard, le plus retentissant des désastres.*"

"It's from an article written by Émile Zola who was pleading for justice for Captain Dreyfus, a Jew. He had been wrongly accused by anti-Semites. Zola wrote an open letter to *L'Aurore*, a newspaper, setting out his polemic. What you said is a line from it. Do you know what it means?"

"Kind of."

"*We shall see whether we have been setting ourselves up for the most resounding of disasters, yet to come.*"

"How do I know this phrase?"

"I visited you in the hospital and read you the entire article by Zola every day when you were asleep."

"Why do I only remember that bit?"

"The mind poses questions that may never be answered."

14

SING

I BURST INTO MR. ERNST's office as he was having a meeting with Mr. Lindey. There was no time for Mr. Ernst to remind me that I should have knocked. I drove straight in.

"Can you tell me what this is?"

Mr. Lindey took the piece of paper I was holding out and read it.

"It's a note, Set," Mr. Lindey explained. "It's about Sam Coleman, the Chief Assistant United States District Attorney."

"And?" I asked.

"Well," Mr. Lindey continued, "this note explains that Mr. Coleman – he's the man we'll be fighting against – says he's read *Ulysses* and he thinks it's a literary masterpiece. However, he also thinks it's obscene."

I looked from Mr. Lindey to Mr. Ernst but I was still confused.

"You might have noticed also," Mr. Lindey added, "that Coleman suggests passing the book around the District Attorney's office because, he thinks, it's the only way they might get a literary education. Quite funny, don't you think?"

"But who wrote this note?" I asked.

"Well, you see at the top, it says it's from A. L. That's me, Alexander Lindey and then it says it's to M.L.E. That's this man here; Morris Leopold Ernst. It's what you might call an internal office memorandum."

"Mr. Lindey, your office ain't that far away from here. Why, I'd say it's a good ten seconds walking distance. You know how many of these I have to file? Maybe next time, Mr. Lindey, you might just wear out a bit of shoe-leather to tell Mr. Ernst what's happening. Sorry for not knocking but I felt this was important."

"Yes," Mr. Ernst said.

The note or, as Mr. Lindey called it, the internal office memorandum was discussed at the next meeting. Mr. Klopfer was the last one to arrive. He was quiet and told us he had seen a ghost.

"A ghost?" Miss Kreiswirth inquired.

"Definitely a ghost," Mr. Klopfer replied. "Out there, a figure all in black. Elf-like."

"That's our trash-burner," Mr. Ernst explained.

"Yeah, Squeaky Molloy, the rat-catcher," I added.

"I'm sure it was a ghost," Mr. Klopfer said.

"Can we begin?" Mr. Cerf asked.

"Set has something to show us," Mr. Ernst announced.

I took up my map of the United States and held it in front of me so they could all see.

"This is a map of the United States," I explained.

"No?" Mr. Klopfer said.

"Anyway, you see here, all these red dots. They mark all the libraries that have said they want to stock *Ulysses*. Looks good, don't it. Better than reading them all out to the jury. And look here, there's two in Texas."

"We mightn't have a jury. We might have a judge," Mr. Lindey said, "but whichever, this is very good, Set."

"A judge, a jury?" Mr. Cerf asked. "When is this case going to come to court?"

"The Assistant District Attorney," Mr. Ernst began.

"That's Sam Coleman," I explained.

"Yes, Coleman," Mr. Ernst continued. "He's greatly impressed by *Ulysses* but he thinks it's obscene."

"So it's going to court?" Mr. Cerf asked.

"Coleman doesn't want to take on the responsibility of making that decision so he's handed that over to his boss, the District Attorney," Mr. Ernst explained.

"So, he'll make the decision. How long is that going to take?" Mr. Cerf asked.

Mr. Lindey decided to answer. "Mr. Coleman's boss is George Z. Medalie."

"And?" Mr. Cerf asked.

"Mr. Medalie is running for office, the Senate," Mr. Lindey explained. "We, our firm that is, had some success against him in a case recently so he's a bit reluctant to make the call and perhaps lose the case while he's running for election. This means we are unlikely to get a decision until after the polling day in November."

"November," Mr. Cerf said. "Perhaps Mr. Medalie might like to take a vacation then. Wouldn't that be a good idea? And then he could retire and then we could get another District Attorney after another few months and then we could have another election and another delay. Wouldn't that be a good idea? Is there no way to speed this up?"

"The process of law moves at its own pace," Mr. Lindey said.

"Are you sure it moves at all?" Mr. Cerf asked.

"What did you mean about the case being tried before a judge or a jury?" Miss Kreiswirth inquired.

"We would prefer if the case were tried just before a judge," Mr. Ernst explained. "A jury would be asked to put themselves into the minds of John Doe or Jane Doe and what they might think of certain passages in *Ulysses*. In that case, they might become more, shall we say, prudish. A jury is an unknown quantity, not something we want. A judge, on the other hand, is learned, as in, he knows the law. The only problem here is that we have to get the right judge, not so much one sympathetic to our cause but one with an open mind."

"Do they exist?" Mr. Cerf asked. "And if they do, won't the District Attorney object? Surely it would be more beneficial to them if it was a jury trial."

"No," Mr. Lindey answered. "The District Attorney's office wants to see the law enforced in a way that is just. They do not want to win at all costs."

"I find that hard to believe," Mr. Cerf said.

"It's the way we are," Mr. Ernst said. "We have a code of justice and we stick by it, all of us on all sides."

"What the hell is that?" Mr. Cerf asked.

For a moment, I thought he was putting another question about our conversation. We stopped and listened to the sound.

"Is it a woman singing?" Miss Kreiswirth asked.

"That's all we need," Mr. Cerf said.

"Maybe it is," Mr. Klopfer replied.

Our curiosity led us all out of the conference room to where Squeaky Molloy was gathering the trash near the doorway. Papers had fallen onto the floor and he was putting them back. I suppose I was being a bit boastful so I had to tell everyone what the song was.

"It's from *The Bohemian Girl*, 'I Dreamt I Dwelt in Marble Halls' by Balfe, Michael William Balfe. He's Irish."

Squeaky heard me and stopped singing. He turned round. No wonder Mr. Klopfer thought he had seen a ghost. He was covered in soot from head to toe but his most defining features were the whites of his eyes set against darkness of his tiny frame.

"Sorry. Sorry," he said. "Just doling out a few bars of an oul' melody. That's all. I'll stop. Didn't mean to disturb yiz."

"Sing," Mr. Cerf said and surprised us all.

15

SIN

Itold Mr. Finnegan that I must have been getting better because all the coincidences were returning. There was the skewer at the 21 Club which reminded me of the tuning fork, the feather that Ops used to ward off thunder and the knitting needle Mrs. Finnegan had used to direct Tom and me doing our dance routine. Then I told him about Mr. Ernst's daddy coming from Bohemia and Squeaky Molloy singing a song from *The Bohemian Girl*.

"Ah yes, Arline," Mr. Finnegan said.

He told me that Arline was the Bohemian girl who had been kidnapped when she was young and couldn't remember much when she got older. That's what the song's about, 'I Dreamt I Dwelt in Marble Halls'.

"See, there's another one. I lost my memory too."

"But you're fully recovered, Set, aren't you?"

"Well, not really. I keep seeing colors in front of my eyes; purple and blue."

"Must get you to a doctor."

"No. I kind of like it. Mr. Finnegan?"

"Yes, Set?"

"Who attacked me?"

"A gang of nobodies."

"It wasn't them other people, that vice society?"

"No. It was New York or, rather, what it has become, a jungle of marauding thugs. Roosevelt'll it set it right."

Just before polling day, Mr. Cerf heard that someone was planning to bring out a pirated edition of *Ulysses*. I thought Mr. Cerf might give up and drop the whole case but Mr. Lindey sent a letter to the booklegger threatening all kinds of things on him; an injunction, seizing any pirated books and frightened the hell out of him. We didn't hear any more about it but at meetings, Mr. Cerf became quiet and I thought we all knew that this was another thing worrying him.

We put all these worries aside, except for Mr. Cerf maybe, for the presidential election. It was just like the time we heard who had won the Democratic nomination. Mr. Finnegan wouldn't turn on the radio and we had to wait for Mr. Haltigan to stop by. We listened out for his footsteps. I heard Mr. Finnegan whispering at the table. I think he was saying prayers. There were noises on the street but we couldn't make out what had happened.

At around three o'clock in the morning, my heart began thumping faster than normal; certainly faster than Mr. Haltigan's footsteps. Tom and me got up and stood at the table. Mr. Haltigan came in and seemed surprised that we were up.

"Well?" Mr. Finnegan asked.

"I've just come from the Biltmore Hotel. Franklin Delano Roosevelt has been elected the 32nd President of the United States. Hoover rang to concede shortly after midnight."

Tom ran to Mr. Haltigan, hugged him. Mr. Haltigan seemed unmoved.

"We've won," Mr. Haltigan said. "We've won."

"I know," said Tom.

In the morning, Mr. Haltigan took Tom, Finn, Stevie and me to Fifth Avenue where we had our photographs taken by Underwood and Underwood. One was of all four of us sitting down beside each other and then one of each of us on our own; that's five altogether. Mr. Haltigan said the day should be recorded and so it was but we had to wait four months for Mr. Roosevelt to be inaugurated.

✝
✝

December 1932 arrived. Things happened in December. That's what my daddy said. I bumped into Mr. Grenado on my way to work.

"I can't find this goddam place," he said, looking up at the sky instead of looking around at the street signs.

"What you looking for?"

"The place where you work."

"I think I might know where it is. I'm on my way there now. Was this just an accident, Mr. Grenado, us meeting like this?"

"A fortunate one, if there can be such a thing. I have a meeting there."

"With Mr. Ernst?"

"No."

"Mr. Greenbaum?"

"Neither."

"Mr. Wolff?"

"No."

We found Mr. Cerf standing in the lobby, his hands gripping his lapels, head up and eyes closed. There were small office trash cans in front of him as well as Squeaky Molloy, who was singing to Mr. Cerf:

> 'Tis gone, the past was all a dream,
> The light of life is o'er;
> The hope that once so bright did seem
> Now shines for me no more,
> now shines for me no more.

It was a suitable song for someone so, as Mr. Grenado put it, besooted. I went to see Mr. Ernst, in case he had something for me to do other than filing.

"Is this turning into a pantomime?" Mr. Ernst asked me as Squeaky's performance continued.

"Opera. It's from *The Bohemian Girl*," I replied.

"Apologies. Here," Mr. Ernst said, shoving a piece of paper at me.

"For filing?" I asked.

"For reading, then filing. Sit down."

I read.

UNITED STATES DISTRICT COURT
SOUTHERN DISTRICT OF NEW YORK

UNITED STATES OF AMERICA,

Libellant,   A 110-59

—against—

ONE BOOK entitled *Ulysses*
by James Joyce

TO THE HONORABLES THE JUDGES OF THE
UNITED STATES
DISTRICT COURT FOR THE SOUTHERN
DISTRICT OF NEW YORK.

On 9 December, 1932, comes George Z. Medalie, United States Attorney for the Southern District of New York, in a cause of forfeiture, confiscation and destruction under the Tariff Act of 1930, and on information and belief informs the court as follows:

I stopped reading.

"What's all this about, Mr. Ernst?"

"We're going to court. Finally, the decision has been made. Mr. Medalie wasn't elected."

"He has a real strange turn of phrase this Mr. Medalie," I said. "Who the hell does he think he is, some knight on a charging horse?"

"It's the way things are put in legal documents."

"And what are we going to say?"

"Something like, And now Morris L. Ernst, intervening as agent for Random House, makes claim to one book entitled, *Ulysses, et cetera et cetera.*"

"I think you're going to need to work on that some, Mr. Ernst. That *et cetera et cetera* ain't going to wash with the court. They might think you're trying to fool them with all that Latin."

"You're quite right. It needs some work."

Squeaky had stopped singing. Mr. Cerf came in.

"It's good news, Bennett, isn't it?" Mr. Ernst asked. "Finally, your waiting is nearly over. Was there something else?"

"We're going to need a new trash-burner," Mr. Cerf informed us. "Grenado has stolen him. Told him he's going to spend the rest of his life on the stage. Yes. It's good news."

We all slipped from 1932 to 1933 to a year that promised to be brighter. One story that threw some darkness on our hope was the appointment of Adolf Hitler as chancellor in Germany. The *Brooklyn Daily Eagle* described him as a troublemaker. I read the report aloud to the piano tuner in Caffè Reggio.

"Discord," the piano tuner said when I had finished.

Mr. Waugh arrived and sat near me.

"Coffee," he said.

The waiter waved his hands in front of him. This was Italian for, "You're not being served."

Mr. Waugh got up and addressed the waiter. "You are guilty of a great <u>sin</u>."

"Harmony," the piano tuner said.

16

IN

URNING ON THE RADIO WAS never more important. Mr. Finnegan allowed Stevie to do it. Of all the claims made by Mr. Roosevelt in his inauguration address, the one that struck me most was about the money-changers fleeing from their high seats in the temple of our civilization. How I wanted those money-changers to flee the Boldts' house so that my daddy could have his house back. Mr. Finnegan liked another expressed by the President, that these dark days would be worth all the suffering if we learned only that our true destiny is not to be ministered unto but to minister to ourselves and our neighbors.

Mr. Roosevelt took our country out of the cemetery and put it in a cradle. We read about all the ideas he had and all the projects he began. The most telling report of what was happening, for me at least, came from Ops.

Dear Set,

Lukas is planting trees and getting paid for it. Mr. Shaefer bought a new shirt. The queues are changing from ones that lead to a crust of bread to ones that end in work and dignity. I hear laughter from people's conversations. Hope is returning. I thought it had been buried. The dust storms still come but afterwards, when neighbors come round to sweep our porches, they whistle in the same wind. Someone somewhere started singing the Battle Hymn of the Republic the other day. It was in the

*distance. I didn't know who it was. It didn't matter. It was someone like
me, my neighbor, rejoicing. We are seeing the glory,*
With Great Love,

Ops.

The swift and effective actions taken by Mr. Roosevelt to wage war on the Depression contrasted with the delays that kept dogging our own battle to get *Ulysses* legalized. Mr. Coleman, from the District Attorney's office, got real upset because Mr. Lindey had another copy of *Ulysses* mailed to the United States. It was considered under another law and even deemed a classic but this was only in one district so it didn't help us that much. Mr. Coleman thought Mr. Lindey was trying to pull one over on him. He was.

Mr. Ernst got us our trial to be heard before a judge and not before a jury but then came the problem of getting the right judge. Luckily, Mr. Coleman had cooled down so he agreed to work with us on picking a judge that wouldn't be too biased against us.

At meetings in the conference room, Mr. Cerf clasped his hands, shaking his head and sighing at every bad turn that came our way. One judge was not suitable. We were told he was a strait-laced Roman Catholic. Judge Coxe didn't want the case. Judge Knox was ill. Another judge wouldn't transfer the case to Judge Patterson because his child was ill. Mr. Lindey objected to another judge because he was sure this judge would have the entire book read out in court.

"When is this going to end?" Mr. Cerf asked calmly one day

"It has," Mr. Lindey replied. "It'll come before Judge Woolsey."

"What's he like?" Mr. Cerf asked.

"He buys old furniture," Mr. Ernst answered. "His wife sells it and then he buys more old furniture."

"Does he read?" Mr. Cerf asked.

"He has thousands of books," Mr. Lindey replied.

"Does he read?" Mr. Cerf asked again.

The speed of our progress was slackened again when Judge Woolsey said he wanted to read the book. This was in August 1933, about a year and a half since we first started. Two months later, in October, Judge Woolsey came back to say he still hadn't finished the book.

"I think I know what the word eternity means now," Mr. Cerf said.

"Not too long now," Mr. Klopfer ventured bravely.

"I wanted to include a scheme in the book, if it ever gets published that is," Mr. Cerf said. "It explains things about *Ulysses* but Mr. Léon, Mr. Joyce's friend and indeed Mr. Joyce, won't entertain the idea. I'm stalled at every turn. All we need now is for Joyce to come out and scupper the whole thing. We should have someone over there with a gag ready to shut him up if he starts. I know what writers are like and I know what this writer is like. And to top it all off, I get another letter from Mr. Léon telling me of German pirates. They're planning to publish the book in Germany. Can you believe that? How many attacks can one man take?"

"How many attacks can one book take?" Mr. Klopfer asked.

"Not too many more, Donald, not too many more," Mr. Cerf replied.

Our fear that the delays would continue and our worry that we might lose were put to one side when the people of New York voted in Fiorello La Guardia as mayor. It had taken him a long time to get there. We took some comfort from this, all of us except Mr. Cerf who appeared to be at breaking point.

"What's wrong, Mr. Ernst?" I asked when I went into his office. He was standing behind his desk, didn't seem himself. Mr Lindey was there too, sitting down.

"He's fine, Set," Mr. Lindey assured me.

"Are you better, Set?" Mr. Ernst asked.

"Just a cold. Mr. Finnegan wouldn't let me come to work. When you sent the message for me to come back I was coming back anyway. I can catch up with all the filing. You don't need to worry about that."

"I need these," Mr. Ernst said, handing me a piece of paper with a list of documents on it.

"All these?" I asked.

"Yes," Mr. Ernst replied, turning his back to me, looking at the pictures on his wall. "If you can't find them, we'll just, I dunno. The case is tomorrow. I couldn't find them, whatever way you've done it. It's tomorrow. We're up before Judge Woolsey. Tomorrow."

When Mr. Ernst turned round, I was gone. He must have turned round because he was facing me when I came back a few minutes later.

"No, Set," Mr. Ernst said. "No. Don't bring them in one at a time. I need them all together. Could you just do that?"

"They're all here, Mr. Ernst."

Mr. Lindey started looking through the pile.

"So they are," Mr. Lindey said.

"You think I couldn't find them?" I asked.

"Well, *I* couldn't," Mr. Ernst replied.

"You do your job, Mr. Ernst, and I'll do mine. Don't you know the alphabet?"

Mr. Lindey started laughing so much I thought he was going to keel over and then Mr. Ernst started laughing. I didn't see the joke.

"What time will you be back tomorrow?" I asked. "I'd really like to know how it went."

"The same time as you," Mr. Ernst said. "I'll need someone with me to look after my files. After all, you do your job and I do mine."

"Gee, that's great but what'll I do?" I asked.

"You could take notes or doodle," Mr. Lindey explained. "It's just a treat."

"Ain't you afraid about all this?" I asked.

"The only thing we have to fear…" Mr. Ernst replied.

"…is fear itself," Mr. Lindey concluded. "We've been working on that one. Stole it from Roosevelt."

"I better wear my best suit, then, else they might stop me at the door," I said.

"I'm going to do the same," Mr. Lindey said.

"You'll be with us, Set," Mr. Ernst assured me. "You won't have any problem getting <u>in</u>."

I underlined 'in' like I had underlined all the other words: 'startling', 'starting', 'staring', 'string', 'sting', 'sing' and 'sin'. After underling 'in' there was only one word left; 'I' with a capital letter for me.

17

'I'

ITT TOOK TWO AUTOMOBILES TO bring me to where the *Ulysses* case would be heard. The Finnegans and other people I knew came to see me off. It was like my first day at school.

Mrs. Janosik dropped me off at West 44th Street in the heart of Manhattan. I thought she'd drive off but she parked the car and got out. The car behind us stopped too and the people in it got out as well. Guess they wanted to see me going in. Mrs. Janosik told me it was number 42, the New York City Bar Association building, and she pointed to it.

"Go on," she said.

I walked towards the building but stopped and looked back at Mrs. Janosik, the Finnegans, Mr. Haltigan, Mr. and Mrs. Taylor, Jack and Charlie, Mr. Pete, Mr. Grenado and Domenico Parisi, the man who owned Caffè Reggio. There was a small boy with them who was sparkling and visible. Squeaky Molloy had become squeaky clean. He waved.

Mrs. Janosik didn't need to point out the building to me. There was a big crowd outside: photographers, reporters, protestors and policemen. I saw a woman I recognized and went up to her.

"Mrs. Taylor?"

"Yes?"

"It's me, Set. You used to teach me. Remember?"

"Set? How you've changed."

We talked about Pendleton. She asked about neighbors and places, shops and trees.

"What are you doing here?" she asked.

"I'm involved in this case here. And you?"

"Oh, that's so great to hear. I'm just one of these protestors. We came down from New Jersey specially. Can you believe they're trying to publish such a book in this country? What has it come to?"

"I best go in Mrs. Taylor."

"Sure. I don't want to keep you from your important work."

"Mrs. Taylor?"

"Yes."

"I'm on the other side. I'm fighting for the book, not against it."

She stared at me, looked down and then took a sharp intake of breath, before looking up at me again.

"Your mother would be ashamed of you."

"Glad to see you again, Mrs. Taylor," I said. "You were always a fine neighbor."

A crowd pushed between us. They were getting riled. I was pushed this way and that but I didn't mind. I looked up at the building. It seemed like a palace. It was made of granite, mahogany, marble and a few other things, I guess. Mr. Lindey found me, grabbed me by the arm and led me in. We went to the sixth floor where there was another crowd of people in the corridor including Mr. Cerf, Mr. Klopfer and Mr. Ernst.

"This is Mr. Sumner," Mr. Klopfer said, introducing me to the head of the New York Society for the Suppression of Vice. "John S. Sumner."

"And what's your take on all this, young man?" Mr. Sumner asked.

"It's busier than all get-out," I said.

"All get-out?" Mr. Sumner asked.

"Yeah," I replied. "It's what we say in Texas, like it means it's real busy."

"You're not in Texas now, boy," Mr. Sumner said.

"Darn right, Mr. Sumner but you know what? Texas is in me."

He turned his attention to Mr. Klopfer.

"Are you going to read out any of the Anglo-Saxon swear words or phrases in your defense, Mr. Klopfer?"

"I'd much rather utter them all here to you personally and with great feeling."

After a while, all the people filed into the oval courtroom. I was the last to go in. There's wasn't room for a fly to land so I stood just inside the door beside an old man, the bailiff.

"Hi, I'm Set," I said. "Can I stand here?"

"Sure," the man said. "My name is George. Should have had today off but here I am."

"Well, you'll have tomorrow off. It's Saturday," I replied.

"Don't get me wrong," he said. "You see, I'm also Judge Woolsey's chauffeur so I had to be here. In fact, I want to be here."

"Oh," I said. "Why?"

"Well, that's a long story. It's because all my life I've been drinking water, and getting buses and sitting in waiting rooms."

"Don't understand."

"They all had the sign 'Colored' on them. This trial here, is about whether or not we can speak. Liberty of expression. Liberty for books is the same as liberty for me. Liberty is not like money, it don't have an exchange rate or different currencies. It's all the same."

"Morris is looking for you," Mr. Lindey said.

I got real worried as I made my way through the crowded courtroom. Had Mr. Ernst asked me to bring something? Maybe I had forgotten. Mr. Ernst was sitting on one of three chairs at a table. Mr. Lindey sat beside him and pointed to the third vacant chair.

"Well, aren't you going to sit down?" Mr. Ernst asked me.

"Sit down? Here?" I asked.

"Yes. Ringside seat."

"What about, Mr. Cerf? Shouldn't he be sitting here?"

"Weak bladder," Mr. Lindey said. "Upsets our train of thought. Sit."

"What'll I do?" I asked.

"Take notes if you like," Mr. Lindey said, "or you can just sit and watch the greatest literary trial of the twentieth century."

"How can you be so relaxed?" I asked.

"This is what we do," Mr. Ernst replied.

"That's some table up there, ain't it?" I asked.

"That's the judge's bench," Mr. Lindey said. "Believed to be the finest piece of furniture in the United States. They'll be over in a minute."

"Who?"

"Our enemies. They may try to wrong-foot us. Listen and beware."

"Mr. Ernst, I don't know about these files here. I don't know whether I'll be able to find anything."

"It's all in my head."

Our enemies approached, one by one. First, there was Sam Coleman, the Chief Assistant US Attorney. He seemed nervous.

"I'm not sure about all these swear words," Mr. Coleman said.

"I'll explain them to you," Mr. Ernst replied.

"What I mean is, the Government can't win the case."

"Why such defeatism and at such an early stage?" Mr. Ernst asked.

"The only way to win the case is to refer to the great number of vulgar four-letter words used by Joyce," Mr. Coleman explained. "This will shock the judge and he'll suppress the book but I can't do it. I can't say them here, in open court."

"Why not?" Mr. Ernst asked.

"Because there's a lady in the courtroom."

"That's not a lady, that's my wife," Mr. Ernst explained. "Maggie is a school-teacher so she's seen more swear words scrawled on the walls of bicycle sheds than most people. Besides, she's also been a newspaper gal and you know what they're like."

"Can't do it," Mr. Coleman said and then left.

"That's good, ain't it?" I asked Mr. Ernst.

"We'll see," Mr. Ernst replied.

Next to come over was Nicholas Atlas, the Assistant US Attorney. He chatted for a while with Mr. Ernst and Mr. Lindey.

"Clever idea," Mr. Atlas said, "pasting the reviews into *Ulysses*. Who thought of that one?"

"Our legal advisor," Mr. Lindey replied. "Set Wright."

"How do you do?" Mr. Atlas said. "I wish you all the best of luck."

"May the best book win," Mr. Lindey said. 'By that I mean *Ulysses*, not the Atlas."

"Clever," Mr. Atlas replied and returned to his table.

"They seem like friendly folk," I said.

"You might have noticed," Mr. Lindey explained, "that before a boxing match, the competitors tap their opponents' gloves as a sign of sportsmanship. Afterwards, they begin to beat the hell out of each other. Much the same here."

"What are we waiting for?" I asked.

"The Constitution made flesh," Mr. Lindey explained. "The judge. Judge Woolsey."

I blew out some air. "I don't mind saying. I'm as nervous as a long-tailed cat in a room full of rocking chairs."

"SILENCE IN COURT."

The roar from George the bailiff made me freeze.

"ALL RISE."

We stood up. I was shaking. As the judge came in, George shouted again.

"Judge John Munro Woolsey presiding in the case of the United States *versus* One Book Called *Ulysses* by James Joyce. Mr. Samuel C. Coleman and Mr. Nicholas Atlas for the Libellant, Mr. Morris L. Ernst and Mr. Alexander Lindey for the Claimant."

Judge Woolsey placed a blue paper-bound edition of *Ulysses* and some files on his bench. He really did look like a man who bought old furniture.

"Sit," Judge Woolsey said and we sat.

The silence continued for some time broken only by the noise of Judge Woolsey shifting papers on his bench and someone at the back of the courtroom clearing their throat. "George," Judge Woolsey said, calling to the bailiff, "you will hear many things in this trial so I must caution you not to be shocked."

The judge then lit a cigarette which he had placed in a long holder.

"This trial, as you see, is informal," the judge said. "I am in an extremely difficult position in being required to pass judgment on a book that for ten years has evoked the most violent denunciations and praise from all manner of learned men and women. Mr. Coleman, as Libellant, you may begin.

I picked up a pencil. I looked at Mr. Lindey and he nodded approval. I decided to take notes. I also decided not to underline the letter 'I' as Mrs. Taylor from Pendleton, my former teacher, would have had me do. We had taken different paths.

18

TRIAL BY FURY

NEW YORK BAR ASSOCIATION

The United States *versus* One Book Entitled *Ulysses* before Judge Woolsey

Morning, Friday, November 24th, 1933

Samuel Coleman: I contend that *Ulysses* is obscene and consequently should not be permitted into the United States. Because I contend this, I would ask the court not to think of me personally as a puritanical censor.

    Judge Woolsey: You see, this is what goes on.

    Coleman: Your Honor?

    Judge Woolsey: Obscene. As a judge, a spectrum of adjectives bind me by law: obscene, lewd, disgusting. Tell me, Mr. Coleman, what do you think constitutes obscenity? Hold on. One definition is a thing may be said to be obscene when its primary purpose is to excite sexual feeling. Mr. Coleman.

    Coleman: I don't think that the definition of obscenity should be limited to exciting sexual feeling. I can understand people reading something that does not excite them in such a manner but which they might still pass on as being obscene. I should say a thing is obscene by the ordinary language used and by what it does to the average reader. It need not necessarily be what the author intended. On these grounds, I think there are ample reasons to consider *Ulysses* to be an obscene book.

Morris L. Ernst: What it does to the average reader? Is Mr. Coleman contending that everyone in the United States who reads the book will start hopping into bed with each other? I have yet to find one single instance where it could be proved that the reading of any book has led to the commission of a crime of passion.

Coleman: Your Honor, may I continue? I would like to conclude my point.

Judge Woolsey: You are not alone. Continue.

Coleman: Thank you, your Honor. We approach the book with great respect.

Judge Woolsey: You're welcome.

Coleman: We approach the book with great respect. We realize that the substance of the book is a microcosm, depicted and represented in a most literary, most sensitive and very scientific way. We admit that the book is to be praised for its style, which is new and startling. We distinguish its method and realize that this is a new method in the creation of the novel. Finally we realize that this is literature and poetry.

Judge Woolsey: Mr. Coleman, we need you to say the word, "however", and to proceed from that point.

Coleman: Your Honor, it is important to put on record our context and view.

Judge Woolsey: You have done that. We await "however" however.

Coleman: And so, your Honor, the Government's case against this book relates, in part, to the sexual titillation of episodes, more particularly the dreams at the end of the book.

Judge Woolsey: Mr. Coleman, you are referring to the long soliloquy of Molly Bloom here. I don't believe they are dreams. Fantasies perhaps.

Coleman: Yes, your Honor.

Judge Woolsey: She fantasizes or thinks about men and sex with colorful descriptions of the male and female anatomies.

Coleman: Yes, your Honor.

Judge Woolsey: Mr. Ernst, what is your opinion of the effect this soliloquy might have on a young woman?

Ernst: I don't think that is the standard we should go by. The law does not require that adult literature be reduced to mush for infants.

Judge Woolsey: I see. I have to say here about this, you know, I can't remember the number of times I've read or heard people say that they can't understand the book. So when I started reading it, I have to admit to my shocking surprise that I understood all the passages that had been deemed obscene and marked by Mr. Coleman.

Laughter in Court

Judge Woolsey: As I've said, this isn't an easy case to decide.

Coleman: With respect, your Honor, I hadn't finished.

Judge Woolsey: Neither had I, however. I think things ought to take their chances in the market-place. My own feeling is against censorship. I know that as soon as you suppress anything the bootlegger goes to work. The people see about as much of the prohibited article as they otherwise would and the profits go into illegal channels. Still, still there is that soliloquy in the last chapter. I don't know about that. But, go on with the case.

Coleman: Thank you, your Honor. If I might repeat, the Government objects to the sexual titillation of episodes. This includes the lurid and obscene passage at the end of the book. We also object to the use of unparlorish words.

Judge Woolsey: What are they, Mr. Coleman? Words that may be used in the kitchen only or, perhaps, the bedroom only?

Coleman: I am referring, your Honor, to expressions, allusions, clichés, and situations which, even in this day and age, could not be mentioned in any society pretending to call itself polite, and certainly not in mixed company, no matter how free that mixed company may be.

As Mr. Coleman continued, Mr. Ernst whispered to Mr. Lindey that they needed to make something of the word "polite". Mr. Lindey seemed to go into a world of his own, staring at the table in front of us but came back to life a few moments later. He took my notes and pointed at a line.

"Here it is," he whispered to Mr. Ernst. "Woolsey said he had read the passages deemed obscene which were marked by the Government. I would go for anti-Semitism and royalty, Deasy and the Citizen."

"Perfect," Mr. Ernst said, showing that he understood whatever code they were talking in.

"Do you need page references?" Mr. Lindey asked.

"No," Mr. Ernst replied.

✝
✝

Judge Woolsey: Mr. Ernst? Mr. Ernst? Whenever you're ready.

Ernst: We've been ready for some time, your Honor.

Judge Woolsey: We have been ready for some time at this time. Mr. Ernst.

Ernst: Thank you, your Honor. This word "polite' or the phrase "polite society'.

Judge Woolsey: You're welcome.

Ernst: The Government puts forward the argument about words that could not be mentioned in any polite society. I refer your Honor to the conversation between Stephen Dedalus and Deasy, the headmaster; the conversation about Jews.

Judge Woolsey: Yes. I know it.

Ernst: Joyce celebrates his native city, Dublin, and indeed its people but he's not so blind as to paint them all in glory. In this conversation, he exposes Deasy as a rabid hater of the Jewish people.

Judge Woolsey: Yes he does.

Ernst: Later, in another section the Citizen speaks of the British monarch, King Edward the Seventh.

Judge Woolsey: This is when Leopold Bloom is in Barney Kiernan's pub?

Ernst: Yes, your Honor.

Judge Woolsey: And which page is that, Mr. Ernst.

Ernst: Page 330, your Honor, the section I'm referring to carries over to the next page, page 331.

Judge Woolsey: Very helpful. Thank you, Mr. Ernst. A moment, please. Yes, here it is. Continue.

Ernst: The Citizen has a go at the British king, saying that he is more pox than pax, meaning he's more affected by syphilis, the pox, than by peace, pax, even though this sovereign's supposed reputation is as a peace-maker.

Judge Woolsey: And your point is, Mr. Ernst?

Ernst: My point is; what is the Government's definition of polite society. The Government has marked passages in *Ulysses* that it deems obscene. The anti-Semitic ravings of Deasy are not marked by the Government, meaning that the Government does not deem them to be obscene, yet does, as you see your Honor, deem the attack by an Irishman on a pox-ridden white Anglo-Saxon king to be obscene. Is the contention of the Government that anti-Semitism should be encouraged or left unchallenged if brought up in polite society but that those who drink from dainty china cups should grovel to an unelected, white Anglo-Saxon ruler?

Coleman: I object to that, your Honor. Mr. Ernst is making out that I am a racist.

Ernst: My point was directed at the Government.

Coleman: I represent the Government and, as you know very well Mr. Ernst, I marked those passages.

Judge Woolsey: Gentlemen, gentlemen. Please desist. This is informal.

Ernst: If I may, your Honor?

Judge Woolsey: Yes.

Ernst: Mr. Coleman is a highly skilled and honorable lawyer and carries with vigor his duty of searching for the truth. He is not a racist. If the point I have made remains, I accept, as Mr. Coleman has argued, that people might construe something else from it. Therefore, your Honor, I withdraw the point I have made.

Coleman: Thank you, Mr. Ernst.

Judge Woolsey: You know, since I've become identified with the case I've received many letters about the book. A man from Lynn, Massachusetts, wrote me that this book was the most precious thing in his life and another man wrote me that it had seared his soul. Someone else said that he had found in it "life's greatest pleasure". This is what goes on, you see.

Gentlemen, there is another legal matter, separate to this case, which I must attend to by telephone. Excuse me. We'll adjourn for a brief moment. Some of us might even enjoy a coffee from dainty or undainty tea-cups, depending on the company, polite or otherwise. I use a flask myself.

Bailiff: All rise.

✝
✝

Mr. Cerf came round and stood in front of us. He was careful to smile because the members of the press were behind us. However, his anger came through his fixed grin.

"Let me get this straight, Morris," Mr. Cerf said. "You've insulted the former king of the United Kingdom, America's closest ally. You're saying the book we're defending is anti-Semitic?"

"He didn't say that," Mr. Lindey said.

"Let me finish," Mr. Cerf replied, continuing to hold a false smile. "And on top of that, you've been forced into a humiliating climb-down. Can we talk outside?"

Mr. Cerf and Mr. Ernst left the courtroom.

"That didn't go too well," I said.

"It went perfectly," Mr. Lindey replied. "Normally, there's just a bit of sparring at this point. This was a targeted blow, below the belt. It's scared the hell out of them, including the judge."

"But Mr. Ernst had to apologize," I said.

"He apologized to Mr. Coleman. He didn't apologize to the Government. Don't underestimate Morris. The point may have been withdrawn but, like the stench of an abattoir, it remains in the mind long after you've left the building."

Mr. Lindey called over George, the bailiff, and whispered something to him. George went off and came back with a pile of note-paper which he placed in front of me. It was as high as a sheep's leg.

"You will see, Set, that trials are sometimes about appearance," Mr. Lindey explained. "Thanks, George."

"How so?"

"Mr. Coleman is reluctant to fight this case despite how it appears," Mr. Lindey said. "Morris will expose this. He'll draw Coleman out, allow him in when he interrupts. This will appear as if Morris is being courteous. The judge will see the weakness of the Government's arguments. You see, Coleman's heart really isn't in it."

"Yeah, but then Mr. Coleman'll get to talk," I said.

"That's what we want. We want the judge to see he has no case, that all Mr. Coleman will do is attack our argument and put forward nothing himself. Judges don't like that. It's all about appearance."

As soon as Mr. Ernst returned, the bailiff roared at us all again to stand up and Judge Woolsey took his seat.

The judge began a sentence saying, "I" but then stopped and looked at the high pile of note-books in front of me. I guess it looked as if we were in this for the long haul. The judge then looked scornfully at Mr. Ernst before laughing to himself. It was all about appearances.

NEW YORK BAR ASSOCIATION

Early afternoon, Friday, November 24th, 1933

Judge Woolsey: Mr. Ernst, perhaps you could give us a broad outline.

    Ernst: Thank you, your Honor.

    Mr. Ernst waited for a few seconds, staring at the bench.

    Judge Woolsey: You're welcome, Mr. Ernst. Proceed.

    Ernst: Who are we? What are we? The Government has sought fit to confiscate a copy of *Ulysses* because the Government deems it obscene. It's up to the Government to prove this. It confiscated the book, we didn't.

    Coleman: The burden of proof is clear. It is up to Mr. Ernst to prove that the book is not obscene.

Ernst: This is a clear point of law. The Collector of Customs, acting on behalf of the Government, has libeled the book on the grounds of obscenity. It is up to you, Mr. Coleman, to explain yourself.

Coleman: The manner in which I discharge my brief is my business, not yours, Mr. Ernst.

Judge Woolsey: Gentlemen, gentlemen, gentlemen. Be gentle. This is informal. Perhaps you might both appreciate and understand that I am the judge in this case. Neither of you is. Put forward your arguments. The decision rests with me alone. Do not presume, either of you, to decide for me. Continue Mr. Ernst. Go gently into the afternoon.

Ernst: First, the book. *Ulysses* is unlike any other work that has preceded it. Joyce has embarked upon uncharted literary seas. There is every reason, therefore, why the rules of law which are invoked in ordinary cases, should be applied here with exceptional care.

Coleman: I disagree. The court should not show favoritism. This is like saying that a rich man should be treated in a different manner to a poor man. All stand before the court equally.

Judge Woolsey: A point well made, Mr. Coleman, even though, this judge here, sitting before you, is quite well acquainted with the law, with justice and does not need a lecture. I suggest that Mr. Ernst be given space to argue. Fluidity is important in the search for meaning. Continue.

Ernst: James Joyce has exerted a profound influence on the world of letters, possibly greater than any other person before him. He has steadfastly scorned self-exploitation. He has delivered no lectures, given no interviews, posed for no newsreels, attached no explanatory prefaces that might yield him some harvest. Nearly as blind as the Greek master from whose epic he borrowed the name of his novel, he has lived apart. He has revolutionized expression. He stands as a kind of colossus of creative writing, dominating his age. Not since Shakespeare, it is said, has the English language reached such heights as in *Ulysses*.

The distinguished American critic –

Judge Woolsey: All critics appear to be distinguished, like professors.

Ernst: I disagree, your Honor. Fluidity, if I may? The distinguished American critic, Stuart Gilbert, wrote of *Ulysses* that it is, and I quote, "A power beyond the scope of any but the greatest". Rebecca West says that Joyce is a writer of majestic genius. Arnold Bennett says that he is dazzlingly original.

Coleman: May I interject?

Judge Woolsey: Mr. Ernst?

Ernst: Yes.

Coleman: I can find an equal if greater number of critics, distinguished or otherwise, who put forward a counter view. Mr. Ernst quotes Arnold Bennett selectively. Bennett said he was revolted by *Ulysses*. The American novelist, James Branch Cabell, said that in eight years during which the book had lain by his bedside, he had never become excited sufficiently to read beyond page forty. Professor John Dewey, the educational reformer and philosopher, curiously enough, called *Ulysses* a great book without ever reading it at all.

Judge Woolsey: Mr. Coleman, I think we should come back to this. I am not ignoring your point but I would like to hear the remainder of Mr. Ernst's outline. Mr. Ernst.

Ernst: Thank you judge for giving me space. I have no objection if Mr. Coleman wishes to make some points.

Judge Woolsey: Up to you. Mr. Coleman, you wish to make some points?

Coleman: Thank you, I will, your Honor and thank you, Mr. Ernst. You will know, your Honor, that Mr. Ernst, in his written submission, cites several works that have come before the courts because they were thought to be obscene. I accept that in each case, the courts decided that they were not obscene. Let's take a look at them.

Judge Woolsey: I am acquainted with all of them for professional reasons. I felt I had to add that last bit. Continue.

Coleman: First, there is *Madeline*, purporting to be the autobiography of a prostitute set, in part, in a brothel. Any obscene words? None, unlike *Ulysses* which is teeming with them.

Second, *Mademoiselle du Maupin* by Gautier which abounds in passionate and amorous descriptions. The main sexual encounter is written in a style of great linguistic reserve. No obscene language, no bawdy scenes.

Judge Woolsey: Théophile.

Coleman: I beg your pardon, your Honor?

Judge Woolsey: Gautier's first name: Théophile.

Coleman: Thank you, your Honor. Third, we have *Casanova's Home-coming*. Again, without any unprintable words. Even the descriptions of nudity are not obscene.

Ernst: If they were unprintable, it's no wonder they weren't printed.

Judge Woolsey: Let's dispense with flippancy, Mr. Ernst.

Coleman: Your Honor, I now draw your attention to two books of old Chinese stories. These are *Eastern Shame Girl* and *Adventures of Hsi Men Ching*. The boldest incidents in these stories are treated tastefully with the usual Chinese sophistication and delicacy.

Ernst: What a pity.

Coleman: Mr. Ernst also mentions another book in his written submission, one by Pierre Louys, entitled *Woman and Puppet*. The story is that of the deep, burning, inevitable and disastrous love which a Spanish gentleman has for a girl of doubtful ancestry. Even the description of when he does finally possess her is accomplished by inference rather than by blunt obscenity.

Judge Woolsey: Are there many more of these?

Coleman: Just two more, your Honor. One is *Female*, a book written for popular consumption and not intended for the discriminating mind. It concerns a promiscuous woman in an age of clandestine drinking. In accord with modern popular taste, the author has given this prostitute the traditional heart of gold as she reaches the zenith of her career in protecting innocent young girlhood.

Judge Woolsey: Strangely, I have forgotten all about this book.

Coleman: An occasional word is offensive to general taste, but according to the standards of the law, the book cannot be held to be obscene. I might add, your Honor, it has nothing to recommend it to the intellectual mind and undoubtedly has a great deal to recommend it to the prurience of shop-girls, grocers' wives and probably to some stenographers.

Judge Woolsey: I have a higher opinion of these women than you appear to have, Mr. Coleman. Are you nearly finished?

Coleman: Just one more, your Honor – *Flesh*.

Judge Woolsey: Well, I wonder what that's about?

Coleman: These are sketches of perversions. As far as I can now remember, there is not one word in it which *per se* is obscene or filthy. And so, the point I am making is that Mr. Ernst, in citing these books, appears to contend that therefore *Ulysses* cannot be obscene. This is spurious. *Ulysses* is in a league all its own when it comes to disgorging the entrails of a filthy mind into an obscene and pornographic morass littered with four-letter words.

Judge Woolsey: Mr. Ernst.

Ernst: The American writer and critic, Edmund Wilson, says that Joyce, "Soars to such rhapsodies of beauty as have probably never been equaled in English prose fiction".

It is, I contend, monstrous to suppose that a man of the stature of Joyce would or could produce a work of obscenity.

The claimant, Random House, was established to print and distribute books in America of significant content and typographical distinction. Its publication of *Candide* with illustrations by Rockwell Kent was described by *The New York Times* as the most beautiful book ever produced in America. Its current list includes works by Chaucer, Emily Brontë, Herman Melville and Voltaire.

Judge Woolsey: And to quote from another Frenchman of letters, Descartes: *Je pense, donc je suis*. I think, therefore I am going to break for lunch.

Bailiff: All rise.

Over lunch, Mr. Cerf wondered how we had ended up with Judge Woolsey after passing up on so many others and asked if we could have him replaced. No-one answered.

"Couldn't you argue, Morris," Mr. Cerf suggested, "that dumbbells in search of smut would certainly throw down the book in hopeless disgust after trying to wade through the first two chapters?"

"If you want me to?" Mr. Ernst replied.

"I'll leave it up to you," Mr. Cerf said, before leaving to make a call.

The mood changed.

"Do you see what they're at?" Mr. Ernst asked.

"Yes," Mr. Lindey replied.

"What are they at?" I asked.

"The other side is not really arguing its case," Mr. Lindey explained. "They're vulturing on what we have said. Sure, they've set it out briefly but they're waiting for us now to prove that the book is not obscene."

"Can't you do that?" I asked.

"We'll try our best," Mr. Ernst replied. "The problem is that every point we put forward, no matter how strong, will be knocked down by Coleman."

"This means," Mr. Lindey continued, "that the last bell ringing in the judge's ears will be the one sounded by Coleman, not by us."

"To paraphrase Homer," Mr. Ernst said, "generally, the audience applauds the last song the most."

"He's unhinged," Mr. Cerf said when he returned. "The judge."

"You obviously don't know many judges," Mr. Lindey said.

When we returned to the courtroom, Mr. Lindey urged Mr. Ernst to press home the issue of the law.

NEW YORK BAR ASSOCIATION

Mid-afternoon, Friday, November 24th, 1933

Bailiff: All rise.

Judge Woolsey: Sit. Well, who'd like to start?

Mr. Ernst waited but Mr. Coleman didn't offer to speak.

Ernst: If I may, your Honor? We contend that the test of obscenity is a living standard and *Ulysses* must be judged by public opinion of the day. I have provided your Honor with citations from the law on this.

Alexander Hamilton, in the early days of our republic, protested against the use of the maypole in America, claiming that the dance had phallic significance. Now our parks and playgrounds are filled with maypole parties and the custom appears obscene to no-one.

In Rome, remarriage was deemed adulterous and a third marriage was severely punished. Today the notion that remarriage is immoral has been rejected.

In 1900 any female who appeared on a bathing beach without sleeves and a long skirt would have been jailed. By 1911, bare knees could be legally displayed at the seashore, but legs still had to be covered. Today swimsuits leave very little of the human form concealed.

A woman superintendent in the Children's Department of the Brooklyn Public Library once charged that *Tom Sawyer* and *Huckleberry Finn* were corrupting the morals of children.

It is clear that *Ulysses* must be judged by present-day views. The standards of yesterday, the abhorrence of any mention of certain biological functions, the excessive prudery, the sex taboo, are as definitely dead today as the horse-drawn carriage and the donkey-engines.

Coleman: If I may, I appreciate the eloquence of Mr. Ernst but is he suggesting that in a few decades from now, murder may become legal because it will then be acceptable? Obscenity is a crime and it will always be a crime.

Ernst: Murder will always be a crime. That which is deemed obscene changes with each generation, even with each passing day. This is my point. We must judge obscenity by the standards of the day.

Moral standards are not of static nature. In St. Hupert Guild *versus* Quinn, the Court insisted that literature of its time must be judged by current opinion.

Viewed against our contemporary background, *Ulysses* clearly does not violate our obscenity statute. Statues of the naked human form stand undraped and unashamed in the lobby of the Roxy Music Hall for New York's millions to behold. The fig-leaf has become a thing of the past unless of course it's for the polite company which Mr. Coleman keeps.

Coleman: I suggest that Mr. Ernst does not reduce this to personal attack.

Judge Woolsey: I, too, would feel attacked if someone accused me of keeping polite company. Come now, gentlemen, this is informal. I am jesting, Mr. Coleman. This is informal. We are not averse to robust debate. Mr. Coleman, perhaps, you would like to make some submissions?

Coleman: I will give Mr. Ernst the courtesy he deserves to finish the points he wishes to make.

Judge Woolsey: I see. Mr. Ernst.

Ernst: Thank you, your Honor. We contend that *Ulysses* is not obscene according to the accepted definition of obscenity as laid down by the courts.

Judge Woolsey: You're welcome.

Ernst: Thank you for allowing me to finish my sentence this time. *Laughter in court.*

Judge Woolsey: You're welcome. Proceed.

Ernst: I contend that to uphold the libel, the court must find not only that there are reasonable grounds for believing *Ulysses* to be obscene, but also that it is obscene by a majority of evidence. The sole evidence is the book.

Coleman: I disagree, your Honor. In this book, which numbers more than 700 pages, or indeed in any other, any passage can be deemed to be obscene and the rest of the book not.

Ernst: I refer to the case brought in the past few months by Mr. Sumner of the New York Society for the Suppression of Vice, who is attending this court today, against Erskine Campbell's *God's Little Acre*. Magistrate Greenspan ruled that in order for the prosecution to be sustained, the court must find that the tendency of the book as a whole, and indeed its main purpose, is to excite lustful desire. Does Mr. Coleman disagree with Magistrate Greenspan?

Coleman: I am referring to *this* case.

Ernst: The points of law are the same.

Judge Woolsey: Your point is noted, Mr. Coleman.

Ernst: I hope mine is too, your Honor.

Judge Woolsey: Mr. Ernst, I was attempting to draw a line under this argument because I understand it and so that you might be allowed to continue. If you wish me to say each time you make a point that I understand it, I will. My way of working is to intervene when I do not understand a point or seek elaboration. Now, gentlemen, this is not a playground where the participants should seek regular or indeed any reassurance. Continue.

Ernst: Your Honor, Mr. Coleman and I are sufficiently qualified in the law not to be besmirched as spoilt urchins demanding our turn on the swing. Do you accept that point your Honor?

Mr. Lindey hung his head.

Judge Woolsey: The trial, as I said, is informal, Mr. Ernst.

Ernst: And, as I said, do you accept that point, your Honor?

Judge Woolsey: I do.

Ernst: May I continue, your Honor?

Judge Woolsey: You may.

Mr. Lindey lifted his head.

Ernst: *Ulysses* is a many-faceted crystallization of life and thought with the quality of universality. Sex is present, to be sure; but sex is part of man's existence. One can no more say that *Ulysses* is obscene than that life or thought is obscene.

Coleman: I submit, your Honor, that life is not on trial here, *Ulysses* is.

Judge Woolsey: For a moment there, I thought I was on trial.

Ernst: I come to my next point, your Honor. *Ulysses* is a modern classic. The United States Government has officially acknowledged it as such. It cannot, therefore, be deemed obscene.

Judge Woolsey: I believe you are referring here, not to the original copy of *Ulysses* sent from Paris to Random House, which was confiscated and which is the subject of this trial, but to another copy of *Ulysses* sent in that was confiscated in May of this year.

Ernst: That is correct, your Honor.

Judge Woolsey: And this copy, the second copy, if you will, was sent in at the behest of your colleague, Mr. Lindey, I see there sitting beside you?

Ernst: Yes, your Honor.

Judge Woolsey: And Mr. Lindey, as I understand it, petitioned the Treasury Department for this second copy to be admitted but under another provision.

Ernst: Correct, that provision being the discretionary authority granted to the Secretary of the Treasury under section 305 of the Tariff Act, 1930, to admit a book if it is deemed a classic.

Judge Woolsey: And, as I see from a letter here, that permission was granted.

Ernst: Correct, your Honor. In other words, the United States Government has deemed *Ulysses* to be a classic.

Coleman: Your Honor, I object. This particular copy of *Ulysses* is not the subject of this trial.

Judge Woolsey: How does it differ from the one that is on trial?

Coleman: It's a different copy.

Judge Woolsey: In what way?

Coleman: It's the same book but it's a different copy, your Honor. In any case, it is not evidence, it is not before the Court.

Judge Woolsey: The matter is dealt with at length in the brief submitted by Mr. Ernst and Mr. Lindey and therefore can be addressed. It is, indeed, similar to the reviews pasted into the first copy, they, too, can be discussed here because they are part of evidence.

Coleman: The issues surrounding the second copy are not in dispute.

Judge Woolsey: Do I take it from what you say, Mr. Coleman, that the United States Government, which you so ably represent, accepts, as you did earlier this year, that *Ulysses* is a classic?

Coleman: Yes, but that is not the point.

Judge Woolsey: I want to hear the remainder of Mr. Ernst's argument on this before establishing what you contend to be the point. Mr. Ernst.

Ernst: Let us be clear; the Federal Government has officially paid tribute to the greatness of *Ulysses*. It has deemed it to be a classic. The words "classic" and "obscenity" represent polar extremes. They are mutually antagonistic and exclusive.

Judge Woolsey: Mr. Coleman.

Coleman: The provision in law which allowed this second copy in is for book-collectors, a niche market, not for the general public. Medical books with illustrations of the human body are sold to a very specific strata of society, they are not for public consumption because of their graphic nature. People with depraved minds might salivate over them.

Judge Woolsey: I see.

Coleman: Mr. Ernst quoted selectively from Arnold Bennett. He does so again when quoting the Treasury Department. Its discretion is to allow books in that are obscene. Deeming it a classic does not eradicate its obscenity.

Ernst: That which is obscene, corrupts and depraves cannot be of the highest class and of acknowledged excellence.

Judge Woolsey: I think, gentlemen, we will take another break. Some of you, no doubt, might drink a cup of coffee, others might even like to take a turn on the swing.

Bailiff: All rise.

✝
✝

Mr. Ernst went off to talk to Mr. Cerf and Mr. Klopfer.

"Why did he go at the judge like that?" I asked. "If this is like a boxing match, why did Mr. Ernst punch the referee in the kisser?"

"Earlier," Mr. Lindey replied, "Morris had a sound argument but withdrew it, apologized because Mr. Coleman took offense. He didn't have to do that. It was a noble gesture, letting the judge know he's honest, a man of integrity, not afraid to admit when he's wrong. Just now, Morris defended himself but, more important, he defended Mr. Coleman against the judge's charge that they were acting like spoilt kids. Here again he was showing his integrity and honesty but this time to authority. Integrity and honesty are powerful weapons in a courtroom. Would you believe a thief or would you believe a man of honesty and integrity? That's why he took the judge on."

"Another noble gesture?" I asked.

"We think the judge is of the view that because Coleman is not making any original points himself that the Government is just going through the motions. I think the judge felt that before he came in, hence all this talk of informality. However, the District Attorney's office is infested with members of the anti-vice society, so if the Government loses, it's likely to appeal. That's what Morris is trying to tell the judge, why he referred to Mr. Sumner's case and pointed him out in court.

"Morris is also letting the judge know that the trial is not really informal. Much is at stake, including, as I said, the possibility of an appeal. If that happens, the judge's comments and the manner in which he conducted the trial will come under scrutiny. Judges don't know it all. Morris was giving him a polite nudge to wise up."

"Didn't seem that polite to me," I said.

"If you need to make a point in court, you need to make it forcefully or else don't make it at all. Besides, politeness is not an issue here. The judge already said he wouldn't like to be accused of keeping polite company. Courtrooms have their own code."

"Still, it seemed a bit strong," I said.

"Maybe it was," Mr. Lindey replied, "but as you've seen, it hasn't done any damage. Afterwards, the judge seems to have gone with us on the issue that *Ulysses* is a classic and therefore cannot be obscene."

When Mr. Ernst came back, he told us how he was going to approach the next session. "Coleman keeps knocking us down. There's only one way around it. I'm going to fire bullets."

NEW YORK BAR ASSOCIATION

Late afternoon, Friday, November 24th, 1933

Bailiff: All rise.

    Judge Woolsey: Sit.

    Ernst: May I continue, your Honor?

    Judge Woolsey: Please do.

    Ernst: Thank you, your Honor.

    Judge Woolsey: You're welcome.

    Ernst: The nature of the book and elements outside it negate any implication of obscenity. The title, *Ulysses*, gives no indication that it is obscene. Illustrations, such as pornographic pictures, enhance the potency of what is published. There are no illustrations in *Ulysses*.

    Coleman: Excuse me…

    Ernst: May I finish, your Honor. I have given way several times. Fluidity.

Judge Woolsey: Let Mr. Ernst finish.

Ernst: Joyce has not hidden behind a pseudonym that *might*, I say *might*, give rise to the integrity of the work. It has been published openly by Shakespeare & Company in Paris and has always borne Joyce's name. The element of concealment, almost invariably present in a work of pornography, is wholly absent here.

The length of the book may confer immunity. A reader looking for obscene matter in *Ulysses*, which has 725 pages of closely-printed pages, would get tired of wading through it. The first passage dealing with sex occurs deep in the book.

Coleman: Your Honor, I must be allowed to reply to these points.

Judge Woolsey: I agree and in time. Do not interrupt again unless it is on a point of law. Do I make myself clear, Mr. Coleman?

Coleman: Yes, your Honor.

Ernst: Your Honor, I look forward to debating each and every one of these points with Mr. Coleman and, indeed, any points he may wish to make himself. I come to the matter of Joyce's style or indeed styles. The worst Chinese obscenity cannot be understood by anyone not acquainted with the tongue.

Style. Each episode in *Ulysses* has its scene and hour of the day, is associated with a given organ of the human body, relates to a certain art, has its appropriate symbol, a specific technique and has a title corresponding to a character or episode in the *Odyssey*. Certain episodes also have their appropriate color.

For instance, the episode in the office of the *Freeman's Journal and National Press* is entitled Aeolus; its Hour is 12 noon; its Organ the lungs; its Art rhetoric; its Color red; its Symbol, editor; its Technique enthymemic.

Judge Woolsey: Enthymemic, meaning an argument in which the conclusion is not expressed. From the Greek, *enthuméma*, first theorized by Aristotle.

Lindey: Correct, your Honor.

Judge Woolsey: Thank you, Mr. Lindey.

Ernst: How can this style be known immediately or innately but by those who have knowledge of it? It can't.

Coleman: We're not talking about style, we're talking about obscene words.

Ernst: Words, their use, and style, its use, are inextricably linked. To appreciate the text fully, both must be understood. As I said, the worst Chinese obscenity cannot be understood by anyone not acquainted with the tongue.

Coleman: Four-letter words, as used in *Ulysses*, can be understood by everyone. And to come back to your point about *Ulysses* bearing Joyce's name, you interpret this, Mr. Ernst, as some kind of safeguard against it being obscene. I interpret it as temerity. Joyce has the audacity to put his name to obscenity. It is not bravery, foolhardy perhaps.

Judge Woolsey: Thank you, Mr. Coleman. Continue, Mr. Ernst.

Ernst: Certain exterior factors have a bearing on *Ulysses*. Among these are the author's literary reputation, the opinion of critics, the attitude of librarians, the acceptance of books in representative libraries and institutions.

About a year ago we sent a questionnaire to hundreds of librarians around the country.

Judge Woolsey: Yes. Yes, Mr. Ernst. I have a map of the United States from your submission pinpointing all the responses from libraries.

Ernst: That's correct. With scarcely a dissenting voice, the librarians conceded the greatness of *Ulysses*. They describe it as superb and classically exquisite. Ethel McVeery, of the North Dakota Agricultural College, said she found it compelling and provocative. Mrs. Ruth E. Delzell, of the Free Public Library in Amarillo, Texas, said it is a masterpiece.

Coleman: Are we leaving the judgment of this case up to librarians in the backwoods?

Ernst: All are equal before the law, Mr. Coleman, from those who live in our cherished countryside to those who live in our great cities, from those who are rich to those who are poor.

Judge Woolsey: Your points, those from both of you, have been made and I have understood them. Continue, Mr. Ernst.

Ernst: It goes without saying that pornography finds no place on the shelves of reputable libraries. Many of the librarians who answered our questionnaire stated that they had copies of *Ulysses*.

The Library of Congress has the English original and the French translation, the Widener Library at Harvard University has two English copies, the general catalogue of the New York Public Library lists more than thirty items: books, pamphlets, magazine articles, all dealing with James Joyce and/or *Ulysses*.

Coleman: This has no bearing on the case.

Judge Woolsey: Mr. Ernst?

Ernst: It would be absurd to assume that an obscene work would appear as assigned reading in our leading institutions of learning. Yet no course dealing with twentieth century English letters, given at any of our colleges or universities, fails to include Joyce and *Ulysses*. For instance, the book has been on the reading list at Harvard in connection with English 26, given last year by T. S. Eliot, the distinguished poet and, three years ago, by I. A. Richards, Professor at Cambridge and Peking.

Coleman: Again, I submit, your Honor that it is not up to outside institutions to decide what is obscene or not. After all, that is why we are here before you. Is it not?

Judge Woolsey: I think we may conclude. You want to say something else, Mr. Ernst?

Ernst: If I may?

Judge Woolsey: Please.

Ernst: Pornography bears the stigma of stealth and secrecy. Printed smut is produced anonymously, is distributed though subterranean channels and is sold at back doors or counters. Random House proposes to publish *Ulysses* in this country, openly and under its own imprint. The claimant's reputation, the high character of its list, are persuasive indication that what the claimant is eager to do is to add another classic to its roster, not to circulate pornographic material.

Judge Woolsey: Thank you, gentlemen. I am concerned about this method Joyce employs, this stream of consciousness or inner monologue. There are passages of literary beauty, passages of worth and power. I tell you, reading parts of the book drove me frantic. There are sections that are so obscure, so vague that it was like walking around without your feet on the ground. Take the passages where Stephen

Dedalus was tight and everyone else was tight. They had visions and dreams that to me were perfectly phantasmal. This stream of consciousness; I do not know. I do not know. In any case, we will resume tomorrow morning.

Coleman: Excuse me, your Honor, it's Saturday. Tomorrow.

Judge Woolsey: Yes, Mr. Coleman, Saturday invariably follows Friday, just as Mr. Ernst reminded me, unnecessarily also, that page 331 follows page 330.

Bailiff: All rise.

✝
✝

We sat around the table in the conference room at the offices of Greenbaum, Wolff & Ernst.

"Well, whatever else happens," Mr. Cerf said, "you've made the book unsellable – 'wading through the pages, impossible to understand, like Chinese'?"

"It's a trial, Bennett," Mr. Lindey said, "not a book review."

"Well, perhaps it might be a good idea then," Mr. Cerf suggested, "not to have any more goes at the judge."

"You do your job and we'll do ours," Mr. Lindey said.

"I don't understand this Coleman character," Mr. Cerf said. "All he has to do is concentrate on the four-letter words and he's won, hasn't he? What's he doing? Waiting until tomorrow, when he can land the knock-out blow. Fuck?"

"He's not going to say the word in court," Mr. Ernst said. "He told me he wouldn't."

"Well, that's something, I suppose," Mr. Cerf said, getting up to leave.

"It's up to me. I'll have to say it," Mr. Ernst said.

NEW YORK BAR ASSOCIATION

Morning, Saturday, November 25th, 1933

Ernst: *Ulysses* has been generally accepted by the community and hence cannot be held to break the law. This philosophy has been tersely expressed by former Justice Wendell Holmes of the United States Supreme Court. He said, and I quote, "The first requirement of a sound body of law is, that it should correspond with the actual feelings and demands of the community whether right or wrong".

Public opinion furnishes the only true test of obscenity. Such opinion is definitely discernible. It is true that people, as a mass, are inarticulate. The body politic registers its will through representatives chosen at the polls. By the same token, the community makes its moral reactions felt and its judgments pronounced through responsible people, who, by reason of their respective endeavors, furnish an accurate social mirror.

When newspapers, college professors, critics, educators, authors, librarians, clergymen and publishers rally to the defense of the book, they do more than express their personal views. They speak for the body social.

To say that *Ulysses* is obscene is to brand eminent persons in various walks of life as champions of obscenity; and on top of this, it would mean that our libraries and universities have been guilty of the criminal offense of disseminating salacious material.

Judge Woolsey: Mr. Coleman.

Coleman: If Mr. Ernst wishes to pursue this point yet again, I will tell the court what some of the people he's referred to have been saying. I quote, "Decidedly overrated, a psychological extravaganza rather than a work of fictional art". That comes from a librarian and Professor of English at Hunter College. He was talking about *Ulysses*, by the way.

Judge Woolsey: Is that against the law, Mr. Coleman, to be overrated?

Coleman: No, your Honor, but it goes against Mr. Ernst's line of argument. Here's another, "*Ulysses* is literary jazz for sophisticated half-morons". That's from Johns Hopkins University.

And here's an interesting one from a public librarian in Riverside, California, who says that queries about the availability of *Ulysses* come mostly from army officers and men of leisure.

Ernst: I don't doubt that these people said these things. I don't doubt that the last librarian quoted looks down on army officers serving our nation as a sub-human species. I don't doubt that another uses the phrase "sophisticated half-morons" which is a contradiction in terms. I don't doubt, either, that the vast majority of librarians feel that the publication of *Ulysses* is worthwhile and that the novel has literary and psychological importance.

Judge Woolsey: Any other points? Mr. Ernst.

Ernst: Your Honor, *Ulysses* must be judged as a whole, and its general purpose and effect determined. On that basis, it must be cleared. In Halsey *versus* the New York Suppression of Vice, the Court said, and I quote, "No work may be judged from a selection of such paragraphs alone. Printed by themselves they might, as a matter of law, come within the prohibition of the statue. So might a similar selection from Aristotle or Chaucer or Boccaccio, or even from the Bible. The book, however, must be considered broadly as a whole".

I contend that the book should not and cannot be judged on the basis of isolated passages. Granting that it contains occasional episodes of doubtful taste, the fact remains that obscenity is not a question of words or of specific instances, nor even of whole chapters. It is a question of entirety. To justify the condemnation of *Ulysses* it must be deemed to violate the law as a whole.

The Court has read the book and knows that such portions of it that may conceivably be challenged are a negligible fraction of the whole.

Coleman: You see, Mr. Ernst accepts that passages of *Ulysses* can conceivably be challenged.

Ernst: Challenged, yes. It's similar to what you have been saying Mr. Coleman. It is a fact that the majority of librarians and indeed literary figures and writers consider *Ulysses* to be a masterpiece. The majority. Your contention, Mr. Coleman is to take a few of these people and spuriously argue that they represent the whole. They do not.

Coleman: My point is that there is not a blanket praise for *Ulysses*.

Judge Woolsey: Let's move on. Mr. Ernst.

Ernst: Let us come now to the work "fuck". Tastes change, taboos vary, but man has always found a new combination of letters to convey a concept if the old word is deemed disgusting. No better series in our own generation can be found in the travelogue of the bathroom, toilet, water closet, W.C. gentleman's room, john, can, and now "I'm going to telephone'. No-one is ever really deceived.

With regard to the word "fuck", one possible derivation was "to plant" – an Anglo-Saxon agricultural usage. The farmer wants to fuck the seed into the soil. I like the word. I don't use it in parlors because it makes me unpopular but the word has strength and integrity. In fact, your Honor, it's got more honesty than phrases that modern authors used to connote the same experience.

Judge Woolsey: For example, Mr. Ernst?

Ernst: "They slept together", for example. It means the same thing.

Judge Woolsey: That isn't even usually the truth.

Ernst: I agree, your Honor.

Judge Woolsey: Mr. Ernst, let me ask you something. Have you actually read *Ulysses*?

Ernst: Yes, judge, and while reading it I was invited, in August, to speak to the Unitarian Church in Nantucket on the New Building Act and on banking.

Judge Woolsey: What's that got to do with my question?

Ernst: Well, I addressed about four hundred people. I was intent on what I was saying. And still, when I finished, I realized that while I was talking about banking, I was also thinking, at the same time, about the long ceiling-high windows on the sides, the clock and eagle in the rear, the painted dome above, the gray old lady in the front row, the baby in the sixth row, and innumerable other tidbits.

I went back to my reading with a new appreciation of Joyce's technique, the stream of consciousness put into words. And now, your Honor, while arguing to win this case I thought I was intent only on this book, but frankly, while pleading before you, I've also been thinking about that ring around your tie, how your gown does not fit too well on your shoulders, and the picture of George Washington at the back of your bench.

Judge Woolsey: I've been worried about the last part of the book but now I understand many parts about which I've been in doubt. I have listened as intently as I know but I must confess that while listening to you I've also been thinking about the Hepplewhite chair behind you.

Ernst: Judge, that's the book.

Judge Woolsey: Interesting individual, Hepplewhite. You know, many date his fame from the time of the publication of his book on cabinet-making and upholstery, 1788, but of course he had been dead two years by that time.

Ernst: He was around the time of Chippendale, wasn't he, your Honor?

Judge Woolsey: Yes, that period when hoop-skirts and stiffened coats went out of fashion.

Ernst: And with them, the need for large chair seats.

Judge Woolsey: Exactly, but we digress. Let's return from the grace of the Hepplewhite chair to the disgrace, as you view it, Mr. Coleman, of *Ulysses* on another item of furniture, the bookshelf. But first, a short adjournment.

Bailiff: All rise.

We stood in a circle in the corridor.

"I don't see the point," Mr. Cerf said. "Why did you have to say it?"

"Fuck?" Mr. Ernst asked.

"Yeah, that about sums it up," Mr. Cerf said.

"Why are you so willing then to print a book with the word in it?" Mr. Lindey asked. "We've taken the monster out of the cupboard, unshrouded it and shown it for what it is, just a four-letter word. Did you notice, no-one gasped? The judge didn't object. Coleman didn't even argue it? None of the papers will print it. They're not brave enough."

"This isn't about bravery," Mr. Cerf said.

"Yes it is," Mr. Ernst said. "We've told the emperor he has no clothes."

"I don't believe emperors like hearing that," Mr. Cerf said.

"This is a court of law," Mr. Ernst said. "The truth is at home here, nothing but the truth, no matter how fucked up it is."

NEW YORK BAR ASSOCIATION

Early afternoon, Saturday, November 25th, 1933

Judge Woolsey: Gentlemen, I feel the points have been well argued. It's time to approach the finishing line. Mr. Coleman, excuse me, before you begin, I'd like to say I'm still worried about this stream of consciousness, what is expressed. Sorry, Mr. Coleman.

Coleman: Your Honor, we have standards in life and there are standards in law. There are also standards in literature. I have mentioned some of the other books that have been before the courts. They concerned serious, bold and sensitive issues. The authors dealt with these scenes in a prudent manner.

Joyce brings the standard of literature down to the level of the sewer and revels in it. He curses and blasphemes his way through narrative and calls on us to sink to his own despicable level, glorifying the demons of life, celebrating them, telling us there's nothing wrong with them. We are a society with standards. We must keep them for ourselves and for our children. To allow the standards of our own lives to be lowered would be wrong. The law is part of the standards of our lives. It sets a bench-mark that we must adhere to so as to remain a civilized society. Joyce wants to destroy our lives. Allowing the standard of literature to be lowered will bring about a weakening of other standards in life.

Ulysses is damnable, hellish filth from the gutter of the human mind. I contend and plead that this book is obscene. All anyone has to do is read it and I ask that no-one be allowed to. It will corrupt them.

Judge Woolsey: Mr. Ernst.

Ernst: Joyce does not call on us to do anything. He makes no suggestions. The sole evidence presented is *Ulysses*. The question is: Must the obscenity of the book be proved by a fair preponderance of evidence, or must it be proved beyond a reasonable doubt? It is submitted that it must be proved beyond a reasonable doubt.

This is like a capital case. *Ulysses* stands before the court as defendant charged with being a menace to public morals. It faces possible annihilation, no less complete than that of hanging or electrocution. Before it is turned over to the executioner, its guilt should be shown beyond a reasonable doubt.

It is a noble citizen whose stature has been almost universally conceded. It may be that in *Ulysses*, Joyce has seen fit to cast light into some of the murky chambers of the human mind. What Macaulay wrote in his essay on Milton applies with equal force to Joyce. He wrote, "There is no more hazardous enterprise than that of bearing the torch of truth into those dark and infected recesses in which no light has ever been shone".

A libel against spoiled food-stuffs is different to a libel against a book. If the Government prevails in this case, it is not a cargo of maggoty meat that is destroyed. A book is imprisoned on death row. Nor does it mean a physical book consisting of a cardboard cover and paper pages. No. It means that ideas are suppressed, that freedom of expression is fettered. The condemnation of ideas should be much more reluctantly ordered than the destruction of rotten vegetables.

Ulysses bears a universal message – a weird cry from the very depths of Dublin to the rim of the world – the cry of tortured conscience. To ban it from our shores, to brand it obscene, to compel our libraries and universities to sweep it from their shelves, is to assure for ourselves the lasting derision of generations to come.

Coleman: Your Honor, I contend that *Ulysses* is not only spoilt literature but it will spoil minds. It is a textual plague that must be quarantined and, yes, destroyed. The Europeans can make their weird cry from their tortured conscience in their own bailiwick. We don't need to hear it.

Mr. Ernst talks about the generations to come and what they might think of any adjudication here. Mr. Ernst does not wish to live in the present. He says we should be governed by whatever whim certain people have outside this courtroom. Well, that may be the case if that whim becomes law. Obscenity has not become legal. He talks of our descendants and their opinions. Well, in case Mr. Ernst hasn't noticed, they haven't arrived yet. It is laughable to think that any court should make its judgment on what people think and even more so on what people who haven't been born yet, what they might think.

Milton wrote *Paradise Lost* not obscenity found. Eradicating filth from libraries would be a godsend not an order from Satan. If *Ulysses* is confiscated or electrocuted, as Mr. Ernst so colorfully puts it, the only cry that will go up won't be from the dirt-filled pages of *Ulysses* but from the wholesome populous of the United States who will cry freedom. Freedom from obscenity.

Ernst: Your Honor.

Judge Woolsey: Gentlemen, we must conclude. I must take a short adjournment.

Ernst: Your Honor.

Judge Woolsey: Mr. Ernst, I am the judge. You are not.

Bailiff: All rise.

✝
✝

Mr. Cerf and Mr. Klopfer came to our table. We remained standing.

"For someone who's not supposed to have his heart in it," Mr. Cerf said, "Mr. Coleman seems to be doing a fine job."

"Methinks the lady doth protest too much," Mr. Lindey said.

"What does that mean?" Mr. Cerf asked.

"You're right, Coleman doesn't have his heart in it," Mr. Lindey said. "He doesn't want to win the case but he's an attorney to the core. Anything he says is on the hoof and he's good at that. That's why he keeps chipping away."

"What do you think, Set?" Mr. Klopfer asked.

"Pity we can't say something that Mr. Coleman couldn't respond to," I said.

"That's a good idea," Mr. Ernst said.

"Good luck with that," Mr. Lindey said.

Bailiff: All rise.

Judge Woolsey: Sit. Now, gentlemen, as I've said, this isn't an easy case to decide.

Ernst: Your Honor, if I may.

Judge Woolsey: We must conclude, Mr. Ernst.

Ernst: Your Honor, Mr. Coleman began this case. I will conclude it. Are you disallowing me from doing this?

Judge Woolsey: Relax, Mr. Ernst, this is informal.

Ernst: It is also a court of law, and as I represent the claimant, I have the right to be the last voice heard from the floor of the courtroom, not Mr. Coleman.

Judge Woolsey: Go ahead, Mr. Ernst.

Ernst: I feel, your Honor, that this is no ordinary case. I also feel that you need to hear our arguments fully. In that respect, when I have finished, I have no objection to Mr. Coleman responding. I will have no more to say after this.

Judge Woolsey: Very well, Mr. Ernst. Your final submission please.

Ernst: You mentioned your worry about Molly Bloom's soliloquy at the end of the book. So what is it? Dozens of pages, blocks of text of only eight sentences and no other punctuation at all. No capital letters. A stream of consciousness. What does it make the reader do? We read one sentence but we career into the next because there's no period, no signpost. We must retrace a word or two to take our bearings, earn understanding. We're in the stream ourselves but we don't know we are. It's like when we think, we don't think that we are thinking. It's choppy but fluid again in a moment. We want to know what's happening. Our eyes dart forward. Lost again. Our senses demand order. Our eyes reverse and once again the message becomes clear. Our interaction with this slab of text has become like the dashing thoughts of the human mind, going this way and that, order but spontaneity, constantly changing course, flowing, stopping, confusing, making sense, sorting things out. The text, devoid of apostrophe, comma, poverty-stricken in periods, is undressed, naked, taking on a meandering course all its own, reflecting Molly's thoughts, her own apparent physical nudity, sensuality, sexuality. Our focus is on rowing with two paddles; one representing our ability to read, the other, our will to comprehend. We float through rapids at times, then serene seas, sailing, not at our own will, within this normal woman's consciousness, entering her mind and therefore her very spirit. She is more intimate with us now than she has ever been with her husband or lovers. We are with her now. No-one else. And on this journey, this odyssey, we're led, without realizing it, by Joyce. Invisible. We've forgotten we're reading. His voice is not heard. Hers is. He has distracted and ushered us by means of entertaining and effective literary devices, devised and sculpted, honed and fired, lit and sparked; this colossus of writing. The privilege of reading it, this spectacular assembly and positioning of words, sprouting images in our own imaginations, making them more fertile than they have ever been. This enormous cascade of thought, set in majesty on the tallest column of literature, the tallest it's ever been. This most sublime form of human expression, this explosion of thought brushes the Heavens, basking in the sun, soaking in the rain, huddled in the snow, blurred in the mist, vivid at noon, electrified by the most powerful lightning storm, to remain breath-taking for our eternity. The most eternal it's ever been. Yes.

When Mr. Ernst had finished, we all remained quiet. I looked over at Mr. Coleman whose head was down.

Judge Woolsey: Mr. Coleman? Mr. Coleman?
　　Coleman: No. Your Honor. No.

Judge Woolsey: Very well, I will adjourn until after lunch when I will conclude this trial.

Bailiff: All rise.

✝
✝

NEW YORK BAR ASSOCIATION

Mid-afternoon, Saturday, November 25th, 1933

Judge Woolsey: I must apologize for having taken so long to bring the case to a hearing. If the conclusion is that the book is pornographic, that is the end of the inquiry and forfeiture must follow. I have further to consider, namely, Joyce's sincerity and his honest effort to show exactly how the minds of his characters operate. If Joyce did not attempt to be honest in developing the technique which he has adopted in *Ulysses*, the result would be psychologically misleading and thus unfaithful to his chosen technique. Such an attitude would be artistically inexcusable.

This book still leaves me bothered, stirred and troubled. This is what goes on.

I know Mr. Ernst that your client is anxious to learn one way or the other about this book. Still I must take a little more time to make up my mind.

I must reserve my decision.

Bailiff: All rise.

I became lost in thought. Mr. Ernst's final submission had dazzled me.

"Set."

I realized I was the only one in left in the courtroom apart from Mr. Lindey who was peeking in the door.

"Come on," Mr. Lindey said. "We're having a meeting now. In the office."

"A meeting? About what?"

"You," he said.

The offices of Greenbaum, Wolff & Ernst on Madison Avenue, number 285 that is, in New York.

Mr. Cerf was lost in thought. The rest of them were just sitting there.

"Did you hear what the judge said?" Mr. Lindey asked me.

"Yeah. Don't seem too convinced yet."

"No. What I mean is, what he said about Joyce?"

"Yeah."

"You see, Set," Mr. Ernst said. "The judge is worried about Joyce, his intentions. What if the judge goes off to consider everything but while he's doing that, Joyce says something?"

"Like what?"

"Like, judges are idiots or there's no justice in America. Joyce might be offended by things Mr. Coleman said when he gets the press reports."

"Well," I said, "I guess the judge'd be none too pleased."

"That's right," Mr. Ernst said. "There's another thing. Joyce might say, for the fun of it, that he *is* a pornographer. I'm not saying he will."

"Well that wouldn't be too helpful either," I said.

"Mr. Haltigan's brother lives in Paris," Mr. Ernst said. "He's been keeping an eye on Joyce for us, just in case."

"Of course, he might not say anything at all," Mr. Lindey said. "But it's better we take precautions."

"Sure," I said.

"The only thing is," Mr. Ernst said. "Mr. Cerf thinks that Mr. Haltigan, the one in Paris, could do with a little help. It might be better to have someone as an official representative of Random House over in Paris; a kind of double safety measure you might say. The Mr. Haltigan in Paris has other work to do. We need someone who can spend all their time at it."

"And?" I asked.

"So we were wondering, would you be willing to go over to Paris to do this for us?" Mr. Ernst asked.

"Me?"

"Yes."

"Why me?"

"Mr. Cerf thinks," Mr. Ernst explained, "that this job needs someone who knows about the case and more important than that, someone with a bit of spunk, someone not easily shut up, someone passionate about what we've done, who knows what's at stake and who could stop anything untoward happening."

"Ain't there anyone else who could do it?"

"Mr. Cerf wants you to do it," Mr. Lindey said.

"Well, I can't. Don't have a passport."

"Mr. Haltigan," Mr. Lindey said, "the one in New York, that is, has arranged one."

"Has? Don't I need to apply and sign something?"

"Mr. Haltigan has taken care of it," Mr. Lindey said. "We know what your signature is like from the letters you signed. We kept copies, as we do."

"Don't I need a photograph?"

"Mr. Haltigan," Mr. Lindey said, "already had a photograph of you."

"How did he get that?"

"I don't know," Mr. Lindey said.

"Oh, I remember," I said. "The day after Roosevelt was elected. You've been planning this for some time behind my back, haven't you?"

"Yes," Mr. Lindey said. "The decision to send someone to Paris was raised several times but after the judge's comments today, Mr. Cerf thinks we really need to send someone over."

"I see," I said. "I really don't think I could stop Mr. Joyce from saying anything and I really don't think that's the reason you're sending me over."

"Correct," Mr. Lindey said. "See, I told you we couldn't fool him. It's like this, Set, there's not much to do now except wait. We wanted to give you a present for all the work you've done for us. We just thought that Texan pride of yours might refuse such a kind offer. And so, the jig is up. What do you say?"

"It's real kind of you," I said. "My daddy said never to refuse a kind offer."

"Tonight," Mr. Lindey said. "The *Europa* leaves at midnight."

"Tonight? Mrs. Finnegan is coming back tomorrow."

"You'll see her when you get back," Mr. Lindey said. "So you'll go?"

"I guess."

"You hear that, Bennett?" Mr. Klopfer said.

"What's that?" Mr. Cerf said.

"He'll go," Mr. Klopfer said.

"Who'll go? Where?"

"Set will go to Paris. He's agreed," Mr. Klopfer said.

"That's good," Mr. Cerf said. "He deserves a vacation after all he's done. That's good. Did we all do our best, do you think?"

"Even if we did," Mr. Lindey said, "it may not have been enough."

Mr. Finnegan had my suitcase all packed. Everyone seemed to have known about this except me. He had shepherd's pie ready. Tom kept asking me to get him the address of a French girl, any French girl. Finn wouldn't eat his meal. He sat on the bed, sulking because I was going away. When I finished my meal, I went over to him. He punched me in the arm and turned away.

"I'll bring you back a present. Won't be so long."

"Go away," he said.

When I was just going out, Mr. Finnegan asked Finn if he wanted to say goodbye to me.

"Gotta headache," Finn said from his bed.

I left.

Mr. Haltigan drove me to 58th Street Brooklyn. We waited at the dock.

[218]

"Do you think we'll win?" I asked.

"Judge Woolsey comes from a long line of distinguished Woolseys," Mr. Haltigan explained. "Merchants. The name carries with it a reputation. His family is of high standing. Has to consider his judgment carefully. If he decides that *Ulysses* can be printed in America, the Court of Appeal might overturn his decision. He'll become known as seedy Woolsey, dirty Woosley. All the high standing built up over the generations will be knocked down to the gutter."

"Yeah."

"You have enough money?" Mr. Haltigan asked.

"Bundles and, before you say it, no, I won't lose it. How'll I know your brother?"

"He's not like me."

"I was thinking more of a physical description."

"He'll start roaring your name if he doesn't find you first. After all, I found you and I didn't need to scream at all. Wears a green fedora. He'll introduce you to Joyce. You deserve to meet him."

"I ain't going to spy on him."

"I know."

I embarked, first time I ever used that verb about me. I stood on the deck and looked down at the waving families and friends of my fellow passengers. Mr. Haltigan waved and left. He wasn't one for sentimentality.

For some reason, might be called intuition, I felt that they weren't sending me over to spy on Mr. Joyce. I also felt they weren't sending me on a vacation. There was some other reason.

"A very good vessel this, you know," an Englishman said to me.

"Is it?"

"Oh yes, sister ship of the *Bremen*."

The *Bremen* was the ship that had brought over the copy of *Ulysses* which was now awaiting its fate. Coincidences were going to follow me across the Atlantic. I thought of Joyce and what he had done with the English language and challenged myself to play with words as he had done. I wanted to go from "startling" to "I" in one sentence with all the words in between. The ship left port at midnight and, a little way out, I completed my mind game but not with as much success as Mr. Joyce would have enjoyed.

It was *startling* to be *starting* a new life, *staring* at the *string* of people on deck, feeling the *sting* of the cold November wind and hearing the birds *sing* before they flew back to the land of our past *sin*, a country *in* a state of Depression-ridden disgrace because of the adherence by some folk to being too long too selfishly too *I*.

1 9

THE HUT OF AMOS I.

FUNNY, I THOUGHT, ME SPENDING the guts of the past two years fighting tooth and nail for Mr. Joyce to be heard only to find myself sailing to the other side of the world to help shut him up. I wasn't going to do that even if I could. They wouldn't entrust me with that. They were kind enough to give me a vacation but I knew I'd spend it trying to figure out the real reason they wanted rid of me. Something in my Texan bones told me there was something else afoot.

The *Europa* docked at Cherbourg where it was raining and so, for the first time in almost a week, I set foot on wet land. (It had been raining in New York when we set sail.) I had spent part of my journey thinking of Columbus. Then I had a nightmare that the ship would fall off the edge of the world. What a waste my voyage would have been! I thanked Columbus for letting me know we were living on a ball and not a plate.

I had a lot of time to think. I was fixing to write a diary. Mr. Finnegan suggested I should. I planned to read it to him when I returned. Mr. Finnegan said I should put dates at the top of my entries because I didn't have an actual diary. I didn't like that idea. It was too easy, too obvious, too boring. I wanted to be like Mr. Joyce. I wanted to make words walk around the city, walk around the world, float across the ocean.

An idea came to me during the voyage. It's difficult for some folk to find their sea legs. They get struck down with *mal de mer*: that's French for puking over the side of a ship. I didn't, but the salt air and being surrounded by a seemingly eternal sea temporarily made my thoughts wander into strange places. I never thought like that before.

Some thoughts were dumb. Like, I asked myself what the names of the seven seas were. I didn't know the answer. That's when I got my idea. I decided I'd write my diary under seven headings with all the headings beginning with the same letter. The seven 'C's.

COINCIDENCES

Friday, December 1, 1933

I passed through immigration into isolation. There was no man with a green fedora. I heard a voice behind me.

"I'd say you're the fellow I'm looking for."

I turned round and found a burly man with a brush moustache.

"Socrates is the name," he said holding out his hand.

"I'm waiting for a Mr. Haltigan," I said.

"That's me. Socrates Haltigan."

"So what's my name?" I asked.

"Ah," he said and then became lost in thought before giving me an answer. "I've forgotten."

"You should be wearing a green fedora. Why ain't you wearing a green fedora?"

"Well, you see," he replied but didn't say anything else.

"What's your brother's name?" I asked.

"Stephen," he replied.

"No, it's not," I said. "It's John."

"That's what we call him, John, but his name is Stephen. I thought you were trying to catch me out."

"Think I'll make my own way to Paris," I said.

"No, no, don't do that," he pleaded. "The wife is waiting in the car. We're to bring you to Paris."

"Why ain't you wearing a goddam green fedora?"

He couldn't answer.

"What's going on?" a woman asked as she hurried towards us. She was smiling but knew something was wrong. She seemed like a joyous woman but overtaken now by the confused situation she found herself in. I walked away with my suitcase but I could still hear their conversation.

"He thinks we're trying to kidnap him," Socrates told her.

"Sure why would he think that? Come on into the car, won't you? We've been so looking forward to seeing you," she pleaded. "Socrates, what did you say to him? For God's sake. Ah Lord."

Her disappointment baffled her. She uttered the phrase "Ah Lord" in a high-pitched child-like voice of wonder. It broke me up. Their conversation turned to a mumble and disappeared as I got further away from them. I thought of hitching a ride to Paris from one of the other passengers. My suspicions had been heightened by the attacks on us by the New York Society for the Suppression of Vice. I wondered could I get a train or a bus or a taxi? I was tired after the long sea voyage. Did I have enough money for a taxi? The man wasn't wearing a green fedora. I should have asked the woman her name but it was too late now. He would have told her to say it was Haltigan. He was Irish, the right nationality. I wasn't sure. She didn't look like a woman who was about to abduct me. I was being dumb again. Of course they were the right people.

"Young man, young man," Socrates said as he caught up with me. "Please. Please. I've made a dog's dinner of this. I lost the cablegram, you see, and yes I've forgotten your name but I remembered the name of the ship and when it would arrive. I'm all at sixes and sevens and I've had a long drive. I'm sorry. Please. Come with us. She's been cleaning the house up all week up and the neighbor is putting a dinner on to coincide with our arriving back. Lamb."

"Why didn't you wear the green fedora?"

"We were in a rush. Please? If only for her. Do it for her. She's awful disappointed now. She was so looking forward to everything being right for you. Please don't do this to her."

"There's a blanket there for you on the seat," Mrs. Haltigan said as I got into the back of the car. "You might want to rest. Isn't he an awful man altogether forgetting your name like that? We were in such a tizzy you see. I don't know what you must think of us at all, Mr. Wright."

Being called Mr. Wright shot through me. I flinched at getting respect like this only because I was being stubborn. I said nothing because I was ashamed and proud and tired and stubborn.

She went to say something else but Socrates shushed her.

"Ah Lord," she said, reluctantly accepting the ruination of what should have been a happy first encounter. It was because of this and not because I was in a foreign country that I didn't feel at all at home. I should have. Goddam hat.

I dozed and slept, tossed and turned as we made our way eastwards towards Paris. The great excitement I felt at the prospect of seeing the city flowed through me in waves. Once we began driving up the rue de Belleville on the north-eastern side of the capital, I sat up and came fully back to life. The more I saw of the moving city, the more I thought it had been sculpted by angels. We stopped outside the church of Saint Jean Baptiste de Belleville. Socrates and his wife had a brief and whispered conversation outside the car. Then she led me down the rue de Palestine and into a building where the couple had their apartment. Socrates did not follow us in.

"Is Mr. Haltigan not joining us?" I asked as the tasty aroma of lamb and mushroom soup tantalized my senses.

"Later," she replied. "Call me Anna and himself is Socrates. Now, get that inside your shirt."

She placed the bowl of mushroom soup on a linen table-cloth. The china was, no doubt, her best. The cutlery was gleaming; her best too. She had set another place for Socrates and I wondered when he might return.

"Thank you so much, Anna," I said. "Don't know why I was such a pain. It's not me. I'm not like that."

"Don't mind any of that. He shouldn't have forgot your name. Eat up," she said and joined me at the table with a bowl of soup for herself.

"He worked in Galway for a while, the West," she said. "That's where he got the accent. He can't understand how our daughter doesn't speak with an Irish accent. Isn't that funny?"

She laughed. I smiled.

"She was born here, you see. He often says that she has my legs and his intellect but he can't understand how she doesn't have an Irish accent."

"What's her name?"

"Aurora. She was the second. We had a little boy, Raymond. When we left Dublin we lived in Bayswater for a while. That's in London. Then we took off for Maine. It's in the United States – but sure you know that – on the border with Canada. Ah, the poor lad. He died there. Lovely, he was. The doctor said he was a time-bomb. There was nothing we could've done."

"I'm sorry."

"He fell ill and then he died. It wasn't long. Himself was a great one for the hats; thought they brought him luck. So he used to always wear a fedora, a green one. John, that's his brother – oh but sure, you know John – he used to rib him about the green fedora, saying he was getting notions above himself. When Raymond died, he didn't wear it after that. We came here after. He does a bit with the horses. He loves the oul' horse."

The conversation stopped as she served the second course.

"I hope this is all right," she said.

"It's much more than that, Anna," I said.

"Isn't is great about Roosevelt getting in?" she asked.

"Yes."

"And he's done so much for them now, the ordinary souls," she said. "Sure, we never get a chance. I don't know how he's done it. Himself got into an argument with some fellow the other day, some fellow who said that Roosevelt shouldn't be president because he's not able to walk on his own two feet. Wasn't that an awful thing to say? Himself said, 'Sure what does it matter if he's able to make the rest of us walk again?' That softened his cough, whoever that fellow was."

She started laughing before telling me more.

"I had to tell him about it, that Roosevelt was elected. He didn't know. Normally he's the one with all the great news. I was on the Métro reading the newspaper, nearly missed my stop. There it was. I read it all the way out of the station, the Métro Marbeuf. It's just around the corner there on the Champs-Élysées. Funny name for a station, Marbeuf. I wish they'd change it. So that's that anyhow.

"You're here to see Joyce. Socrates knows Jim all his life. Joyce. Remembered him writing a story with another boy, Raynold, when they were very young. Austin was his name. Yes that's it. Austin. Austin Raynold. Lived on Carysfort Avenue."

"Do they keep in touch here; your husband and Mr. Joyce, I mean?"

"A little. Joyce only ever has one strong friendship anywhere. He was always like that."

She served the dessert, rhubarb pie, which she called rhubarb tart, telling me it was made by Joyce's wife, Nora.

"She's from Galway," Anna said. "Socrates didn't know her when he was there but they talk about the city like they need to remember it, like it's a comfort to them both. Will you have tea?"

"No, thank you."

"Coffee, something else?"

"No, thank you, Anna. Couldn't swallow another crumb. This is really so kind of you. Will Socrates be back soon?"

"He's waiting in the car for to bring you to your hotel," she said. "It's not a long journey and he's a very good driver."

"What's he doing in the car?"

"Waiting for you. There's no rush."

"Why didn't he come in?"

"He felt you might need a rest after being stuck on the journey back with him all that time," she said.

"I feel so bad about all this. What I said."

"Sure you didn't say anything. He forgot your name. Anyway, he loves playing the martyr. Don't mind him. Are you sure you won't have a cup of tea?"

I got up.

"You're very kind. I better go. Best meal I ever had, ma'am."

"Oh I doubt that," she said. "And it's Anna."

"I won't ever forget your name," I said.

"I'm sure he won't ever forget yours," she said. "Sure we'll be laughing about all this in the future. Wait'll you see."

✛
✛

Socrates was leaning against the driver door of his car. I took him by surprise.

"Pity, me coming all this way over the Atlantic to make friends only to fall out with the first one I meet."

"Sure, we *are* friends," he said.

"I was hoping you'd say that," I said.

He didn't drive off immediately because he became distracted by something in the skies.

"Look," he said, "a red balloon. It's drifting south. Maybe it'll land in the Parc de Belleville and make a child happy. Still, there'll be another one bawling its eyes out over having lost it."

We began our journey.

"Is that why they call you Socrates?" I asked.

He stopped, got out, checked the engine and then got back into the car again. As we took off, he strained to listen to the noise of the car and then relaxed.

"That's fine," he said.

"You know about cars?" I asked.

"Ah, I do a bit of engineering. What were you saying?" he asked.

"Seems to me you were philosophizing about the balloon. Is that why they call you Socrates?" I asked.

"No. The mother gave me that name. She was into philosophy," he explained.

"So your brother, he's called after a philosopher?" I asked.

"No," he said. "The mother went through phases."

As we neared our destination, he pointed out the Arc de Triomphe even though it was impossible not to notice it.

"I do a bit of taxiing as well. An English Lord was complaining to me about that structure there. Said the French make a meal out of describing things and that in English it would be the Triumphal Arch and not the Arch of Triumph. I told him that the French have the right idea. They put the noun first, the main thing, and then describe it. We do the same in the Irish language."

"What did he say to that?" I asked.

"He said the Irish were wrong as well so I kicked him out of the car."

"Don't you like English folk?"

"No. I just detest their overlords. Now, we have to turn here, up the rue Galilée. This is where your hotel is. The Hotel Galilée. Sure what else would it be called?"

We stopped outside the hotel. It was an imposing building; a little eccentric. The steps up to the entrance were parallel with the sidewalk and fitted neatly into a large recess so that they were flush with the entire frontage. Nothing stuck out.

"Joyce lives over there," Socrates said, pointing to a house on the corner. "Number 42, third floor."

We went into a narrow lobby and I checked in. Socrates returned to the car to fetch my suitcase which I had forgotten. Me and suitcases seemed hell-bent on adventure when arriving into a city. While Socrates was gone, I looked around the lobby. There was an elderly man sitting in a chair smoking a cigar. In between blowing out rings of smoke, he smelt the side of the cigar which had a good length of ash still attached. I heard a gasp. It was the tiny elevator being pushed up by a fat shiny tube smeared with engine grease.

"You'll be staying with Mr. Ibsen," Socrates said when he returned.

"Oh," I said.

"He has two rooms," Socrates explained. "He doesn't use one so you'll have privacy. He doesn't come out much. Painter. That's how I got to know him. I do of bit of painting myself."

"Ibsen?" I asked.

"Yes," Socrates replied. "No relation."

We took the stairs. When we reached Mr. Ibsen's room, Socrates knocked at the door and went in leaving me in the corridor. He emerged a few moments later with a key which he used to open the door opposite. I followed him in. It was a bright room with two beds,

[228]

one at the window and another in the opposite corner close to the door.

"Are you all right for money?" Socrates asked.

"Sure," I replied.

"Don't be afraid to ask me for anything," he said. "The receptionist speaks English so she can arrange meals for you whenever you want. I'll be back at midday tomorrow and every day after that and, by coincidence, I have to come here on Tuesday. There's a do. The aeronautical club. Rossi and Codos'll be here. They flew across the Atlantic. New York to Syria. Longest flight ever. Last August. I'm in the club; the aeronautical club. I do a bit of aeronautics."

"Should I go and see Mr. Ibsen?" I asked.

"Best to leave him alone," Socrates replied.

"When should I go and see Mr. Joyce?" I asked.

"I'll arrange it but it'll probably be mid-afternoon tomorrow," Socrates said. "He doesn't start drinking until eight in the evening. I'll leave you then. Here's a newspaper. You can read about the looming menace. Make sure to lock the door. Hotels are always full of strangers. Anything else?"

"No," I said. "Thanks so much."

"*Au revoir*," Socrates said.

"*Merci, monsieur*," I said.

After unpacking my things and putting them away, I looked out the window and saw number 42 rue Galilée, where Joyce lived on the third floor. I was filled with a sense of disbelief that I was in Paris and so near the man whose work had dominated my life for the past two years. Something else caught my eye but it disappeared.

I lay on the bed and began reading the newspaper Socrates had given me, *Le Petit Parisien*. I read that *The Devil's Brother* was being shown at the Eldorado. It was a Laurel and Hardy film I had seen with Tom back in May. On the front page, there was a story about a big Nazi meeting in Berlin with a picture, the looming menace.

Before I went to sleep, I heard voices on the street, two women talking. I couldn't make out what they were saying because it was in French but wondered were they talking about me or the looming menace or perhaps about the red balloon drifting above the street which I had spotted from my window.

†
†

CONFUSION

Saturday, December 2, 1933

When I got up, I noticed a note had been slipped under my door.

Come see me before breakfast. Ibsen.

I knocked.

"In," Ibsen said.

I went in. Ibsen was standing at a canvas with brush in hand. He wore a suit and looked more like a clerk than an artist, no large hat or smock.

"Ah," he said. "Ain't you never seen no black man afore?"

I didn't like him mocking my accent.

"Why do you ask?"

"You seem surprised."

"I'm not."

"I must be wrong then."

"Darn right you are."

"You appear to have got out of the wrong side of the bed or, as they say incorrectly in America, gotten."

"Bed's beside the wall. Only one side to get out of. Haven't yet learned how to go through walls like you."

"I can't go through walls."

"Bet there's a ton of folk would like to help you with that."

He laughed and then laid his brush on a palette which was resting on a hip-high table with narrow legs. His accent was clipped and upper-class like the way folk spoke in the British films.

"I can tell the future," he said, "but more of that later, in the future. Do you find this city talks to you? It talks to me. I respond. Out loud. Do you find this?"

"Not so far," I answered.

"Would you like to see my painting?" he asked.

"Sure," I said.

He held up his hand as a sign that I should not move towards him. "Maybe later."

My blood began to boil.

"Maybe never," I replied. "I'll be out of your way today. Thanks for allowing me to use your room."

"Is it because I'm black?" he asked. "Prefer to breakfast with the two Nazis downstairs?"

"No. It's because you're an asshole."

I closed the door behind me and heard him howl with laughter.

The breakfast didn't fill me up so I ordered another one. I kept trying to identify the Nazis. There were two men sitting opposite me but I couldn't hear their conversation. There were another two men sitting beside each other at the window, one with a red beard, the other with a black beard. They were having orange juice and croissants. French? The others were families and the cigar-puffing guest who approached me.

"Don't blame you," he said as he stopped at my table. "See you've had two breakfasts. The French can do everything with an egg but fry it. Their hens lay poor eggs."

He left me in a scented cloud of cigar smoke.

"*Mademoiselle*," I said but then forgot the word for bill in French.

"*Oui, monsieur?*"

It came to me.

"*L'addition, s'il vous plaît.*"

"*Socrate*," she replied.

What was that? Two syllables; soh-krat. Socrates in French. He's paying the bill. That's what she meant. Socrates was getting the bill. I'd never get used to this. Ibsen came down the stairs and sat in front of me.

"What time did Socrates say he'd be here?" he asked.

"Noon."

"Ten o'clock then or two in the afternoon. The Irish are always either two hours early or two hours late. Never on time. You threw me off when you came into my room. I was expecting a woman. Portuguese. She wants me to do a portrait of her."

"Maybe she's late," I said. "What time did she say she'd be here?"

"They're the ones by the window."

I turned my head. Mr. Blackbeard and Mr. Redbeard caught me looking at them.

"She didn't give me a time," Ibsen said. "In fact, she hasn't even contacted me."

"Well how'd you know she wants you to paint her picture?" I asked.

"I can see the future. I just have this feeling that such a thing will happen," Ibsen said. "Make sure to knock later on once you've seen Joyce."

Ibsen got up and shouted across at the two Nazis.

"Good morning, gentlemen," he said and they nodded.

"Laryngitis?" he roared. "In both your cases, arsenic would be a suitable potion, continues the ailment for eternity."

I decided I needed a walk. Socrates was wrong about the hotel being full of strangers. It was full of nut-cases.

✝
✝

Socrates found me in the garden at the back of the hotel. It was freezing so we walked around.

"Did you read the newspaper?" he asked.

"Not all of it," I answered. "Read the bit about the Nazi meeting in Berlin."

"There's another more important story beside it," Socrates said, "about the superiority of Nazi air power over the rest of us. I know a bit about aeronautics. They're not seeing the signs here, the Government. All the young men who should be leading this country were cut down in the war in Passchendaele or on the Marne. Everywhere. We're left with old men with no ideas. Decadence."

"Ibsen had a go at two of them," I told him, "in the lobby."

"Good."

"I didn't say nothing."

"Better."

"When I left Pendleton, I figured on seeking out all the bad things in the world rolled into one. Now that I've found them, two of them anyway, I didn't do nothing. I don't know. Maybe, I should keep my head down. That's what my daddy would say. Keep my head down, until the time is right."

"Better again," Socrates said. "Come on. There's only so many times I can walk around a garden."

We went back through the hotel, out onto the rue Galilée and made our way towards the Arc de Triomphe. We walked down the Champs-Elysées. I saw a cinema, the Elysée-Gaumont, in the distance and tried to remember what film was showing there. I couldn't remember. We stopped at a coffee shop and sat down.

"I need to tell you about Joyce," Socrates said. "He's being put through the mill at the moment. His daughter, Lucia, is out of her mind. They've had awful problems with her. Then there's his sight. I don't know many blades have been cut into them. No anesthetic. Then there's the book."

"*Ulysses?*" I asked.

"No," Socrates replied. "The one he's working on at the moment. Ten years or so he's been at it. *Work in Progress*, he calls it. Some of it has appeared. Pound has deserted him; that's Ezra, the poet. Stannie, his brother, tells him he's being a fool, wasting his talent. His benefactress, Miss Weaver, isn't enthusiastic either but she's still helping him out. He's more or less on his own. And then, as you said, there's *Ulysses*, the court case in New York. It'll be a blow too much if it goes against him, I think."

"We've done our best," I said.

"I know," he said. "John's told me."

"What about Mr. Léon?" I asked. "What's he like?"

"You wouldn't meet a finer man if you sailed the seven seas," Socrates said. "They're very formal with each other but the best of friends. They have rows every now and then but they always make up. Léon calls Joyce *Starik*, Russian for old man. Joyce doesn't like that. He loses friends, very close friends, very easily. I think he believes we're all out to betray him. He's fragile, be careful with him. So now, let's go and meet the greatest author on earth."

✝
✝

I waited on rue Galilée outside number 42 as Socrates made my imminent arrival known to Mr. Joyce. The porch door was open and I noticed the white terrazzo floor of green leaves and orange tiles. I became nervous. The concierge, a large woman, eyed me suspiciously. After a while, Socrates came out with someone else. He introduced him as Paul Léon, a studious-looking man.

"Third floor," Socrates said and I was left alone.

I went in and looked around at the spacious lobby, then up a couple of steps towards the stairs which wound around an elevator just like the one in the Hotel Galilée. Then I was standing at the door or two doors together, big ones, number 3. I rang the doorbell and waited.

After we had introduced ourselves, Mr. Joyce's wife, Nora, brought me into the kitchen where a kettle was boiling. There was no sign of Mr. Joyce.

"No news from New York?" she asked.

"No," I replied.

"You can't imagine what it's been like for me to be thrown into the life of this man," she said. "He should have stuck to music instead of bothering with writing. And to think, he was once on the same platform as John McCormack. Tea or coffee?"

"Coffee please."

"Oh thank God for that," she said. "Some that come here are too polite to say either. You know, he spent nineteen years thinking about *Ulysses* and seven years writing it, and what has it got him? I don't know whether he's a genius or not, but I'm sure of one thing, there's nobody like him."

"You make a great rhubarb pie," I said. "Mrs. Haltigan gave me some."

"Faith, and I wasn't expecting that."

"Did I say something wrong?"

"Will you stop?" she said. "It's just that most people who come here only ever ask about him. I must make her another one. You're much younger than I thought. Come on, I'll bring the coffee out to you."

She led me into the drawing room which had parquet flooring. The room was furnished with a piano, a book-case, regal-looking chairs and paintings on the walls. Nora sat me on a sofa facing Mr. Joyce who was sitting in an armchair looking at the window. He was wearing a blue jacket, dark trousers and slippers of white and blue check. His glasses were thick and dominated his thin face. Every now and then he took a silk handkerchief from his pocket and used it to wipe his glasses.

"Do you know the Colums, Padraic and Mary?" Nora asked me. "They're great friends of ours."

"Oh yes," I said, "the writers. Well, I don't know them but I heard tell of them."

"Well," Nora continued. "When we were waving them off on the boat-train from Paris to New York once, Jim told them that they'd be safe in America. That's what he said. He can say nice things. Sometimes. This is Set, Jim, the young man you were expecting, all the way from New York."

"Hello, Mr. Joyce," I said.

"Sure, chat amongst yourselves there," Nora said and returned to the kitchen.

When we were left alone, I guessed that Mr. Joyce was suspicious of me. He hadn't said anything. I didn't blame him. I was sure he was wondering why I had come all this way when I had no news to report.

"Mr. Cerf, he's the publisher," I said, "he was kind of keen that I come over here. He's afraid someone might misquote you, something like that. Then the judge might get to hear of it and go against us. It's not that Mr. Cerf doesn't trust the reporters here, he's just a whole lot nervous is all."

Nora returned with a cup of tea for Mr. Joyce and a cup of coffee for me. She had to take Mr. Joyce's left arm and guide it towards the cup which she had put on the table beside him.

"That's where it is, Jim," she said and then went back into the kitchen before returning with plates of almond cakes, one for Mr. Joyce and one for me.

"Jim," she said, "he likes me baking. Said he enjoyed the rhubarb tart I gave Anna Haltigan. I'll leave you be."

Alone with Mr. Joyce, I thought the silence meant that he didn't want me there.

"I like the way you speak," he said.

"My accent?"

"That too."

He fumbled for the cup and nearly spilt it.

"I always have the sense that it's evening," he said and then sipped his tea and bit into one of the almond cakes. "There's a pigeon that arrives at the window-ledge almost every day. Do you know what she says, my wife? She says, 'There she is again'. That's what she says. Then it flies off and, when it returns later, she says, 'Oh look, *he's* back again.' That's what she says. Do you understand why she says that?"

"No," I replied.

"I doubt if she does. Where are you staying?"

"Hotel Galilée."

"Miss Weaver stayed there," Mr. Joyce said, referring to his patron. "Tell me about the guests."

"There's this painter, Ibsen, he's letting me stay in one of his rooms."

"Ibsen? Any relation?" Mr. Joyce asked.

"No," I replied. "Then there's an Englishman, I think he's English, who smokes cigars. Says the French can't fry an egg and that French hens don't lay good eggs.

"Ask him if *he* can lay a good table?"

"Then there were two Nazis in the lobby this morning."

"They will end up with few admirers," Mr. Joyce said.

"I don't like them either because they burn books."

"I was talking about the hotel owners," Mr. Joyce said.

He became silent. I looked at the book-case beside me.

"Do you have anything to read?" Mr. Joyce asked.

"No, just newspapers."

"They tell people about the extraordinary. I write about the ordinary. Take some books."

I took one and read the title aloud. "*Les lauriers sont coupés.*"

"Why did you choose that one?" Mr. Joyce asked.

"It was upside down."

"My wife," Mr. Joyce said. "It's a feminine trait to put books upside down. That book is where I got the idea for the interior monologue in *Ulysses*. It's by Édouard Dujardin."

"Did he mind that you took his idea?" I asked.

"No. People kept asking me how I had come up with the method of writing people's thoughts into the narrative. I told them again and again that Dujardin's book gave me the idea. All of a sudden then, this forgotten writer, undeservedly forgotten, got a new lease of literary life and deservedly so."

"There's some paper that's fallen out," I said.

"If it's a bill tear it up," Mr. Joyce said. "Read it."

"It's a list of names," I said.

"Who are they?"

"Famous people. There's Arnold Bennett, Édouard Dujardin, Albert Einstein, T. S. Eliot, E. M. Forster, John Galsworthy, Ernest Hemingway, D. H. Lawrence, Wyndham Lewis, Thomas Mann, W. Somerset Maugham, Luigi Pirandello, Bertrand Russell and lots more besides."

"Ah yes, I know what that is," Mr. Joyce said. "People who signed the petition against Samuel Roth. He pirated my book in America. Miss Beach, that's Sylvia Beach, who first published *Ulysses*, she organized it. Someone was looking for that. Who was it? Oh yes. Budgen. Frank. He's writing a book about me. The telephone number here is Passy 98.06, if you hear anything from New York."

"Sure," I said and took this as a sign that I should leave and maybe not return again. "I'll just say goodbye to Nora. She asked me to call her Nora."

"Come back tomorrow," Mr. Joyce said. "The afternoon. I like the way you speak."

"In," Ibsen said after I had knocked on his door.

"Did the Portuguese woman call?" I asked.

"No," he replied. "Are you going to ask me that every day?"

"You should know? Thought you could tell the future."

"I don't scoff at other people's talents," he said. "Don't scoff at mine. I interpret things."

"Really?" I asked.

"Hardly unreally," he said. "Do you want to hear any of my interpretations?"

"Can't wait," I said.

"Sarcasm suits no-one. To *Ulysses*, the book. My interpretation. Strip away all focus on the styles, the characters, the secondary characters and what are you left with? Molly Bloom, her husband, Leopold, and Stephen Dedalus. What is at the core here? Another being. His name is Rudy, son of the Blooms. He died young. This unspeakable tragedy understandably drives a shaft between the couple's relationship. They try to come to terms with it. They remain together, unbroken but damaged. Bloom is a Jew. Don't you think it's odd that Joyce doesn't tell us how Rudy, the child of a Jew, died? He's mentioned several times but only when Leopold is pining about him. The reason for his death, the death of the Jewish child, is not explained. Don't you see? It's a metaphor not only about the future but about all futures. No-one else has this interpretation. It's mine."

"Other folk have other interpretations," I said.

"And I have other interpretations," Ibsen said. "Here's another. Simpler, so even you can understand it. It's a book but it's more than a book. There are things that people haven't seen like a magnificent world deep in the universe or splendors they haven't experienced like being carried down a huge waterfall and landing safely, refreshed and exhilarated. It's in that realm but it's different. It's a human phenomenon, up there in the Heavens and careering down a waterfall; an outstanding achievement of the human mind pervading our lives even though we might never touch it or read it. It's just there; another wonder of the world, sparkling yet invisible to most."

"Have you finished?" I asked.

"No," he replied. "I have another interpretation. I call it *the* interpretation. Ready? Why is it a good book? Why is it not a bad book? Does anyone know? I do. Let's go to the Louvre. The *Mona Lisa*. Is it a good painting? Why is it not a bad painting? She's perhaps an unconventional beauty. Is she smiling? Is she not? Is that it? A great painting must have a little gimmick? No. It's to do with absence. Someone or some people stole the painting in 1911. What happened? People queued all day at the Louvre to gaze at the easel or the wall where it rested or hung. Why? What moved them? It's beyond description. A mystery? No. Some things are like this. They defy description. They defy explanation. They are, in other words, great works of the human mind. The academic and the imbecile (sometimes, by the way, these are one and the same) are bereft of an answer. Why? It is beyond description but it is great. Back to *Ulysses*. My answer is this; listen carefully. It is much more than a book. Even when it is absent it is present. If this does not satisfy you, then answer fully this question; why is it not a bad book? Answer carefully."

"Well you got it all sorted out," I said. "Ain't you?"

"Correct," he said. "Now come look at this."

I stood in front of his paintings, three in all; two finished or nearly finished, the third, a blank canvas.

"It's a triptych," he explained. "A rustic scene. That means country-side. One sees a man, the swineherd, like a shepherd except he looks after swine. Then there's a hut and empty sties where pigs are penned. They're being walked. A chap approaches. He's old, or made to appear old, a beggar. The sky is deep blue, azure."

"What's that?" I asked.

"A purple tunic, a reference to generosity. It's the story of Emaues from the *Odyssey* by Homer. When Joyce moved in across the road, it inspired me to paint this. His novel, *Ulysses*, is based on the *Odyssey*. I find that the city talks to me. I respond to it. Out loud. Do you find this?"

"No," I said.

"No?" he asked. "People keep saying that to me when I ask them. In any case, there's a chap in the *Odyssey* called Emaues, almost like my own name, Amos. By the way, I must tell you this. It's a burden for an artist like myself to have the name Ibsen. One is asked if one is related to the Norwegian playwright. That's where he was from. If I sign my paintings, they wonder if, in fact, Ibsen the playwright was also Ibsen, the painter. So I have had to take pre-emptive action. I sign my paintings, Amos I."

"Good idea."

"Or, more correctly, great idea," he said. "Now, look at the second painting. The old man, the beggar has approached and is sitting down eating roast pig which the swineherd has cooked for him. There are other men there too. They have returned with the pigs which are now penned in the sties. You see? I interpret my own work. I interpret things."

"What'll the third painting be?" I asked.

"Have no idea," he said. "I'm stuck. I knew I would be. Someone else will finish it."

"Who?" I asked.

"Someone in the future," he replied. "I have two chunks of news for you, by the way. While you were out, Socrates called and invited you to Sunday lunch. Said he'll pick you up at midday tomorrow."

"That's kind of him," I said.

"When you come back, there'll be a change," he said. "That's the second chunk of news. My nephew, an impossible organism, is arriving from England. He always arrives in the afternoon so you won't see him until you get back. You'll have to share the room with him. Do you mind? It's only for a few days. He's an orphan. Great aunts look after him in England but they can only take so much and need a break every now and then. Do you mind?"

"Guess not," I said.

"Well, tell me about Joyce?"

"I don't know," I said. "Didn't say much."

"Did he eat anything?"

"Eat anything?"

"Yes, it's when you insert nourishment into your mouth, chew and swallow. Did he fucking eat anything?"

"He had an almond cake, maybe two."

"You have no eye for detail. You should know how many."

"He had two."

"Get out."

✝
✝

I went back to my room. The door wouldn't open completely so I had to squeeze myself in. I tore the newspaper as I pulled it from underneath the door. There was a letter as well from Socrates telling me he'd call at midday the following day. I sat on the bed and ignored stories about the Third Reich. A picture of a frozen little waterfall in the Bois de Boulogne caught my eye. Beneath it there was a story about the cold snap. I thought of turning the pages to find out what picture was showing in the Élysée-Gaumont but then decided to take a walk and find out myself.

The air was chilly. All the people were wrapped up in winter clothes. I stopped at the edge of the sidewalk, turned and looked at the Élysée-Gaumont. In big letters, the hoarding announced the film, *I was a spy*. Ibsen's words came to me, about the city talking to him. I decided to do as he had done, respond.

"No, I'm not. I told Mr. Joyce I was not a spy," I said out loud.

A couple walking past the cinema glanced at me and then laughed among themselves.

COMPANIONSHIP

Sunday, December 3, 1933

Twice Anna Haltigan had to repeat my name to get my attention. "Set. Set." I was not able to stop looking at her daughter, Aurora. She was about my age and had inherited her mother's brown eyes and unbroken cheerfulness though I didn't know if she had her daddy's intellect or her mother's legs.

When Aurora showed me saddles that her father kept in a closet she turned and stared at me like I was supposed to react with wild enthusiasm.

"What do you think of them, Set?" she asked. "Aren't they all shiny? Daddy loves the horses."

"I thought you'd have a French accent," I said.

"Ah, I do sometimes," she said. "I put it on and Daddy gets all confused. We do laugh at it, Mammy and me."

I managed only a quiet response which made her giggle. Anna went about the task of serving lunch with great excitement. I felt this was not only because I was in their apartment but because I had been introduced to Aurora.

"Aurora helps the nuns out with the young girls that are starting school," Anna said. "Ah, sure it's hard for them at first. The nuns have great time for her. Don't they Aurora? They have great time for you."

Aurora blushed at the attention she was getting. At Anna's suggestion we all made our way to the nearby Parc de Belleville after lunch. We went in twos, me with Socrates. When we got into the park, Anna ordered Aurora and me to walk around it while she and her husband would walk the other way. She told Socrates that young people should be on their own. There was no argument. We took off as separate pairs in different directions.

Aurora told me about having been to Nice with her classmates under the supervision of two nuns, their teachers. When she tried to walk over a tricky mound of turf she reached out her hand to me. I took it and she steadied herself before jumping back on level ground. She did not let my hand go. She swung her arm and made mine swing too. I felt very conscious of myself. Holding her hand changed me. I didn't want to let it go. It was a super kind of feeling of being alive. There was nothing calculating about her. I thought, though, that she felt she had found a friend in a school playground and nothing more.

I let her hand go as her parents turned round towards us. It was too late. They had seen the connection we had made. Aurora giggled again. Anna decided we should go around as separate pairs again and so we did. We did not stop.

Aurora told me that a lot of boys wanted to kiss her so I asked her if she had kissed many boys. She told me she hadn't but that many boys had kissed her. I asked her if I could be one of them and so she kissed me quickly on the lips. There didn't seem to be anything daring about it. It was a childhood kiss to a childhood friend as if still in childhood. She asked me why boys always wanted to kiss girls so I told her it was the only way to stop them talking. This set her into a fit of giggling. I pleaded with her not to tell her parents what I had said. I thought it might sound bad.

We found ourselves facing each other, looking into each other's eyes.

We made our way home in pairs. This time I was with Aurora, holding hands, ambling behind Anna and Socrates. There was something very loving about it, daring even.

┼
┼

Later that afternoon I was back on the sofa in Mr. Joyce's apartment. I noticed a piece of paper on the floor, maybe another page from the petition against Samuel Roth. I picked it up. It was a real long strip of paper with printed text. It was something else.

"This was on the floor," I said and handed the paper to Mr. Joyce.

"It's a galley proof from Budgen's book about me," Mr. Joyce said. "They keep slipping off onto the floor. He's a good writer, Budgen. Told him so too, but couldn't resist adding that it was only because of his association with me."

"Thought it might be from your own book, *Work in Progress*," I said because I wanted to let him know I was interested in his work.

"No. Do you miss your family in New York?" Mr. Joyce asked.

"The Finnegans put me up in New York," I said.

Mr. Joyce sat bolt upright in the chair.

"What?" he asked.

"I'm sorry," I said. "Probably should have told you that before. I came from New York but I'm not from there. I'm from Texas."

"Who are these Finnegans?" he asked.

"They're the family looking after me in New York," I said. "Do you know them?"

"No," he said, relaxing. "So your parents live in Texas then?"

"My daddy does," I said. "My mother's dead."

"Did you know her?" he asked.

"Not really," I said.

He became silent again so I continued.

"She died when I was real small. I was in bed. Something woke me up. A noise far away. I didn't know what it was. I know now. It was Mrs.

Taylor, our neighbor, she was playing a gramophone record. Caruso. The wind was blowing in a particular way so I could hear it, just about. Then I heard my mother calling me. She called twice. 'Set. Set.' I got out of bed and went to my mother's room. She was dying. Told me to comfort one of the little Mexican girls who was crying. I gave her my teddy bear. She stopped crying and then I went back to my mother and she just died."

"I'm sorry," Mr. Joyce said. "I nearly met him once, you know. Caruso. He was in Dublin. I spoke Italian, you see, so I wrote to all the newspapers offering them a story if I could get an interview with him but they all refused. Played the Theatre Royal. Wore green socks and a shamrock in his button-hole in honor of the Irish. 1909 it was."

"What a pity you two didn't meet," I said.

"Yes. The newspapers went against me. Then recently, this man Harold Nicholson wanted to give a talk on the BBC about me but the censors there wouldn't allow him to mention the title of my book, *Ulysses*. Is there no end to their attempts to try to crush me?"

I heard a noise and saw Nora in the kitchen doorway. She had been listening. "Now, Jim, now, Jim, we've heard all that before."

I told Ibsen about my conversation with Mr. Joyce.

"You've heard, I presume," he asked, "about his mother's death?"

"Yeah," I said. "She wanted him to say there was a God when she was on her deathbed but he refused."

"I must interpret this for you," Ibsen said. "I interpret things. If there is a God and Joyce had soothed his mother by saying he believed, then God would have told her in Heaven that her son had lied. As it is or was, God, if he exists, told Joyce's mother that her son had told the truth. Surely that is what God wants."

"What about the distress he caused her?"

"There is no distress. *We* know about it but if this God is so benevolent, then he would have wiped the memory from the mind of Joyce's mother once she had landed in Heaven where we're told there is no pain. Getting back to the issue of Joyce refusing to tell his mother that he believed in a God, I don't believe that Christianity preaches it is a sin to tell the truth."

"That's one way of looking at it, I suppose," I said.

"Would you like to hear about my mother?" Ibsen asked. "It seems to be a day for talking about mothers."

"Sure," I said.

"So would I," Ibsen said. "When I was an infant, I was lying in my African village that had been plundered by the unfriendly inhabitants of a neighboring village. My parents lay dying beside me. A man came along, English explorer. Before my father died he told this explorer that he, my father that is, was the village witch-doctor. Could see into the future and that I would inherit this facility. He asked the explorer to take care of me and so he did.

"I was brought back to England and realized later in life that I was living in an estate house the size of a country's parliament with a court-yard that would hold its own with any of the great squares of European cities. I had four new brothers who have since done what all proper upper-class English children do when they grow up, including me. I became the artist. One is in the army, or was. He died. Another is a doctor, the third went into the City, that's London-speak for Wall Street, and the fourth, poor thing, into the Church where he will eventually get promoted to high office and wear the important Church color of purple. That reminds me."

"Of what?"

"There's a deranged priest in the hotel," Ibsen said. "Limps. Uses a blackthorn stick, the walking aid of choice for leprechauns. Dark and shiny, just like his soul, no doubt. Looking for Joyce's address. Probably wants to tell him that he's going to hell. Imagine that. My brother, the officer, made me legal guardian of Robert even though he had a doctor and a clergyman to choose from."

"Who's Robert?" I asked.

"My dead brother's son," he replied. "My nephew. The one who has just arrived and is ensconced next door. He calls himself Robbo, by the way. There are other names that might suit him better but I will desist from listing them."

"What about his mother?" I asked.

"Do try to keep up," he said. "I told you, he's an orphan. She predeceased her husband by a year. That's the way of it. I am the legal guardian of this creature. That's why he's here."

"Do you remember the last thing *your* mother said to you?" I asked.

"I was only a baby, I told you. Do you?"

"Yes," I answered. "She told me to look after the little ones."

"A worthy last request. How was your lunch with the Haltigans?"

"Fine. We went for a walk after, the four of us."

"Aurora?"

"Yes."

"Thought she was in Nice. You know, if you weren't here, they, the Haltigans, that is, would be looking after my nephew. I'm an artist. I need time alone. Distraction is the great leveler of artists. Normally comes during the holiday when the Haltigan girl can look after him. I thought she was in Nice."

"No. She's back. I told you," I said. "Can I go see him? Robbo?" I asked.

"Please do. Be careful. I told you."

I knocked at my door and heard a spirited voice. "Is that you, Set?"

When I opened the door I saw a young boy. He immediately launched into an introduction.

"My name is Robert but you see in school, in school, there are three Roberts. Robert Palmer, Robert Woodman and then me. So, so. Do you want to know what their fathers do?"

"No," I said as I stood bewildered by his irregular jumps.

"Well, I might tell you later," he said. "So, Robert Palmer, he's called Bob and then Robert Woodman is Rob and I'm Robbo because, you see, it would be really confusing for everyone if we were all called Robert. Are you from America?"

"Yes," I said.

Robbo twirled his fingers in front of him as he spoke and, at other times, stood on one leg as he swung the other.

"Maximilian Archer, he's in my class, his brother is in America. He works in Detroit. That's in the middle. I've put all my things away in the drawers and, and, I put my case under the bed so it wouldn't clutter. Oh and I put my sailor suit in the wardrobe. It isn't really a suit but that's what it's called. Is that all right?"

"Sure," I said. "Are you hungry?"

"Oh, yes please," he said. "Shall we eat here?"

"No," I said. "Downstairs. Are you ready?"

"I don't have any money," he said.

"I have."

"It really is very kind of you to pay for it." he said. "I don't get an allowance. Bob Palmer gets lots of money."

"Well, are you coming?"

"Oh yes. I am rather famished."

On the way downstairs, Robbo told me what the fathers of his namesakes did, that he didn't like eating rabbit and that Greenland was very cold. His loud and endless chit-chat at the dining table amused the other guests who looked over at us and smiled. As I looked around, I noticed a figure dressed in black and presumed it was the mad priest Ibsen had told me about. I could see a crooked, spiky walking-stick tilted against his table.

"Will you read me a story before I go to bed?" he asked. "I saw the book you have and I opened it. I hope you don't mind. *The laurels are cut*. I can speak some French, you see. Will you? Will you read it to me? I read myself but I like it when people read books to me. Maybe just a little. Will you?"

Three men sitting at the table beside us sniggered. I didn't mind people being amused by Robbo but they seemed to be laughing at him and at me. I banged the table, making everything on it jump.

"Got a problem?" I snarled.

Even though it was three against one, the clatter and my unexpected challenge threw them off and they shook their heads but said nothing. My outburst silenced Robbo who seemed to become a little afraid.

"Do you want anything else?" I asked.

"Well, I wouldn't mind some dessert. I like ice cream."

I looked over at the three men I had challenged. They had become sheepish. The other guests too had stopped smiling at us. Robbo ate his ice cream and licked the front and back of the spoon many times before announcing to us all that he was stuffed.

Robbo's wittering continued all the way back from the dining table to our room. I had stopped listening. The book Mr. Joyce had given me was no longer on my bedside table but on my bed where Robbo had left it. A sheet of paper stuck out from the pages. It was the copy of the petition against Samuel Roth that I had mistakenly taken with me when I borrowed the book. A slight sense of panic burst through me because I remembered Mr. Joyce had told me one of his biographers had been looking for it. I began listening to Robbo again.

"I have two great aunts," he said. "They look after me, you see."

"Robbo," I said. "I have to go out for a minute or two. Don't leave the room and lock the door."

"Don't leave the room and don't lock the door?" he asked.

"No. Don't leave the room and do lock the door."

"Where are you going?"

"Just across the road," I said. "Won't be long."

I ran out. As I crossed the road, I decided to push the list under the Joyces' door rather than disturb them. I arrived just as Nora was about to enter the apartment and she insisted that I follow her in.

"I took this by mistake, Mr. Joyce," I said. "It's the list of people. The petition against Samuel Roth. You said Mr. Budgen might need it."

"Ah, yes," Mr. Joyce said and took the list. "Sit down. My son has a friend. Laubenstein, an organist. He's taught me phrases from your country. I like them. 'Bought the farm' for someone who moves to the countryside. 'Hell's Bells' to express surprise. You must have ones in Texas as well."

"Lots," I said. "There are Texas Germans there too. Still speak German."

"Tell them to go up on the highest hill and speak their language," Mr. Joyce said.

"Why?" I asked.

"So everyone will hear them," he said. "Their heritage will drift down across the plains and root itself in the soil, there to flourish when the sun comes up."

We both stopped talking because of a noise, like a beat of a drum. It was accompanied by a chant. Someone was coming up the stairs.

"What's that?" I asked.

"It will become clearer in time," Mr. Joyce said. "It approaches. It is ascending."

The clatter of someone jumping with two feet onto each wooden step towards the Joyces' apartment became louder and clearer. Each clatter was followed by a phrase, "Here is me. Here is me." Then it stopped and we heard a quiet knock.

"And who is this young lad?" Nora said in the hall-way.

"Robbo. Is Set here? I've had to knock on all the doors."

"Oh no," I said out loud.

"Look who's here," Nora said as she came into the room with Robbo. "Is he yours?"

"No," I said. "He's just staying with me in the hotel. No relation."

"No-one appears to be related in that hotel," Mr. Joyce said.

Robbo approached Mr. Joyce and then looked at Nora. "Is this your father?"

Mr. Joyce put his head back. "Ha," he shouted, before laughing.

"Did you ever hear the like?" Nora said and she laughed too.

"My name is Robbo. In my class, my class at school there are three boys, well there are more, but there are three and they're called Robert. So, so it's really confusing you see…"

The same story he had told me earlier went on and on before coming to a grinding halt.

"Will you have something?" Nora asked Robbo as she bent down to him. "Some lemonade and a biscuit?"

"Oh yes, please," Robbo said. "What's your name?"

"Nora."

As soon as she had left, Robbo began again. He twiddled the tips of his fingers in front of him and twirled around every now and then.

"I stay with my two grand aunts," he said. "You can call them grand aunts or great aunts. It really doesn't matter. I don't go to school anymore because a governess teaches me at home. I said, you see, that I was enjoying school and then, and then they took me out of it."

"I thought you were stuffed," I said.

"That was earlier," Robbo replied and sat beside me on the sofa.

Nora handed him a glass of lemonade and a large biscuit.

"Thank you very much, Nora," Robbo said. "When I was at school..." Robbo continued but stopped as he bit into his biscuit, chewed and swallowed his drink.

We all waited.

"When I was at school, the teacher, Mr. Parsons, he asked us what animal we would like to be. What animal would you like to be?" he asked.

"A deer," Mr. Joyce replied, "with flashing antlers."

"My name's Robbo. Oh, but I told you that already. What's your name?"

"Babbo," Mr. Joyce said.

"That's what we call him," Nora explained as she put down a cup of tea on a table beside Mr. Joyce and guided his hand towards it.

"Will you have something?" she asked me.

"No thank you, Nora," I said. "I've just eaten. So has he."

"May I call you Babbo?" Robbo asked as biscuit crumbs fell on his trousers.

"It's my name," Mr. Joyce said.

"And what would *you* like to be, Set?" Robbo asked. "I mean what kind of animal?"

"Don't know," I replied. "What about you?"

"An Alsatian," he replied.

"Why?" Mr. Joyce asked.

"Because there was this story one time in school about an Alsatian killing two people and I'd like to be an Alsatian so I could kill my two great aunts and then I wouldn't have to go to prison because dogs don't go to prison. Babbo? Why did Nora take your hand and push it towards the cup?"

"I can't see very well," Mr. Joyce replied, still laughing about Robbo's murderous intentions.

Robbo ate the rest of his biscuit, finished his drink and then sat on the floor at Mr. Joyce's table.

"I'll sit here, Babbo," Robbo said, "and when you want to drink some tea, it is tea isn't it?"

"Yes," Mr. Joyce said.

"When you want to drink some tea, just tell me and I'll hand you the cup. That way, you see, you won't spill it."

"I'm afraid of dogs," Mr. Joyce said.

"Maybe I could be something else then, Babbo," Robbo said. "I wouldn't like to frighten you. Does anything else frighten you?"

"Thunder," Mr. Joyce said.

"Babbo, do you think Nora would give me another biscuit?" Robbo asked.

"Yes, of course," Mr. Joyce said.

Robbo skipped into the kitchen. His voice became a muffled unbroken burr punctuated by Nora's laughter.

"I could listen to him all day," Mr. Joyce said. "I love his endless chattering."

"You can have him," I said and Mr. Joyce laughed again.

'Come on, Robbo. Best get back," I shouted.

"Do you think they could all be wrong?" Mr. Joyce asked, as he held up the list of names I had handed him earlier.

"No," I said and got up.

"A lion," Mr. Joyce said.

"What's that, Mr. Joyce?"

"A lion," he said, "you'd be a lion."

"Do I come across that fierce?"

"They protect their young like no other," he said.

CONFLICT

Monday, December 4, 1933

Nora Joyce brought me peace after breakfast when she came into the hotel and offered to take Robbo for a walk. He jumped at the chance.

I would have gone along except I saw Aurora in the hotel helping her father prepare a banquet room for the aeronautics event that was being held the following evening. As soon as Robbo skipped out with Nora, I made my way to the banquet room to see Aurora but Socrates cut me off at the pass and asked me to sit down in the lobby with him.

"Got a cablegram from the brother in New York. No news yet," he said.

"Mightn't be for a while," I said. "That judge certainly likes taking his time mulling over things."

"You must be bored here with nothing to do all day," Socrates said.

"No. I have my hands full looking after Ibsen's nephew."

"Robbo?" Socrates asked. "When did he arrive?"

"Yesterday."

I thought Socrates might offer to put Robbo up in his apartment like Ibsen said he had done before. Nothing.

"Hands full is right," Socrates said. "You should take him up to the square there. It's just up the road past where the Joyces' apartment is. Opposite."

"I'll see," I said.

"There was a young boy who was here a few months ago with this family," Socrates said. "He loved it up there. They had a peculiar name. What was it? Brombert, that was it. Came from Leipzig through Switzerland. Parents had to tell the young lad to stay in his compartment in the train until they crossed the border into Switzerland. They heard the word *Juden* being mentioned. That's Jews in German. It's blowing in the wind from the east. This."

"Do you want a hand setting things up in there?" I asked.

"No," Socrates replied. "Let me know when Robbo is back. Aurora would love to see him."

Socrates returned to the banquet room. The priest, who had been sitting behind him, turned his head to me.

"You know Joyce?" he asked.

I remembered that Socrates had mentioned the Joyces' apartment during our conversation.

"Yes."

"I have a book I'd like to give him," the priest said. "He's been looking for it for a long time. Collector's item."

"I can't tell you where he is, I'm afraid," I said.

✝
✝

Aurora knocked at my door as I was resting in bed reading a book.

"Come in," I said, thinking it was Ibsen or a hotel maid.

I shot up.

We sat on the bed and talked. I told her I had never kissed a girl. She told me she had never kissed a boy but that boys had kissed her. We stopped talking then and looked at each other. I closed my eyes. My lips tingled as they touched her lips. We drew apart. I opened my eyes. She laughed. I smiled. She left. I stayed. I closed my eyes again hoping the past would come back, the past of a few moments ago when we had kissed. The future seemed more important now than it had ever seemed; the future when I would meet her again and kiss her again.

✝
✝

"A visitor, had we?" Ibsen asked.

"You keep your nose out of my business."

"Oh, really? Business? She charged a fee, did she?"

"I don't like the way you talk."

"Interesting you command me to keep my nose out of your business. Might the rest of my body intrude into your business? I'll still have my brain, I suppose. Being noseless, however, will put me at a disadvantage. You see, I use it to sneeze and to sniff out the guilty secrets of sap-rising creatures such as yourself."

"That's because you got nothing in your own life."

"Let down the draw-bridge. What's it like, love?"

"I ain't in love."

"Oh, for God's sake. What's it like? I'm an artist. I want to know what others feel. Well? You can trust me."

"I can trust you to laugh at me."

"I will not laugh. What is it like? Come on, tell me."

"Real good, I guess."

"Real good? Real good? That's wonderful! I haven't been to Texas but I imagine if a cowhand there sought the opinion of another on the mending of a wheel-barrow, he might just hear his straw-chewing pal passing such a judgment. Real good? Might you expand on your terse explanation?"

"You said you wouldn't laugh."

"I'm not laughing. I'm enraged. How would you describe the sun? Why, I figure it's a big ol' orange ball up there in the sky and, I reckon, it's hotter than them there chicken legs on Granma's griddle. Take my advice. It comes from an artist and is therefore of the highest caliber. Don't ever write a love scene. I feel I would be so excited by your descriptive powers that I might even jump out the window with excitement. Real good? You are a disgrace."

I made my way over to the Joyces' apartment, being careful to ensure that the prying eyes of the priest did not follow me. Mr. Léon emerged from the apartment door as I was about to ring the bell.

"There's news?" he asked.

"No."

"He's on his own."

I entered the apartment and asked from the kitchen door if I could come in. Mr. Joyce, sitting, facing away from me, gestured toward the sofa beside him. I sat down.

"Mrs. Joyce and Robbo are gone for a walk," I said.

"They'll both be delighted with that," he said. "Do you know the French phrase, *un mot d'escalier?*"

"A word of the stairs?"

"Do you know what it means?" Mr. Joyce asked.

"No."

"It's when you have been taken aback or outraged but cannot think of what to say until later, perhaps on the stairs going up to bed," Mr. Joyce said. "There's nothing comparable in English. I'm just thinking aloud. Your mother said your name twice, you said, when she was dying. Is that right?"

"I think so."

"Did she pause in between?"

"No, not too much, if at all."

"Must get back to my book, thinking about it," Mr. Joyce said. "You can read there if you like."

I looked at the bookshelf and saw novels by Gabriele D'Annunzio and Rudyard Kipling. I chose *Anna Karenina* by Tolstoy, a big book and began to read. Mr. Joyce appeared to be dozing. I wondered what was going on inside his head. I had read a good way through the first chapter when he whispered to me. I thought he was dreaming.

"Who are you?" he whispered.

"It's Set, Mr. Joyce. Your wife'll be back shortly."

He said nothing more so I tried to find the point in the book where I had left off.

"Who are you?" Mr. Joyce whispered again.

"It's Set, Mr. Joyce, from across the road, the hotel."

He seemed to settle back down again. I went back to reading.

"I'll put it another way," Mr. Joyce said. "Where are you from?"

So I put the book down and looked at him but he looked like he was asleep.

I told him. The conversation that followed was one I wouldn't easily forget. Aposiopesis. Nora returned shortly afterwards.

"Ah there you are," she said." Will you have something?"

"No," I said. "Thank you, Nora. Better get back."

"He's waiting for you," she said. "Up to high doh, he is. Bought a present for you. Turkish delight but don't tell him I told you. Sure, bring him over this evening, won't you? You'd like to see him, Jim, wouldn't you?"

"Dearly," Mr. Joyce said.

✝
✝

I reached a turning point on the stairs of the Hotel Galilée when Robbo shouted down to me. I looked up and saw his head peeping over the banisters.

"Come quickly, Set," he shouted, all excited. "I have a present for you."

The priest called after me. "Young fellow."

He found it difficult to climb the stairs. His blackthorn stick seemed more a hindrance than a help. He paused for breath as he reached me and used the rail to steady himself.

"You sneaked out there a while back when I wasn't looking," he said.

"I could hardly sneak out if you were looking, now could I?"

"Never have so many obstacles been put in the way of a kind deed," he said. "I just want to give Joyce a book."

"How do you know he wants it?"

"He wrote about it."

"Where?"

"In one of the papers."

"Which one?"

Robbo came down the stairs and stood beside me. "Set, come on."

"Can't remember which one it was," the priest replied. "What does it matter?"

"What's the name of the book?" I asked.

"What's it to you?"

"Have you got the book with you?" I asked. "I'd like to see it. I could give it to him for you."

"I need to give it to him myself."

"Why?"

"Now look here," he said pointing his blackthorn stick at me.

"Look where?" I asked. "You want me to look at the top of your stick?"

The priest breathed heavily. He was angry.

"I'll find him another way, if you don't want to help a man of God," he said.

"So that's how you describe yourself?" I asked.

"Set, come on," Robbo said, tugging at my sleeve.

The priest's anger rose even higher. As he turned to go back downstairs, he tightened his grip on the blackthorn stick, swung back and whooshed it horizontally through the air belting Robbo on the upper arm. Robbo grabbed his shoulder. He mouthed a big and slow "Ow" but didn't utter a sound. I was caught between running after the priest, who was scuttling down the stairs, or tending to Robbo, who was looking to me for help. I wasn't able to move. Everything became unreal. Robbo wet his trousers and a dark stain of urine crept out from underneath his shoes on the red carpet.

Aurora appeared at the bottom of the stairs. She laughed because she didn't know what had happened and probably thought we were playing a game on the stairs. The anger that was building up inside me came out.

"It's not funny," I roared. "He hit him. He hit him. The priest hit him."

We helped Robbo up the stairs to our room. Aurora took charge, giving me orders as she saw to Robbo. I brought her a basin of water and a sponge. I fetched clean socks from the chest of drawers and the trousers of his sailor suit from the wardrobe. I put his shoes near the window to make them dry quicker. There was nothing more for me to do.

"You'll be all right now," Aurora kept saying to Robbo, along with other phrases aimed at comforting him.

I became redundant and began thinking of when me and Lukas used to wash Mr. Boldt. For a few moments, I was back in the past, under the Texas sun, hearing people speak with my own accent, at home.

"I'll get rid of this," Aurora said, taking the basin and sponge out with her, leaving me alone with Robbo. I went over and knelt in front of him. I looked down at the clean white socks he was wearing and at the trousers she had put on him. I looked up. He was still gripping the place where he had been hit and staring at me, not being able to understand why anyone would want to hit him. His eyes were watering. I released his grip and saw there was a tear in his jacket, a spike of the blackthorn stick had ripped it. I took off his jacket and his shirt and saw that the blow had punctured his skin. There was a little blood. Aurora returned and I shouted at her again.

"Get a doctor!"

"What?" she asked.

"Get a doctor. Get a doctor."

I put Robbo sitting on his bed. He kept staring at me.

"Doctor's coming," I told him. "Fix you up real good."

Robbo's breathing quickened, became gasps and then he broke, collapsing into helpless, choking and uncontrollable crying. My attempts to soothe him didn't work. I was distracted by other bruises on his body that had not been inflicted by the priest.

The doctor arrived and began tending to Robbo. As he did so, Aurora and myself stood in the other corner of the room, silent and not looking at each other.

"I'm sorry," she said. "I was a bit slow realising that he'd been hit."

"Oh, no. No," I replied. "No, you wasn't. I shouldn't have hollered at you. Oh, I feel so bad."

"Sure no matter," she said, brightening up. "Would have been worse if you hadn't felt the need to roar. I'm proud of you."

✝
✝

"In," Ibsen said so I went into his room and sat down.

"Make yourself at home," he said, posing in front of his unfinished triptych.

"The mad priest attacked Robbo, hit him with that stick of his, injured his shoulder."

"Is he all right?" Ibsen asked.

"Had to get a doctor, bandaged him up."

"I'm wondering are the colors too dark in the middle painting," Ibsen said.

"Ain't you going in to see him?" I asked.

"I know what he looks like."

"Why don't you care about him?" I asked.

"He's all right, isn't he? Boys are used to rough and tumble."

"He was attacked," I said.

"You've said that already."

"What kind of a person are you?" I asked.

"I'm an artist. I can't have any encumbrances."

"He's a little boy, your nephew. You're his legal guardian."

"Just other descriptions of the same thing."

"You're not an artist," I said.

"And, how should I take this hill-billy criticism, I wonder, with gravity or levity?"

"Whoever is taking care of him in England is beating him," I said. "He has bruises on his body. Did you know this?"

"Probably from fighting with other boys," he said. "It's what they do."

"Why don't you care about him?"

"If *you* care about him so much, why don't you take care of him?"

"You ain't got no soul," I said.

"Haven't. *Haven't* got *any* soul," he said.

"Don't tell me how to talk. I don't tell you how to paint."

"You can't paint. I can. You can't talk. I can."

"Could you paint humanity?"

"Of course. It would have to be abstract."

"No. It should be concrete. You're not an artist."

COLOR

Tuesday, December 5, 1933

Aurora was helping Socrates put the finishing touches to the event they were planning for the Aéro-Club that evening. Every time we tried to talk, her father intervened and asked her to do a chore. We didn't get much of a chance to be together.

It was made even more difficult because I was taken up with minding Robbo. His responses were quiet. He grasped my hand when we went downstairs for breakfast and clung to me as we went past the spot where he had been attacked. He acted like a child on the best of behavior for all the wrong reasons. When I encouraged him to get dressed, to put on his sailor's hat and to follow me downstairs for breakfast, he obeyed. When I told him he looked mighty fine in his sailor's suit or praised him for eating up most of his breakfast he became unsettled, preferring that I didn't draw attention to him. His head was down most of the time.

Socrates approached our table after he had helped another man put up a sign, *L'Aéro-Club de France*.

"I just got word a few minutes ago," Socrates said. "Cablegram from the brother. There's just so much to do."

"What's it say?" I asked.

"Tomorrow," Socrates said. "The judge is delivering his ruling tomorrow."

I took the cablegram and read it.

"What's he doing in Texas," I asked.

Socrates took the cablegram back and read it. He hadn't noticed where it had come from.

"I don't know," he said. "John's always some place."

"Furthest I've known him to travel is Staten Island," I said.

"Better let Joyce know," he said.

"I'll tell him," I said and saw Robbo looking up at me. "We'll tell him, Robbo, won't we?"

"Do," Socrates said. "Still have plenty of work here and I have to set up the teleprinter after. For tomorrow. It's like a telephone except it prints what it wants to say from all the way over across the Atlantic."

"The judgment?" I asked.

"Yeah," he said. "I'll get one from Léon Bailby. He's the editor of *Le Jour*. The lads here'll help me set it up when this other thing is over. They know about communication."

I kept on wondering why Mr. Haltigan was in Texas.

Nora put Robbo sitting up beside the sink and questioned him about the assault after I had told her about the priest's attack on him. She urged me to keep Mr. Joyce company in the sitting room while she turned her full attention to Robbo.

Mr. Joyce greeted me with the usual gesture to sit on the sofa.

"We thought you'd come back yesterday evening," he said. "Has he found playmates in the hotel and is avoiding us again today?"

"No," I said. "He's here."

"I didn't hear him," Mr. Joyce said. "Where is he now?"

"In the kitchen with Nora."

Mr. Joyce raised himself and angled his head.

"I can't hear him," he said. "What's wrong with him?"

"Someone hit him in the hotel," I said. "With a stick. Nothing broken but he ain't himself."

"They've knocked the living daylights out of him, Jim," Nora said as she led Robbo into the sitting room. "The poor lad."

Mr. Joyce lifted Robbo up onto the armchair. Robbo rested his head on Mr. Joyce's shoulder and began playing with Mr. Joyce's lapel.

"By God, and I'll fling him into a bunch of nettles if I get hold of him," Nora said.

Mr. Joyce began singing. When he had finished, Robbo lifted up his head.

"Babbo? Are you going to have a biscuit today?"

"I can't," Mr. Joyce said.

"Why not?" Robbo asked.

"I can only eat a biscuit if someone else near me eats a biscuit."

"Babbo? I think I could eat a biscuit."

"Nora!" Mr. Joyce shouted.

"I heard," she said.

"Mr. Joyce," I said. "The judgment will be delivered in New York tomorrow."

"What are you talking about, Set?" Robbo asked.

"We'll know tomorrow if Babbo's book can be sold in America," I said. "That's why I'm here, to tell Babbo about it."

"And what will you do after, I mean, after we know about Babbo's book?"

"Well, I guess I'll go back to New York."

"Babbo, I couldn't understand the song," Robbo said. "It wasn't in English."

"Here," Nora said as she brought in the biscuits.

Robbo eased himself onto the floor.

"Babbo, I can give you your tea again. I don't mind. Is Babbo getting tea, Nora?"

"If you want him to have tea, so he'll have it," Nora said.

"Babbo, I didn't understand the song."

"It was in Italian," Mr. Joyce said. "It's from *Madama Butterfly.*"

"Will you tell me what it says, Babbo? And Babbo, will you tell Set to stay? What does it mean, Babbo, the song?"

"*Un bel dì, vedremo / levarsi un fil di fumo / sull'estremo confin del mare,*" Mr. Joyce said. "*One fine day we'll see / a pillar of smoke floating up / over the sea's horizon.*"

"Is Set coming back, Babbo?" Robbo asked.

"*E poi la nave appare. / Poi la nave bianca / entra nel porto, / rumba il suo saluto. Vedi? È venuto!*"

"Is he, Babbo?" Robbo asked.

"*And afterwards the ship will appear. / Then the white ship / will come into the harbor, will thunder / a salute. Do you see? / He's arrived!*"

"It's about you, Set," Robbo said, smiling. "You're coming back."

Robbo ran in to the kitchen to tell Nora his news.

"I wish," Mr. Joyce said, "he would decide my future too."

Mr. Joyce didn't seem one for starting or continuing a conversation so I decided to ask him a question. "Did it really take you seven years to write *Ulysses*, Mr. Joyce? Nora told me."

"Nearly didn't finish it; illnesses," he replied. "I was going to surrender it to another writer to finish, James Stephens. Smallest man I've ever seen. I'd like to tell you something about him."

"Sure."

"My name is James. His name is James. Stephen is the hero of my books. His name is James Stephens. He was born in Dublin on 2 February 1882. Do you notice anything strange about his birthday?"

"Is it yours too?"

"Yes. He and I were born in the same country, in the same city, in the same year, in the same month, on the same day, at the same hour, six o'clock in the morning. I am fond of coincidences. Are you?"

"Don't have much choice in the matter. They keep following me around."

✝
✝

The Hotel Galilée was abuzz with excitement. I found a table in the corner to watch all the guests who had been invited to the event by the Aéro-Club. While Robbo immersed himself in the crowd, Aurora joined me at a table in the corner of the banquet room. Finally, I thought, we'd get a chance to be together.

"Big crowd," I said. "Your daddy must be pleased."

"Here he is now," she said.

"Set, I want you to meet Louis Blériot, the first man to fly across the English Channel in a heavier than air aircraft."

"What's not heavier than air?" I asked.

"Hydrogen," Socrates said. "Another Frenchman, Blanchard, crossed the channel in 1785. Got there before us."

"The things you learn," I said to Aurora.

"And this," Socrates said, "is Colonel Frank P. Lahm."

"I'm from Ohio," Colonel Lahm told me.

"Texas," I replied.

"Colonel Lahm," Socrates said, "knew the Wright brothers and he's the US army's first certified pilot."

Then came Paul Codos and Lieutenant Maurice Rossi who had flown across the Atlantic just a few months before, followed by the French Aviation Minister, Pierre Cot, Mrs. Codos, Mrs. Rossi and an engineer by the name of Zapata. The introductory bombardments by Socrates continued, preventing any opportunity for Aurora and me to escape other company.

"Daddy has arranged a taxi home for me, a cab as you call it," she said once the event had ended. "I'll see you tomorrow. I hope."

That word "hope" was greater than the sum of its parts. We would see each other the following day. She hoped. I hoped. We hoped. I looked forward to that time when we were not reduced to just exchanging smiles across a hotel lobby. I went upstairs and realized that I was at a higher altitude than all those pilots downstairs had ever been. Then I remembered that the announcement of the judgment on *Ulysses* would interrupt our love. I would be busy. Amos I. was right. I'd never write a love scene – too many interruptions.

In the middle of the night, a crack of thunder woke me in time to see lightning brightening up the room. It was directly overhead. I put my head back down and turned to go back to sleep. My eyes opened quickly. I went to Robbo's bed. He wasn't there. My heart sank. I thought it was about to stop. I didn't know what it felt like to be scared of thunder and lightning but I knew it couldn't be greater than the terror bouncing around inside me. Nothing could. He wasn't with Ibsen. Ibsen wasn't in his room. Robbo didn't appear to be anywhere else in the hotel. I kicked and banged and roared and shouted. My own death would not have caused me as much distress. I checked if Socrates had left a note. Surely he would have told me if he was taking Robbo home with him. Nothing. My mind was swirling. I would kill anyone who might harm him. I dressed frantically and made my way over to the Joyce's apartment.

The doors were open. I uttered a weak "Hello" not wishing to startle anyone as I went into the kitchen. I opened the door to the sitting room. The light was off but more bolts of lightning lit up the room. Robbo was lying on his side on the floor and had his arm over Mr. Joyce who was also lying on his side.

"Jesus of Nazareth," Mr. Joyce said, "King of the Jews, from a sudden and unprovided death, deliver us."

As Mr. Joyce cowered, another light from the Heavens helped me see how frightened he was. He was shaking. Robbo looked up at me and put his index finger to his mouth. "Shush."

I left them; a bright boy protecting flashing antlers.

COMMUNICATION

Wednesday, December 6 1933

In the morning, Nora brought Robbo back to the hotel. Over breakfast, he became distracted by the engineer, Zapata, who had stayed up all night to install the teleprinter in the lobby. Socrates was helping him and it was obvious from their conversation that the machine was kicking up.

"Let's go over and help them," Robbo suggested.

"Let's not," I said.

Socrates and Zapata stared at the teleprinter. There was a clackety-clack but just one clackety-clack.

"It's happening," Socrates shouted and hugged Zapata.

The teleprinter remained silent but then burst into life; the paper spewed up and the clackety-clacking began. Zapata and Socrates tore off the sheet together and read it.

Socrates brought the sheet over to us and handed it to me. "We have a connection," he said. "News Report: Prohibition ended. Now they can legally toast *Ulysses* if all goes well."

Later, Socrates, Robbo and me made our way over to the Joyces' apartment. Nora introduced us to Paul Léon (she didn't know I had already been introduced to him by Socrates) and his wife, Lucie, and then to Eugene Jolas and his wife, Maria. All the seats were taken so Robbo sat on Mr. Joyce's lap. I followed Nora into the kitchen.

"Thanks for taking care of Robbo last night," I said.

"It was the other way round," she said. "Wasn't it kind of him of come over?" He remembered Jim's fear of the thunder."

"Yes."

"They'll all be asking you about Jim in New York now when all this is over," she said.

"They'll be asking about you too."

"Ha," she said. "I wouldn't think so. You can tell them I serve biscuits and lemonade."

"I know you do much more than that, Nora."

"You have no idea what simple people I come from," she said.

Socrates asked me to return to the hotel and wait for news of the judgment. When I got back, Zapata handed me a sheet of paper. It was the judgment with Zapata's inky thumbprint. The teleprinter was still typing. I ran to the Joyces' apartment.

All the heads turned towards me. Robbo was kneeling on Mr. Joyce's armchair, facing me. Mr. Joyce was standing behind him at the window. The Jolases occupied the settee, the Léons were on chairs and Nora was standing by the piano smoking a cigarette. Socrates was pacing about but stopped when I came in. I handed him the sheet and he began reading:

> *"I have read Ulysses once in its entirety... The reputation of Ulysses in the literary world, however, warranted my taking such time as was necessary to enable me to satisfy myself as to the intent which the book was written... If the conclusion is that the book is pornographic that is the end of the inquiry and forfeiture must follow."*

Socrates looked up at me.

"Go back," he said. "There's more."

Zapata was waiting for me at the door of the hotel with another page. I took it, ran back to the Joyces' apartment and handed over the second page which seemed long and difficult to understand, for me at least.

> *"If Joyce did not attempt to be honest in developing the technique which he has adopted in Ulysses,"* Socrates read, *"the result would be psychologically misleading and thus unfaithful to his chosen technique. Such an attitude would be artistically inexcusable."*

There was much more but that's all I could take in.

"He's writing a book himself, this judge," Mr. Léon said.

When Socrates had finished reading, we still didn't know. He looked up at me and nodded. I ran back. The teleprinter was throwing another tantrum but Zapata managed to get it to belch out another page. I took it and, as I reached the door of the hotel, I thought I heard him calling me back but I ignored him.

Socrates gave up reading and instead started commenting on what Judge Woolsey had said.

"The judge says he gave the book to two friends to read. They thought it was tragic, powerful and then he says, '*I am quite aware that owing to some of its scenes, Ulysses is a rather strong draught to ask some sensitive, though normal persons, to take.*'"

Mr. Léon stood up and then sat down immediately. "How long is this going to go on?"

There was still no indication of the ruling. I ran back again to find Zapata at the door of the hotel with another page.

"This is it," said. "No more. Just one last line."

It was the judgment.

As I walked the short distance from the hotel to Joyce's apartment, I decided not to find out the fate of *Ulysses*. I would wait. Instead, I thought of all the filing I had done, all the worry pent up in Miss Kreiswirth and the powerful submission made by Mr. Ernst to Judge Woolsey. I thought of how much the judgment would mean to Mr. Klopfer and Mr. Cerf. I thought of the success enjoyed by Mr. Roosevelt, now President Roosevelt and Mr. La Guardia, now Mayor La Guardia. I imagined Mr. Finnegan pacing up and down his apartment betraying how much the judgment meant to him. I thought of the people who had attacked us and imagined how overjoyed they'd be if we lost. I asked myself, not for the first time, if I had done my best and answered truthfully that I had. I hoped that this would be enough but feared the worst. I thought the journey from the hotel to Joyce's apartment was not as short as I would have liked. I wanted to keep travelling hopefully, never to arrive. I was afraid.

"This is it," I said and handed the page to Socrates.

"I can't," he said and walked away from me.

"Here," I said to Robbo. "You read it."

Robbo took the page and looked at it.

"U ... , Ulys ... , Ulys, ..." he said, stumbling to pronounce the first world.

"Oolisays," Mr. Joyce said.

Robbo began again:

"*Oolisays may, therefore, be admitted to the United States.*"

Mr. Joyce turned towards us, his head back, looking like a man who could not see very well.

"Thus one half of the English-speaking world surrenders," he said. "The other half will follow."

✝
✝

CLAIRVOYANCE

Thursday, December 6, 1933

I was just about to get ready for bed when I heard Ibsen going into his room. Even though he lacked many things, he had allowed me to stay in one of his rooms and so I decided to give him the courtesy of thanking him.

"In."

I sat down.

"Make yourself at home, why don't you?" Ibsen said. "Congratulations."

"I'm heading home tomorrow," I said. "Just wanted to thank you for putting me up."

"Don't come back," he said. "Find something else to do other than this. Stand back and take a look at your life. Ask yourself what it's saying to you. Don't come back here."

"You working for immigration now?" I asked.

"I can see the future. Don't come back. They'll kill you. Will you promise me that you won't come back?"

"Still haven't finished the painting?"

"Will you promise me that you won't come back?"

"No," I said.

"Don't come back. I can see the future."

20

TEXAS, PARIS

A FEW DAYS AFTER RETURNING to New York, I found myself in the conference room on one side of the table facing Mr. Ernst, Mr. Klopfer, Mr. Lindey, Mr. Cerf and Mr. Haltigan.

"Can we hold this meeting in English?" Mr. Klopfer asked me. "My French ain't what it used to be."

"What's all this about?" I asked.

"Set," Mr. Haltigan said. "I want you to listen very carefully. We, all of us here, are not without ways and means. What I mean is, we can do things. So, we've done something. We've got your father's house back."

"Oh," I said.

"I'd understand if, maybe, you're upset," Mr. Haltigan said. "Perhaps, it's something you wanted to do on your own. In fact, you did. We just helped out a little."

"How?" I asked.

"We found out the details of what happened to the Boldts," Mr. Haltigan said. "The exact poor investment that Mr. Boldt had made. That was the easy bit. Then, I went down in a big truck with a gang of workmen from the Lower East Side, carpenters, builders, that type. I told Mrs. Boldt that I was from the Government and had come to offer her an apology about the money that been stolen from her. She said it hadn't been, that her husband had invested unwisely. I told her there had been an investigation and that, indeed, it had been stolen by unscrupulous persons and that the Government was very angry about it. Before she could say anything else, I gave her a letter with President Roosevelt's signature on it saying that these men were here to restore her house. We had a budget, I told her. After a while, she believed us. The letter from the president sealed it. In no time at all, we found ourselves in the hardware store with Mrs. Boldt picking out new chairs, carpets, many things. Took only a day's hammering and sawing before everything was declared suitable by Mrs. Boldt. An achievement in itself. The papers are all signed. We had a good attorney by the name of Lindey.

"Well?" Mr. Klopfer asked. "What do you think of all that?"

"Why did you do this?" I asked.

"Because of what you've done for us," Mr. Klopfer said. "Well, are you still talking to us?"

"Guess so. I knew you were all up to something before I left. Thanks," I said, still trying to take it all in.

"You see?" Mr. Klopfer said. "I told you he'd be full of gratitude."

"Won't you get into trouble" I asked, "forging the president's signature like that?"

"Maybe it's not a forgery," Mr. Haltigan said.

THE HOUSE

When I returned home I didn't dress too fancy or too hobo – something in between.

I wanted to get my fill of Texas again so Daddy and me went to Deer Creek and sat down some distance from curious and wary antlers.

"I'm worried about the Boldts," Daddy said. "You might have cottoned on to Mr. Boldt's wheezing. Legs ain't what they used to be. Mightn't last beyond the Fall."

"He don't look the best, Daddy."

"She'll be alone, you see, Mrs. Boldt. She's getting on too. Wouldn't like her rattling around without no one near, even though she's back in her own house now. Well, if Mr. Boldt goes before her or maybe she'll go before him, I'll be spending as much time up there in her house than in our own house looking after her."

"Yeah."

"They're neighbors. We must look after them."

"What you two talking about?" Ops said as she arrived.

"The future," Daddy answered.

"I think I might go back to Paris," I said.

"Don't go back there," Ops said. "It ain't safe."

Out of the corner of my eye, I saw antlers flashing.

CONVERSATIONS ON A HOMECOMING

Lukas fiddled with an oil can in one of the outhouses as he spoke to me, remembering funny things that happened. He laughed more than I did.

"Staying long?" he asked.

"Few days."

"New York?"

"For a while."

"Then where?"

"Paris."

"I heard you was there about some book or other," he said. "I got it all planned out. Been saving. Now, the way I look at it, I can start building a place of my own and then later I'll get married. We're going to take a few years before we have children hollering around the place."

"What's her name?" I asked.

"Haven't met the lucky lady yet," he said.

I laughed.

"What's so funny?" he asked.

"Just the way you said it?"

"You find the way I speak funny?"

"No, Lukas."

"Well anyway, I reckon this plan of mine'll take a few years. So I was fixing on me and my wife taking a vacation before that. Things is picking up, you see, and I reckon they'll pick up even more. So maybe, I reckon, we could go over and visit you in Paris. What you think of that? Good plan, ain't it?"

"I don't know," I said. "It's not looking too good over there, you know?"

"Well, *you're* going there, ain't you?"

"Sure, but —"

"Oh, I see," Lukas said.

"See what?" I said.

"You just don't want to have us folk letting you down among your fancy friends over there?"

"Don't be so dumb," I said.

"Oh yeah, well what is it then? What is it?" Lukas asked.

"There might be a war. Things are getting bad over there."

"Might be a war? Why you going there then?" he asked.

I couldn't answer. I just didn't want Lukas, my friend, to be harmed in the future. Didn't want to tell him that neither. Might think I was calling him weak.

"Knew it," he said and then threw the oil can at the wall of the out-house before walking off.

I called after him but he kept on going.

Mr. Shaefer and Lukas stopped by at our house later for some lunch. Lukas looked like he wanted to be somewhere else, anywhere but near me. We all sat around after, talking. I entertained them all with stories of my adventures in New York and Paris. Lukas didn't seem none too impressed. Mr. Boldt shuffled in the chair and sat forward.

"Set, Set," he said. "You know I'd really like to ask you a question."

"Oh now," Mrs. Boldt said. "I'm sure young Set doesn't want to be answering no silly questions."

"I'm sure it's not silly Mrs. Boldt," I said. "Go on, Mr. Boldt."

Mrs. Boldt was surprised. Even though I was polite, I had never tried to overrule her on anything. She went quiet. Mr. Boldt shuffled in his chair again.

"You see, Set," Mr. Boldt said. "I've got to wondering, you know, all these writers down the centuries, why, there must be hundreds of them, thousands, maybe millions."

"Honestly, what kind of a question is this?" Mrs. Boldt said, looking away from us now.

"Well," Mr. Boldt continued. "There's just such a fuss kicked up about this book you've been talking about. *Ulysses.*"

"We've heard about all that," Mrs. Boldt said.

"I know that," Mr. Boldt said, "but what I want to ask is, well, the whole world seems to be talking about this here book. Been in court and everything. I was just wondering about this man, Joyce. How can he reach so many people? You said you met him. I just want to know, what he's like. What's he like, boy?"

"Oh Lord, what a question," Mrs. Boldt said and laughed.

"Guess he wouldn't have much to do with us folk, now would he?" Lukas asked. "Living like a lord in some castle in Paris with fancy friends. Why, we'd be only dirt to him. That's what those folk are like. People who've been to Paris. Ain't it?"

"Lukas!" Mr. Shaefer said.

"I can reply to both your questions with one answer," I said.

"I didn't ask no question," Lukas replied.

"You did," I said sternly.

"What's he like, Set?" Mr. Boldt asked again.

"Well, Mr. Boldt, Lukas," I said, "I used to sit with Mr. Joyce in his small apartment. He doesn't live in a castle. One time, I was reading a book. Mr. Joyce was asleep, at I least I thought he was. Then he said something. I could hardly hear it. He asked me my name."

"Thought you said you knew him," Lukas said.

"Lukas, stop it!" Mr. Shaefer shouted. "Go on, Set."

"Well, I said to him that I was Set, that I was staying across the road and that his wife would be back shortly. Then he asked me again and I told him I was Set, that he knew me, that I was in Paris because of his book *Ulysses*. He didn't say much then. I went back to reading and then he said, 'I'll put it another way. Where are you from?' So I put the book down and looked at him but he was still looking like he was asleep. So I said, 'I'm from Texas, Mr. Joyce. Near Troy. Between the Piney Woods and the Hill Country. A little place called Pendleton. My father lives there. That's where I'm from'.

"Then, after a few moments, Mr. Joyce sat up in his chair and held his hand out to me, but he kept staring at the window. Well, I held my hand out too and, as we were shaking hands, he looked at me.

"'So am I,' he said."

✝
✝

Lukas didn't come to say goodbye when I was about to leave for New York. I asked Mr. Shaefer to tell Lukas that I always regarded him as a friend if anything happened to me. This amused Mr. Shaefer who wanted to know if I was dying. I didn't answer and he wasn't amused anymore.

✝
✝

TOO LATE FOR LOGIC

Back in New York, people were excited that La Guardia had become mayor of the city but I wondered about him being like the rest of those politicians. Didn't bother me much because I was more interested in making up my own mind about what I would do. Would I really go back to Paris? It was odd that everything became clear to me only when New York descended into darkness.

Mr. Haltigan asked me to help him deliver furniture to a family that had just arrived over from England. Folks did that; helped each other out. I had to meet him on the Lower East Side at 9 o'clock on Friday morning, May 11. We had heard that a dust storm was making its way over from the northeast and had already engulfed Chicago but we never thought it would be anything like it was.

I was up early and made my way out into a dark and dusty city. The cloud of grit was thousands of feet high. The Statue of Liberty became a gray figure on a slightly darker background – so much so that I felt it was only my imagination that allowed me to see it. As I made my way up to the Caffè Reggio I heard people complaining about the government again. They said the topsoil from the valleys of the Missouri and Mississippi rivers were now swirling about Manhattan and all because of drought, all because no measures had been taken to prevent erosion. They said the wind found it easy to lift the dry soil and transport it to the cities across the United States.

I fell over a body lying on the street.

"Hey, watch it," a voice warned me.

When I sat at the Caffè Reggio, I found I could write my name in the dirt on the table. A waiter asked if I wanted coffee but before I had any chance to decline, he was off to get it. Two dark figures sat near me; one was the piano tuner, the other could have been anyone.

The coffee was served in a cup on top of which there was a square piece of card-board with a straw piercing it.

"Us Italians can adapt, don't you think?" a familiar voice said.

"Baa Baa, is that you?" I asked.

"Yes," he said. "This reminds me of King Lear except there's more than one fool."

"It's me. Set," I said.

"I know who you are," Baa Baa said. "I know where you're from."

"Have to meet Mr. Haltigan down the Lower East Side," I said. "No idea how I'm going to get down. Can't see too good."

"I'll bring you down," the piano tuner said. "Makes no difference to me."

The piano tuner left me at the place where Mr. Haltigan said he'd be and, Mr. Haltigan being Mr. Haltigan, was there. We walked down the street and stopped. There was a queue of people standing outside a relief station waiting to get interviewed, waiting to get food, waiting to get clothes. Mr. Haltigan took off his coat and put it around a woman who was holding a baby. Even though it was summer and would have been a day of brilliant sunshine, the dusty cloud had brought a chill with it. We looked inside the relief station and saw all the people who should be interviewing the poor, instead reading and talking to each other in the heated office.

Just then a limousine, a Chrysler Imperial, drifted towards us. It stopped. The back door opened and a small man got out. It was Mayor La Guardia. He walked with a determined air to the door of the relief station and reached it just as a tall man with a hat and smoking a cigar was about to go in.

"Where do you think you're going, buddy?" the tall man said.

"Don't, don't ever, ever speak to a citizen of this city like that," La Guardia said and then flicked the man's hat off before knocking the cigar out of his mouth. La Guardia went in. All the magazines went down. The chattering stopped. He took off his coat and we heard him telling the man who had tried to stop him at the door that he was fired. La Guardia, the mayor and La Guardia, the lawyer, sat behind a desk and gave orders to open the doors and let the people in. He then began processing all the requests.

Mr. Haltigan and me watched all this.

"Did you see that, Mr. Haltigan. He clear knocked that cigar out of that feller's mouth. Brought down the Cyclops, he did."

"Let's go."

"Ain't you getting your coat back?"

"No. Too late for logic."

THE ORPHANS

I returned to Paris in August 1934. After the ship had docked, I took the boat-train to Paris and made my way to the Hotel Galilée. I thought I'd just stay a few nights before moving to another hotel. I didn't expect a welcome from Ibsen.

After leaving my suitcase in the care of a coin-hungry porter, I made my way upstairs and knocked on Ibsen's door.

"In."

I went in. For a man who was so convinced he could tell the future, he seemed very surprised to see me.

"You're back?"

"Good to see you too," I said.

"I told you not to come back," he said.

"I don't do everything you say."

"They'll kill you."

"Who?"

"Nazis. Best to go back."

"Can't see any of them around."

"They'll be here," Ibsen said. "In the future. Go back."

"I'm staying."

"I knew this would happen," he said. "One more attempt then."

He went to the window and looked out raising his hand which, I guess, meant I should be quiet. He started shaking his head. The witch-doctor was coming out in him. I sighed and shook my head. It had only taken me a few seconds to become fed up of his games.

"Are you listening?" he asked.

"No choice."

"Correct."

He turned around, closed his eyes and began.

"The future. I need to tell you what will happen. It begins:

"Where the Truth becomes the first and last casualty so inundated by deceit that crooked waves drown the young deer from sea to lake.

"Where there is false appeasement; nations and friends are soft-soaped so much they will slither and suffocate in their own suds.

"Slippery and predatory – the dart of the conger eel.

"Where scoundrels of the street send up scandal to the sill.

"No doubt you've heard.

"Where action is taken only to destroy or steal wealth, never to build or help.

"The red of the cunning and the yellow of the cretin merge to form a bitter color.

"Where fear is engendered about the future, a fictional apocalyptic future.

"Where the air is made unclean unnecessarily; people will be starved of air from a whistle in the dark.

"Children will be made into orphans.

"Where blame is laid on the weak and vulnerable, on the poor and hungry for things they didn't do.

"Where women are reviled. Where rape and foul thoughts splutter into the verbal dollar currency.

"Where violence is placed front of stage but peace put trembling behind bars.

"Where racism is made normal, the texture and fabric of conversation, woven by the debased, the depraved.

"Where the powerful are defended and the vulnerable are cast aside.

"Where no one is safe; all the enemies kept close are made suddenly remote to be replaced by new and dangerous clowns."

He opened his eyes and came back to normal, if normal was ever anything Ibsen could come back to.

"You really think all those things are going to happen here?"

"Yes, in the near future and then they'll all happen again somewhere else in a distant future."

"I'm staying."

"Nothing to be done then. You can stay in your room. I'll be gone in the morning, to the south. The light is better there."

"Don't let me drive you out," I said. "Going to stay somewhere else anyway."

"No," Ibsen said. "You'll stay here. This is the way it is. I will leave my key under your door."

"I don't understand you," I said.

"I'm an artist."

"Ain't artists supposed to be understood?" I asked.

"Yes," Ibsen replied, "but not by people like you."

"Gee, thanks," I said.

"The Portuguese woman," Ibsen said.

"What about her?" I asked.

"She hasn't called."

"Well, maybe that just means you can't tell the future," I said.

"Yet," Ibsen replied. "The time will come when you need to be intrinsically yourself, to let loose the imagination of courage and humanity."

He hadn't made a sound. When I woke, I found his key shoved under my door. After getting dressed, I used the key to open the door to his room, half-expecting to find him there laughing at me. He was gone. He had placed a squat swivel-chair in the center of the room. It looked inviting. I sat down and faced the half-opened door. To my right was the triptych. The blank canvas remained blank. It seemed to scream at me.

THE WAKE

Later that day Aurora called and we went to a little café near the hotel which the porter had recommended. As we drank our coffees, no fewer than four people approached us but not all at the same time and not all for the same reason.

"You look real nice," I said quietly.

"Thanks," Aurora said and blushed.

"Well, look who it is, and Aurora too," Nora said arriving with Mr. Joyce.

She sat down at our table and questioned me about when I had arrived and what I was doing back. I stumbled out an answer as I helped

Mr. Joyce to find his seat. Soon Nora and Aurora were chatting away amongst themselves.

"Did you hear about the Appeal, Mr. Joyce?" I asked.

"Another victory."

"And *Ulysses* is selling real good. 30,000 copies so far, Mr Cerf told me."

"We've moved," Mr. Joyce told me. "Rue Edmond Valentin. Socrates told me you sought our address. Were you planning to come and say hello?"

"Yes."

"People think that but they always end up saying goodbye. There's incendiarism in the air. Have you noticed?" he asked.

"Yes."

"I feel the need to leave. You mightn't get the opportunity to say hello or goodbye to anyone again if you stay here."

"So folk keeping telling me."

"After I have said goodbye other writers will follow. I sense the arrival of a playwright. His works will make apt headlines. Logic will follow Famine. Epitaph will precede The Wake. Your mother said your name twice, didn't she, before she died?"

"Yes," I replied.

"In my next book, you might find that Texas is mentioned the same number of times, twice," he said, "but not close-set. There'll be space in between. Vital text. In your honor."

"*Work in Progress*?" I asked.

"It'll be called *Finnegans Wake*. Same name as the people you were staying with in New York but I had decided the title before, in the past."

"What's it about? Waking up? The things folk do when they get up in the morning?"

"No. What happens before that. The night. Nighttime."

"Come on, Jim," Nora said, getting up. "We'll leave these two in peace."

Nora and Mr. Joyce said their goodbyes and moved off but Nora returned briefly to our table.

"Ye'll be very popular now," she said, looking around. "They'll come asking about him. For a while anyway."

Before I could say anything, the third person arrived at our table. He excused himself in French but before he had a chance to ask me if he could get an introduction to Mr. Joyce or if I knew where Mr. Joyce lived, I saw him off.

"They all want to know him now," I told Aurora. "Here's another one."

An exotic-looking woman started speaking French to me but, like her predecessor, I interrupted sharply and in English.

"He was only looking for directions," I told her. "Don't know who he is."

"You speak English," she said. "That's good. My English is better than my French. No. The man in the hotel said you will be here. Mr. Wright?"

"That's me."

"I am looking for Mr. Ibsen," she said. "The hotel said you know him."

"He's gone," I said. "South. Won't be back for a while, maybe not at all."

"Oh," she said. "That's a pity. I wanted to ask him if he'd paint my portrait. I suppose I should have written to him first. Wasted journey. I'm sorry for disturbing you."

"That's all right," I said. "Where are you from?"

"Portugal."

TOWN WITHOUT LAUGHTER

Robbo jumped from behind the door of the Haltigans' apartment and announced his presence.

"Hello Set. I'm here."

He turned and began jumping. "Here is me. Here is me."

Over lunch, Socrates told me that Ibsen, as Robbo's legal guardian, was leaving Robbo in their care, that he would not be going back to England.

"Sure Lord, we had a little boy before," Anna said. "Do you remember me telling you, Set?"

She turned to Robbo and cupped his face in her hands.

"And I keep telling this little man, that's he's not a replacement, he's an addition."

"I'm an addition," Robbo said while chewing sweets.

"Don't speak with your mouth full," Aurora told him.

"I do apologize," Robbo said, his mouth full.

Socrates, usually serious and unemotional, broke into a fit of laughter, his body heaving up and down, his face changed from stern to that of a big child.

"Isn't it great about the book?" Anna said. "Sure, what got into them trying to lock it away? Have they no sense, these people? Still, didn't it work out well all the same in the end. Didn't it, Set?"

"Yes, Anna," I replied. "It did."

The lunch was served, the plates and cutlery washed and put away. Anna then told me that Socrates, Robbo and herself were going to the next apartment to visit a neighbor. Aurora and myself laughed at the same time. We knew what they were up to – match-making.

"You don't seem to be yourself," Aurora said.

"I'm afraid of what's going to happen to you."

She laughed.

"All these people in New York who helped me. Lot of them were Jews. You know, a Rabbi even gave me a suit and his son gave me his coat. That's what they did. They're in my house now. I want to be a teacher. I'm going to learn French real good. They'll be forty brown eyes staring up at me in the classroom. Twenty children. I'll ask them about short cuts. Kids always know short cuts. I'll know them all so when they come, the Nazis, I'll know all the short cuts and I'll be able to save them."

"God, that's a great idea," Aurora said. "Why didn't I think of that?"

"But it'll be dangerous, don't you see?"

"Daddy'll help too and Mammy. She knows how to fling a cooking pot."

"Aurora, your Daddy told me, these people, they got superior air power. Don't you see, it's going to take more than a cooking pot to stop these people?"

"Sure Mammy has a press load of them and she can get some from the neighbors."

"Aurora, Aurora, they'll kill you. They're going to kill me."

"I wouldn't worry about them. Daddy can be handy enough in a fight as well. Knocked a man out one time they were in Dublin. Over a horse, it was. Or was it a pony? Some old four-legged thing anyway. You're getting yourself all worked up. Do you want another cup of tea?"

"No," I said and got up.

"It's over, Aurora. I can't bring you into danger. My mother told me, you see, to look after the little ones."

She smiled at me as I left.

The door to their neighbor's apartment was open and Anna spotted me leaving.

"Ah, you're not going yet?" she asked.

"Something to do," I said. "Thanks for the lunch."

I made my escape down the stairs out onto the rue de Palestine.

"Set, Set," Anna called from the doorway.

I turned round but didn't walk back.

"Set," she said. "What happened?"

"I have to go," I said.

"But, Set, she's a grand girl. We brought her up real well."

"I know that," I said.

"And she'll do well in her exams," Anna said. "The nuns said they expect her to do real well."

"I'm sure she will."

I turned and walked away.

"Ah Lord," Anna said. "What's happened?"

Though I couldn't see Anna, I imagined her in the doorway, disoriented, deciding to follow me but then, a moment later, deciding to go back upstairs to her daughter. Anna didn't know what to do. In my mind's eye, I could see her arms waving about like she was conducting an invisible orchestra. She couldn't understand. Her body, like her mind, was drenched in disappointment and grieving for the sudden loss of her daughter's hope and happiness.

✝
✝

FAMINE

I turned the corner out of sight but not out of misery. During the long walk down the rue de Belleville into town, no other thoughts came into my mind. I wondered what the Haltigans were doing. I wondered was Anna now telling Aurora that there would be another young man she'd find. I wondered what Socrates would be thinking but, most of all, I couldn't get the image of Aurora's utter disregard for my warnings out of my mind. It was a strange walk, a walk where the city didn't speak to me. It had stopped talking and so, I suppose, had I.

By the time I reached the steps of the Hotel Galilée, I was exhausted. Numbness had already set in but now I seemed to be living in an unreal body and in an unsettling world. When I got to my room, I stopped and decided, instead, to go into Ibsen's room. The chair invited me to sit down. It didn't have to say anything. So I sat down and swiveled a little to the left and a little to the right. I stared at the half-open door. I looked to my left through the window at the building opposite. I looked to my right at the triptych and the blank canvas. I slouched in the chair and put my head back, closed my eyes and gave in to exhaustion. I descended into my imagination, becoming intrinsically myself.

I hear music. It comes from the future. I know what it is. The song, the song about Caruso, the song the piano tuner told me about. Caruso is dying and he sings to the woman he loves. I can't describe music beyond *boing, boing, boing.* Someone in the future will compose this. I see them dipping the stem of a plucked rose into an Italian coffee, circling and stemming notes on a music sheet, the thorns of the stem bite into the composer's fingers like a blackthorn stick would into the shoulder of a child. Blood mixes with the blue ink, purple appears. A red balloon drifts past Mars and disappears into the redness but I know it's still there. A spherical Statue of Liberty in the Heavens. The music sheet expands, flies upwards and covers the sky, the stars now taking the place of the musical notation. All the spheres, great and forbidding, pulsate with light and become the signals of sound. Death seems sweet.

I see my class, the little children staring at me. They are under a bridge in Paris. It is night. Nighttime. It is time. The boat creeps in. Their bodies rock as the waters fight against them. The boat, now full, drifts off, a teddy bear falls into the water and floats away. Its owner, a boy, reaches out and rescues it in time. Nighttime. He looks back at me. This is what happens before they will get up in the morning. Socrates is there. We wait as thudding boots beat their drum above us on the bridge. The soldiers are gone. I will remember the short cuts. There will be no forgetting them. I will not need a word on the stairs. *Un mot d'escalier.* I will have remembered the short cuts. There will be no Famine of recall. I climb up and walk away. A shout. They've seen me. I run. I slow down so that they'll keep chasing me. The little ones will escape. I have distracted their killers. I stop at street corners until the moving column of death appears again in the distance. Another shout. They've seen me. I reach the steps of the Hotel Galilée and wait. Here they are again. Another roar. It drowns out the music. It drowns out 'Caruso'. Discordant replaces accord.

I sit in the swivel chair and wait. They're coming. I hear them downstairs. Words on the stairs. Doors are kicked open. Women and children scream. They hadn't paid for this. Death ascends towards me. I wait. In my imagination, I see all the people who have helped me when I had nothing. They appear behind my chair as a family portrait. My mother is there, grayer than the rest. So is the piano tuner. So is Nora. So is Mr. Joyce. He speaks:

✚
✚

"Do you really want to do this, Set? Have I inspired you only to place your-self in jeopardy, to perish? You can't do this, your voice won't be heard."

"It's the only way I can live," I roar. I am a dying lion.

✚
✚

Roosevelt is standing now, facing them like I am. Integrity set in granite. For a moment, I see a sign for the Métro Marbeuf. It changes to Métro Franklin D. Roosevelt. La Guardia is holding a cigar, waiting to knock the eye out of the Cyclops. Mrs. Janosik is smiling, conducting my imagination. The blind piano tuner can see. Lukas puts his hand on my shoulder. Still my friend.

Coincidences collide. Hidden ones emerge. "I am so," Lukas shouts. The letters walk around and become Amos. I. Will they walk around again and become: "So am I"?

✚
✚

I hear the boots on the stairs, closer. Here we are. Here we are, they seem to say. Robbo is behind me, the English boy, and he says to them defiantly, "Here is me. Here is me". "Go on, git," Lukas roars at them. It's some comfort but no use. I know absolute silence will ensue. *Il s'est alors produit un silence absolu.*

They don't have to burst open the door but they do. A soldier appears with a bayonet poised. Others join him in the background. He's as young as I am but I don't have a uniform. I come from between the Piney Woods and the Hill Country. He lunges at me. There's nothing except my body jolting. The future fails. Another lunge and jolt. I am bayoneted alive. Will I be buried dead? My killer has the face of someone doing something he doesn't want to do but doing it anyway, trying to appear brave; an armed man against an unarmed civilian. Somehow, I don't feel brave.

They wait, watching me die. I look to the right and there it is, the unfinished triptych with the blank canvas, not blank any more. It's splashed with blood. I have finished the painting. A red balloon drifts across the room. It turns blue and purple, the colors of my schooling of what I was taught to be. Free in the air.

"What's the matter?" Aurora asks.

I've returned to the present. She followed me down. I rest my elbows on my knees and look down at the floor.

"Go, Aurora," I say. "I want you to live. It's not only what my mother said. It's what *I'm* like. I'm driven to do this, to protect children. This is me. Here is me. They're going to kill me for this."

She's still holding my hands. She squeezes them gently and raises me up. I have to stand but I'm still looking down. Someone is holding my hands and trying to help me. It's her.

"I'm like this, you see. This is what I'm like," I say and then I look up at her.

She says nothing for a while but then she changes all our futures.

"So am I."

A NOTE ON THE TEXT

*U*LYSSES SPENT JUST ONE DAY before Judge John M. Woolsey. Two days are given over to the proceedings in this novel for dramatic effect. The ruling by Judge Woolsey was upheld by the United States Court of Appeals for the Second Circuit. Judges Learned Hand and his cousin, Augustus N. Hand, agreed with Woolsey. Chief Judge Martin Manton dissented. In a later case, unconnected with *Ulysses*, Manton was jailed for conspiracy to obstruct the administration of justice and to defraud the United States.

Readers wishing to hear more about *Set at Random* and learn of new books by Declan Dunne can subscribe to his newsletter by filling out a two-line form that can be found on this link: www.setatrandom.com

BY THE SAME AUTHOR

MULLIGAN'S
Grand Old Pub of Poolbeg Street

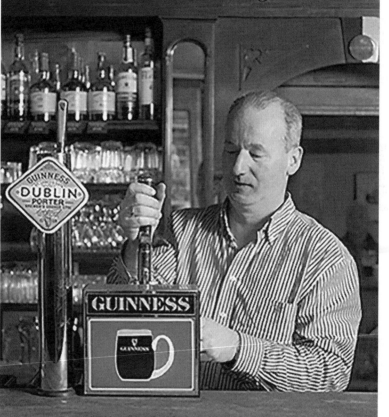

Declan Dunne

MULLIGAN'S

Grand Old Pub of Poolbeg Street

ISBN: 978 1 78117 348 0

Mulligan's is more than a Dublin pub; owned and managed by Gary and Gerry Cusack, it is an Irish cultural phenomenon. It has a unique and colourful history, spanning two hundred and thirty-six years. Mulligan's has hosted the famous; Judy Garland, Seamus Heaney, Con Houlihan, James Joyce, John F. Kennedy and, indeed, the infamous – police arrested a kidnapper there. Quirkiness pervades its atmosphere. The ashes of a US tourist are interred in its clock. Barmen have seen ghosts on the premises. For decades, performers at the Theatre Royal thronged to Mulligan's, mingling with journalists from The Irish Press who smoked, fumed and interviewed celebrities in it.

This fascinating book captures the atmosphere and essence of an Irish institution, loved by both natives and tourists alike.

www.mercierpress.ie

PETER'S KEY

PETER DELOUGHRY AND THE FIGHT FOR IRISH INDEPENDENCE

Declan Dunne

PETER'S KEY

Peter DeLoughry and the fight for Irish Independence

ISBN: 978 1 78117 059 5

In February, 1919, three Irish revolutionary prisoners walked out of Lincoln Jail without having dug a tunnel or fired a shot. The escape was the culmination of months of planning that involved some of the greatest intellects in Ireland and Britain. Peter DeLoughry (1882-1931) was one of the founding fathers of modern Ireland. His most famous achievement was to make a key that allowed three of his fellow prisoners in Lincoln Jail to escape in February 1919. The key became a symbol of the success that could be achieved by co-operation and hard work. However, as the years went on, the key became a matter of poisonous dispute between DeLoughry and Michael Collins on one side and Eamon de Valera and Harry Boland on the other. The key emerged as a symbol of the hatred and bitterness that welled up and overflowed in the nascent years of the Irish Free State. DeLoughry was also Mayor of Kilkenny for six consecutive years, a record not surpassed before or since. He served in the upper and lower houses of the Irish Parliament where he became embroiled in issues such as divorce, film censorship and, most important of all, the Anglo-Irish Treaty, which he championed. He lived through an age of political and social turbulence; his childhood and adulthood bridged the time of Parnell and the birth of the Irish Free State.

www.mercierpress.ie

28077415R00186

Made in the USA
Columbia, SC
10 October 2018